M2

I0588050

Rise of the Giants

Millennium Series

Staci Morrison

First published by Alanthia Publishing 2021

Copyright © 2021 by Staci Morrison

ISBN: 978-1-7365520-4-9

First edition

For Michelle, muse, encourager, and cheerleader, who kept assuring me the work was great and worth the cost. She loves these characters as much as I do. Thank you for the inspiration, writing and otherwise. You are a gem, a true friend.

Table of Contents

Enter the Millennium

Welcome back! The reader will recall that years in the text are indicated with ME, Millennial Era, instead of BC or AD. Thus, 999 ME is 999 years into the Millennium.

Character names use a Hebrew construction, whereby 'ben' means child of, so Josiah ben Eamonn means Josiah son of Eamonn.

So, what is the Millennium, and when will it occur?

It is a prophetic time, the next great age. Our world today will not continue ad infinitum. At some point in the future, the Lord will appear in the Heavens and call His church to Himself. This global cataclysmic event is called the Rapture and sets off a series of events that will usher in the Tribulation, seven years of wars, famine, earthquakes, fire, and pestilence; hell on Earth. But in the end, the evil forces are defeated. The Lord returns to rule, ushering in the Millennium, one thousand years of paradise, a return to what was lost in Eden.

Series Notes

As the series progresses, there is a clear dividing line in the story; before Prince Eamonn's murder and after. I used that as the anchor point while writing, and perhaps it will help you.

Many readers requested glossaries, lists of character names, and a timeline of events. There is a massive one I built whilst writing the series, which needs to be updated after the overhaul I did of M1, and nobody wants a twenty-page color coded (by book) document, right? Well, some of you might, and I really love you for that. The timelines are book specific, so the spoilers need to be hidden. I will share what I can on Alanthia.com.

I am honored and humbled to have you back, so from the bottom of my heart, thank you. Take my hand; I am going to tell you an amazing tale.

"When man began to multiply on the face of the land and daughters were born to them, the sons of God (elohim) saw that the daughters of man were attractive. And they took as their wives any they chose. The Nephilim were on the earth in those days, and also afterward, when the sons of God came in to the daughters of man and they bore children to them. These were the mighty men who were of old, the men of renown."

—Genesis 6 1-2,4.

Part 1 - Prologue

October 23, 985 ME (Six Months into Rebellion)

The Chosen Ones–New City Palace, Alanthia

Royal protocol dictated the New City Palace should still be in mourning, its windows draped, its inhabitants dressed in black. Ruling Prince Eamonn and his son, Prince Josiah, had been in their respective graves for less than six months, a fact that had not escaped Prince Korah ben Adam's notice.

When rumors of a coronation celebration raced through the Palace grapevine, the remnant of his mother's cadre of old biddies marched into Korah's office, outlining in painstaking, tedious detail why it was unseemly to hold a ball. However, Korah did not particularly care for the rules of polite society, had despised his mother, and if possible, liked her gaggle of old busybodies even less. After Princess Mary's death, Eamonn put up with the ancient crones; Korah had no intention of doing the same.

The day after the courts declared him the rightful heir to the Alanthian throne, the Palace major domo informed the ladies that their services were no longer required. Their fussy, overly embellished guestrooms were packed up, and they were shipped off to resentful relatives or the rarely used royal estate in Saskatchewan. They left in a cloud of musky perfume and barely suppressed outrage, all rustling silks, thumping canes, and wobbling chins.

Korah and Peter shared a rare smile. Even Alexa breathed a sigh of relief, glad to see the last of them.

In his first decree as the Ruling Prince, Korah declared himself a man of the people and announced he would not travel to the Golden City for the coronation. The ceremony and celebration would take place in the New City.

His critics decried the move, which severed a one-thousand-year-old tradition. Every Ruling Prince in the Millennium received his crown by the hand of the Iron King. Eamonn's advisors were especially vocal in their protestations, however Korah gave as much credence to them as his mother's old biddies. They were cut from the same cloth as far as he was concerned.

But the truth was, Korah had no real choice. Having secured his throne by another power, he held no illusions about who he owed his loyalty to, or where his source of power sprang. The Coronation Ball had been Marduk's idea.

So, on the evening of October 23, 985 ME, dignitaries from nine of the ten kingdoms packed the New City Palace. The jubilant guests partied in an atmosphere that bordered on mania. Heedless of the consequences and blind to the evil lurking behind the man they had just placed on the Alanthian throne, they drank and danced, offering toast after toast to the handsome monarch, who opened the festivities with his lovely wife, Princess Alexa.

An Indian summer wind blew through the open windows. The heat in the crowded ballroom made the maidens simper and flush. They deployed their decorative fans with flirtation and guile, enticing suitors who sought their favors. They did not realize there was one among the crowd they needed to avoid, one disguised as a man, who was not, and he was hunting. Marduk, the immortal Prince of Persia, the fallen angel, wore a facade, posing as the elegant, urbane, Palace advisor, Secretary Tristin.

He moved through a flowing sea of delicate ladies, draped in silks, watching them, choosing. Gliding over to an icy Scandinavian beauty with clear green eyes, he departed disappointed. She was not fertile. They had a scent when they were breeding, which was the goal tonight, the entire purpose of this ball. Risky, to be sure, but he had not broken bonds before everyone else to play it safe.

He ignored the daggers Eamonn's former advisors shot him from across the ballroom; as if he could not discern their thoughts, could not hear them plotting. He focused on the ringleader, speaking into the man's brain, "Don't cross me, you little worm. I will destroy you." He sent a warning pulse through the ether and grinned as the man paled and staggered backward, clutching his heart.

Message received.

He nodded in feigned polite acknowledgement and turned back to the ladies. There would be time enough to deal with the troublemakers. This was a party, after all.

The Greek delegation looked promising, no morals in the lot of them. The Ruling Prince was a wild card, mercurial, temperamental, but in a manner reminiscent of the ancient Roman emperor Caligula, and his sort always ended up in a bad way. As a strongman, Korah was a much better choice. He would leave Antiochus to Zeus, if the bastard ever broke out.

But Antiochus' sister, Philomela, was another matter, a first-class bitch, to be sure, but Secretary Tristan was not hunting a wife. And he had never liked Zeus, so dallying with a Greek Princess made selecting her all the more enticing.

Employing his most humble demeanor, Marduk escorted Philomela to the dance floor, inhaling her scent, oh yes. The force of his desire must have transmitted itself because she trembled under his hands as they waltzed. When she tried to pull away, he locked an arm around her waist and flicked his tongue over the tender olive skin just below her ear. "Thou hast the most enticing scent, reminiscent of the Aegean Sea, warm, dark, and beautiful. I would like to bathe in thy deep waters, slick and wet."

"Thou art impertinent, sir." Philomela drew back, shocked. "I shall inform my brother of thy scandalous tongue." She wrenched free, departing the dance floor in a huff.

Marduk grinned. There was the first one.

He scanned the rainbow of gowns, spotting a Creole belle in rose satin and lace. Ah, he knew her, read the intent behind those clear gray eyes. She had been watching him, though she would never admit it. Oh, this one might prove entertaining.

He decided to play her game.

Striking a formal bow, he presented an offering, coconut water sweetened with cane syrup. In perfect French, he flattered, "*Mademoiselle Charlotte, je suis ton humble adorateur.*" I am your humble worshipper.

The fair-haired beauty inspected him as if he were a rooster in a livestock fair. He preened in his outward perfection. She gave him a haughty stare and turned away, pretending indifference, but Mademoiselle Charlotte Durant took the glass from his hand and drank.

Number two.

The last maiden posed a bit of a conundrum. Marduk vacillated between the Russian with glacial eyes and firm calves and the Kenyan with ebony skin and graceful limbs. But in the end, the little horse dancer captivated him. The most unlikely of the attendees, a rancher's daughter from rural Alanthia, she floated in his arms like a memory of a time lost eons ago.

Monsters Under My Bed - New City Palace - Prince Peter

Seven-year-old Prince Peter ben Korah's knees shook as he slid open the secret panel into his mother's bedroom. He had run through the passages, and in the silence, his breath came in shuddering gasps. He feared when he turned, there would be something coming through the narrow, dark spaces. He closed his eyes, inching the panel closed, certain someone or something was going to reach out of the darkness and grab him.

The night Josiah escaped, Peter woke from a nightmare where people turned into serpents and coiled around his legs, their fangs dripping poison and false promises. The dream, and what he and Josiah overheard outside the tomb room, scared him so badly he slept in his mother's room for a month. That ended abruptly, when his father, who also apparently wanted to sleep in his mother's bed, found him curled up with her. He jerked Peter by the arm, marched him out the door, and banished him. His father's threat was implicit, conveyed and clearly understood because Korah flashed that particular look, which always recalled the nightmare with vivid clarity.

So, every night since, Peter forced himself to stay in his own room, even when he grew certain something hovered in the shadows, watching him. He hadn't been inside the passages for months, avoiding them, saving them in case he needed them, like tonight. He risked his father's wrath, not daring to remain by himself, huddled under the covers, waiting. Because what he had seen lurking in the guest wing was neither dream nor his overactive imagination.

Every hair on his body stood on end as he rushed across the woven carpet on tiptoes, scared any noise might be detected, the faintest whisper overheard. "Mother?" he croaked, trying not to cry as he burrowed under the blankets.

She made a sleepy sound.

He cupped his palms around her ear. "I think there is a monster in the house. It smells like rotten eggs, and it is hunting."

3am - Redding, California - James ben Kole

Two hundred miles north of the New City Palace, James ben Kole did not give more than a passing thought to the Coronation Ball. He had a mare in trouble. She thrashed, her sides heaving, blood oozing from her body, and still the foal did not present. James ran his callused hands over her quivering flank as another contraction rocked her with nothing to show, save crimson.

He buried his face in her glorious white mane, whispering, "You can do this. I know you can, lass."

His fiancée, Persa ben Yereq, would be heartbroken if the mare did not survive the birth. Lightning had been her faithful mount as a child, her mother's before that. The horse was ancient, no one knew how old. Lightning was as much a part of Rivergate as the thoroughbred barn or the main house, a fixture and greatly beloved. The foal represented a promise of new life, James and Persa's future, their beginning. She had to make it.

Changing the blood-soaked hay, panic crept along the edges of his brain. He fought it down, for Lightning's sake, for the sake of everything. The horse's labored breathing echoed off the fine stall, a shudder to it, heretofore not present. The other animals kept a quiet vigil, and as much as he railed against it, the atmosphere shifted, becoming a death watch. He threw aside the bedding fork and fell to his knees. "No, lass. No."

Lightning gave a tired exhale and closed her extraordinary blue eyes. James felt her give up.

"Looks like you need some help," a voice said from the shadows.

James raised his head from his murmured prayers. "I wouldn't be opposed," James said through the lump of grief lodged in his throat. He considered the stranger, trying to place the man. He looked familiar, yet he did not know him.

Moving into the stall, the man extended a gloved hand. "Name's Joshua. I heard you were looking for help."

"She's been in foal for ten hours, started bleeding about two. She's aged." James stroked Lightning's heaving sides as another futile contraction seized her. "You have experience?" he asked quietly, the hint of an Irish burr softening his words.

"I know a little." Joshua looked around the well-appointed stable, "Where's everybody at?"

James shrugged. "I haven't a clue, but it seems it's just you and me."

"As it will be, James."

July 16, 990 ME (Five Years into Rebellion)

In for One, In for All - Taylorsville, NC - David and Zanah

"What exactly do you want me to say, Zanah?" David ben Jesse murmured, staring at the scratched kitchen table covered in bills. "I thought we couldn't lose. The opportunity looked so good." His hand squeezed his temples, hiding his shame, trying to explain. "I did it for us, for you, for Davianna, for our future."

"You've lost everything, all of it?" Zanah ben Joseph shrieked. "The house? They are foreclosing on my house?"

He nodded, refusing to look at her, could not bear the contempt flashing in her big brown eyes.

"We'll have to leave Taylorsville. You've humiliated me in front of everyone I know," her voice cracked, on the verge of tears.

He rose to comfort her, but she spun away, her lovely features contorted in rage and scorn.

"You are such a loser."

David's shoulders sagged. He deserved that. "Zanah, I'm sorry. I should have never trusted him. I guess he was a con artist, but he just seemed like such a helluva nice fella."

January 24, 1000 ME (Fifteen Years into Rebellion)

When the Devil Comes to Call – Louisiana Bayou - Beau

"*Voila merde*, Miss Pink!" Beau Landry cursed into the phone. "You sent the Devil to my house. Now I've got a backyard crawlin' with snakes and a burnt-up pot of etouffee!"

"Don't you yell at me, Beau Landry," Alaina ben Thomas retorted. "What's happened? Did Korah's men find them?"

Beau's skin crawled, erupting in big goosebumps. His voice, when he stopped yelling, grew hoarse. "Not that devil, *chèr*, the old dragon himself."

Alaina gasped. "Have mercy. The literal Devil?"

"In the flesh." Beau peered out the kitchen window, staring into pitch black. It seemed as if all the light in the world had been extinguished when Lucifer landed in his backyard.

"Are you okay?" Alaina breathed.

He paused. Old terror, the sort that stalked his nightmares and hid in the recesses of his mind, slithered up his spine. He had not forgotten; it was more like a closet he never opened, whose contents were once known, but remained too terrible to remember. Tonight, the door to that closet blew off its hinges, and all sorts of nasty things spilled out. Alaina asked if he was okay. She, of all people, understood the danger he was in. "I'll make it."

Panicked now, Alaina shouted, "Let me speak to Peter!"

Beau laughed, a bit unhinged. "Prince Peter ain't here, *chèr*. He and the rest of them been taken off by angels."

"Angels? Like real angels? Seriously, they're gone?"

"In a flash, *mon chèr*. It was quite a sight."

She gasped, "So, you are alone?"

"Unless you count the snakes."

Alaina let loose a string of oaths straight out of a Mississippi beer joint. It was so incongruent with her normal modulated, cultured speech that he grinned. He remembered that girl. She covered the phone, but he discerned the high-pitched questions from her companion.

When she returned, her fingers pounded the keyboard. "I have to call you back." She sounded distracted, preoccupied. "Stay there."

"*Êtes-vous fou?*" he asked, lapsing into French, which he was wont to do when he got agitated.

A ghost crept over the line. "I'm not crazy, but neither are you."

He laughed in bitter irony. "There are a few doctors who might disagree with you, *chèr*. But I ain't hanging around here, waiting on the Devil to come back for a repeat visit, perhaps he be wanting some of this burnt-up etouffee. I'll leave it for him, but I'm gone."

"There's more than the Devil in that bayou, Beau. I remember."

There it was, at last, the truth. The thing neither dared speak to another living soul, even to each other, and they had seen it together. His voice lost its customary teasing sarcasm, sounding haunted, full of ancient regret. "*Mo chagren*, Alaina." I am sorry.

Pregnant silence filled the airwaves. Long history vibrated and shook them, mixed with terror, memories and heartbreak. But beneath all the pain, there was a glimmer of hope and rediscovery, resurrected over a phone line.

"Where are you going?" she whispered.

He made a sound in the back of his throat, heat and frustration, mixed with promise. "I think it's time I come find you, Jolie Catin. We got some unfinished business, no?"

The line went dead.

Part 2 - Persa and James

April 8, 985 ME (One Month before Rebellion)

Champions

On the evening of the 985 Equestrian World Championships, they scalped tickets for the vaulting event at six times their face value, for one reason only. The powerhouse duo of Persa ben Yereq and James ben Kole were going to attempt a feat never accomplished in the long, illustrious history of the sport. The crowd fidgeted in their seats, craning their necks in anticipation, checking and double checking their programs. They calculated refreshment and bathroom breaks to not miss their favorites. They applauded politely for the competitors who came before, because, after all, the athletes were the best in the world. But the event organizers knew their business, so James and Persa were last in the line-up.

A staple in the circuit for a decade, all week they hinted this may be their last performance. If it was, the rabid equestrian fans wanted to say that they had been there, had watched it happen. Millennials were horse crazy, the races of course, polo for the more refined, and steeplechases for the adventurous. However, the artistry of dressage and vaulting captured the beauty of the age, the elegance of man in harmony with nature. The sport, relegated to half empty, tiny arenas, and no real renown in the Last Age, exploded in the Millennium, turning their athletes into super stars. And every three years, the best of the best, gathered for the World Equestrian Games, which in 985 ME was held on Alanthia's own New City Equestrian Grounds.

"Ladies and Gentlemen," the bearded announcer called, as the gas lights focused, and the restless crowd fell silent. "The duo you have all been waiting for, our last competitors of the evening, James ben Kole and Persa ben Yereq."

Shouts, applause, and deafening cheers greeted the pair as they jogged in perfect synchronicity into the arena. The little girls wanted to be Persa; they wanted to marry James. The men attended because their wives and daughters loved the sport, but secretly, they thought it was all right, offering their expert opinions, booing the judges, protesting with the loudest fans at scores they disagreed with. Tonight, even the men felt the excitement, the energy contagious. The home team might pull off one of the biggest upsets in history. Alanthia had not won a vaulting World Championship in almost two decades, the Europeans dominating the sport with monotonous regularity.

The music began, a big band inspired, upbeat tune that had the crowd on their feet, bobbing and dancing. It was one secret to the pair's success. They always chose fantastic music. Vaulting required athleticism and strength, but there was a level of dance that derailed most male athletes, who came off effeminate. James ben Kole was a master, evoking an aura of a great entertainer, the consummate showman.

Persa ben Yereq looked to all the world a little fairy, floating above it all, making impossible feats of acrobatic skill look simple, effortless. But she was a fierce competitor, and anyone who caught the look in her hazel eyes did not doubt that behind that fluttering silk lay the stalwart heart of a warrior.

"I have you, go," James urged Persa as their vaulting horse, Rain, cantered under him.

Persa gave him a knowing smile, squeezed his hands, and pushed into a handstand. With her pointed toes fifteen feet in the air, James held her aloft. They maintained the position for a count of four. Then he launched her. She spiraled into a backflip, catching James' outstretched hand on her way down. Her feet hit the ground with the horse still cantering in a circle. The crowd held their breaths. She bounced, momentum and her partner carrying her into the air, where she flew onto the back of the mare, landing in a solid, unwavering stance. Persa threw out her hands with a flourish and struck an impish curtsy to James, who pumped his fists in triumph.

The packed arena erupted.

They were the only athletes in the history of pas de deux vaulting to pull off that trick, and on the evening of the Equestrian World Championship, the unstoppable duo of James and Persa executed it flawlessly.

Continuing their routine, they orchestrated a series of graceful and intricate lifts, holds, and impossible turns on the padded back of the horse, delighting the cheering crowd. Nothing penetrated their concentration save the music, attuned to each other, and the rhythmic horse beneath them. They dismounted to thunderous applause and a standing ovation.

Later, as they stood on the dais, the announcer proclaimed, "Ladies and gentlemen, winning gold in pas de deux vaulting, Alanthia's own, James ben Kole and Persa ben Yereq!"

James raised the silver cup over his head, his broad grin showing a full mouth of straight, white teeth. Persa held a bouquet of lavender roses aloft and gave a jaunty wave. The head judge, sporting substantial gray muttonchops, placed the gold medals around their necks, a reward for a decade of grueling work.

A trumpet split the air, filling the arena with the soaring notes of the Alanthian National Anthem. The victors lent their voices to the haunting song and closed their eyes, savoring the moment. James reached for Persa's hand. She took it without looking, clasped it, and squeezed.

Three hours later, at the Champion's reception, they still held hands as they wound their way through the receiving line. James leaned in, his breath tickling the pink shell of Persa's ear. "We did it, Fey."

The corner of her mouth lifted, and she sent him a sidelong glance. "We did it, Jay."

The orchestra warmed up in the club ballroom, most of the guests already taking advantage of the open bar. Candles shimmered in crystal chandeliers, a cool spring breeze making their wicks flutter and dance. Formal attire replaced boots and jeans, yet the sweet smell of hay exuded from many who spent their time in the company of horses. An air of expectancy tempered what would normally be a lively crowd, but royalty graced their presence tonight, and everyone, from the master of ceremonies to the lowliest groom, felt the unspoken pressure to be on their best behavior.

Inured or oblivious to the eager crowd's craning necks and nervous energy, the urbane and handsome Prince Korah ben Adam's hazel eyes glimmered as he greeted James and Persa.

Persa curtsied, spreading her green and gold gown around her in a sparkling puddle. James bowed low, holding the pose for the requisite two seconds.

Korah extended his open palms and bid them rise. "Well done, Alanthian Champions." He lowered his voice, adding in a conspiratorial whisper, "The pair of you gave the best performance of the night."

Persa clasped her hands, concealing a nervous tremor, but her lowered chin did not hide her pleased smile. Stealing a glance at the Ruling Prince's charming brother, she accepted the compliment. "My Esteemed, we are humbled. Thank you for your kind words."

Prince Korah nodded, a smile playing at the corner of his mouth. "You are stunning, my child, a rare talent. I sat captivated and spellbound throughout." He winked at James. "I am heartened to have two Alanthian champions this night. I fear our European counterparts continue to dominate our esteemed sport."

James nodded in thanks. "My Esteemed, Persa and I have always endeavored to bring honor to the King and our kingdom."

"I would say you accomplished it. Well done." Korah placed a strong hand on the shoulder of the squirming boy beside him. "Take note, Son, how these young Alanthians, through hard work and discipline, bring glory to our kingdom."

The golden-haired boy looked up, wearing an expression of weary defiance, telegraphing he heard the message, again. He turned to Persa, giving James the cut direct. "It was obvious which of you is the talent in the pair." Korah's fingers squeezed, but Prince d'Or gave Persa a sunny smile, ignoring his father. "Please allow me to escort you to the refreshment table."

Peter shrugged off his father's grip, taking the tiny girl by the arm and pulling her away. Feeling his father's eyes burning a hole in the back of his head, he thought he might pay for that later, but took his chances. He had enough of that ridiculous receiving line anyway, and the girl by his side was the closest thing he had seen to a potential friend all evening. Up close she was older than he first thought, but not much taller than him. Besides, it annoyed his father, and he could get away with that sometimes, in public.

As he retreated, Peter failed to see the strained expression on his mother's face or the deft way she diverted Korah's attention to the next guest.

"What was your name again?" Peter asked, studying her from under a raised golden eyebrow.

Persa chuckled, "I am Persa ben Yereq, my Esteemed."

"Are you hungry?" he asked, stealing a glance over his shoulder, checking for pursuit, "because I would much rather go see the horses."

"I would rather be with the horses, too." She plucked at her dress, adding, "Alas, I am in silk, and there are official duties that will require my attention."

Peter's chest lifted in a sigh of resignation, familiar with official duties. The way she spoke made him realize she was not as young as he first thought. "How old are you?"

Persa drew herself up, and Peter saw her flush, revealing a dusting of freckles, not quite obscured by the makeup she wore. "I'm nineteen. How old are you?"

"Seven," he replied, looking her straight in the eyes. She did not blink or look away, which was unusual. Most people got nervous around him. "You gave a good performance tonight. How long have you been vaulting?"

"Ten years."

Peter gestured over his shoulder. "Is he your brother or your boyfriend?"

The corner of her mouth twitched. "He is my fiancé."

"That is a shame." Peter flashed her his best smile. "Well, if we cannot go see the horses, we will at least skip this bloody long line."

Persa followed helplessly as the crowd parted for the little Prince. Several friends cast her speculative stares, which she answered with a sheepish grin and a slight lift of her shoulders, conveying she did not know what this was all about either. She refused to consider what James was going to say when he finally caught up with her.

Bowing with practiced elegance, Peter swept a hand toward the long buffet table. "As promised, my Lady."

Persa made murmured apologies to the people queued up and took her place at the front of the line, trying to control the hollow growl her stomach emitted. She never ate before competing and realized an apple dumpling at breakfast was the last thing she consumed. The lemon pasta with chicken and capers smelled delicious. Peter sent her an exaggerated wink and began dishing his plate.

Across the room, James stood open-mouthed as Persa finally caught his eye and mouthed, "Sorry."

He spotted Persa's father, Yereq, and remarked with wry irritation. "I fear Prince d'Or has stolen my date."

"I see that." Yereq narrowed his eyes.

James' friend, Andrew ben Nathaniel, elbowed him. "If he were a few years older, I'd be worried, man. Have you seen him ride?"

James laughed, "I am not terribly concerned about a kid."

"Well, he might not be stealing your fiancée, but it looks like he just hijacked your dinner date." Andrew pointed to the pair, settling at the head table.

Yereq pinched the bridge of his nose and turned away, muttering a curse. The three of them worked for more than a decade for this night, for this celebration. It was their crowning achievement, and on a whim, a royal robbed him and James of their victory dinner with Persa. However, there was not a thing he, or anybody else, could do about it.

Andrew read James' glare, threw back his head, and laughed.

Don't Be Mad

Two hours later, Persa found James brooding alone on the veranda that overlooked the club's immaculate lawn. He sent her a baleful look, then returned to his intense study of a horse topiary. Persa slipped her slender arm through the crook of his elbow and joined him in his reverie, keeping silent.

He raised his chin, ignoring her, never taking his eyes from the topiary. At length, he moistened his lips and asked, "Did your wee date have to go night-night?"

Persa snorted, a giggle caught in the back of her throat. "Yes, I believe the Prince retired for the evening."

James glared down at her.

Persa shrugged, adopting a chagrined, beguiling innocence. "What was I to do? He escorted me to the table. Then Prince Korah and Princess Alexa joined us. They are lovely, by the way. I could not just leave."

James sucked in a deep breath, held it for a moment, then exhaled in an audible rush. "This was our night."

Persa pulled his arm tighter and knocked his shoulder with the top of her head, coaxing, "It's still night, and the band is still playing. Come now, don't be mad. I couldn't help it."

Strawberry-blonde tendrils, loose from her up-swept hair, fluttered in the temperate breeze. She looked up at him with lovely hazel eyes, and he was lost, had been since he was Prince d'Or's age. His Fey, so named because she reminded him of a tiny fairy, lithe and elegant, utterly captivating. He harrumphed and said, "Keep that little pipsqueak away from me. I'd like to thump his ear."

She shouldered him playfully as they strolled toward the ballroom. "He's actually quite charming."

James growled, "Don't push it."

"Ha! You are jealous."

With practiced athletic grace, he turned and lifted her. Bringing them nose-to-nose, he murmured, "If I did not know, Persa ben Yereq, that I have your heart, I would be jealous of the wind that caresses your skin."

Persa kissed the tip of his fine straight nose. "Very gallant of you, my love. Now, let's go dance. It is not every day we win a World Championship."

"Aye, we did." James set her down, sadness clouding his soulful eyes.

She caught the look. "No sadness. We agreed tonight we would enjoy ourselves. We will discuss tomorrow, tomorrow."

He bowed his head, nodding. She was right, yet he could not shake the deep sense of melancholy. This part of their lives was ending, however triumphantly. Tomorrow, they would retire, and real life would begin.

May 2, 985 ME

Death of the Monarch

James and Persa's victory parade, planned in their small town of Redding, California, was canceled as the kingdom mourned Prince Eamonn ben Adam. The news of his unexpected death rocked Alanthia. Long-life was a mainstay in the Millennium, so to lose the Ruling Prince at the tender age of forty-five felt ominous, an omen of evil foreboding. Persistent gray clouds covered the region from Vancouver to Guadalajara as the sky cloaked itself in mourning.

For years, Alanthians flirted with rebellion. They pushed boundaries, flouted their loyalty to the Iron King, and dabbled in the forbidden. Tantalized by the secrets of the past, an unspoken fear crept over the kingdom that their misdeeds may have cost them a righteous leader.

They could not say why they felt so anxious or why Prince Eamonn's death affected them so deeply; but it seemed like a wall had crumbled, and an enemy breached their defenses. There was no war, not for a thousand years, no marauding army laying siege. However, they knew in their hearts something was desperately wrong.

Tucked among the stalls at the Rivergate thoroughbred ranch, Persa and James sat together in an empty stall. "As sad as this is, it changes nothing," Persa said, taking James' hand. "The contract is still in place. You work here for two more years. When we both turn twenty-two, Dad will give us our starter stock and the Pepperwood property. After you add the money you will inherit from your grandfather's trust, we are all set."

She smiled up at him and laughed. "And it wasn't like we needed Prince Eamonn's blessing."

"True," James agreed, draping an arm over her shoulders, and kissing the top of her head. She was right, yet in the kingdom's collective mourning, everything felt less concrete.

A crash in the stall beside them shattered their cocoon of peace, giving them something tangible to worry over. Their beloved vaulting horse lay in her stall, convulsing and thrashing, her great brown eyes rolled back in her head. Thirteen hours later, Rain was gone, and with her the unshakable assurance of a bright future. Something wicked loomed over the Alanthian horizon. James felt it.

September 4-5, 985 ME

Who Runs the Show?

Rain's death, as much as the upheaval in Alanthia, brought an uneasiness to the ranch. Rivergate had not lost a horse to sickness or accident in living memory. The barn, once a perfect haven, became tainted for Persa. Where laughter and song once reigned, grumbling and murmuring took root. Ranch hands slipped away, lured to the New City by the promise of a life that did not involve shoveling manure.

On September 4th, the ranch shucked off the dark clouds of uncertainty and prepared for a birthday party. James ben Kole, the future son of the house, turned twenty. The date also marked the end of the first year of their three-year betrothal, and Persa vowed today was going to be special.

The morning of the party, Persa faced Cook with her hands on her hips. "I do not care if you think it is below the dignity of Rivergate. It is what he likes, and it is his birthday."

"Chicken fried steak?" Cook blustered. "Whoever heard of such an abominable dish?"

"We had it at a competition in Houston three years ago. He loved it, and we have not had it since. He still brings it up. So, that is what we are having." Persa raised on her tiptoes, attempting to look taller... it did not work. At 4'10", the top of her head came to Cook's shoulder.

He snorted, pounding out the flat steak as if it were the enemy. "I'm not necessarily opposed to it," Cook said over the racket. "But this sort of thing is a ton of work." He gestured with the mallet toward two workstations where helpers should be. "And I hate bloody frying, dangerous, messy business."

Persa tilted her head, not giving an inch. "It's his birthday."

"Yes, it is," Cook snapped. "And it will be my luck that every hand on this spread gets it into their head they want this for their birthday, and I'll be making the blasted dish twenty-five times a year."

"Fine," Persa relented, pulling his ruddy cheek down for a kiss. "I will decree that only James gets chicken fried steak for his birthday."

He narrowed his red-rimmed eyes, calculating. "All right," he grumbled and gave the flat steak a mighty whack.

"Still keeping everyone in line, I see," said a teasing voice from the doorway.

Persa spun around with a squeal of delight. "Ian." She rushed forward and threw herself into his outstretched arms.

"Hello, Pers." James' brother picked her up and gave her a spin.

"Oh, Ian, it's good to see you." She looked around, adding in a conspiratorial whisper, "He hasn't seen you, has he?"

"No. But it was a blasted long walk. Mother and Father dropped me at the south pasture before we drove up. I assume James is settling them at his place," Ian said, referring to the guest house James occupied.

"Excellent, I shall hide you." Persa pulled him by the arm out of the kitchen. "We'll go to Dad's study." Persa peaked around a corner before scampering across the hall, her high ponytail swinging back and forth.

Safely hidden, she shut the heavy brown door with a thunk, noting the upper corner needed to be planed. "Hang on," she said, retrieving a notebook from her pocket and adding 'Door to Dad's study' to the long list of house repairs she started keeping last week.

Looking up, she grinned. In the year since she had seen him, Ian ben Kole had changed. His resemblance to his older brother became more pronounced, only their eyes and builds differed. Where James' eyes were a soulful brown, the color of milk chocolate, Ian's were a smoky gray blue, like dawn on a winter's day. Tall and square-jawed, Ian remained lean, but ripcord muscle lay just below the surface, saving him from gawkiness. At sixteen, James had filled out. Ian looked like he might not, though it suited him.

Ian met her smile with his own toothy Kole brothers' grin. "I see you haven't grown."

She pursed her lips at him. "I see you have."

"In more ways than one, Pers."

"You've lost your accent among all those fancy people at the Royal Military Academy," she teased.

Their regional accent held strong hints of an Irish burr, inherited after a large influx of horse ranchers immigrated to Alanthia, bringing their finest stock, their food, and a fervent desire to be as far away from London as possible. Raised an hour south of Rivergate, James and Ian sounded more cultured than she did, though years on the ranch and countless hours of training with her father softened James' clipped tones. Yereq's grandfather, the founder of Rivergate, had been one of the original settlers. He sponsored dozens of families, bringing them to Redding to work the ranch. Thus, plucking any stable hand out of Rivergate and dropping them in a Galway pub would have caused only the natives to notice the nuances adopted from years among the Alanthians. Persa thought they sounded melodic and liked the way they spoke.

"Aye," Ian said with a nod, exaggerating his cadence. "'Twas easier to do than constantly explaining where I'm from, lassie."

"I imagine," she smiled. "But I know where you come from, boyo." Persa poked him, and he deflated like a balloon, blustering all over her.

"I am proud of you," Ian said, picking her up and grinning. "World Champion."

She swatted his shoulder. "Put me down."

Ian dropped her by her father's big leather chair and flung himself onto the matching sofa, stretching and yawning. "How is he, Pers?"

She frowned. "He works too hard. We've lost half a dozen hands in the last few months. But he has only replaced one. On top of that, they've begun construction at Pepperwood, so he rides over every day to supervise. I've told him I would help, but he insists on doing it himself."

"If I know my brother, he is driving everyone crazy."

"He is not that bad."

Ian raised a straight eyebrow at her. "He is a perfectionist."

Persa crossed her arms and slouched in the leather chair. "He is exacting, but that's not always a bad thing." Her eyes moved to the silver cup, displayed among their numerous other trophies.

"Granted," Ian chuckled. "But I do not need to tell you that my brother has always been an overachiever."

"No, you do not."

"Do you miss it?" Ian pulled a blanket up to his chin, snuggling into the sofa, though his ankles hung off the end.

"Vaulting?" At his nod, she gave a small shrug. "A little. But we were ready to stop. We made the right decision."

Staring out the office window, she did not confide that she still woke every morning carrying the expectation they would saddle Rain and fly together. Neither did she mention retirement was proving quite different from her expectations.

As the staff shrank, the demands of Rivergate did not. James was not the only one doing the work of three people, so their time together dwindled to hastily eaten meals accompanied by her father and a dozen hands. Evenings found them both so exhausted they barely stayed awake to kiss goodnight.

She shook off the maudlin turn of her thoughts, fixed a smile, and said, "Well, I would love to stay and visit, but I have a thousand things to do before tonight. Come with me. I'll show you to the guest room. You look as if you are about to drop."

"Aye, I am. The military has an aversion to sleep." He yawned loudly to emphasize his point. "Bless you."

"If you weren't a surprise, I'd put you to work. You know I would."

"I know, little general," Ian said, following her efficient, quick steps through the door. She walked with determination, her shoulders back, her head up. Her diminutive stature and swinging ponytail belied the veritable force of her personality. "Your father and my brother may think they run Rivergate, but the rest of us know the truth."

Persa shot him an annoyed look. "You make me sound like a shrew." Her voice broke as she added, "Now, go in there and take your nap."

Birthday Celebration

All the planning, preparation, and subterfuge were worth the effort when James saw Ian. He gave a whoop of surprise and ran across the lawn. After a brief back pounding hug, they turned, wearing identical smiles across their handsome faces. For a moment, the relentless gray sky parted, and they stood tall and strong, their brown hair glimmering with flashes of gold and red.

Beside Persa, Salome beamed with maternal pleasure. "They are extraordinary, my boys, are they not?"

"Yes, they are, though I am partial to one," Persa said, giving Salome a tentative smile.

Salome walked away without a word.

Certain every eye watched her as she glided across the lawn to join her sons, she carefully avoided any stray horse apples that might litter the grass. Truly the whole place had gone downhill since last she was here. She planned to have a word with Yereq about it, but not today. Today they were celebrating her first born's twentieth birthday.

She smiled, hugging her boys, presenting an image of a proud mother. There were several neighbors in attendance, including a few vintners who were making a name for themselves. Salome knew how people gossiped. Let them think she was pleased her eldest son settled for this life and a future with a little nobody. They would never guess that privately she railed against James' choices, not only of a bride, but that blasted contract that practically indentured him to Yereq in exchange for four horses and a property in the middle of the redwoods without so much as a proper road running to it.

He was not even capitalizing on his World Championship by using his own name for the ranch, which had a time limited value. In five years, no one would even remember him, but Pepperwood? No one knew what that was, or where it was, for that matter. Did James expect anyone in polite society to travel four days north through dense forest to find a place called Pepperwood? To Salome's way of thinking, James willfully threw away all the opportunities she and Kole had given him, and she was certain her friends thought so, too.

She endured their pitying looks at her last charity luncheon. Sarah ben Paul's uncouth sons were attending law and medical schools. They just elected Beth ben Terry's middle son to the legislature, and witless Eliza ben Thomas' son, with his weak chin and watery eyes, had made junior partner at Anderson, Bradly, and Todd, the New City's most prestigious accounting firm. In Salome's opinion, James outshone them all, and he was wasting it. She could claim him as a World Champion, but that was already wearing thin. She saw it in her friends' eyes, knew what they said behind her back.

Noble blood ran through her son's veins, on his father's side, but that was no matter. She brought enough money to the marriage that Kole's entire blue-blood family was saved from penury, so the scales balanced out. But she raised her boys to want more, to aspire to greatness, to become men of renown. Ian was well on the path, as for James… two years, she still had two years.

Dinner provided the second surprise of James' twentieth birthday celebration. When Cook placed the heaping plate of chicken fried steak in front of him, the grin he flashed made every grease splatter worth it.

Persa tilted her head and gave Cook an 'I told you so' look. Cook grunted and stalked back to his messy kitchen, resigned.

As the party wound down, James and Persa strolled toward the stables. "Your mother still hates me," Persa said in a conversational tone.

James stiffened. "My mother does not hate you. She simply wants me in law or medical school." He shrugged. "Which is one reason I love Ian so much. She can heap all that maternal ambition on him."

"Did you catch her expression at dinner?"

James detected the hurt behind her words and gave a nasal snort, trying to diffuse the situation. "It made more chicken fried steak for me. She plays the martyr to the hilt. I let her. That was delicious, by the way. Thank you."

He maneuvered her into the shadows outside the barn and took her in his arms. She rested her ear against his chest and relaxed.

"I miss touching you," he murmured.

"And I miss being touched," she said into the folds of his shirt.

"Even if we weren't, you know... I still had you in my arms."

She ran her hands up his sides, feeling the hard planes of his body. "You feel nice."

He groaned.

From the time they were nine, their training put them in constant physical contact. Six to eight hours a day, they touched. As they grew older, they pushed boundaries, sneaking off, away from the watchful eyes of her father and their coaches. One night, after an intense session of adolescent petting, they discovered the dangers of playing with fire. A barn cat interrupted them, and they stopped just short. Afterward, they realized anything more than a chaste kiss, a touch of a hand, or a quick hug ignited the flame. However tonight, relaxed after several glasses of celebratory wine and enjoying their first intimate moment in months, neither felt inclined to follow a set of rules established when they were thirteen.

James buried his face in Persa's neck, whispering, "I am on fire all day, every day. Two more years feels like a prison sentence."

Persa pulled his mouth down to hers, and a lifetime of pent-up passion blazed.

"Fey, I'm dying." James ground his new jeans into her softness, feeling her yield beneath him. "I want to touch you, make love to you."

She was almost sobbing in frustration. "Jay, I need you. I don't care anymore."

He buried his face in her neck, seconds from losing control. One term of their marital contract was that Persa remained chaste, but he'd been thinking on the matter for quite some time. There were ways around that. "I'll not take you in the dirt, not our first time. I'll honor our contract, but I'm going to touch you, and you can touch me."

He pulled the shirt out of her waistband and ran his hand up her belly, settling on her small breast. She moaned and with an arch of her back fumbled for the hooks on her bra. His tongue on her nipple turned them both to liquid fire.

He felt her heat, heard the desperate sounds she made as he slid his fingers inside the waistband of her jeans. Attuned to everything about her, the scent of her arousal drove him mindless. Persa unsnapped her jeans and freed the zipper, guiding his hand to her, as desperate to have him touch her as he was to do it.

A shrill voice shattered the night's passion. "James ben Kole!"

They froze, but James did not move, shielding Persa. His voice, when he spoke, held such a note of command and fury that, for once, his mother did not argue. "Go back to the house, Mother. I will see you shortly."

At the sound of her retreating feet, James groaned and dropped his forehead to Persa's. With their labored breaths mixing in the evening air, he closed his eyes. "I am a rutting billy goat, molesting you in the grass."

She giggled, snuffling his ear. "You don't smell like a billy goat. I like your new cologne, by the way, all warm sandalwood and sea."

"Mother bought it for my birthday," he said absently, studying her through hooded eyes, trying to cool the fire flowing in his veins. "You are so beautiful. Forgive me, Fey."

She brought her delicate hands to the sides of his face. "I am not beautiful. I am a wanton trollop who loved every second of taking a quick tumble with you in the dirt. There is nothing to forgive, Jay." She kissed the end of his nose and added, "I have a present for you, and it wasn't this, although I dare say that would have been more fun." She laughed low and husky, giving him a seductive wiggle.

"Quit!" He threw himself off her, his forearm covering his eyes. "I can't even think about it, or I will start again. That is dangerous fire."

Persa sat up, straightening her clothes. "Then I shall be sure to have a bucket of water in our bedroom on our wedding night."

James snorted. "If you have a cold bucket handy, I could use one about right now."

"I am sure your mother has one waiting." Persa flushed, growing red with embarrassment, and burying her face in her hands. "Now, she truly hates me."

He chuckled, "Yeah, she does." Her open-mouthed expression was exactly what he'd been after, and he burst out laughing.

She punched his shoulder and sauntered away, swishing her little hips on purpose.

He was on her in a second, scooping her up with one arm around her waist. "Where do you think you are going?"

Persa gave a grunt of mock struggle, then she twisted, throwing her arms around his neck, and wrapping her legs around his waist, a trick they practiced thousands of times. "Take me to see Lightning. That's where your present is."

He tilted his head, puzzled, but carried her into the barn, enjoying the feel of her in his arms. Touch restored without the flame, for now.

They stopped in front of Lightning's stall where a whimsical nameplate, painted in a girlish hand, decorated the door. Persa gestured to her beloved horse then back to James, beaming.

James bit his bottom lip, looking between them. "Um… okay. Good evening, Lightning, lovely to see you. Can you please tell me what you and Persa are up to?"

The horse shook her head no. They burst out laughing. Persa slid to the floor, going to Lightning, and scratching the spot she loved just below her ear. "Look at her, Jay. I mean really look at her."

He blinked, clearing away the fog. Lightning was such a fixture on the ranch, no one paid much attention to her. With so many other things pulling at his mind, he might not have actually seen her in months. "Jupiter's Moon," he exclaimed, "she's in foal." He moved into the stall, examining her. "When did this happen?"

Persa threw up her hands in shared surprise. "I do not know, neither does Dad. From the looks of her, I suspect it had to be last winter."

James picked up a brush and stroked her fine white flanks. "Lightning, it seems Persa is not the only little trollop around here."

"Hey!" she protested, coming into the stall. With a devilish grin, she wrapped her hands around his waist, running her palms up the front of his thighs.

He stilled mid brush stroke.

"If you are going to call me a trollop, I may as well reap the rewards."

His mouth went dry. "Stop."

She giggled, nipped his back, and pressed her body against his. Then turning on her heel, she left him frozen with the brush held aloft, his jeans growing uncomfortably tight again. They breached a dam, and spill water flowed up the banks.

He put the brush back on its shelf and stalked her.

She backed away, laughing, and held up a hand for him to stop. "Wait, there is more. The foal is yours, for working so many extra hours these last few months. Dad said when it comes, it's yours. It will be our first baby."

He stopped, then pounded a loose fist over his heart, and brought it to his smiling lips. "That is a great birthday present, Fey."

"It's not a present. You earned it. Just as you've earned everything else. You don't have to do what you do here. Your mother is right. The entire world is open to you, yet you stay here... for me. I know that, so does Dad. I don't know what we would do without you."

He gathered her in his arms. "Well, I guess you will never have to find out because I'm not going anywhere."

Invitation

At breakfast the following morning, a housemaid rushed in, flushed and excited. "This just arrived by a special messenger from the Palace." She handed Persa a heavy envelope with calligraphy script on the front.

Ian looked up from his heaping plate of bacon, toast, tomatoes, sausage, scrambled eggs, and black pudding. "What do you have there, Pers?"

She shrugged and turned the letter over, her eyes widening. "It has a royal seal."

Salome leaned forward and snapped, "Well, open it."

Persa schooled her features. She wanted to lift her lip and snarl but did not. James was already in the barn, and last night she vowed to try to make peace with Salome.

Kole ignored his wife, engrossed in his newspaper.

Persa's small intake of breath stopped all movement in the breakfast room. "It's an invitation to the Coronation Ball."

Salome snatched the letter out of Persa's fingers. "Let me see that."

Kole dropped his paper and sent a baleful look at Salome but remained silent.

Salome shook the invitation at Persa. "How did you get this?"

"Now see here, madam," Yereq interjected. "I don't care for your tone." Holding out his hand, he added, "Give it over."

Salome drew back, affronted. However, she recognized the steel in his brown eyes, so she relented.

Yereq examined the letter, frowning. "Well, this is surprising. Quite an honor." His expression belied his words. He looked sick. "Persa, you seem to have made an impression on the royal family."

Kole took a sip of tea, sending a speculative look at his wife. Salome sputtered. She refused to support James and Persa's sporting career and thus, was absent the night they won the World Championship. Kole knew she omitted that pesky detail when she bragged about James' victory. That he had a partner or that Salome did everything in her power to sabotage his training did not merit a mention either. He had not told her Persa sat with the second family at the reception, had not wanted to hear her ranting over why it should have been James at the table and not Persa. Kole crossed his arms, enjoying his wife's obvious discomfort.

Salome did not sleep with him for three months after he allowed James to move to Rivergate and train with Yereq. He saw the dynamic developing and orchestrated the move to prevent his domineering wife from browbeating their quiet older son into submission. It was a decision he never regretted. Ian held his own with his mother; James might not have, at least when he was younger. So Kole sent him to the one place where James might grow into the man he knew he could become, and it was not Salome's version of him. His strategy paid off. Despite what Salome thought, James was an extraordinary young man.

Staring at the invitation, Salome took refuge from her embarrassment by adopting a haughty tone. "I am sure James' invitation is at his residence."

Yereq raised a ruddy eyebrow. "One messenger, one invitation, and it's to my daughter." He emphasized the latter half of the sentence. "Plus a guest, so by default they invited James, too."

"Where am I invited?" James asked, coming through the door, the smell of hay and horses clinging to his clothes.

"Persa received an invitation to the Coronation Ball," Salome said, her words dripping with accusation.

James read the room and grinned. "Prince d'Or is making his move."

Persa burst out laughing, though she tried to smother it when Salome sent her a quelling look.

Ian glanced between them, his eyes sparkling. Persa wrote to him about the incident with the little Prince, regaling him with James' jealousy.

"What is the meaning of this?" Salome blustered.

James kissed her cheek and sat beside her, knowing the smell of the barn would annoy her. "It's a joke, Mother. Draw in your claws."

Persa hid her amusement behind a hand, her head turned away, studying Kole's newspaper, but her shaking shoulders ruined the charade.

Salome looked from face to face, everyone in some state of suppressed mirth. "I do not think it is funny. Not at all."

James had pity on her. "Prince Peter spotted Persa at the reception, thought she was a seven-year-old like him, and they became friends."

Persa threw her napkin at James. "He did it to annoy his father, and you, if the truth be told." She quirked an eyebrow at James, then added in a conciliatory tone to Salome. "Prince Korah was praising James, and it struck a nerve with Prince Peter. So, the little rascal pulled me out of the receiving line, and I ended up eating dinner with the royal family. It was a pleasant evening. He is quite a charmer."

Kole tapped his paper. "There are shady goings-on at the Palace right now. This cockamamie story they floated about Prince Josiah does not add up. And that ruling that came down last week declaring Prince Korah the heir without a proper inquest?" Kole shook his head. "There are too many unanswered questions about the whole affair, something's rotten." He leaned forward. "Persa, I don't think you should go."

Yereq nodded. "I agree, Kole."

"Don't be ridiculous." Salome waved a dismissive hand. "Kole, you are reading too many conspiracy papers. This is a high honor, one James and Persa would be foolish to pass up."

"When is it?" James asked between bites.

Yereq looked at the invitation. "October 23rd."

James pursed his lips and shook his head. "There's no way I can go unless Lightning foals before then. From what I gathered from the records, they left her unattended one afternoon in December and found her the next day. Calculating forward, that puts her due date right around that time."

Persa shrugged, indifferent. They attended dozens of balls, met many important people. Nothing was more important than their first foal. "Then we won't go."

"Persa you must go, even if James cannot. Think of it, who buys more horses than the royal family? What might a contract with them mean for you and James?"

James regarded his mother through narrow brown eyes, but he could not fault her logic. It was unlike her to be so conciliatory.

"I shall chaperon," Salome declared in triumph, then added in an unctuous tone, "It will give Persa and me a chance to get to know one another better, plus provide me an excellent opportunity for me to instruct her in proper deportment, decorum, and etiquette." She turned to Yereq. "Which is part of her education you have neglected. I will require it when she marries James. As you know, our family travels in a higher social circle."

Yereq could not help the twitch of his lip as he glared at the self-important, detestable woman.

The pained smile on Persa's face fooled no one. She sat, clearly horrified at the prospect but utterly and completely trapped.

October 23, 985 ME

Midnight Rider

Back at her future in-law's townhouse, Persa fell onto the small double bed with a sigh. Her feet were killing her after hours in satin shoes, that while stylish, had paper thin soles and zero arch support. The left one had been a smidgeon too tight, and there was an angry spot on her big toe where the strap rubbed the cuticle raw. The injury was likely exacerbated by the aggressive pedicure Salome insisted she get, declaring in front of everyone at the shoe store that Persa's toenails looked like an eagle about to catch a fish. Persa honestly never noticed, wearing boots or trainers her entire life.

Examining the torn cuticle, she wondered idly if she had embarrassed herself at the dozens of receptions she attended throughout her career by having eagle toes but dismissed the thought. Her only pair of dress shoes were close-toed, flesh-colored pumps that went with her three best gowns, servicable, practical, and less to pack. Nobody looked at her feet, anyway.

She closed her eyes, letting the silence of the house surround her. There was noise from the street, and it seemed to Persa the New City never stopped. Even at this hour, she heard people talking, carriages jingling, and the faint notes of a drunk singing down the block; quite a change from the crickets and nightbirds at Rivergate.

Salome spent the trip making veiled excuses about why their townhouse was not in the most fashionable part of the city, like Persa would know or care, but each time Salome mentioned it she made a point of staring at Kole. He ignored her. From what Persa gathered, this had been his great-aunt's house, and at one point it *had* been in the most fashionable district, but tastes and locales changed in the last fifty years, relegating Andrew's Square to the second tier in high society rankings. Salome hinted they might someday build another and give this house to James. Persa kept her opinion on that to herself, merely stating Ian might make better use of it. James was right, allow the woman to heap her unrelenting maternal ambition on Ian. She and James would never come to town. It would be an absolute waste.

Kole and Salome spent most of their time at their sprawling manor in Leggett, where James was born, about an hour south of Rivergate. The trip to the New City normally took four days, three on a fast horse, six if pulling a team with a ponderous amount of luggage. It took them six.

They arrived a week early, a fact that chafed Persa because she had no news from home and wondered every hour if Lightning had foaled. The baby represented so much, their future, their hopes. Stud or mare, the foal would play a major role in the establishment of Pepperwood.

However, she kept her worry to herself, vowing to use this trip to build a bridge between her and her future mother-in-law. Whether it worked remained to be seen, but she thought she made progress. At least she hoped she had, otherwise two weeks spent in the company of the odious woman had been for naught. She smiled where appropriate, did her best to make small talk with the parade of fashionable matrons who flocked to inspect her. She drank more tea and said more, "Yes, madams," than in her entire life.

They dressed, coiffured, painted, and corseted Persa into a gown that even she admitted flattered her pale complexion and complimented her strawberry-blonde hair. Most colors looked ghastly on her, which was why eighty-five percent of her wardrobe was green. It suited her, and even Salome gave up the plums and pinks, the en vogue colors of the season, when she saw how putrid they made Persa look.

The ball had been a crush of people, food, smells, and frenetic energy. Persa had never seen the New City Palace and marveled at its opulence. Prince Eamonn commissioned a restoration project in the early 70s that took ten years to complete. Inside and out, the Palace felt more like a municipal building than a home, which she surmised made sense since it served as both. Persa could not imagine living in such a place but got a behind-the-scenes tour by the most unexpected escort, Prince d'Or.

He had been the highlight of the evening. Seeking her out and greeting her like his long-lost friend and personal guest, he once again pulled her out of the receiving line, much to the delight of Salome, who shooed her off, beaming with social triumph.

Peter insisted on showing her his horses, and took her through the family wing, declaring it was the most direct route to the stables. That was likely when the blister began. The dancing shoes were not meant to tramp through grass, across lawns, and down to the barn. However, the Prince's charming smile, the excitement in his emerald eyes, and enthusiasm to show her his new yearling, propelled her along. Inside the rich, quiet stables, her mind settled for the first time in two weeks, and they passed an enjoyable half hour.

His nanny, a formidable woman of indeterminate years and kind eyes, found them and hustled them back to the ballroom in time to watch Prince Korah and Princess Alexa open the ball. From then on, Salome attached herself to Persa like a limpet, and other than a single dance, her fun with the little Prince drew to a close.

To Salome's credit, she ensured Persa did not become a wallflower, and her minor status as an equestrian helped bolster her popularity. The only time she escaped the dancefloor were the few powder room breaks she sneaked in. It was a pleasant evening, but she was supremely relived to have it finished.

Persa was ready to be home. The constant barbs and endless lecturing from Salome strained her patience. Her face hurt from smiling. But most of all, she missed James. They had not been apart this long since they were nine, and she felt like her right arm was missing. She kept turning to say something before realizing he was not there. The experience disconcerted her, and she vowed to never take another journey without him.

Changing into soft pajamas, she snuggled under the itchy bedspread, which was beautiful but offered little by way of comfort. An odd trembling came over her body, from too much stress, an overload of nervous energy, and too many dance partners. She yawned and stretched.

A soft ping against her window caught her attention. She dismissed it. When it came again, she padded over to investigate.

In the courtyard below, James sat astride a magnificent black stallion, leading a dappled gray mare. She opened her mouth in exclamation, ready to call out, but he raised his finger to his lips. Persa glanced around her empty bedroom and instantly understood. She held up a finger, signaling she needed a minute.

He had come, which meant their foal was born, and all was well. Of course, James missed her as much as she missed him, and he would provide a welcome buffer against his mother, a prospect nearly as appealing as seeing him again.

She changed out of her pajamas and slipped on her favorite jeans, riding boots, and a soft cashmere sweater because the evening had turned cool. Tiptoeing down the steps, she clung to the shadows and hoped the butler was in bed. He should be, but she was not taking any chances.

The front door was out of the question, too big, too locked, too loud. But there was a side door through the kitchen, and the lights were out in there. The banked hearth cast the rustic room in an orange glow, and she rushed through, keeping her head down, determined to ignore anybody who might be in there. Nobody saw her.

Closing the door quietly, she sagged with relief. It had been years since she snuck out of the house. Turning, she grinned. The light of the crescent moon shone watery and weak, but he was there, waiting for her. He held up a finger, signaling her to stay silent. She nodded, her eyes suddenly filling with tears.

"Get on," he whispered and flipped her the gray's reins.

With a dancer's grace, she mounted the horse and followed him into the night. When they were a fair distance from the house, she drew up beside him. "Where are we going?"

"A special place, I prepared just for you."

"Are you sick? You sound terrible." Persa squinted in the dark, his beloved face cast in shadow.

"Throat's sore. Just a long journey, come on." He spurred the horse ahead.

Persa drew her brows down in confusion; something was not right. His seat was wrong, the set of his shoulders tense. Her heart fell. The foal? Had something happened to it? First Rain… now their baby? "James," she called through strangled vocal cords.

He did not stop, beyond the sound of her voice, the beat of the hooves drowning out everything.

They were in an unfamiliar part of the city, but all parts of the New City were unfamiliar to her. James had spent more time here than she, so she followed him into the night.

He did not slow, did not speak, keeping just ahead of her, such that she could not voice the increasing worry pressing in on her. It must be bad, otherwise he would not be acting this way. Her lungs refused to breathe as a band of dread tightened over her chest like a vice.

They rode hard.

James turned off the main road onto a cobblestone drive, his exuberant whoop of laughter lifted her spirits. "We're here," he said, turning with a grin.

"Where?" she asked, looking around at the stone walls and hedge lined property.

"Come on," he urged, and cantered down a torch-lit path that ended in a magnificent garden illuminated by a thousand candles.

Persa dismounted and tied the reins to a hitching post. "James, what is this place?"

"They call it the House of Amah." He lifted her to him for a fierce kiss.

Passion erupted between them.

If the foal had died, he would tell her. He would not bring her to an enchanted garden and kiss her that way.

Breaking the kiss with a groan, he pulled her down a path to the center of the hedgerows, where a merry fountain danced in front of a bed of red silk covered in rose petals.

"I cannot wait any longer," he declared, tracing a gentle finger over her jaw.

Persa smiled, feeling shy. "Nor can I, my love."

They touched, tender and warm, their clothes shedding, hurried in their passion, a whirlwind.

But as he entered her, breaking the barrier, taking her maidenhead, his face changed, and Persa ben Yereq froze in pure terror. In that horrifying instant she knew the man inside her was not James, not her love, not her friend, but a monster.

She screamed into the empty night, "No! No! No!"

He bit her, drawing blood.

"You aren't James!" She pushed, fought, and screamed for help, but Persa was a tiny woman and no match for Marduk.

He pounded into her body with brutal force, his face changing between James, one of the men she danced with at the ball, and then something far, far worse.

Violent convulsions shook his body, and he cried out, "Ilsidor, I have missed you."

Persa sobbed; trapped, violated, raped.

October 24, 985 ME

Reminiscence

After the ball, Marduk, the Prince of Persia, did not go to Princess Philomela of Greece as a man, as an ardent lover seeking stolen kisses in the moonlight. He came into her room as himself, brutal and terrifying, eternally wicked. Even the Hosts of Heaven trembled before him. Philomela did more than tremble, she would have screamed. She would have told. She would have run her mouth. So, he cut out her tongue with a single flick of his talon and pumped his black seed into her belly.

To Mademoiselle Charlotte, he brought a young rooster and slit its throat above her naked, questing body, bathing her in blood before he fell upon her in lustful fury. She took him inside with greedy pleasure, milking him, demanding what he offered.

But for Persa, there was seduction. A midnight ride under the stars, into the labyrinth, where he laid her down and forgot everything for a brief moment.

He could still hear her crying through the locked doors. She needed to stop. He had not hurt her, not really. All her yammering about him stealing something that had not belong to him… who cared, he took what he wanted, and he wanted her.

Even if she was a bit of a sniveler, Persa made him feel. The first time when they danced, and tonight when he took her. Perhaps she could give him that feeling again, which was why he locked her up while the others were free. She was his now, and she better get used to it.

In the grand scheme, the Creole wench was a better fit, wicked thing that she was. But Marduk had seven thousand years of wickedness. The little fairy woman sparked something; a glimmer so foreign he almost forgot it existed.

Wandering the garden, melancholy stalked him; the rumpled bed of silk mocked him. He had not imagined he would be lonely, released into a world where he was the only one of his kind, but he was, which was part of the reason he took the monumental risk tonight. And it worked. The women were already breeding. He felt his seed take hold while his body still throbbed within them. It was heady.

Four thousand years passed since an elohim put a spawn on a human, creating a Nephilim, a Giant. It was a daring plan from the outset, one that yielded mixed results in the First Age. Sexual desire ensured there was no lack of volunteers. However, the beauty of the Daughters of Eve, was a mere bonus, their ultimate goal was corruption. With their seed firmly embedded in human DNA, it would only be a matter of time before the bloodlines of man became unalterably polluted. There could be no Messiah if they accomplished that. They nearly succeeded. Only a dozen pure humans remained before the flood.

After the water cleared, they tried again, changing tactics, and manipulating the cellular structure of their offspring, so the second-generation Nephilim did not attain the great height of the first, the Titans. They also curbed their barbaric and bloodthirsty tendencies, reasoning the Most High may not wipe them out.

The second generation possessed incredible intelligence and cunning, making great advances in mathematics, science, astronomy, architecture. They built standing stones and pyramids, the ruins of which, survived to this day. Writers immortalized their great feats in the tales of the demigods, the mighty men of renown. History disregarded them, relegating them to myth. Scripture recorded them, but those passages were layered in mystery. Most failed to understand the words and certainly did not discern the Nephilim tribes recorded, assuming the names were nothing but recitations of long dead ancients. But Marduk remembered them, especially the Amalekites, his particular favorites.

For a time, the Nephilim spread across the globe, concentrating in the Levant, where everyone believed the Most High would try to bring forth the Messiah. Though they suffered terrible defeat when Joshua led the Israelites out of the desert. He and the rest of those filthy Jews slaughtered most of the Nephilim. Only a remnant escaped. But for four hundred years the Rapha remained defiant in Canaan before being cut down by that little pissant David.

Marduk knew the risk, lying with three human women. He refrained from doing it in the Last Age because things had not ended well for his brethren who had. It was long forbidden and always roused his enemy. But he was not yet in the abyss, and for that, he garnered a measure of satisfaction. The Most High ignored him since his escape. Perhaps He had grown old. The thought cheered him.

As if conjured, golden light blossomed at the center of the garden. He brandished his sword and prepared for battle, expecting the swine Gabriel, but it was not Gabriel who came to him. His visitor proved to be someone even more terrifying. Marduk fell on his face.

He had longed for her, now she was here, after seven thousand long years. "Ilsidor!" he sobbed.

"Marduk," she spat the name given to him at the fall. "Oh, look what has become of thee."

"Hast thou come to slay me?"

"The hour of thy death is not mine to decide, but thou hast been dead to me for eons, from the moment of thy rebellion."

"I was deceived," he protested, "beguiled and fooled by Lucifer. It was not my fault."

"Thou art as much a liar as he. Thy forked tongue speaketh only deceit." Ilsidor took three steps forward. "I was there. I beseeched thee. So do not lie to me."

To anyone else, Marduk would have argued, to Ilsidor he could not. He might beg for forgiveness, but there was none. There was no pardon, no redemption, no Savior for the fallen elohim, and Marduk knew it well. So, he just stared at her, his beautiful, perfect Ilsidor with her copper-gold hair, tiny stature, and ivory skin. He loved her once beyond reason, yet he let her go for a phantom promise of power and worship. He cursed himself for a damned fool.

"Marduk, tonight thou hast committed great wickedness in the eyes of the Most High." Her words hung in the garden's silence.

He awaited the sentence. If it was to come, let it be by her hand.

She hovered above him, shimmering in magnificent golden light. "However, the Most High foresaw thy deeds before He laid the foundations of the Earth. Thy punishment was long decreed. But this warning I give to thee, do not defile another daughter of man. Gabriel awaits his orders with great anticipation."

Marduk eyed her with deep suspicion. It was a stay of execution. As she faded, he called after her, "Ilsidor, say it, say my name."

Ilsidor looked down on the abomination he had become, no trace of his former glory. He had once been beautiful. With tears in her voice, she cried, "I cannot. You killed him!"

Then she vanished, and he was alone with the echoes of Persa's tears ringing in his ears.

November 985 ME

Sacrifice of the Heart

He said his name was Tristin. Persa did not believe him. It was too beautiful a name for what he was. He thought she did not see, that she did not know, but for a second that horrible night in the garden she glimpsed what he was. He was not the cool, handsome, urbane advisor to the Ruling Prince. He was a monster, and she was his captive.

Persa cried for a week straight. She refused food, refused water, had lain in her silk prison cell and willed her body to die. But then she learned he could make her do things. He invaded her mind and overcame her will, mucking about while he was in there, he saw James.

Persa fought him off, emerged from the mind rape to find him seething with rage and jealousy. He would have killed James if she had not bargained for his life. Holding his gaze, she recognized the power she exerted over him. The babe growing insider her mattered to him, even if it meant nothing to her. "You shall not harm him, for if you do, I will kill myself." She lifted a knife to her throat.

Marduk's nose flared, and his rancid breath filled the chamber with the stench of rotten eggs. His true self flashed.

She stood her ground, glaring at him.

"You would go straight to the eternal fires of Hell, Persa. Trust me, it's not a place you want to be." The Tristin persona shape-shifted back into place.

"I am already in Hell, but I'll not let you touch him. Promise me!" Persa screamed.

He looked at her without emotion, only when a drop of blood ran down her neck, did he shrug, "Yeah, okay." He could stop her, make the knife fly from her hand, but he could not be with her every minute.

Persa knew he was lying. He did that as easily as breathing. "Swear to me."

He flicked his hand in dismissive exasperation. "Whatever, I swear."

"Swear on her name, swear on the name of Ilsidor."

Marduk spun on her and growled, "You do not speak her name."

She hissed back, "You do not speak his."

"Put the knife down, Persa. I believe the time has come for us to make our agreement, and it is exceedingly difficult to do so with a knife at your jugular."

They negotiated for ten days. The little human amused him. Fairy creature she may appear, she possessed an iron will. It was that core of strength that told him her threat of suicide was no mere ploy.

She knew she held her strongest position while she carried the babe. She controlled the power of life and death, and he wanted this baby.

As with every successful negotiation, no one got everything they wanted, but they struck a deal. Persa exchanged her life for James' and the people he loved, which included Persa's own father. Marduk agreed not to bedevil or curse James, he was to be left unharmed. Persa agreed to stay with Marduk of her own accord. He would release her from her cell and give her freedom, but she must never seek James or her family, and she could never tell them why. Persa agreed to carry the baby to term, Marduk promised to protect her from it. Persa granted him a dance once a week. Marduk bought her horses.

"One weekend a month I walk through those doors, and you do not follow me. I get one weekend free of you." Persa pushed the parchment across the table.

Tristin exploded from his chair. "I will never allow that."

"What do you want in exchange?" Persa's voice was bitter. She expected the price would be sex and was prepared to pay.

He read it in her eyes and leered. There was a line he could not cross, but that did not mean he could not keep her bound to him in other ways, though it might prove dangerous. "You submit to me the night before you go."

Persa lifted her chin. "For one hour only, no blood, no bruises, and you stay Tristin, no morphing or shape-shifting, you bastard."

Already she understood him. "Two hours."

She rose from her chair and pulled the dress over her head. "Ninety minutes, and it can start now." Persa ben Yereq had Satan's number two general by the balls, and she knew it.

"Then you call me Tristin," he growled and reached for her.

"Tristin, you now have eighty-nine minutes."

Fey, the girl she had been, the vaulting champion, the betrothed and beloved of James, died at that moment.

James ben Kole, sixty miles away on a desperate search, overwrought with grief and worry, felt her go. His soul ripped in half as he fell to his knees in agony.

December 12, 985 ME

Horses and Truffles - New City, Alanthia

Persa rode through the gates of the House of Amah, breathing for the first time in five weeks, which was how long it had been since the last time she escaped. She could have left last weekend, but today was her birthday, and she was not spending it with him. She rode a fine mount, her one source of pleasure behind those walls. True to their contract, the stables brimmed with horses.

Tristin was rarely in residence, which gave her a measure of peace. Yet he maintained no set schedule, which disconcerted her, by design. Persa did not think she had any more tears to cry, but each morning she woke with her pillow wet, and her heart broken. Yet she rose, went to the stables, worked with the horses, and somehow kept breathing.

Funds did not concern Tristin. The wealth and gifts he lavished upon her were obscene. She forbade live-in servants but permitted a staff of rotating maids, cooks, gardeners, and stable hands to work the vast estate. Persa kept her face hidden and spoke only the most cursory commands. She isolated herself from every living thing except the horses. They kept secrets.

One hand stood out among the rotating help. He came the day Shalimar fell into distress. He was kind and worked with her long into the night as they walked the mare through a bout of colic. Around 3am, she fell asleep on a wooden bench, using a leather saddlebag for a pillow.

At dawn, he said, "My Lady, the crisis has passed."

She rubbed sleep from her eyes and gave him a weary smile, realizing he had covered her with a clean blanket. Her veil had fallen away.

He returned her smile, warm and genuine.

She looked beyond him to Shalimar, who appeared sound. Persa went to her with an outstretched hand. The groom had seen her face, so she did not linger. Over her shoulder, she called, "Thank you, Joshua."

He had not returned, and their encounter remained the only human interaction she permitted herself since Tristin took her prisoner fifty days before.

She kicked the horse into a trot and left the House of Amah behind, focused on her destination, Zuzah's Chocolates and Confections. It was her birthday, and she wanted her truffle. After that, she did not know.

It should have been a straightforward exchange, less than five minutes in the store, then back into the shadows. Had she hoped he would be there? Had a deep part of her mind wished for a glimpse of him so desperately that she rode to the one place, on the one day, where she might find him? Did she risk his life and her heart for a piece of chocolate? Or had she known he would be here and known she must set him free?

It was her dismount that caught James' attention.

He had not known what else to do. So he sat across from her favorite chocolate shop, watching and praying, a half-eaten box of truffles beside him. His heart lodged in his throat, and he leapt to his feet, running across the park. She dressed in midnight blue from head to toe. Her face, her hair, everything, was hidden. But he knew Persa's dismount like his own face in the mirror. It was her.

James stood by her horse, looking through the glass. His mind warred with his heart. It could not be her, yet he knew it was. When she pointed to the chocolate cherry truffle, he was certain. Why was she hiding? Where had she been? Oh Lord in Heaven, thank you! She was alive!

Persa froze in the doorway. He could not see her face but the person behind her bumped into her when she stopped, jostling the bag of chocolates, which fell to the ground.

"Persa!" he croaked.

She ran but did not get far. He was stronger, faster, and unencumbered by long robes. He caught her by the arm. For an instant, she clung to him, making a sound like a wounded animal. It ripped his heart out.

She smelled different, she felt different, something was wrong, something was very wrong. Then she pushed him away, and he stumbled back in surprise. "Persa, my God! You're alive!" Tears stung his eyes, and he wanted to fall to his knees and weep.

Turning away, she hid behind the veil and croaked, "No, you are mistaken. Go away, I don't know you."

The accent was wrong, the voice low and deep, but his soul knew. "Persa, where have you been?"

"If my husband finds out... Go away, leave me alone." She tried to push past him.

He grabbed her shoulders and shook. "Stop!"

Her voice broke in a sob. "He will know. Let me go!"

James reached out and pulled the veil away and saw her hazel eyes red with tears. He swayed, a wave of dizziness overtook him at the sight of her. "Why are you doing this? Fey... I don't understand."

She covered her face and turned away, her voice cold and cutting. "I did not want to hurt you, but I see you will not let me go unless I do. I do not love you, James ben Kole. I have not loved you for a long time." She stared at the ground, sounding hoarse, her entire body shaking. "I met someone else and was too much of a coward to tell you, so I used the Ball to run away. We have been lovers for months, and I married him on October 24th."

Persa whirled, her nose flaring in anger. She grabbed his hand and put it to her belly. "I am pregnant. So, leave me alone! I have moved on. You need to do the same. Goodbye, James."

The expression on James' beloved face was one that she would never forget. It seared on her brain forever; shock, disbelief, and betrayal at a level so deep neither of them would ever recover.

James did not hear Persa's choked sob as she rushed past. He did not see the look of utter desolation on her face as her soul rent in two, because his own cry of anguish shut out everything. He fell to his knees, and the world went black.

December 21, 985 ME

Solstice

Persa heard Tristin enter the stables, even if she had not, the horses would have alerted her. They became restless when he was near, whickering and stamping in their stalls, tossing their magnificent manes and tails in agitation. She gathered herself, put the shield over her mind, and turned to face him.

To the human eye, he was brutally handsome, olive-skinned with dark hair and brows, his manner and attire elegant. In public, women turned to stare. They cast him sly sidelong glances, which he always returned. They did not understand who they flirted with, but Persa did. His voice gave him away, deep and gravelly, hollow and echoing. It rose out of the dank place that burned behind his eyes.

She crossed her arms over her chest, rested them on the swell of her belly, and glared at him.

Tristin gave a mocking snort of laughter, amused by her scorn. "Good evening, my dear. You are looking well," he lied. She was pale and terribly thin, despite her bulging pregnancy.

He gestured to a hook on the wall. "Put on your cloak. We are going for a stroll. It's the Solstice, one of my favorite nights."

The belligerent set of her shoulders conveyed her reluctance to go anywhere with him, but she pulled off her work gloves and capitulated. There were battles to fight, and a walk was not one of them. She controlled an involuntary flinch when he took her elbow. She would not give him the satisfaction of pulling away, refusing to feed the sadistic pleasure he garnered by controlling her, hurting her.

Outside, the air felt frosty, and a persistent wind ruffled her hood and reddened her cheeks. She focused on the crunch of gravel under her boots, saying nothing.

He opted for a companionable tone. "For thousands of years, men celebrated this night in fantastic fashion. Alas, that is something else lost in this soft age."

Persa remained silent.

Undeterred, he said, "I shall endeavor to revive the practice, perhaps I will teach our son."

Her head snapped around. "Teach him what?"

Tristin grinned and turned his head slowly. The veneer shifted for an instant, and she glimpsed the reptile. Hunger burned in his snake eyes. "The old ways."

Persa repressed a wave of nausea and tried to pull away. He held her close and with a lift of his lip, pressed a long finger to her temple. Visions of burning trees, humans in cages, skinned corpses, and orgies flashed across her mind. She swatted his hand away, disgusted and ready to fight. "Don't do that!"

"You've seen him," he growled.

Persa looked ahead, remaining impassive, and continued walking. With a monumental force of will, she made her mind blank. "I left him."

"You long for a man, when I am a god."

Persa's blood ran cold. He never admitted what he was, but she was quite certain he was no god. "You are a fiend."

"I should cut your tongue out."

She gave him a narrow-eyed glare. "Then I could not say your name."
She softened her gaze and played the lover, stroking his cheek. "Tristin."

"Bitch." He looked away.

She laughed, a broken sound, full of bitter irony. "I wasn't... until I met you."

February 11, 986 ME (Nine Months into Rebellion)

Lightning Crashes

Sixteen weeks after the Coronation Ball, three creatures were born. When the unholy pains began, Princess Philomela of Greece fled her home alone, hiding in mute shame and horror.

Deep in the Louisiana Bayou, Mademoiselle Charlotte writhed in ecstasy and pain, her blood staining the white silk coverlet as she labored beneath an immense canopy embroidered with scenes depicting the rise of the Loa. Voodoo drums drowned out her screams of travail.

Persa cried in the arms of her dark suitor, her captor, her enemy. Marduk held her while she pushed.

March 15, 986 ME

Don't Touch It

Persa stood at the back wall of the House of Amah, staring at nothing. She escaped outside, seeking what little solace was available in this walled prison. Tristin was with the baby that was not a child. It was a monster, like his father. If she had comprehended what she carried, she would have slashed her throat that day in the library. Tristin named it Rapha. Her personal name for it was Spawn.

Her entire life she secretly dreamed of a baby, one she could pour her love into, nurse and hold, cuddle, and care for. What she gave birth to was more vicious than a rattlesnake and three times as dangerous, a vile creature. Her first sight of it shattered any illusions she might have harbored as it feasted on its own umbilical cord. He bawled like an angry gorilla, grating and horrible. Born with a full head of flaming red hair, teeth, six fingers and toes, his elongated face and skull marked him as decidedly not human. He glared at her with orange hell-fire eyes full of hatred not native to this world.

Tristin cared for it, which was well enough because Rapha tried to kill her anytime she got near it. Tristin adored it, if such an adjective could be applied to him. Persa determined he was incapable of natural affection or tender emotions. Wickedness polluted every atom of his being. And in the month since he was born, it was clear his son inherited that.

Trapped with two of the evilest creatures on Earth, Persa rested her forehead on the cold stone wall and tried to feel nothing.

September 11, 986 ME

Unleashed

On September 11th, less than a year after Prince Korah ben Adam ascended the throne, the Alanthian Legislature lifted the ban on technological exploration. Across Alanthia, bells rang from steeples, marching bands paraded down Main Street, and vendors sold their wares to the ecstatic crowds who gathered to celebrate the momentous day.

Well, half the kingdom partied; the other half looked at each other in silent dread or carried warning signs, picketing the celebrations. Organizers relegated them to the outskirts, where the celebrants jeered at them, and the press labeled them doomsday conspiracy theorists. For the protestors, full-scale rebellion loomed, whether they liked it or not.

In front of the Alanthian Capitol Building, the biggest crowd in the kingdom gathered to listen as the Speaker of the House read the official proclamation. Prince Korah's supporters erupted into frenetic celebration when he mounted the dais. Delivering a rousing speech, worthy of the famous orator, he declared the hardest fought battle of Alanthia's life was behind them. They were no longer held in bondage, free to pursue a dream, illuminating the way for everyone on Earth, and retaking what had been denied, technology! Together they would usher in a New Age with Alanthia in the vanguard.

"As we speak, the first automotive plant of the age is gearing up. By spring Alanthians will once again travel by car."

The spectators shouted their approval.

In a dramatic moment, Prince Korah raised his hands for silence. The crowd grew still, mesmerized by his charisma and charm. A tinny ring came from the podium. Korah looked right then left, a smile spreading over his handsome face, as he reached into his suit pocket to pull out a phone. "Hello?"

The crowd went wild.

Holding the phone aloft, he proclaimed, "Soon, every Alanthian will have their own, thanks to the actions we have taken today."

Fifty feet below the podium, dressed in their finest, Royal Military Academy cadets, Beau Landry and Ian ben Kole stood alongside the elite fighting units of all branches of the Alanthian Military services. Their presence was largely ceremonial, but their sidearms contained live ammunition and their swords were honed steel.

As the Speaker read the proclamation, Beau Landry shot a mischievous look at his best friend and roommate, Ian ben Kole. Dreams of cars, phones, computers, and everything in between danced behind a pair of extraordinary cobalt blue eyes. Neither Beau nor Ian cared a fig about the political intrigue and drama playing out on the stage behind the Ruling Prince. They gave little to no thought about the ramifications of lifting a ten-century ban on technological exploration. No, the primary preoccupation of the two young bucks was the thirty-six-hour pass that began as soon as Prince Korah finished yapping.

The speech ended with a rousing, "Long live Alanthia!"

Beau and Ian removed their covers and waved them in celebration. A sea of blue and white Alanthian flags fluttered in the cool September wind, and the cheers of the crowd drowned out the distant thunder rumbling in the clear sky.

Turning to leave, a flash of color caught Ian's eye, and he stopped cold. Twenty yards away, dressed in midnight blue, stood Persa. She looked like a doll posed for a painting, no life in her once animated face. A man of middle eastern descent held her hand as he spoke to an ecstatic Prince Korah. Fury erupted in Ian. He stormed up the steps, ready to confront her.

Beau called after him, jostled backward by the streaming crowd.

Terror flashed across Persa's face when she saw him. She glanced at the man beside her, her eyes alive and huge. "No!" she mouthed, giving her companion a pointed look. "Please!" she begged, shaking her head, and backing away.

Ian stopped, studying her.

Her face morphed, turning banal and bored, but an instant too late. Her companion caught her.

His black eyes scanned the crowd, and the unbridled evil behind his look took Ian's breath away. Ian averted his gaze, but not before their eyes met. "Jesus!" he muttered, then covered his mouth, abashed that he dared utter the holy name.

Beau came alongside him. "Why are we up here, man? You seen a ghost?" Beau looked around. "*Mon Dieu*, who is that?"

Ian dared a glance and saw the man fixated on them. His insides froze, as pain exploded in his head. "Beau," he choked, "let's get out of here."

Beau grimaced as the black-eyed man turned away. "*Allons!* That is one wicked Loa!"

Ian felt like an ax had cleaved his skull in two. Blinded by the sudden migraine, he grabbed Beau's arm. "Stop."

Beau swore, standing stalwart with his friend as the crowd teemed around them. "Ian, *ca va?*"

"Speak English, you ridiculous Cajun. No, I'm not okay. My head is killing me, and I cannot see." He rubbed his eyes hard, trying to clear away the darkness. At length, he muttered, "We have to find James."

"*Merde*, your brother? I thought you did not know where he was?"

Ian turned and stumbled down the steps, still holding Beau's arm. "I have a good idea where we'll find him."

Interlude with the Prince

Prince Peter spotted Persa from his place behind the podium while his father gave another speech. By habit, he found someone or something to occupy his mind while the adults spoke. Today, he settled on the little horse dancer. She looked different from the last time he saw her a year ago, and she was with Secretary Tristin, who gave him the creeps.

She seemed sad, wearing the same far-away expression his mother often had. It seemed strange no one noticed, only seeing a pretty face, but since he had one of the most beautiful faces ever created, beauty never fooled him. Peter read what went on behind the mask. Studying Persa, he recognized a girl who needed a friend and perhaps a laugh. He determined he was going to make that happen.

Once the speech ended, well-wishers crowded the stage, but they parted for him as he headed toward Persa. But before he reached her, she paled, growing still, her eyes wide with horror. He followed her line of sight to a young cadet racing up the steps. She signaled him to stop, cutting a look at Secretary Tristin.

Peter hung back.

Secretary Tristin grew angry, scowling at Persa and the cadet. He had one of those faces that only smiled on the outside, but not on the inside. Peter decided it was his eyes. That guy had the meanest eyes Peter ever saw.

Persa stepped in front of him, but she was too short to block the Secretary's line of sight. She hissed something, and Tristin turned his mean look on her. Peter nodded in admiration as she lifted her chin and gave it right back, not backing down. The confrontation ended, and she moved off by herself, staring into space, her expression one of absolute desolation.

Peter moved beside her and whispered, "What do you need, Persa?"

She turned, startled by his presence. A smile broke across her face, they were almost eye to eye now. "Peter," she said in her soft Irish burr. He always liked the way she spoke, liked that she called him Peter instead of my Esteemed.

Her eyes darted toward Tristin, and she relaxed, finding him occupied. "You look quite well."

"You look like a spooked colt. Come with me."

"Okay." Persa smiled, her first genuine smile in almost a year. Then it faded as she added, "Let me tell Tristin where I am going."

Peter rolled his eyes.

"That was a paltry excuse for an escape," Peter scolded as they wove their way through the crowd into the Capitol Building. "What fun is that, if you tell them you are leaving?"

"Fun that can go on for more than two minutes and might forestall negative consequences," she retorted, her heels beating a rapid staccato as they bounded down an empty hallway, skirting security.

"Forestall negative consequences?" he laughed. "Which is a fancy way of saying it keeps you out of trouble. And do you know what sort of adventure ends without being in trouble?" At her shrug, he declared, "The boring kind! Come on, before I leave you behind because you have gotten old."

"I feel a hundred," Persa said, an edge to her voice.

"Well, you are not," Peter countered.

"Where are we going?" Persa jostled past three men in suits who stared after them in dismay.

He raised a golden eyebrow and quipped, "I do not know, this is a spur-of-the-moment adventure."

She threw back her head and laughed, then pulled him into a hug. "You have no idea how wonderful it is to see you."

"Prince d'Or, spreading sunshine wherever he goes." He gave her his winning smile, awkward in his eight-year-old face, but wondrously charming, with hints of the devastating weapon it would become.

As the day wore on, Persa rejected painting fake mustaches on the portraits in the gallery. She liked his idea of toads in the punchbowl. Sadly, the procurement of said toads proved impractical. In the end, their adventure amounted to little more than roaming the halls of the Capitol Building, laughing uproariously at whatever outlandish scheme one of them proposed, and arriving slightly late and a bit disheveled to the State Dinner.

For Persa, it was a lifeline, for Peter a pleasant diversion, for Marduk it was seething jealousy and hatred. He focused on a new target, one not covered by their deal.

Off to the Races

It perturbed Beau Landry that instead of celebrating with the rest of the kingdom, perhaps finding a pretty lady to spend some quality time with, they were on a mission to locate Ian's erstwhile brother. He understood family responsibilities but still felt entitled to a mild case of the snarls. "I don't understand you, Ian. You catch a glimpse of that *fille* who jilted your brother, then run off to tell him about it? What good can come of that? You said he's in a bad way since she left him. How's this going to help? It seems to me it will make things worse."

"It's hard to explain, man. I've known Persa my whole life. She's like my sister. She and my brother have been crazy in love since they were seven or eight years old. And the whole thing, it never made sense, that she would leave. And now that I've seen her? It's just wrong. You saw that guy."

A chill slithered down Beau's spine. "That dude had some bad *juju* as we say down in the bayou."

"Right! She is afraid of him, and when he looked at me… something is not right."

They found James three hours later, sitting in a rundown bar, disheveled and drunk. He gave Ian a bleary grin and slurred, "Just the man I was hoping to see."

Ian embraced him with a backslapping hug. "How's that, Brother?"

"You have talent, boyo. I've been trying to get a race up all afternoon, and none of these *eejits* will take me on because they know… But you?" He sighed heavily. "You drum up a race for us, cause I'm running out of money." James looked at his empty glass, forlorn and disgusted. "I think I'm *fluthered*, too. But I ride fairly well when I'm drunk."

He pulled Ian's jacket and tried to whisper, which in his condition meant he just slurred an octave lower. "Sometimes, I even pretend to be smashed, drives up the stakes." He got a big smile on his face. "They don't think I can ride, but I can always ride. One of these days, I plan to ride right out of here."

"*Ivre comme un poisson!*" Beau shook his head, saying, he is drunk as a fish.

James' head fell back, and he grinned. "Frenchie!"

Ian snorted. "He's not French. He's a bayou rat, though it comes in handy with the ladies."

James lost his smile and gave him a world-weary look. "Bah! I hate 'em all. Treacherous banshees."

"Speaking of her," Ian began.

James held an open palm up to his face. "No! Not another word. I don't wish to talk about her. I choose not to think about her." His head bobbed as he squinted out of bloodshot eyes. "Get us a race, Brother. That always cheers me up."

"*Merde*, how long have you been drinking?" Beau took a step back, waving away the fumes of alcohol rolling off James.

James gave him a crooked smile. "What day is it?"

A heavy, bearded man called from across the bar, "I'll race that drunk son of a bitch. It'll be the easiest money I've earned all year."

James waggled his eyebrows at Beau. "Now, that is more like it!"

Within an hour, they set the race, four riders, one mile. Beau, with an eye for an opportunity, became stakeholder and bookmaker. He strutted around the dusty bar in his fine uniform, rousing the crowd, calling the odds. He had seen that crazy drunk ride. These hayseeds did not know they were about to race a World Champion, drunk or not. James on a horse was a sight to behold, no distinction between man and beast. He rode like the wind, fearless.

Later, counting up their winnings in James' shabby rented room, Beau thought he might have found his new calling. James lay passed out on the floor, a stack of cash on his chest. Ian prowled the room, thinking about Persa and that evil-eyed man.

And So it Begins

Coordinated terrorist's bombs exploded in and around the State Dinner, rocking the occupants and sending a tray of wine crashing into the head table, bathing Prince Korah in merlot and fine crystal. Plaster fell from the ceiling in sizeable chunks, statues crashed to the ground, as the air filled with white dust before black smoke smothered it, sucking breath and light from the room.

A second firebomb exploded, and chaos ensued.

The attacks came in waves through the night and the next day. The violence spread across the kingdom. Alanthians hid inside their houses, some in fear and trembling, crying out for mercy, and blaming Korah for bringing this upon them. Others shook their fists to Heaven and hardened their hearts. The terrorists laughed with delight, corrupted and twisted in their zealotry, they claimed fealty and allegiance to the Iron King, who did not know them. The king they knew was an imposter who appeared in their midst as an angel of light, their old god, one they should have known, but did not; Marduk.

He orchestrated it.

It was enjoyable, watching them blow themselves to bits. But it also served a purpose. He understood true rebellion could not occur if half the kingdom fought everything he was doing. Better to flush them all out and be done with it. Nothing stirred up people more than a little terrorism. Besides, this date held fond memories for him.

Even the anti-technology opponents would rally behind Korah against jihadists. It was brilliant. Give them a common enemy, and they would unite. Make them afraid, and they would surrender their freedom. Give them a martyr, and they would die for a cause.

Autumn 986 ME

Miscalculation

It was the response to the terror attacks that went badly. The sheer brutality of the governmental action against the jihadist groups turned the stomachs of the peace-loving Alanthians. Marduk miscalculated their bloodthirstiness, too many years of peace softened them, and he failed to anticipate it. He assumed they would react like men from the Last Age, but they had not. He ruled different men in the past, and he had forgotten who he was dealing with, Alanthians. They recoiled in horror at Korah's actions. Instead of uniting, they splintered.

In bars and across dinner tables, Alanthians went to war among themselves. They argued over the public executions of the terrorists, the midnight raids, and kangaroo courts. They debated about their loyalty to the Iron King, rebellion, and technology. A new and powerful anti-royal sentiment ran among Korah's enemies. The agnostics persecuted the faithful, and the young fought the old. The South stayed loyal to the Iron King, and the New City rejected him.

No matter whose side they were on, all Alanthians looked out their windows with increasing concern as the earth changed. It dried up and withered as the kingdom bubbled in a cauldron of rebellion and chaos.

Choosing Sides

Anyone who spent time with Beau Landry would assume there was nothing he liked about life at the Royal Military Academy. From the food, to the hours, to the discipline, which he and Ian found themselves subject to often, he painted a picture of drudgery. The truth was Beau loved the place; it just did not fit his personality or his image to admit it.

He was an exceptional student, but he approached his studies with such nonchalance that it annoyed his instructors and his fellow cadets. Everyone knew with the slightest application of his mind, he would have supplanted the tight-ass sycophant that rose to the top of their cadet class, Emerson ben Palmer. Pompous, arrogant, and self-important, Emerson was the scourge of the younger cadets, the bane of his classmates, and the favorite of only those social climbing, like-minded, windbags who sought to align themselves with his family and their connections. Ian hated him. But for three years, Beau had not given a damn.

It started with a wedgie. Simple really, and it should have never escalated into what it did. But the origins of the great schism, were just that, a wedgie, given to the wrong person, on the wrong day, at the wrong time. The first-year cadet was a small boy, delicately boned with thick glasses and long fingers, he quite resembled a tree frog. He was also Beau Landry's third cousin.

By November, the Academy split, Emerson's side entrenched with Prince Korah. Beau's clan, and most of the class behind them, Prince Josiah's former classmates, professed loyalty to the Iron King. In the way of young men, they saw no gray areas and did not cloud the issue with nuance or honed arguments and persuasions. It was one or the other. And the Academy, like the kingdom, was about to explode.

October 23, 986 ME

One of These Nights

On the one-year anniversary of the Coronation Ball, James sat alone in a bar, listening to a half decent band, and watching hundreds of yellow bubbles climb to the top of his beer glass. It was hard to get drunk anymore, or impossible to tell if he was ever sober, he was not sure which was true. He'd crawled into a bottle that dark day in December and stayed.

Ian's insistent ranting that something was wrong with Persa haunted him, if he let himself think about it, which wasn't often. Most of the time the thought intruded while he slept, so he took care to drink enough that he passed out rather than slumbered.

He knew where she lived now and knew every four weeks she left for a weekend. She would leave next weekend, alone. James also knew about her husband, the special advisor to Prince Korah, who seemed to only have one name, Tristin.

He drained the beer, even the thought of his enemy's name tasted bitter in his mouth. There was no child, or none that he or anyone else ever saw. He watched the place, paid off a few servants, but they had little to report other than she was in residence and seemed in good health. There were no bars on her windows or chains on the doors. Ian was wrong, she was no prisoner.

But he was. Imprisoned in his pain, in drunkenness, in despair. It was not getting better.

The only time he felt alive was when he raced, which he did with deadly abandon, and thanks to Beau Landry's industriousness, great financial gain. Since the night of the terrorist attacks, Alanthians needed diversion. With the skill of a brilliant entrepreneur, Beau seized upon the sentiment and arranged weekend races in and around the New City. James hustled his own through the week, but on the weekends, he made his living. If what he was doing could be described as living.

He remained indifferent to the tumult brewing around him, even now a loud argument broke out in the bar. If James had to choose, he fell on the side that favored returning to full obedience to the Iron King because Korah employed Tristin, and that was reason enough. He planned to kill that son of a bitch.

October 31, 986 ME

Wild Heart

The interlude with Prince d'Or saved Persa's life. She had been dead since the rape and abduction; dead in her mind, her will, and especially her heart. The carefree afternoon spent racing down the hallways and laughing, sparked a flicker, at least in her mind and her will. Her heart still struggled.

The afternoon of October 31st, with the feel of Tristin's hands still on her body, the stench of his tongue lingering on her skin, she saddled the horse and galloped through the gates of the House of Amah.

She threw off the veil, left her black cloak in the drive, and shed the malignancy of the place. Crisp autumn wind loosened her hair, as dust billowed behind the pounding hooves. She leaned forward in the saddle, spurring her mount.

He would not keep her prisoner forever.

An hour later, she checked into her favorite hotel, showered, and ordered room service. Stepping outside, she looked across the water, letting the gentle waves of the Bay soothe her mind. The sun set, turning the sky behind the mountains a vivid blaze of pink and orange. Persa sipped a glass of wine, enjoying the kiss of the breeze, the soft fluttering of her hair around her face.

'If I did not know, Persa ben Yereq, that I have your heart, I would be jealous of the wind that caresses your skin.'

"Oh, Jay, I miss you," she whispered.

Within earshot, a music festival began, a female singer taking the stage. Persa listened idly, not particularly attuned, but the notes wove a spell, sweeping her away. In a surreal moment, she knew the song carried a message. She took the words, bound them to her heart, fashioning a shield.

On that balcony, Persa ben Yereq vowed to fight.

November 8, 986 ME

The Match

In the course of a kingdom's life, there are pivotal moments, imprinted on the psyche of all who lived through them. November 8, 986 ME was one such moment. The kingdom awoke to the tragic news that Princess Alexa ben Seamus had been murdered.

Alanthians went into shock, and even Korah's enemies were broken-hearted. The lovely Princess had been a fixture in Alanthian life for two decades. Her regal grace and kind smiles captivated and charmed her subjects. Noteworthy humanitarian efforts, charitable foundations, and famous style made her a favorite of ladies' magazines and the press. Alanthians were proud of their beautiful first family, and her death, so soon after the tragedies of Eamonn and Josiah, rocked Alanthia.

A talented artist immortalized their heartbreak with a sketch of

Prince Peter, standing with his small hand resting on his mother's casket. Alone. His shoulders slumped, his eyes shut tight against the grief, the image captured the salient moment and seared itself onto the collective consciousness of the kingdom.

Officials claimed those who opposed the repeal of the technology laws murdered Alexa. The opposition denied it, asserting that like Prince Eamonn and Prince Josiah the year before, the true villain was Prince Korah.

By November 15th, Alanthia was at war with itself.

February 20, 987 ME

Encamped

It was a bloody conflict. Visions of valor, great honor, and gallantry never materialized. Those glorious dreams were trampled, buried beneath the mud created by the blood of dead men. The kingdoms of the world did not send troops to support those who fought against Korah. The Iron King did not intervene. By February 987 ME, the opposition force was ragged, cold, and ready for their last battle.

Strangely, war revived James ben Kole. When the fighting broke out, he joined his brother's company from the Royal Military Academy. Restored of purpose, clear of mind, and sober of body; he thrived. Unflinching under fire, capable of phenomenal endurance and speed, he distinguished himself on the field of battle, becoming the greatest mounted horsemen of the age.

His quiet dignity and deadly calm drew men to him, and he rose through the ranks to Major. The enemy feared their mounted cavalry unit, which earned the respect of men on both sides of the conflict. Ian and Beau served under him as First Lieutenants, his closest comrades. He recruited fifty of the best riders in the kingdom, men he raced against in the previous months.

Much of his former personality asserted itself. James, once again, became disciplined in his manner and speech. He stopped drinking but was rarely seen without a large cigar. Unerringly kind and steadfast, the only temper anyone ever saw from him was when he witnessed a drunken man abusing a horse. The encounter had not gone well for the drunk.

Major James ben Kole led the rawboned, starved, and paltry looking horse through the camp, enduring good-natured taunts and much ribbing. James bore up under the guffaws with a knowing gaze and insisted the animal was of the finest quality, much to the hilarity of his fellow soldiers. He named the hapless animal Joey because the stallion's starved appearance gave the impression of a great kangaroo. To the dismay of all, within weeks, James coaxed the animal back to health and proudly sat atop his now devoted warhorse. Beau ran book on it, and he, Ian, and James made a tidy profit on the resurrection of Joey.

"Bloody Hell, Beau, you could figure out how to make money off these ants." Ian watched a line of them trundle off with a bread crumb he'd dropped in the dirt.

Beau lounged on his cot, studying the ants, and calculating how he might do just that. "Talk about." His handsome face broke into a wind-burned smile. "It runs deep in my blood, *mon amie.*"

"None of which we will spill tomorrow." Ian stuffed the last of the stale sandwich into his mouth.

Beau gave a very French shrug. *"C'est la vie."*

James left them to their discussion and strolled out of the tent. Murmuring a cursory greeting toward two privates coming off guard duty and sprinting toward the mess, he walked to the edge of the camp, looking at the afternoon sky. The fighting he did not fear, but the long hours of anticipation tore a man's guts to shreds. Once the cannons roared, the bullets flew, and the horse galloped under him, all thoughts receded to the background.

He did not have a death wish, per se, he simply did not care whether his body lived or died. The men he served with thought he was brave. James knew better.

He worried about Ian and Beau, but war taught him that indecisiveness cost lives. Trying to protect them could just as easily get them killed as not. Their orders tomorrow were simple, breach the enemy lines and take out the command. James volunteered for it, nay fought for it. Personal vengeance drove the request. According to their intelligence, Korah would be on the battlefield tomorrow and with him, Tristin.

Would Persa hate him for killing her lover? He could find no official record of a marriage, yet she lived in his house and claimed a wedding had taken place. Did it matter? Did it matter if she hated him? His rational mind said no, but his heart broke at the very thought of it.

At night, without the alcohol, he flew with her. He would wake, with the feel of her body next to his, the sound of her laughter ringing in his ears. In the dark, he experienced her loss all over again. He only permitted tiny moments of it now, fleeting seconds where the pain would pierce the wall and smite his soul. Sometimes Ian caught him, and the pity on his brother's face was more than he could bear. So, he guarded his emotions carefully, especially if Ian was about.

Vibrations ran through the camp, as battle loomed. By mutual accord, the results would determine the future course of the kingdom. The winner would rule, the loser would pardon the opposition, and Alanthia would return to peace, a civilized ending to a barbaric and bloody conflict. Beau was ready to go home. Ian did not know what his future held. And James planned to die, but before he did, there was one thing left to do.

Chain

Persa felt eyes upon her. James was close. She knew he watched her periodically, their connection soul-deep and true. In the months since she vowed to fight, she conceived no plan that would preserve their lives, saw no way to defeat the beast that held her.

She took great care not to let either the times when James came near or her determination to escape enter her conscious mind. She could not. Tristin often caught her unaware and would snoop inside her brain, especially while she slept. Rapha was learning the same, wicked creature that he was. So she pretended she did not know James came, pretended, even to herself that she did not feel him, long for him, would die just to be near him again. She settled for these moments when he watched her.

The sun set over the horizon, casting the sky in pink and leaden gray. Persa turned toward the place where she felt him the strongest and held her arms out as if she were embracing the light, her head thrown back in entreaty. She held it for a count of four, imagining Rain cantering beneath them as they flew.

The pounding hoofbeats shocked her. He never came near, never broke cover. She dared not let that image enter her mind. The gallop thundered in her ears; she could feel it pounding under her feet as he drew closer.

"Hayuh, Fey!" he called.

From ten thousand repetitions, she dropped her left arm and with her right, took his wrist and swung behind him. Persa did not open her eyes but hugged his waist, letting him spirit her away.

He'd saddled the horse with their vaulting tack. They slowed to a canter, and she slid around his body, practiced and smooth. She found his lips and kissed him. He tasted like cigars and smelled of horses and saddle oil, and him, just him.

They had been dead, both of them. They breathed, yes, but neither lived. There was no life for Persa without James. As they kissed, she realized the same was true for him.

He kissed her neck, his voice ragged. "Fey, the battle tomorrow, I could not go without seeing you one last time."

She clung to him. He was fighting. Somehow she knew, if the fighting did not kill him, this ride would. Persa opened her eyes, damning the consequences and said, "Then love me, Jay."

"Oh God, Persa," he cried.

All conversation stopped. Brokenness, longing, and pain, a lifetime of love exploded between them. Hands, lips, and bodies moved as Joey continued to canter, a rhythm as natural to them as breathing. They flew, choreographing an erotic dance, touching, kissing. The world no longer existed. It always receded when they rode, primal and divine. When he entered her, she screamed and threw back her head in ecstasy, the beat of the horse driving him deep inside.

He cried out, thrusting into her hard. "You are mine."

"Yours!" she answered, tears streaming down her face.

The climax when it came was not sweet or soft, it was a violent reclaiming, with teeth, claws, and wracking shudders that threatened to topple them from the horse who stopped and waited while its occupants groaned atop its back.

As the last waves abated, Persa sobbed into the crook of James' neck, clinging to him, her legs intertwined with his, still joined. "I've just killed you. Oh, my love, my perfect, precious love, please forgive me. I am so sorry, so sorry." She groaned with inhuman anguish, then became frantic, pawing at him, touching his face, covering her own. Her hands fluttered everywhere, until at last they fell limp, and she collapsed, weeping.

"Persa! I'm here." He squeezed her tight. "Tell me what is wrong. Tell me!" He was rocking her back and forth, pleading with her.

"I can't. I promised I would stay away, to save you." She grabbed the sides of his face, looking into his beloved eyes. "Now?" Her forehead fell to his chest.

Still joined, anger erupted in his soul as he held her. "No! You belong to me," he growled, "since we were born. My wife, my love, my heart, my breath, Persa ben Yereq, you are my everything!"

Persa met his force with her own. Leaning back, she looked at him full in the face, her expression fierce, determined, defying the gates of Hell. "Husband, as long as we both shall live. In Jesus' name."

February 21, 987 ME

The Waiting

No one slept, not with death knocking on the door. The day dawned gray and cold. A fine mist soaked hair and chilled skin. His men tended their gear, girding their loins and their beasts with the armaments of war.

James stepped away. Still rocked from the night before, he took a moment of peace to himself before the fighting began. He closed his eyes and whispered a silent prayer.

"I hear you are looking for men," said a vaguely familiar voice.

He turned and broke into a brilliant smile when he recognized the speaker, "Joshua!" James strode forward with his hand outstretched.

Joshua pulled him into a hug. When he stepped back, he unsheathed a magnificent sword, and his countenance changed. "I will fight beside thee today, friend James, and beside thy brother, and thy friend."

Not Flesh and Blood

In the months and years that passed, Beau never quite recalled the exact sequence of events that day. His mind refused to process most of what he saw. It came back in fits and starts, creeping in when he was not on guard, overwhelming him with terror. He heard the screams of dying men, smelled gunpowder, smoke, and the sickening stench of dead men and horses. Through the ages, survivors learned to live with the aftermath of battle, bearing the scars it left on their souls. And had it been an ordinary battle, Beau never doubted he would have coped well enough, but there was nothing ordinary about the closing moments of the Alanthian Civil War.

Three hours in, a thousand men down, and death surrounding them in clouds of smoke and red mist, his company finally broke through enemy lines. They had a clear shot, eyes on the command, riding hard and fast, when the Black Rider emerged out of a sulfurous mist. Armored like a medieval knight, his stallion breathed fire. The warrior screamed in a filthy language as his sword cut through a line of men like butter.

Beau drew up beside Ian and James, with four riders on either side. They reformed their line, preparing a charge as the berserker wended his way through their ranks with deadly efficiency. When the rider annihilated the last man, he turned his horse to face them.

Wickedness emanated from him, so palpable Beau's horse reared. The evil rider laughed, a terrible sound that cleaved soul from spirit, flesh from bone.

Raising his gauntlet, he pushed the air. Four riders to Beau's left choked and grabbed their necks, blood pouring from their eyes, noses, and ears right before they blew apart where they sat. Then the black-gloved gave another flick, and the heads of the four riders to Ian's left fell to the ground, splattering in the dirt, smashed like ripe pumpkins. The rider called Beau's name, and his body lifted from the saddle. As he rose, his cells splintered, blowing apart, and Beau knew he was going to die.

There was a blinding flash.

Then nothing.

February 22, 987 ME

MASH

James ben Kole's first conscious thought when he woke was that no one's mouth should taste like his did, vile, worse than any hangover, and for him, that was saying something. His second conscious thought was that Persa was there, lifting a cup of water to his parched lips. "Fey," he croaked.

"Shh," she soothed. "I'm here."

He cracked a crusted eye and reached for her, lest she evaporate into the fog of his dreams. "Really here?"

"Yes, love, really here." Persa squeezed his hand.

James squeezed back, her small fingers solid. "Ian? Beau?"

"Right beside you, Jay," Persa whispered, but something lurked beneath her tone.

"What's wrong?" he slurred, breathless and exhausted.

"Everything is all right," Persa crooned. "Rest now. I'll be here when you wake up."

James sighed, drifting off, the chapped corner of his mouth lifted. "Be here, when wake up… love you, Fey. All my heart."

Persa laid her head on his chest and hugged. She felt him lapse into sleep and sat up, rubbing grit and tears from her eyes.

Ian lay awake, his cheeks gaunt, his eyes haunted. She moved to his bedside, pouring him a glass of water. His hand shook as he reached for it. Persa steadied him, helping him drink. He fell back into the pillow, exhausted by the effort. He raised his striking thick eyebrows and asked, "Why are you looking at me like that?"

Persa set the cup down on the small table and touched his hair, running her fingers over his scalp, keeping her expression enigmatic. "Your hair is white, Ian."

Confusion clouded his face, and he drew away from her touch. "What?"

"It's pure white," she said in a halting voice. "You are still handsome, but it's a wee bit shocking."

"The hell you say! Pers, that's not funny."

"I'm not joking, E. I'll get you a mirror."

Ian's eyes rolled to the top of his head, and he pulled at the short hairs, trying to see. But his regulation haircut left him with less than an inch, so his efforts were futile. Persa returned a few moments later with a mirror.

The image struck him dumb. His face looked the same, thinner, a bit haggard, older. However, his hair and eyebrows had turned snow white. His hand fell limp, the mirror slipping from his grasp. He closed his eyes and turned away. *"Mon Dieu!"* he declared, using Beau's favorite expression. "Pers, I am old."

Ian ben Kole was eighteen.

"No." She punched him in the shoulder, using a lighthearted, teasing tone. "You just had a fright. I am sure it will grow back." She schooled her features and met his watery blue-gray eyes.

"That thing on the battlefield," his voice trailed off as he reached for her hand. "I experienced that once before, when the man you were with at the Capitol looked at me."

Persa squeezed his hand, and her face contorted in pain. She turned away, her chest heaving in shallow pants. "He was there, and you faced him? Ian, how are you all not dead?"

"Persa, what was that thing?" he asked, trying to control the rising panic in his chest.

She hugged herself, and something dark flashed behind her hazel eyes, hatred. "A beast, from the pit of Hell. I think he's a fallen angel."

"Jesus," Ian exclaimed and did not even flinch at the use of the Holy name.

Persa bowed her head as she ran her hands over her forearms. "He kidnapped me."

A warrior's rage and adrenaline surged through Ian. He sat up, dragging Persa onto the small cot, wrapping his body around hers, holding her as she shook. "Tell me what happened."

"He lured me from your parent's house the night of the ball." She grabbed his face, bringing them nose-to-nose, desperate for him to understand. "I would have never gone with him if I had known. I thought... I believed he was James. He disguised himself." A dam burst, and she uttered the words she had never spoken aloud. "And he... took me... raped me."

Ian clung to her, weeping, and whispering her name, as guilt crashed over him. He had known something was terribly wrong. James was too heartbroken to see it, but Ian witnessed the malevolence of the man. It struck him blind. He saw her terror and left her to it. "I'm so sorry," he cried and kissed the top of her head as she wept.

She could not tell him the worst of it, could not form the words. The shame of it, to be bred like a broodmare, was just too horrible. She squeezed him and cried, thinking of the vile creature she had birthed, a baby that tried to kill her every time she got near it.

Ian lay motionless, as she sobbed.

"I traded James' life, your life, Dad's life. He said if I stayed, he would not kill you. I didn't know what else to do, Ian. But I, but James... when he came for me yesterday?" She sat up, scrubbing her cheeks, and looking at James. She shook her head, defeat and fear etching her face. "I couldn't do it anymore. I could not stay, even if it meant we all died." Her hand convulsed on Ian's chest, clawing. "I'm sorry, Ian. I just couldn't let them keep doing it." She squeezed her temples. "They can invade your mind. And Tristin, he does terrible things."

"Persa, we left you there," Ian cried.

"No, Ian, I stayed. I thought I could do it. That if I was strong enough, that if I loved you all enough, I could bear it." She closed her eyes and whispered, "But I couldn't. He will surely kill us all now. I can't believe we are still alive."

Sealed

"He does not have the ultimate power of life and death," a voice said from behind Persa.

She turned in surprise, blinking several times. "Joshua?"

"Persa," he said with a smile and held out his arms.

She flew into his embrace. "What are you doing here?"

There was a touch of humor rumbling in his chest when he answered, "I came to visit the sick and wounded. I have a talent for that, you know."

She drew back and smiled. "That you do."

"You are exhausted." He motioned to an empty cot an orderly placed beside James. "Rest now, sweet Persa. All will be better when you wake." He walked her to the cot, laying a hand on her forehead, murmuring comforting words as he eased her down. Persa fell asleep instantly. Joshua settled the blanket over her and smiled.

Ian paled.

"Yohanan," Joshua said, using the Hebrew pronunciation of Ian's name.

Electricity flowed through Ian's body, as he held perfectly still.

"Beloved, I give unto thee, the keeping of the truth of the tale which thou hast learned. For whence they awaken, neither shall recalleth the horror of these last 11,688 hours. A latter rain of mercy falleth upon them, as their tears called out to the Most High, and He restoreth what the locust destroyed."

Deep inside Ian's soul, he knew who spoke, so he blurted, "My Lord and my God!"

Joshua's smile was infinite and kind. He sat on the cot, taking Ian's hand. "Twas not fear that turned thy hair white but thy witness of the Shekinah glory. Let it serve as a remembrance unto thee. This day, Yohanan ben Qowl, I charge thee to holdeth the truth of these matters in thy heart and not speak of them to anyone, until the time of the end."

Joshua nodded to the still form in the cot beside Ian. "Assist thy friend, Beau Landry, to his home and his people. His purpose and path will be difficult, but I am with him."

James rolled in his sleep and took Persa's hand.

"I, myself, will tendeth to Persa and James, to see them home." Joshua paused and turned his dark hazel eyes to Ian, his expression deep and unfathomable.

Under his gaze, Ian felt filthy. He wanted to turn away in shame, the weight of his sin resting on his chest like a millstone. "Forgive me, Lord, for I am unworthy," he whispered. "I have sinned against you in thought, word, and deed, by what I have done, and by what I have left undone. I have not loved you with my whole heart. I have not loved my neighbor as myself. I have broken your commandments, but I beg you to forgive me. Create in me a clean heart, oh God, and bestow the gift of your spirit upon me."

Joshua looked upon Ian with the fondness of a father toward a beloved son. "Thou art true to thy namesake, for he was one such as thee, faithful and true, but brash and brave beyond reasoning. Doest thou knowest what thou asks of me? For that gift hast not been given unto man in this age."

Ian bowed his head. "I am unworthy, yet humbly do I beseech thee, Lord. For in my own strength, and in my own power, I can never accomplish the task thou set before me this day. Lest I cut out my tongue and cleave my hands from my body, I fear I shall tell or write. For it is a dreadful thing that happened to my beloved sister and brother, and it was a frightful beast we faced on the battlefield."

Ian gasped, squeezing the Lord's hand in entreaty. "I will fail in my own strength. But by thy power, by thy glory, and by thy might, I can do all things through you, my Lord. Strengthen me and deliver thy Holy Spirit. I will serve you every day of my life."

Joshua looked pleased. "For thy faith and for my glory." He made the sign of the cross on Ian's forehead and disappeared.

A mighty rushing wind filled the tent. Sick men sat up in their beds, praising the Lord. Nurses shrieked in fear. The sky cracked with thunder, and the Holy Spirit filled Ian ben Kole as He had not done in a millennium.

Father and Son

Marduk, in the guise of Tristin, stormed through the manor house, screaming unholy wrath. Rapha toddled by his side, making his own peculiar screeching noises. He summoned his father to inform him of his traitorous mother's departure, not for love or longing, but delight, though he feigned the hurt of an abandoned boy. "She has left us, Papa. You will punish her?" Rapha could not quite keep the anticipation out of his burnt orange eyes.

Tristin paused and picked up his son. "Oh, yes, I shall. Would you like to take part this time?"

A slow smile broke across Rapha's face, exposing sharp teeth. "Can I eat her?"

"May I," Tristin corrected. "Son, I believe the time has come to make fine sport of your mother and those she loves."

"The horses? She took those," Rapha said with gravity.

Tristin's nose flared. "We shall make her watch. Come, let us concentrate together, and we will find her with our minds."

They closed their eyes.

But the Most High had other plans.

Throne Room

Transported in the spirit, Marduk fell on his face in abject terror. He knew where he was, a place he never wanted to be again, in the presence of the Iron King.

On a magnificent throne, sat the great I AM. Behind Him, a rainbow of emerald-green pulsed with living light, pleasing in sight and wondrous to behold. From the throne came flashes of lightning and rumblings of thunder. To either side and above hovered four unfathomable creatures, full of eyes in front and behind, the seraphim. Marduk huddled on a raised island, surrounded by a sea of glass that shimmered like crystal. His enemies, the Hosts of Heaven, stood guard with their swords drawn, magnificent in glory and power, the perfect elohim.

Marduk rose against his will and faced The Most High. He met the eyes of his enemies: Michael, Gabriel, Uriel, and Raphael. Ilsidor was not there. The facade of Tristin fell away, and he stood exposed for what he was, a black reptilian elohim, corrupted beyond redemption.

"Marduk!" The chamber reverberated.

Marduk flinched. The weight of the thunderous voice carried the gravity of his crimes and held the sentence therein. They had not called his name in this chamber since the end of the Last Age, when he and the rest of his brethren were expelled, exiled, and bound to the Earth. He hoped to never hear it spoken again in this place. Judgment loomed, he could only hope for the Abyss, the alternative was worse, the Lake of Fire.

"My Lord." Marduk bowed, going to a knee in submission.

"Thou hast failed to keep thy natural place, Marduk. Through connivance and scheming, thou escaped thy rightful bondage 666 days hence and hath gone about as thou did in days past, in sinful disregard of the laws thou knowest well. Marduk, thou hast corrupted and defiled, committed murder and terror. Thou broketh the law and laid with the Daughters of Eve, begetting three foul and damnable beasts. Thou hast raped, tortured, and defiled innocents. Their cries cometh before my throne." His voice shook the foundation of Heaven and Earth. "What say you, Marduk?"

In ages past, he would have claimed his legal rights under the Earth Lease, which was their writ of permission. But Marduk knew that statute had long since expired. He stood before the Most High without a defense, excuse, or a single true recourse. In desperation, he used the old standby. "I was deceived by the wickedness of thy servant, Lucifer. He beguiled me with his false words and promises. I am thy faithful servant, if thou wouldst redeem me, I would return to thy bosom and serve thee well, my Lord, as I did in times past. Let me resume my rightful place, and I will devote unto thee my unwavering loyalty."

The Iron King sat back, regarding Marduk with omnipotent eyes. He snapped his fingers and behind the throne, scenes played like a video from the Last Age. Tristin arguing with Ilsidor, his words contradicting his claim of deception. Ilsidor's pleas, her warnings, and the consequences of his actions echoed through the chamber. The scenes kept coming. Marduk's own words, actions, and innermost thoughts played for everyone to see. He condemned himself.

Marduk saw Gabriel's sneer and met it with a ferocious growl.

The sea of glass turned to fire. Marduk drew back in agony. He saw them writhing in pain, alive amidst the flame, the false prophet and the antichrist. "I beseech you, Lord. It is not yet time!" Marduk cried.

"Since when art thou a respecter of time?" asked the King.

"Please, my Lord, I will abide by thy terms," Marduk pled.

"Thy fate was sealed at thy rebellion, long past. Hear this foul beast, no more wilt thou present thyself to man to walk among them. No more shall thee defile the Daughters of Eve, nor the Sons of Adam, by lying with them. Thou shalt not touch Persa ben Yereq, nor shall thy go unto thy wicked offspring, who are cursed, and bound to their own territory lest they die."

With a flick of His hand, He banished Marduk, but not before allowing his foot to graze the eternal fire that waited for him.

When Marduk regained his wits, he was in the House of Amah. Rapha sat cross-legged on the floor, bawling. Marduk knew he had only a moment. "Rapha, I will send servants, but you must always hide. Do not eat them. I will provide you food, books, and lessons, but you cannot leave this place, and no one can see you, or you will surely die!"

As an impenetrable force descended over the property, Marduk heard them coming, the Hosts of Heaven.

He fled.

Awakenings

The clatter of a dropped instrument tray startled Persa out of her slumber. She sat straight up in bed, her hand over her heart. James did the same. They looked at each other in bewilderment, then noticed their identical positions, and burst out laughing.

"Morning, Fey," James said with a smile, falling back onto his pillow.

"Morning, Jay." Persa grinned. Casting a furtive look around, she jumped in bed with him. "I feel like I haven't seen you in years."

He chuckled and kissed her strawberry-blonde hair. "Silly wife, I saw you yesterday as I was falling asleep."

Persa lifted her head, her eyes crinkled at the corners. "We were quite wicked to do that, Jay. I am certain Joey will never forgive us."

James brushed his lips against hers. "I was not going into that battle without marrying you, my love, and I was damn sure not going to die a virgin."

"Well, I suppose it was the most appropriate marriage bed for the two of us," Persa whispered, her eyes dancing with mischief.

The corner of James' mouth twitched. "You should not have traveled from Rivergate. I will brain Joshua. I cannot believe you convinced him to bring you here in the middle of a war."

"Pfft," Persa snorted. "Did you see the fine horses I procured on the way down? Six of them, beautiful fine creatures. When you add those to Bayard, Lightning, and the ones Father promised us, we have our stock."

"Indeed, we shall be the greatest horse breeders in the land."

A throat cleared to their right. Persa scrambled up, smoothing her clothing, looking abashed. "Ian, good morning."

James did a double-take. "Brother, what on earth happened to your hair?"

"The doctor said it's rare, but it sometimes occurs after a battle." Ian shrugged, rubbing his scalp. "If this is the only wound I bear…" He looked to the bed that held Beau.

James' face clouded, and he sat up. "How is he?"

Ian shook his head. "He has puncture wounds over ninety percent of his body, but there is no shrapnel. They don't know what did it. He has not stirred since I brought him here."

James rubbed his hands over his face. "I don't remember any of it. Do you?"

"Enough." Ian shrugged. "I'm glad you don't remember, don't try. We lost. It's time to leave." He looked between them and added, "It's time for both of you to go home."

Persa stretched where she stood. "I'm ready."

Ian's eyes closed. When he spoke, his voice was rough with emotion. "Then home you shall go, dear Sister. I will wait for Beau to wake up and assist him back to Louisiana where he has promised me unlimited crawfish, biscuits, and something he calls a *fais-do-do.*"

James laughed. "There is plenty of do-do back at the ranch."

"Ian," Persa wrapped a slender arm around James' waist, "James and I married each other the night before the battle."

Ian's mouth fell open in shock.

Persa laughed. "I hope that is all your mother will do. I fear she is going to have a conniption fit."

Joshua joined them. "War does that Persa, she will understand. I am sure a reception will placate Salome's displeasure, one that you will let her plan, right?"

Persa blinked up at him. "I think I shall. A big celebration sounds wonderful. We'll have it at Leggett."

James snorted. "And that way she won't drive you mad with the details and the planning. You will just show up, wearing your boots and your jeans?"

"And give her a fit!" Ian laughed.

Beau moaned from the bed behind them.

Joshua and Ian moved to his side. Joshua looked at Ian and nodded. Ian laid hands on Beau and prayed.

After a time, Beau's eyes blinked open, blue and black, confused. He moistened his lips, and at another nod from Joshua, Ian brought a glass of water for him to sip.

Beau exhaled like a draught horse. "*Mon Dieu*, get these bandages off me. I feel like Lazarus."

For some reason, Ian and Joshua thought that was hysterical.

February 28, 987 ME

Rivergate

Officially discharged from the Army, James said an emotional goodbye to his men and his brother but wasted no time lolling around the disbursing force. The terms of the amnesty stated that the rebel army was to disband within a fortnight. After months of war, no one wanted to linger.

In the confusion, Persa misplaced her belongings. She had the clothes on her back and nothing else. Much to her consternation and James' teasing, she wore one of his shirts rolled at the cuffs six times, the collar points extending to her shoulders.

James changed from his dashing officer's uniform into plain clothes. Persa studied him as they rode, the war had hardened him. His face was no longer that of a youth but a battle-toughened warrior. Never gregarious, he spoke less now than he had before the war.

However, James was not the only one irrevocably changed. She looked like a stranger to herself, as if war erased the doe-eyed innocence and left behind a woman, a married one, no less. She still could not believe they had done it, that wild abandoned ride. Throwing caution and convention to the wind, she supposed it was the looming battle. War changed everything. Salome would be furious, but somehow, she did not think Dad would be too angry. They were six months shy of the three-year contract.

Persa's desire for home became akin to physical pain. She longed to escape the noise of the camp, the stench of the battle. She wanted Rivergate.

Joshua traveled with them, which was a blessing. Alone, they may have had a hard time managing that many horses. During their trek, the old and normally docile Lightning morphed into a force of nature. Ridden by Joshua, she brooked no shenanigans from the rambunctious herd and dominated the younger horses in a manner that amused Persa. The quiet competence of their groom was a joy to behold. What might have been a challenging journey with the spirited beasts, instead became peaceful and serene.

When they crested the last hill, and she saw the sprawling pastures of Rivergate below, her heart exploded with joy. She gave a whoop and spurred her mount, racing home.

Yereq met her in the yard with open arms. She leapt from the saddle and fell into his embrace, overcome with tears. "We are home, Dad. James is fine, and we made it."

"Let me see you, Persa! It's only been ten days, but I swear, Daughter, it feels longer." He picked her up and squeezed.

"It is the strangest thing. I feel the same." She looked around, beaming with pleasure. "I am filthy and need a bath. Somehow, I lost my belongings in camp, and if I never wear this green sweater again, I will not care!"

"Well, take yourself off then," Yereq said, giving her a playful swat on her bottom. As James and Joshua rode over the hill, Yereq grinned. "I see you have not come home empty handed, that's my girl."

"They are magnificent, Dad." Persa twirled in the yard, dancing. She bounded up the steps, spun at the door and called down to Yereq. "I love you. It's good to be home."

March 1, 987 ME

Pepperwood

The sun rode high as James and Persa guided their mounts on a leisurely pace through the cool depths of the redwood forest. In a few places, sunbeams pierced the giant canopy, sending shafts of gold through the dark green and red shadows. Craggy trunks, hundreds of feet in diameter tricked the eye into believing they were mounds of earth instead of trees. Climbing to impossible heights, in the Millennium redwoods stretched three thousand feet into the air. Many survived from the Last Age and stood quietly as ancient sentinels to original creation. They alone reached the heavens.

The soft clopping of the horse's hooves muffled under layers of thick mulch as James and Persa cut a lazy path. They had not taken the road, newly constructed along the southern pasture line of Rivergate, opting instead to travel the path they rode as children when they discovered the Pepperwood Valley and fell in love with it and each other.

Nestled between the hills and the old-growth forest, a prosperous vineyard flanked them on the east, the Connor River to the west. The property was pristine and flat, perfect for paddocks and pasture. And it was theirs.

Persa bubbled with excitement, eager to see the house, their ranch. James had been secretive about the plans, so she had no notion what awaited them.

James rode beside her, equally excited. He dreamed of this moment since he was a boy, now that it was upon them, he could scarcely define what he was feeling. All he knew was that he was bringing his bride home, finally.

Despite their fervor, by mutual accord, neither rushed. This was a moment to savor.

"Fey, do you remember the first time I asked you to marry me?"

Persa laughed and looked up in remembrance. "We were nine. You had dropped me on my head, and I was furious."

"I was distracted by you, even then." James winked at her.

"Ha, you were just afraid I was going to sock you in the stomach again. Remember how mad I used to get if you let me fall?"

James took a deep breath and drew back in mock fear. "Well, it taught me to make sure I did not drop you anymore. You've always been a fierce little thing."

Persa made a great show of flexing her tiny bicep. "You have to be tough when you are my size." Then she added, with the corners of her mouth twitching. "I'll still punch you in the stomach if you drop me."

"When I carry you over the threshold of our new house, I promise I won't drop you."

"At least tell me what color you painted it," Persa coaxed.

James looked away. "It's a surprise." He was as befuddled as Persa over their house, which he knew he shouldn't be. He had built the thing... hadn't he? Yes, of course, he had. It was white, with a wrap-around porch, a green roof and shutters. He sighed, rubbing his temples, and thought for the twentieth time in a week that the final battle had addled his brain.

"We have waited forever. I cannot believe the day has finally come." Persa reached out her hand.

James inched his mount closer and brought her fingers to his lips. "I shall truly make you my wife." He winked again. "Not on horseback this time."

"I am an exceedingly wicked creature, aren't I?" Persa laughed.

"We will let no wickedness enter our valley, aye?" James said in an odd voice. "I believe we have seen enough of that don't you?"

"Oh, I agree with that." Persa rubbed the bridge of her nose. The war, the worry, the separation had taken its toll. His words brought an overwhelming sadness to her heart. "We'll not be separated again, Jay. I cannot bear it."

"As the Lord wills, my love." James smiled in tender sadness.

They rode in silence for a few moments, their heads bowed in prayer.

As they emerged from the cool forest into the sun, they dropped hands. The Pepperwood Valley lay before them. Persa had not come since James began construction, the week after they signed their betrothal contract. She covered a gasp, staring through tears. Nestled in the center of a dozen fenced pastures, the ranch sparkled like a diamond and emerald tiara. Gables and windows, proportioned and functional, the house and stables were perfect, their home. Her hands covered her heart as tears spilled down her cheeks. "Jay... green and white. I love it."

James smiled, glowing with pride. His earlier angst washed away the moment they emerged from the forest. "Wait until you see inside. Come on. I'll race you!" He kicked Joey hard and took off.

Persa cried in protest at his cheating and chased after him. Her laughter carried on the wind as she raced home.

He did not take her to the house; he took her to the stables, which connected to the residence by a long, covered walkway. New wood, bedding, and twenty exquisitely crafted stalls awaited their stock. It was the heart of the ranch, where they would build their future.

James unsaddled their mounts, and Persa collapsed on a small bench watching him work. When the horses were put away, he came and sat beside her.

Silent tears fell down her cheeks. "I have to stop these tears. Everything is making me cry. I cried over my closet yesterday." She brushed them away and gave a self-deprecating laugh. "My closet? I hate clothes."

He bumped shoulders with her, teasing. "You were just happy to have clean jeans."

"Well, there was that." She bumped him back. "This place," Persa's voice filled with awe, "it's amazing, Jay. You did so good."

He stood and offered her his hand. "Wife, come. Let me show you our home."

Persa looked up into his beloved face. His eyes were no longer teasing, but she could see the smudges of fatigue. His jaw, square and strong, was shaven clean. She studied the small indent between his lower lip and chin that she called the well of a thousand kisses. It was the face of a man, masculine and fine. She put her hand in his and rose.

His kiss began, a mere brush of his lips against hers. Before it could deepen, he straightened, and with a growl, swept her up. As he carried her from the stable, she wrapped her arms around his neck and nipped his ear. "Don't you drop me."

"I haven't dropped you since we were fifteen, and I am not about to start now."

Part 3 - Greece

February 12, 986 ME (Nine Months into Rebellion)

Adoption - Athens, Greece

When Lieutenant Orion ben Drachmas found Princess Philomela, his first reaction was to kill the creature feasting on her corpse; the creature had other ideas. Orion reached for his sword, but the thing hurled him through the air with nothing more than its malevolent glare. It snarled and returned to its grisly breakfast. Orion's heels dug deep divots in the dirt as he scrambled away. In his life, he witnessed dozens of atrocities, but nothing came close to the horror in the boathouse.

Orion rolled to his feet and fled, ready to raise the alarm and bring down the fire and fury of the Palace Guard. But something gave him pause, a memory, a flicker... This was Greece, home of the old gods, the old stories. He slowed his pace as his heart hammered and his devious mind calculated. It would be unwise to attack without proper forethought and consideration.

Perhaps there were advantages to be gained.

Daring a glance over his shoulder, he saw the door to the boathouse was firmly closed. No one stirred in this area of the grounds. They had not raised a full-scale alarm in the search for the Princess. Her maid merely took Orion aside and asked him to check the grounds, so he had a moment to think.

If he could tame it or use it, he would become a man of significant power. Alternatively, if he presented it to Monarch Antiochus, he might

earn great reward and stature in the Royal Guard, without direct expo-
sure to that being. The fickle favor of the old gods was legendary. A creature such as that would have the potential to turn on him, and he would
end up devoured like the Princess. However, if he gave it away, well, that
was even better.

He barked an order to his fellow guards patrolling the wall. "Secure
the perimeter. No one approach the boathouse. I am off to retrieve the
Monarch."

Orion brushed passed the servants, strode into the breakfast room,
and fell at Antiochus' feet. "I pray, my Esteemed, please come with me
posthaste. It is a matter of dire importance."

Antiochus regarded the Lieutenant, lifting a brow in disdain. The
man was disordered, his hair disheveled, his uniform covered in grass,
wet with dew. But something about his tone intrigued Antiochus, the
ambitious gleam in his eyes, the purpose in his step. He surrounded himself with men who exhibited potential. After watching the guard kneel-
ing at his feet for months, he decided to follow.

When they reached the lawn, Orion gestured toward the lake, and
asked in a low whisper, "My Esteemed, with thy leave, may I speak
plainly? For I am a simple man of humble origins."

Antiochus gave him an appraising look. He knew his background;
Orion was from the slums. Ruthless and shrewd, he rose in power and
position through guile and industrious elimination of his rivals. Antiochus respected that. "You have my leave, Lieutenant."

Orion steeled his nerve and plunged ahead. "I believe the old gods
paid us a visit last night and left behind one of their own. I regret to inform you, Princess Philomela did not survive, but the god she gave birth
to lives."

Antiochus froze mid-step and turned the full menace of his glare on
Orion. "My sister is dead?"

Orion fell to his knees, his head bowed. "I am sorry, my Esteemed.
She sacrificed herself for her child, who even now bears the countenance
and size of a human toddler. He is surely a god of old."

"What folly you speak! Are you drunk?"

"Nay, my Esteemed. Only check yon boathouse and see the truth for
yourself," he uttered, groveling. "But take care, it is a fearsome sight."

"Arise, Lieutenant, and show me what you claim."

Orion opened the door as if it might explode under his hand. A
vile stench rolled out, assailing their noses like a slaughterhouse. Orion
stepped back, and Antiochus leaned in, his eyes growing wide at the
scene.

The creature sat amid the gore, turning its hellfire eyes toward the Monarch and giving him a bloody grin. He held a severed finger, licking it like a lollipop. *"Patéras,"* it gurgled. Father.

Antiochus' smile grew slowly. *"Yiós!"* he answered. Son.

The Roving One

The creature called itself Zuzite. He was terrible to behold, enormous with six fingers, six toes, and an elongated skull topped with hair the color of blood and fire. The day he was born, Antiochus ordered the guards out of the interior of the Palace grounds, relegating them to the perimeter. He summarily evicted his guests under the guise of mourning over his sister.

For twelve years, Antiochus hid his son.

At three years old, Zuzite stood six feet tall and could eat a cow in a single sitting. He preferred them uncooked and still alive. Antiochus retrofitted a large guest house on the grounds and conducted all official business offsite in the newly constructed governmental administrative offices. He permitted servants in the Palace two hours per day, warning that any who remained past that window placed themselves in mortal peril as two young maids discovered when Zuzite was four. Antiochus erupted when he found them murdered, but the look Zuzite gave him over a bloody haunch warned him that if he was not careful, the next human leg the creature devoured might be his.

Behind the blood lust lay an incredible mind. Advanced mathematics, physics, chemistry, biology came to Zuzite with the ease of breathing, yet they bored him. The only subject that engaged him was military science. The art of war fascinated him, and he devoured Greece's legends and the writings of the ancients. Antiochus commissioned Orion and an elite group of guards to obtain as many artifacts, scrolls, and texts as they could procure. Cost and means were no object. Zuzite absorbed everything.

February 14, 996 ME (Eleven Years into Rebellion)

Pilgrim Massacre

At twenty-six and eleven years into his exile, Prince Josiah ben Eamonn served in the Iron King's Army as a doctor, under an alias. Today, they had called him to a crimes scene to serve as coroner. Doctor Einar ben Yane, Captain of the fourth dragoons, smelled the slaughter well before his horse reached the site. One of their patrols found a lone survivor this morning, a six-year-old boy, under heavy sedation back at the hospital where Josiah was a second-year resident.

As Sergeant Reuben ben Judah approached, he appeared grave, his face bloodless under his olive complexion. "Captain," he saluted, "it is good to see you. Trust you are well?"

Josiah returned his salute, then extended a hand in greeting. "Sergeant, I am well, thank you." He looked around at the draped bodies. "Unlike these poor souls. What is the report?"

Reuben referred to the clipboard. "At approximately 06:00, three of our men on patrol spotted a wounded civilian child." He glanced at his notes and continued, "Jose ben Alvera of Madrid, Spain and his family were on pilgrimage. The child appeared disoriented, weeping, and bleeding from deep scratch marks on his arms and legs. Our medics treated him and upon transfer to the medical unit, he confided that his party came under attack in the night." He rubbed his mouth and glanced up from the page. "The child claimed the assailant was a monster, an enormous beast, a giant."

Josiah's brows drew together. "No doubt trauma-induced."

Reuben opened his mouth, then closed it again. His pensive expression caused the hair on the back of Josiah's neck to stand up. "You need to examine the bodies, Captain."

Josiah stiffened and moved with slow deliberation to his saddlebags, gearing up for what promised to be a grisly task. He had seen death, doctors saw death every day, even in peacetime. But the scene before him was carnage. The first body was that of a woman, her breasts eaten, her arms torn from their sockets, the flesh from her thighs devoured. Josiah recoiled, turning away. "Oh, Father in Heaven!"

Reuben's voice sounded hoarse. "We found one of her arms thirty yards away. We have yet to find the other."

Josiah sucked in a deep breath and turned back to his work. Deep gouges ran the length of the woman's torso, scratch marks, six deep rows. No animal made six scratch marks. They only encountered animal attacks in the last decade; they did not happen in the Millennium. Animal carnage of this nature was the purview of the Last Age, not this one.

Josiah stood up, his face resolute. "This is the work of a man using some sort of tool or glove."

Reuben turned his head to the shrouded corpse ten yards away. "The bite marks on the second victim, you need to see." Reuben motioned to the pale corporal shuffling nearby. "Cover this body, cover it!" The boy gave a convulsive nod.

Josiah walked to the second body, bracing himself. He had never seen Reuben ben Judah shaken, not like this. The victim was a dark-skinned man, heavy boned and muscled, with the leathery skin of a life-long farmer. The attacker had chewed the corpse. His throat was gone, as were his genitalia, but his limbs were intact. Apparently, he had not been too tasty. Double rows of teeth sampled him along his arms and legs before abandoning him where he lay. Clutched in the man's dead hand were several long strands of orange hair. "Collect these hairs as evidence," Josiah snapped.

Two additional victims were identified by their heads, their bodies scattered in pieces across a mile, dropped like crumbs as if they were consumed and discarded as the murderer walked away. Footprints three times the size of a normal man's were cast and sent to the lab for analysis.

Six hours later, Josiah sat on the tail of a wagon, his bloody apron in a heap, his head buried in his hands. The wagon shifted as Reuben sat beside him, pressing a cup of water into his hand. "Drink this, Doctor. It will help."

Josiah rubbed his face before downing the water in a single gulp. "Bloody hell, Reuben."

When Reuben spoke, Josiah could tell he had weighed his words. "This is not the first attack like this. Trust me, I know this is true. It has been going on for a few years. Usually on moonless nights, like we had last evening. The victims speak of a ravenous beast, over ten feet tall, with hair and eyes the color of fire, huge claws, and fangs. You saw the foot-prints, and you have seen the evidence. Doctor, it is a cannibal."

November 1, 998 ME (Thirteen Years into Rebellion)

Lot in Life

"I told you we should have stayed with the caravan going west, but you would not listen to me," Zanah ben Joseph said, vibrating with scorn. "You never listen to me, David, and now look at the mess you've gotten us into." She looked around the desolate campsite, disgusted.

David ben Jesse rubbed his temple, searching for patience, nearly be-yond his endurance at Zanah's incessant badgering. "We both agreed—"

"I never agreed. I never agreed to come on this pilgrimage. This was all your idea."

"I'm going to fill up the canteens," Davianna called from the other side of the camp, sick of listening to this argument.

David's pained expression telegraphed he would like to go with her. "Be careful."

"I will, Daddy." She clattered away; tin canteens strapped across her body.

Zanah glared at David, then turned her back on him. Their fight suspended, for now. David rubbed the bridge of his nose. His wife was right, though he was loath to admit. They were in a jam. He made the decision to follow the pilgrim road south into Greece, to Camp Eiran and from there to catch a ship to the Golden City. However, he never anticipated how deserted and barren the southern road had become. His guidebook, outdated as it was, had failed to mention it.

Drought ravaged lands surrounded them. Davianna found a small oasis and a stream near their camp, but she calculated, and he agreed, they were several days journey to Camp Eiran. There should be others, there were always others, yet they were out here alone. Instead of pulling together, making the best of the situation, as he and Davianna tried to do, Zanah took every opportunity to cast aspersions and blame. She alternated between rage and tears. He never knew which Zanah he was going to get. She vacillated from moment to moment. But that was nothing new.

David could not recall the last kind word that passed over her beautiful lips. Sometimes he wondered if she ever uttered one in her life that did not have an ulterior motive behind it. She was gorgeous, which was why he fell in love with her. But not long after their wedding, he realized Zanah's beauty was her single redeeming quality. He prayed the pilgrimage would soften her heart, reasoning that a journey to seek the Iron King would bind them together on an adventure of a lifetime, just the three of them. But he had long since given up hope of that; it was not to be.

Add that to his long list of failures.

David poked at the meager fire. His unwavering optimism faltered as the shifting sands buffeted his scorched skin. Surrounded by a sea of failure, he let the vortex pull him under, and he drowned in the poisonous waters of regret and self-loathing. He failed at everything, business, marriage, this pilgrimage.

Davianna returned and gave him a smile, causing him to amend his maudlin sentiment. He had not failed with her. She remained the one thing he had not failed at.

With a grunt of exertion, Davianna dropped the canteen and sat down beside him. Zanah emerged from their tent, took a canteen without a word, and disappeared behind the canvas, tying the flaps.

"It was her idea," Davianna whispered. "She convinced you to go south, so we could take a boat for this last leg. You wanted to stay with our companions on the overland passage."

David dismissed the statement with a shrug. "You don't need to take sides, Dee-dee." Though he appreciated her support. "I've made a bit of a mess of this. We are in a tight spot."

Davianna snorted. "Well, constant complaining does not help."

"She is your mother, and I will not allow you to disrespect her."

"Sorry." Davianna hung her head. "I just don't like the way she talks to you."

David put an arm around her. "Your mum is disappointed in the way our lives have turned out." He kissed the top of her head. "I am disappointed, too, which is why we are starting our new life in the Golden City. But you and I have discussed this. I believe once we finish our journey, she will settle, and things will be better."

"I know they will, Daddy," Davianna said through a yawn. "You always make everything better. I know sometimes you don't believe that, but you do." Leaning in, she pressed a kiss to his cheek. "I'll see you in the morning." She stood up and smoothed her plain dress, the firelight illuminating her young girl's fine form.

He smiled up at her, his golden-brown eyes sparkling with affection. "I love you, Dee-dee."

She paused, holding his gaze and standing very still. Swallowing hard, she whispered, "I love you, too, Daddy."

David stared after her, his heart, the joy of his life. From the moment she came into this world, his daughter became the repository for all the love he had, all the love his wife refused to accept. Bright and inquisitive, they were a pair, much to his wife's consternation.

He never intended for it to be that way, but it was.

That Davianna did not see him as a failure was a miracle in itself. Instead, she saw who he was, a well-intentioned man, who never got a break, and for whom nothing ever worked out.

Surrounded by desolation, in what had likely once been fertile farmland, he felt a kinship to this place. Letting the sands run through his fingers, each grain seemed to represent lost chances, opportunities, and men he should not have trusted but did.

No matter how hard he tried, how honest he was, how many times he picked himself up and tried again, it did not matter. David was not blessed, and in an era where everyone around him prospered, it was a bitter lot in life. It was especially difficult because he was a man of extraordinary faith and devotion.

He had been a star athlete, president of his class, and earned a full academic scholarship to the University of Bristol. When he felt called to leave England, and everyone and everything he loved, he obeyed, and not a single thing had gone right since. Davianna believed him when he said they did not have time to visit England when they landed in Europe, but the truth was, he simply could not face the people and life he left behind.

And when he grew convicted to take this pilgrimage, to start again, he felt a glimmer of hope that perhaps this time it would be different. There had always been a calling on his life, something special he needed to do, and on this journey, he intended to find out what it was.

Voice of Truth

The voice, when it came, seemed unreal. David heard it in the dawn, the gentle quiet hour, when the sun peeked above the horizon. At first, he thought he was dreaming, but his eyes were open, Zanah and Davianna sleeping beside him.

He rose, careful not to wake his family, and looked outside. The day promised to be bright and warm, but there was no one in their camp.

He straightened and stretched.

The voice came again, "David."

He walked around the tent. No one was there. "Hello?"

"David," repeated the deep voice.

The hair stood up on the back of his neck. He remembered Samuel and replied, "I am thy servant, Lord."

"I have heard thy prayers, Son. Thy life has not been for nothing. Thy love and faithfulness have always been before me. Thou accomplished what I ordained, to raise and care for thy daughter, who is blessed among the Daughters of Eve, with an extraordinary path set before her, for which thou hast trained and prepared her."

David fell to his knees, covering his face, speechless.

The voice of the Lord continued, "Take up thy weapon, David, and I will go before thee. Great evil is hunting thy daughter. But do not fear, for this is what I have called thee to do. For this moment and in this hour, thou will serve me, and protect thy treasure."

The Holy Spirit fell upon the dusty man.

David rose as a valiant warrior, took up his weapon, and without a backward glance or hesitation went out.

He saw the giant from a distance. Anger erupted in his heart. That thing was not getting close to his daughter. "Stand down, cursed beast," David bellowed, "for the Spirit of the Lord is upon me, and He will smite thee this day."

Zuzite of Greece looked at David and laughed. "You are nothing. I eat three of you for breakfast." His burnt orange eyes glared as he made a great show of picking his double row of sharp teeth. His black robes fluttered in the gentle wind.

The giant towered over him, fourteen feet tall, with a head the size of an ox. He held a sharpened javelin as big as a tree, but he carried no shield, and wore no armor. Clearly, he did not expect a fight. The giant was sorely mistaken.

David faced him without fear. Seeing into Zuzite's black soul, he knew in an instant what he was, a Nephilim. Righteous anger burned in his soul. The enemy of old was trying to regain ground the Iron King had revoked. Zeal for the Lord, protection of his daughter, and a godly man's passion to destroy evil sang in his heart. The sling he swung above his head added to the glorious tune.

David released the rock; Zuzite threw the javelin. Stone and spear passed in mid-air. Zuzite fell dead, the rock embedded three inches into his skull. The ground trembled as he crashed, sending shock waves that woke Davianna a mile away. With a groan, the Earth opened with a great gawking gasp, and took Zuzite's body.

But the javelin found purchase, piercing David's godly heart.

David's bravery was not celebrated, his sacrifice not immortalized in the annals of scripture, his valiant deed unknown, even to those he loved on Earth. In death, as in life, David's purpose, honor, and glory were carried out before the audience of One.

Final Prophecy

On the morning of November 1, 998 ME, Antiochus woke from a nightmare. He threw back the blankets and dressed in a hurry. Heedless of his disheveled appearance, he rushed from his chamber. Only Orion and the other guards occupied the grounds, standing sentinel as Zuzite became more fearsome and unpredictable.

Antiochus had not entered the guesthouse in six weeks. The moment the door opened, he knew Zuzite was not in residence, yet he ran from room to room, calling out. A lingering stench permeated the air, and the house had become disordered, chaotic. Outside the study, he paused, knocking, just in case. Zuzite in the middle of a problem, a riddle, or a calculation would fly into a rage if interrupted. Antiochus' knock rang hollow, and he eased open the door. Expecting to find the room in similar condition to the rest of the house, the ordered and compulsively clean space disorientated him for a moment. A single parchment lay on the enormous writing desk.

Dated three months ago, Antiochus had not seen it before. Zuzite had not shared it. With shaking hands, he lifted the page, staring at the familiar and precise handwriting.

"A maiden will carry the Black Key in a sealed box, a relic from the Last Age. Whosoever shall retrieve the key, will gain everlasting favor with the Prince of the Powers of the Air and rule with him."

Part 4 - Beau and Alaina

July 15, 990 ME (Five Years into Rebellion)

Mississippi Backwoods

Daddy was drunk again, which was okay if it was wine, dangerous if it was tequila. Alaina ben Thomas watched him through the crack in her bedroom door. Was he singing or cursing? Cursing... Blast it!

Deep in the Mississippi forest, tall pines and moss-covered live oaks loomed over the house. At one point Thomas ben Patrick had white-washed the rough-hewn boards and planted a bed of petunias by the walk-up steps. However, the petunias were long gone and only a few peeling flakes of the cheap paint remained.

Alaina wrinkled her nose as he burped a string of obscenities in the general direction of her mother's rocking chair. A shaft of light penetrated the pollen covered windows, casting his lined face in a sickly yellow hue. He snarled at the empty chair and took a long pull from the bottle.

Time to get out.

In a huff, Alaina grabbed a white leather purse, studded with silver stars. It was tacky; the leather was cheap, but she liked it. Muttering under her breath, she shoved her pink heels into the bag's cavernous depths, spit shining a scuff off the back of the left one. Four-inch pumps were not optimal footwear for sneaking out windows and hiking through the woods, but she'd change before she got to the road.

She applied a fresh coat of lip gloss, fluffed her long blonde hair, and pushed her breast up, pleased with the cleavage. With a final sweep around the room, she rucked her mini-skirt to her waist and eased a long tan leg out the window. Alaina did not know it, but that was the last time she would sneak out of that room.

She never looked back.

July 16, 990 ME

Good Directions

Alaina was lost. She hated being lost. Stupid road signs. It seemed like they didn't exist in this backwater, mosquito-infested swamp. Where the hell was New Orleans? This certainly wasn't it. She looked down at the gas gauge with growing trepidation. They would not have any gas around here, maybe moonshine, but not gas. Damn.

She squinted and spied a wagon with a lanky black-haired hottie adjusting the harness on a fine mule. He was hauling a load of food. Her stomach growled. She had not eaten since yesterday.

Beau Landry spotted the strange car from a distance. Cars were not unknown these days, but rare enough for him to pay attention. As the driver pulled up, he thought with some irony that he would have paid attention to the gorgeous blonde behind the wheel if she were driving a dung wagon.

She came to a brake squealing, gravel skidding, abrupt stop in front of him. She tried to cover the fact that she jerked forward in her seat belt but didn't quite pull it off. The breeze from the open car window tousled her hair around her shoulders, and a tawny strand teased the tip of her sun-kissed nose. She blew it away and adopted a trembling bottom lip expression of distress. His insides twisted into an instant knot.

Approaching the car, he leaned down and said, "What you doing out here, *chèr*? You lost?"

Alaina's eyes widened, momentarily shocked at just how handsome the hottie was up close. Soft and sultry, his voice flowed over her like a bayou heatwave. Alaina tucked the tickling lock of hair behind her ear, staring into the cobalt blue depths of his eyes. Leaving her hand on the side of her neck, she answered, "I was looking for some gas and New Orleans, but seems I found you."

A corner of his lip turned up in a devilish smile. "Jolie Catin, you are in luck. There is a store about two miles up the road. A little ways past, you'll come to a crossroads. If you make a left, you go to New Orleans, however a right will bring you back…"

The invitation came through clearly. Alaina moistened her bottom lip, considering him. He was gorgeous. And oh, that voice… good heavens, all Cajun spice, and heat. But she was already in trouble without adding more. Tilting her head, she gave a small shrug. "Sorry, babe, gotta run." She gunned the accelerator, leaving him in a cloud of dust.

Beau kicked the dirt as he turned back to the wagon. This morning's catch seemed to mock him with their glassy eyes. "Fool, that was the best catch of the day, and you let her get away."

It was the police car parked in front of the store that made her take a right. Alaina dug in her purse, applied a fresh coat of lip gloss, and tried to put some order to her hair, which was a tangled mess of yesterday's hair spray, humidity, and road wind. But the black-haired hottie hadn't seemed to mind. Good.

The stop she executed this time was more controlled; her heartbeat wasn't.

He slid down the wagon seat and leaned in the passenger window, wearing a cocky grin. "You're back."

Alaina fluttered her lashes, going full force, damsel in distress. "Well, I am in a bit of a jam. You see, I am hiding from a terrible man, and this car is out of gas." She covered her face, pretending to cry. "And I… I need help."

Beau had five sisters, a mother, and more aunts than he could name. He suppressed the urge to applaud. This was quite a performance, but infinitely more entertaining than talking to a wagonload of fish. "*Chèr*, don't cry. How can I help?"

"I think… I think I need a place to hide this car." She dared a side-long glance before resuming her dramatic sniffling.

Beau raised an eyebrow. Trouble, nothing but trouble. He let his eyes travel the length of her long, tan, shapely leg, and denim mini-skirt and thought she might be worth a little trouble. "Hide a car? Well, I got a place just down the road that'll suit just fine."

She dropped her hands and turned, feigning relief. But behind her doe-eyed expression, he saw calculated awareness. She was wondering if she was about to become alligator bait. "You do?" Her voice pitched higher than before.

"Folks around here call it Landry's. It's my family's place," Beau assured her. "Go down about a mile. Make a right. At the fork, go left and follow that road until it dead ends. You'll see a whole slew of women and kids running around. Tell them Beau sent you, and I'll be along shortly. I can't leave Gladys here on the side of the road." He nodded toward the mule.

"Women and children, huh?"

His black lashes nearly touched his cheeks as he closed his eyes in ascent. "Probably more than you'll want."

For the first time in two days, her heart stopped thundering. His voice was soothing, his manner calm, and there were women and children. "And you'll be along in a bit?"

When he smiled, she could see his back teeth, strong, white, and beautiful. She moistened her lips, tasting the fresh grape gloss.

"I'll run this load up to the store and be straight back." Beau nodded once and hit the window in dismissal. "Go on now. Officer Woodrow finishes his lunch in about ten minutes, he'll be coming this way."

He repeated the directions for her and watched her ease away in the beige car.

"*Laissez les bon temps rouler!*" Let the good times roll, he said as he mounted the wagon seat. The fish reminded him he still did not catch her name.

Oz

Instead of tearing off, Alaina navigated the twisting roads like an old woman, hoping to conserve whatever fumes remained in the gas tank. Bayou water surrounded her. Flat, scrubby bushes and twisted trees shaded the road, but it gave her a break from the heat, because she did not dare run the air conditioner.

She fought off the genuine fear that she might be driving into a serial killer's trap, a pretty one, but she read enough true crime novels to know they were the ones that took a long time to catch. Even if it was not a serial killer's lair, at the very least, she prepared for a white trash compound, populated by mean-faced wrinkled women and dirty kids, but she could deal.

What she found was something beyond imagination; a gingerbread village, with paved drives, landscaped yards, and covered porches full of well-tended flowering plants that spilled their blossoms over white railings. Houses of every pastel shade and hue dotted the wide avenue. Children on bikes and skates teetered in various degrees of skill and speed, and one little boy rolled on the carpeted lawn, surrounded by golden retriever puppies. Beautiful, smartly dressed women smiled and watched with curiosity as she drove in. Several waved.

Awestruck, Alaina stopped the car, inhaling a mixture of flowers, grass, and just a hint of Cajun spice. Calling to one woman, she said, "Hi. I'm a friend of Beau's. Can you tell me which house is his? He said he'll be right along."

The gorgeous creature was obviously one of his relatives, with her indigo eyes, black hair, and effortless grace. "Beau's my brother," the stunner confirmed. "He's staying down with Granny, the yellow one, right there." She nodded to a charming yellow cottage with white gingerbread trim. "You go park. I'll walk down with you."

Alaina's eyes widened, but she managed a pained smile, wondering what in the world she had stumbled into. As directed, she pulled the sputtering vehicle up to the house. Jerking the rearview mirror down, she took a quick inventory. Heat flooded her face as she looked at her clothes. She felt like she'd shown up for a Junior League meeting dressed like a stripper. Damn!

She found a hairband in the bottom of her bag among the coins, a tiny screwdriver, and a book of matches from her father's bar. Fashioning a messy ponytail, she pulled the tank top up to minimize the cleavage and loosened the notch on the wide leather belt so her mini would ride lower on her hips. Shucking her four-inch pumps and throwing them to the floorboard of the passenger's side, she slipped on the white sneakers, grimacing at the grass stains on the soles. As respectable as she could get, she emerged from the car with a high-pitched door squeak and an impossibly long leg. She plastered a fake smile and prepared to lie her ass off.

Beau's sister had gathered reinforcements. Four women and a couple of young girls waited at the bottom of the driveway, ready to greet her. Alaina experienced a moment of panic as she faced them. Her eyes darted back and forth, looking around, contemplating a potential route of escape. But escape to what?

They took matters out of her hands and swept her away. After the rapid-fire introductions, Alaina thought Mr. Landry must have been a busy man. Everyone here was named Landry… everyone. It was creepy, like some sort of Louisiana harem or tribe or some other weird nonsense. When she commented on the strangeness of it, they chuckled and said it was a family tradition. Everyone took the name of the patriarch, like surnames of the past. They lapsed into French when they got excited but checked themselves when they noted Alaina's incomprehension.

Alaina felt like a new hen in a vast hen house. They surrounded, clucked, and clattered. To her immense relief, they did not question her, just welcomed her with pleasantries, acting as if she was a long-lost friend. In a flurry of enthusiastic chatter, they ushered her to somebody named Betty Jean's house where there was lunch. At the mention of food, her stomach responded with such an enthusiastic growl, they laughed.

Plying her with a huge helping of baked chicken and crawfish stuffing, Maryanne, the short-haired one who looked most like Beau, said, "Eat up and enjoy. Betty Jean made it, which means she will never be able to recreate it. Everything she makes is one-of-a-kind."

"Well, at least Andrea didn't cook it," Betty Jean countered.

The women all laughed, and Alaina glanced around the table, trying to remember if she had been introduced to anyone named Andrea.

"She's not here, *chèr*," Sarah Beth, the pudgy one, offered, "And she will admit she is a terrible cook. She fishes most days with the men."

The eldest, Sue Ann, rolled her eyes. "Our honorary brother."

"Stop it," Maryanne chided. "I see the look on Dan's face when you tease her about that. He doesn't like it."

"Well, at least she married somebody who can cook," Sarah Beth said, and the sisters, aunts, nieces, and cousins nodded.

As lunch finished, Sue Ann asked, "Poor thing, would you like to freshen up before Beau gets back?"

Alaina bit her lip and told her first lie, "It's a long story, but I've misplaced my things."

Collective gasps ensued, and they sprang into action like paramedics arriving at an emergency. They scattered everywhere, but not before making her stand up so they could take the measure of her. Alaina mentally prepared herself.

No, she did not play basketball.

Yes, it was nice to reach the top shelf.

And there was no difference in the weather up here.

For once, nobody made a big deal about her height. Instead, Maryanne said, *"Mon Dieu,* isn't she pretty!"

Sarah Beth sighed, "I'd give anything for those legs."

But Alaina's favorite was when Sue Ann said, "Look at her eyes, I have a blue dress that will be gorgeous on her."

Alaina felt like Dorothy arriving in Oz. She started looking in corners for the munchkins and hoped there were no flying monkeys.

Tell Me True

Beau pushed Gladys to a faster pace than the sedate mule was used to going, but he had a clear mental image of what had befallen his visitor at the hands of his sisters and aunts. He drove into a chorus of calls,

"Hey Beau, where y'at?" Which was the standard greeting in the area and meant, "How are you? What's going on?" The phrase was so ingrained in the region, it lent the accent its name, y'at. Preserved through the centuries, the cultural heritage of the Louisiana Bayou blossomed under the blessings of the Millennial Kingdom. Famous for its abundant fishing, music, dancing, and delicious food, Landry's was a Louisiana paradise, untouched by the rebellion sweeping the New City region of Alanthia.

Beau found her in fresh clothes, glassy-eyed, and utterly besieged on his sister Betty Jean's front porch. She was curled into her chest, pulling at her ear.

"I'm here to rescue you." He gave quelling looks to the women crowded around and waved to several who emerged from their houses to watch.

Alaina murmured her thanks, but in her haste to depart, she stumbled on a pair of borrowed sandals that were at least a size and a half too small. Beau steadied her before she busted her ass in front of everyone.

She was reeling. Her mother long dead, her father long drunk, and other than an odd teacher through the years, the only woman she could call her friend was a regular at Dad's bar. Marilyn was sweet, but a hopeless fall-down lush. Her friends, tired of babysitting her, would pull her shirt over the back of her chair to keep her upright while they danced. For Alaina, a striking beauty from the dangerous side of town, female kindness was absolutely foreign. If Beau's sisters were cruel or catty, she would have rolled with it, but their kindness completely unnerved her.

She walked down the sidewalk, trying to regain her equilibrium and get her story straight. She was in deep trouble, and the next few minutes would determine whether she had a place to hide or if she had to hitchhike to the New City. Attempting a casual tone, she remarked an octave too high, "They're nice."

Beau chuckled, low and deep. "They are a force of nature, not sure about nice."

She gave an uncertain laugh and folded her hands, trying to look demure. "Well, that's one way to put it."

They stopped in front of his little yellow house. "*Allons*. I've got to check on Granny." He glanced at his watch, serviceable, its leather strap worn and soft, yet finely crafted and expensive in a way that did not scream new money. "Her afternoon program just ended, and she usually takes a nap." Alaina's pained smile made him chuckle. "She's harmless."

Somehow, Alaina did not believe him, but she squared her shoulders, prepared to meet what felt like her twentieth Landry of the day. However, he was right. They found the wizened old lady asleep in an oversized recliner beside a huge radio that blared commercials at top volume. The radio shared a table with assorted odds and ends; medicine bottles, a half-empty teacup, a store flyer, knitting magazines, and a lopsided pinch-pot painted in a child's hand that held a collection of paper clips, straight pins, and a lemon-flavored lip balm.

Beau turned down the volume, took the empty teacup, and motioned for Alaina to follow him to the kitchen. He deposited the cup in the sink and asked, "Can I get you anything? Do you need some water or tea?"

Alaina swallowed, her throat becoming dry. "Water, please."

Sliding the glass in front of her, he sat across the table, leaning back in a wooden kitchen chair. He regarded her with calm curiosity, as if she were an exotic zoo creature that might bolt at the slightest movement. "So, I suppose, *chèr*, a good place to start would be with your name."

Alaina took in a breath before answering, her alias on the tip of her tongue. She decided at the Mississippi Louisiana line that Diana was her new name. It meant huntress, and she liked that a lot better than Alaina, which meant father of joy, the irony of which was too much to bear.

Beau held up a finger to stop her. "Now before you answer, there is something you should know."

Alaina raised an eyebrow at him. With amused deliberation, she propped her elbow on the table and rested a loose fist under her square chin. "Okay."

"I love women."

The statement hung between them, full of heat and promise.

He broke the spell with his next words. "But I have no illusions about y'all, seeing as I have five older sisters, fifteen aunts, and more cousins than I can count, all who live within ten miles of where we're sitting." He let that sink in for a moment. "I have seen it all, tears, crying, what my *papa* calls histrionics." He smiled, but his blue eyes turned to cold steel. "We have a saying down here, *dis-moi la vérité*. It means tell me true, *chèr*, because I'll know if you're lying."

Alaina regarded him, not intimidated. "Is that a fact?"

"That's a fact." He relaxed his stern expression and added, "Now, what you tell the world can be a tale, but not to me, cause if I am going to hide a stolen car and a girl on the run from the law in my house, I'd like to know what I'm up against."

Alaina pushed her chair back, getting up from the table. She grabbed her studded bag and moved to the side door, panic beating in her chest. Doomed! The very first person she met figured her out in less than twenty minutes. She could flirt. That came as easy as breathing. She could manipulate stupid people, rationalizing if they were dumb enough to be manipulated they deserved what they got. But running from the law? That was something altogether different. She might have grown up in the backroom of a bar, look like a floozy, and have a weakness for bad boys, but she had been in Math Club for goodness' sake. She was no criminal.

He did not stop her, but his words froze her where she stood. "Jolie Catin, where you gonna go? New Orleans? Alone? You're safe here, but you won't be out there." Alaina turned to face him. The sun from the open door hid her face in shadow, but he could see the rise and fall of her chest, her breath coming fast. He waited.

In the cozy kitchen that smelled like biscuits, Beau's words rang true. She didn't have enough money to take her all the way to the New City. She could get to New Orleans. But then what? Disappear behind a bar to make a living? She wanted a different life, a better future, and running without a plan was not a great way to begin.

When she said nothing, he motioned for her to come back. "Why don't you tell me the tale first?" His lip curled into that devilish smile.

"That seems illogical."

"Not at all. It's practice. I'll critique."

Alaina raised a shoulder and plopped down. Adopting a mournful expression, she began. "Well, you see, I am a governess with two young children in my care."

Beau gave an incredulous snort. "You don't look like a governess, *chèr*."

Alaina drew herself upright, bristling. "Are you going to listen or not?"

He shrugged in apologetic surrender, the corners of his mouth twitching.

"I had charge of two children, Elizabeth and Mark. Their mother, Joan, became ill and on her deathbed begged me to take the children to her parents if she died. Her husband is a successful financier, but at home, he is a drunk, who beats the family. Joan feared what would happen to the kids. She passed away last week," Alaina paused and added for authenticity, "ovarian cancer."

"Tragic," Beau said, eyeing her from beneath his long black eyelashes.

Undeterred, Alaina pressed on. "After the funeral, I took the kids to their grandparents. The car was Joan's. She said I could have it, but her husband told the police I stole it and kidnapped the children. Now I am on the run."

The corners of his mouth turned down, and he nodded his head in appreciation. "Very heroic, has all the elements of a great story." He dropped the chair back to all fours and leaned forward, his voice serious. "Now, *chèr, dis-moi la vérité.*"

A daisy sandal tapped a nervous cadence on the bleached wood floor. She rubbed her mouth with her knuckle, thinking. For reasons she could not fathom, she decided to trust him. "My name is Alaina."

His smile began slowly, like a canoe cutting through calm waters. "Alaina," he repeated in his Cajun-spiced accent.

She shifted in her seat, her insides growing warm. He was quite sultry. Alaina looked past his face, focusing on a pen and ink sketch of a dancing pear just over his shoulder. "Yesterday, I met up with a couple of boys, neither I knew very well." Alaina paused and looked up at the ceiling. "We were supposed to go hang out by the river. They stopped to get beer. I waited in the car." Then, with her nose flared, she dared him to judge her. "They robbed the store. I had no idea they were going to do it."

Beau lifted a brow but remained silent.

She rubbed her forehead and sighed, "A couple hours later, they were drunk and started fighting." She did not add that they were fighting over her. Adopting a nonchalance she did not feel, she met his eyes. "I took off with the car, and here I am."

He eyed her with a level gaze, considering.

Alaina leaned back, giving him a defiant tilt of her chin. "I like the governess story better."

"Certainly more color, I'll give you that." Beau stared past her, his keen mind processing her circumstances. "Though kidnapping and grand-theft auto are serious charges, and while it would make for good afternoon drama on Granny's show, it is not a suitable cover story." He tapped the corner of his mouth. "Did anyone see you at the store?"

Alaina looked up, trying to remember. "Not that I know of."

Beau rubbed his strong jaw. "And that car, it belonged to one of those boys?"

"It's Willy's."

"You know that for true? Cause if they gonna rob a store, what's to stop them from stealing a car? Don't strike me as two backwoods Mississippi boys would have the wherewithal to buy one, *chèr.* Do you know how much they cost?"

The blood drained from her face, and her eyes darted around the room. "Damn. I did not even think about that." She rubbed her temples. "I've got to get rid of it."

Mischief had once been Beau's favorite pastime, so he had no trouble forming a plan. "It's safe for now. But when the time comes, I know just the place. I suspect if anyone is looking for anything it's that car, more than likely the law ain't searching for you." He gave her a pointed stare. "Now your family, I expect they are wondering where you are."

"My mother is dead. Nobody is looking for me." Alaina tilted her head to the side and dared him to contradict her.

Beau dropped his chin to his chest and looked up at her with skeptical blue eyes. "You left out of where you from without a change of clothes because that's Sue Ann's dress." She looked away. "You staying with somebody, and they going to be wondering where y'at."

Alaina refused to meet his eyes, giving a derisive snort. "Well, maybe there was some truth to that governess story."

He paused, considered her words, then had mercy, and let it pass. "What's your plan?"

"I'm headed to the New City." Alaina shrugged, then added with a defiant tilt of her head. "I've got some talent. There's money to be made for people like me."

"Tall, beautiful, blondes on the run?" Beau teased.

She batted her eyelashes at him, on comfortable ground. "Tall, beautiful blondes with kick-ass math and computer skills."

Beau considered her through slightly different eyes. "Is that a fact, *chèr*, brains and beauty?"

He stood up to refill her water glass, staring out the kitchen window. "We're not anti-tech here, but we're not fond of the New City or the wicked bastard that rules it. We fought against him in the war, and folks around here remain loyal to the Iron King. I think that's why we are still prospering." He placed the glass in front of her. "You sure about going? I spent some time there in the '86."

Alaina's jaw dropped. He did not look old enough to have fought in the Civil War. "How did you find yourself in that?"

He seemed to shake away a ghost. "I was at the RMA when the fighting broke out."

It was Alaina's turn to see through different eyes. The Royal Military Academy only admitted the kingdom's wealthiest and most influential families. Granted, this place was not a backwater hovel, but she would have never imagined that the Landrys ranked that high on the social scale. He'd been driving a fish wagon.

He read her expression and gave an embarrassed shrug. "Oil."

She dropped her chin, giving him a skeptical look. "And the fish?"

Beau laughed. "We men still work. What else we going to do, lie around and get fat, or worse, let all these women order us around all day? Have you seen this place? You hang around for more than a day, they have you painting, mowing, or digging a garden. Better to be out on the bayou fishing. One of us stays in, to keep watch, and take the morning catch to *Maman's* store."

"So, the police officer eats lunch at your momma's store?" Alaina crossed her arms and studied him.

"Every day. You can set your watch by him. He's a neighbor, and he'll be here tonight. So, we do need to get your story straight."

"What do you mean, he's going to be here tonight?" Alaina asked with growing alarm.

"For the party." Beau smiled with a hint of guilty innocence. "I lured you here to be my date."

"There's no shortage of women around here," Alaina observed dryly.

He chuckled, "There's a shortage of women I'm not related to."

While Granny napped, they concocted her cover story and decided she was his Army buddy's sister, passing through town on her way to New City Technical School. She sent most of her belongings ahead, and in her excitement, put her bag on the roof of the car and drove off, leaving it somewhere between here and Mississippi.

Alaina balked at the suggestion, claiming it made her seem flighty. But when he challenged her to come up with a better excuse, she veered off into the fantastical, creating stories of robberies and narrow escapes. His raised eyebrows had her trailing off, and with sulky acquiescence, she agreed to appear scatterbrained, though it chafed her. Looking the way she did, people automatically assumed she was stupid, or a slut, usually both.

As the story went, when she realized she was without money and luggage, she remembered her brother's friend in the area and sought Beau's help. Clean and simple, no stolen cars, no kidnapping, no robbery, and nobody running from the law. Alaina just had to remember her fake brother's name was Allen, and no one would be the wiser.

She rehearsed the story with him several times before they were both satisfied with the telling. At her fifth yawn in as many minutes, he insisted she rest. Alaina, who had driven through the night, reluctantly agreed.

When he showed her to the guest room, she was absolutely certain she had landed in Oz. The small bedroom contained a high twin bed, spread with a gorgeous hand-stitched quilt of pink and white. Pictures of ballerinas decorated the dusty rose walls, and delicate white lace curtains puddled on the pale oak floor. A thick braided rug of burgundy and rose cushioned her feet, and in the corner, a child's rocking chair held the most exquisite doll Alaina had ever seen.

She whimpered. Faced with the bedroom of her childhood fantasies, tears flooded her eyes. From exhaustion, wonder, or emotional overload, she did not know, but she curled into herself and covered her face, undone by a pink room.

Her genuine reaction shocked Beau, who had never given Granny's spare bedroom a second thought. She kept it for her granddaughters' frequent overnight visits. He gathered Alaina in his arms as he would a heart-broken child. "Jolie Catin, don't cry."

But she did, and he held on until the tears subsided.

Fais do-do

The setting sun cast the bayou sky in shades of orange, pink, and red. Beau escorted Alaina toward the large wooden meeting hall at the water's edge. The sounds of a fiddle, an accordion, and guitars sweetened the night air. Laughter and song floated out of the building. A door burst open with a bang, and three sweaty boys dove behind one of the equipment sheds. Armed with water pistols and dressed in camo, they focused on their quarry, a gaggle of teenagers milling at the end of the dock. The briny smell of bayou and fishing nets mixed with the succulent aroma of smoking meat and spicy Cajun seafood.

Alaina tilted her head and whispered, "Why are you really helping me, Beau?"

"I told you, I needed a date." Beau took her by the crook of the arm.

"Is that all?"

He shrugged. "Hang around here for a bit, I could use the company." She was the prettiest thing he had ever seen, and if he could keep her around for a while, all the better.

Alaina tucked her arm in his as they walked. After a smoke-filled bar, a tequila-soaked father, and the crowning glory of armed robbery and grand-theft auto, Landry's felt like a dream. And the moment they stepped into the meeting hall, the dream turned into a whirlwind.

The Landrys were a force of nature. They plied her with food, ushered her from group to group, and spun her around the dance floor until she bent over, gasping for breath. Loose tendrils of golden hair escaped her ponytail and framed her face, flushed from dancing.

Alaina caught Beau's eye through the throng. But he let them have her. Something told her there would be no stopping them. The old men loved her, as much for her beauty as that she had fresh ears for their old jokes and even older stories. They teased her about her height, but not in a way that made her defensive. As an outrageous and accomplished flirt, they ate her up like spicy gumbo. To Alaina's surprise, nobody got roaring drunk, used foul language, or picked a fight. The bar she grew up in always carried an undertone of danger, as if violence simmered just below the surface. The fais-do-do at the Landry Meeting Hall was simply fun.

As the night grew long, kitchen sounds signaled food being packed up. Old folks said their goodnights, harried mothers chased overtired children around the dance floor, and the band announced their last song. Only then did Beau walk across the hall and offer his hand.

Moving onto the dancefloor, a Louisiana storm erupted between them. It had been simmering around the edges, like distant thunder and flashes of lightning, but at their touch, it exploded with electric brilliance. Beau pulled her to a darkened corner. The music was playful and fun. She draped her arms over his shoulders, and he rested his hands at the curve of her waist. They did not touch otherwise, but the scant inch of space between their bodies came alive with sparks, dancing with flames.

"You did not tell me this was your party," Alaina murmured, her voice low and sultry.

He leaned in, his breath tickling her ear. "I did not want you to think I needed a present, Jolie Catin. This dance is the only present I wanted tonight."

Over the years, Alaina danced with dozens of boys, flirted with even more, and left them all babbling in her wake; except for her friends from the Math Club, she had mercy on them. However, the man in her arms gave her a glimpse into how those babbling boys must have felt. She brushed her body against his, the merest touch, and stifled a groan when the heat between them turned to molten lava.

Beau inhaled the scent of her hair, floral with an earthy undertone, secret and seductive. His chest tightened, and he fought to control his breathing, lest she think him a besotted fool.

In a flash, he knew this was one of those rare moments. The kind that branded on his brain forever. He let it come, welcoming it, willing it to wash away other things branded there. He absorbed the silky feel of her dress under his hands, how she swayed tall and strong, perfectly formed, and graceful. Her skin glimmered in the gaslight, sun-kissed with a dusting of freckles across the bridge of her nose. He contemplated the shape of her face, unusual and striking, not oval, yet not square. Hexagonal he decided. Two tiny brown moles kept her from boring perfection, one slightly off-center between her well-tweezed eyebrows, and the other just north of her full bottom lip on the left side of her strong chin. "Alaina," he sighed, "you are beautiful."

They stood eye to eye. She gave him a half-smile and whispered, "So are you."

The temperature in their corner of the room spiked as the band played extra verses, cognizant of the swaying couple in the shadows. But the musicians were not the only ones paying attention.

Beau Landry's mother, Sarah, watched, a less than pleased expression on her still pretty at fifty-eight face.

"Momma Bear, why so fierce?" Beau's father, Jorge, murmured, wrapping a muscular arm around Sarah's waist, and pulling her close.

Sarah let out a snort and settled back into his embrace. "Was I?"

Jorge nipped her neck. "You know you were."

"We do not know who she is," Sarah said in a low voice only Jorge could hear.

"He says she's an army buddy's sister, passing through town."

"Pfft! I know the names of all his army friends, never once has he ever mentioned an Allen ben Thomas, either waking or sleeping."

Jorge brought his head around to see her expression. "Talk about?"

"True. Don't doubt me on this." Sarah shook her head. "He's just now back to normal." Her mouth tightened as she looked away.

"You think somebody sent her?" Jorge's lips barely moved as he asked the last.

"You know as well as I do, that it is a possibility." Sarah's face became resolute as she crossed her arms. "I made up the guest room. She will stay with us."

Jorge's chest vibrated with a deep chuckle. "You tell him that?"

"No, but I am about to. Your momma is not a fit chaperon, and those two are so hot for each other your Aunt May is over there fanning herself."

Jorge's chuckle turned into a full-blown laugh. "Let 'em dance, it's his birthday."

She gave a long-suffering sigh. "His birthday was last week, as you well know. This crowd will use any excuse for a fais do-do." She used the slang for an all-night dance party, though this one was ending well before dawn. Fishermen left at dawn.

Jorge turned his wife in his arms, guiding her to the dance floor. "Sarah, I want you to hear my words."

She stiffened, both at the use of her name and the tone of his voice.

"He's not your baby anymore. He's a grown man, and by your own words, he is better. You need to think long and hard before treating him like a child in front of that girl."

"But what if she's here to do him harm?"

Jorge gave her a level look. "What if she's not? What if by your actions, you are the one that does him harm?"

Sarah's nose flared, and she stared down at the floor as wisdom battled instinct, age-old and fierce, to let her son go and risk seeing him hurt? She had done it once, when he left for the Academy, and he returned to her brutally wounded. That damn war, he had been too young to see what he'd seen. Sarah would have never allowed him to fight, but he was out of her reach, and she could not stop it. The sparks flying between the swaying couple served as a warning, and this she could stop. She knew she could. But at what cost? "I don't want him hurt again." Her voice was full of maternal anguish.

"Nor do I." Jorge gathered her close and held her as she let go. "Get to know her. She seems like a nice kid. A little bewildered, certainly lost, but there is something about her I like. And you just might, too. You never know, sometimes we entertain angels unawares." He felt her chuckle, low and deep.

"I know one thing for certain, that girl is no angel," Sarah said, raising a sardonic eyebrow.

Jorge's grin turned lecherous. "Neither are you, *Doudou,* and for that, I am eternally grateful. Now, you come home, and let me show you how grateful I still am."

Fire on the Front Porch

"We escaped my mother tonight," Beau said in a half teasing tone as he watched his parents depart.

Alaina followed his gaze. "I met your father. What do you mean, we escaped your mother?" She pulled away, the heat between them snuffed like a candle. This was perhaps the Wicked Witch she had been waiting for. Oz was not complete without one.

Beau let out a shaky laugh and sagged into her with a sigh of relief. "She had that look about her."

Alaina stiffened and lifted her chin. "And what look might that be?"

He rocked her back and forth. "Like she just caught me eating a cookie before dinner."

Her lips pursed. "I suppose in this scenario, I am the cookie?"

"More like a beignet, covered in sugar."

The heat came roaring back. If she could bottle his voice, it would be worth millions on the hot sauce market. A dozen flirtatious retorts came to mind. Yesterday she might have delivered any of them with practiced skill, but he was no simpering schoolboy. "You are a silver-tongued devil, Beau Landry."

Feeling reckless, he pressed his silver tongue in a kiss just below her ear. The tiny gasp she made echoed through his brain.

The band ended their song.

He groaned in frustration. "I think perhaps I misspoke, you are more like a lit stick of dynamite, *chèr*."

She shuddered in helpless surrender as he pressed another kiss to the side of her neck. "I think you're the match."

He threw back his head and laughed, exposing the muscles in his long, elegant neck. She wanted to bite him.

"*Allons*, let's go home." Beau smiled, warm and full of humor.

Home... such a powerful word, spoken without a thought by one who always had one. It was a raw, empty space for the one who hadn't. When she put her trembling hand in his, she silently asked him to take her there. And he did.

Her heels echoed among the quieting houses as they strolled back to the yellow cottage. It was late, and his speech became relaxed, more French. Indeed, several of the partygoers tonight conversed primarily in French, making this place seem even more foreign.

Beau motioned to each house, explaining which sister, cousin, aunt, or uncle lived there.

But after the long night, her mind was spinning, and she could barely follow what he told her.

At her pained expression, he stopped. "I forget the rest of the world does not live in a family compound. It must seem strange."

Alaina thought of the isolated shack she shared with her father. "I think it is strange more people don't live like this. It's wonderful."

Beau scrunched up his face and rubbed his head. "It can be, it is also *ennuyeux*." He smiled and translated. "Bothersome."

He said it with such long-suffering that she laughed. "I can think of worse things."

"*Mon Dieu*, there are at least ten pairs of eyes on us right now."

They mounted the front steps of the cottage, and he steered her toward the cushioned swing. "They will all be watching as I kiss you, Jolie

Catin." He drew her down beside him. "But only a kiss, on my honor, as your gentleman rescuer."

Alaina moistened her lips as the words registered. She was at his mercy. He could take whatever advantage of her he chose. Instead, he offered her safety, his home, and now his kisses without demanding more. The corner of her mouth quivered. "Shall we set your Aunt May to fanning herself again?"

"I say we burn the front porch down." His lips hovered just above hers. "Kiss me, *ma belle fille*."

No power on Earth could have stopped her, and his husky French words were her absolute undoing. Only the knowledge that they had an audience kept her from ravishing him right there on the swing.

Beau tasted her, pulling, exploring. This was no kiss. This was possession. It was an explosion, an apocalypse.

"*Mon Dieu*," Beau gasped, his breath coming hard.

"Have mercy," Alaina whispered, awestruck.

"The porch is not the only thing on fire. We shall have to stop, or I will break my word." He kissed her neck, murmuring, "For I shall take you to my bed and make love to you until the dawn."

She swallowed hard. "I think I would let you." Her aquamarine eyes held a mixture of fear and pleading.

He threw himself back into the cushions, Gallic prayers tumbling from his lips. "We must not, Jolie Catin. You have a place to stay, as long as you want. You're safe here, and I would not shame you in front of my family."

Alaina stood up on trembling legs, smoothing her borrowed dress. "Thank you, Beau." Her heels clicked on the wooden porch, and she turned at the door. "Good night."

He draped his arm over the back of the cushion and rested his head on his hand, his foot nudging the swing into motion. He looked like a riverboat pirate, black-haired, blue-eyed, and dangerous. "Good night, and Alaina?" His voice was serious. "Lock your door."

July 17, 990 ME

Shopping

Sleepy and rumpled, Alaina sprinted to the bathroom in nothing but a long t-shirt Beau loaned her the night before. She squealed when she saw him sitting at the kitchen table, pulled the shirt low over her bottom, and slammed the door behind her.

The teacup froze halfway to his lips at the sight of those gorgeous long legs and a brief glimpse of a shapely cheek.

"*Mon mignon?*" Beau's grandmother, Isabelle, asked, using her pet name for him, which meant my cutie.

He gave an imperceptible shake of his head. "Sorry Granny, I was gathering wool."

She harrumphed, "Like a wolf hunting sheep gathers wool."

He sipped his tea and gave her a heavy-lidded stare. "I was a good boy."

"In your mind, too?" she asked shrewdly, but the teasing light in her blue eyes mimicked his.

"I shall never tell." He raised his brows in comic lechery.

"You going to buy that girl some clothes today?"

"It would be more fun if I didn't."

Isabelle snorted. "Your *maman* is having kittens over there. I'm surprised she's not already here."

A flash in the hallway told him Alaina had sprinted back, but to his disappointment, she had a towel wrapped around her waist. He turned his attention back to the tea and his breakfast companion. "I expect she'll be over soon. She sent Sue Ann to open this morning."

"Oh, you in for it then. You better tell that girl to hurry up." Isabelle motioned to the pink room. "You know Sarah made up a guest room for her last night?"

Beau grew still. *"Dis-moi la vérité!"*

She nodded. "I tell you true, *mon mignon.*"

Beau snorted in exasperation, feeling besieged. "If I did not love you so much, I would already be living in my house. It's almost finished."

"But who would cook for you?"

The corners of his eyes crinkled with a smile. "I will come and raid your kitchen daily."

She winked. "And I will let you."

Alaina padded into the kitchen, barefoot and disheveled, wearing his t-shirt and her denim mini. Her face was bare of make-up, except for the remnants of last night's mascara. She looked between them and said, "Good morning?" Embarrassed uncertainty pulsed off her in waves.

"Good morning, Alaina. Beau was just telling me how he was going to take you shopping today to help you replace your things." Isabelle looked across the street. "I can imagine that is very disconcerting. Now go get your bag and your shoes. Y'all can be off."

Beau raised his palms in surrender. "Looks like we are going shopping, *chèr.*"

Alaina calculated that she barely had enough money for a change of clothes, if they found a thrift shop, and even then, that money was stolen.

Beau read her distress and gave her a half-smile. "*Allons*. We'll send the bill to your brother, Allen."

Isabelle shooed them out the door. "Have fun."

Outside, Beau asked, "Boat or car?"

"What?" she asked, not quite awake, reeling to find herself outside.

"Do you want to go to town by boat or by car?"

"I sort of wanted a cup of coffee and a shower first." Alaina made a pitiful whimper.

Beau laughed. "Granny hustled us out of there. She's running interference with *Maman*."

Alaina grimaced. "I'm starting to be afraid of your mother."

Beau tilted his head. "My *maman* is kind, generous, and very smart." He paused, gathering his thoughts. "But let's just say you want to put your best foot forward when you meet her for the first time."

Alaina raised a tawny eyebrow. "And being a vagabond, in her son's wrinkled T-shirt, and a borrowed pair of sandals might not be the best way to do it?"

Beau's shoulder's straightened, and he looked at her with pride. "Exactly! Now, *allons*, we'll drive."

He guided her through the back yard and down a side street. A stable occupied one side of the road and a large metal building the other. Digging in his pocket, he produced a key to a heavy door and turned on the overhead lights. Alaina gasped, stunned by the collection of vehicles in the garage, fourteen of them. Trucks, sedans, vans, and sports cars awaited their pleasure. Her mouth hung open as she stared at him.

He shrugged and simply said, "Oil."

In Alaina's entire life, she never spent a single shekel without careful consideration. This applied to a dozen eggs, a bottle of shampoo, or a pair of shoes. She weighed every purchase against need, budget, and whether she could find a better price elsewhere. She approached every cash register with an exact total in her head. And to her private shame, she knew exactly how much she shoplifted over the years, to the drachma. She promised herself that one day she would send the money to those store owners. Alaina paid her debts.

Beau never gave money a thought. It was simply there, like air. Essential to life, noticed only if it was absent, but otherwise not considered.

A shopping day revealed their vast differences.

Their first stop was in Delacroix at a large new store that sold everything from car tires to underwear. Beau determined Alaina needed it all, except the car tires. At the fifth aisle, she stopped protesting because he would take a second one of whatever she was fighting him on and put it in the cart with a devilish grin. She died of mortification in the feminine products aisle when he started asking pertinent questions about which she preferred. Her face flamed, and he gave his second simple answer, "Five sisters."

She discovered that Beau Landry knew more about what women had in their bathrooms than any man alive. And he made sure Alaina had everything, plus a big tackle box to keep it all organized. Hair products, brushes, combs, ties, bands, it all went in the basket. Personal care, toothbrushes, toothpaste, deodorant, lotion, everything he chose was the finest quality.

Moving into the hunting and fishing section, she relaxed. She shouldn't have. He loaded boots, camouflage, and rain gear. When he picked up an absurd pink fishing rod, she threw up her hands in exasperation. Secretly, she loved it, and he knew it. The rod joined everything else in the buggy.

As they walked by the luggage section, he stopped. He studied her with an enigmatic expression, then without warning, in the middle of the store, he grabbed her around the waist and kissed her. Carts stopped, employees froze, and the world stood still while Beau and Alaina set the Mil-Mart on fire.

Acting like nothing happened, he pushed the cart down the aisle and picked out a set of pink luggage. Then he sent her back to the front for a second shopping cart.

"We will buy you some nice clothes in New Orleans, *chèr*. They have a few things here to hang around in, and you'll need something to wear into town." Beau contemplated a wall of socks, looked down at her feet, and smiled.

She curled her toes.

"Size 10?"

She drew herself up to her full height. "Thereabouts." She actually wore an eleven, but she was not telling him that.

He moved through the store efficiently, gathering socks, t-shirts, tops, shorts, jeans, bathing suits, workout gear, a bathrobe, nightgowns and his favorite, lingerie. Cotton, silk, satin, and lace, functional and comfortable, it all went into the buggy. Then, they got to the slutwear. Her cheeks flamed when he held up a pair of red lace boy shorts and said, "These are pretty, but they look like they would crawl. What do you think?"

"I think you can't have an ass and wear something like that," Alaina deadpanned.

He hung them back up without another word, though he looked between them and her, wearing an expression that told her he'd like to see them crawl.

The only thing he insisted she needed in housewares was a big coffee mug that said, 'Louisiana' on it.

In lawn and garden, he bought her two pairs of garden gloves. "Trust me. Those women will have you in the garden."

Walking to the cash register, it was the first time in Alaina's life that she did not know what the bill was going to be. Beau pulled the keys from his pocket and handed them to her. "Go pull the truck around, *chèr*. I'll be out in a minute."

Alaina crossed her arms and regarded him, trying to control the emotional overload crashing in from all sides. The contents of the two shopping carts added up to more money than her father had spent on her in her entire life. "I'll pay you back."

Beau made a tsking noise and said, "You do not pay back a gift, Jolie Catin." The corner of his mouth lifted in a teasing smile. "That's rude. Now go get the truck."

La Petit Pishon

Alaina wondered why he had chosen the big-wheeled truck for their shopping trip, now she understood. It wasn't a road they slogged down, more like a muddy winding path. But Beau drove it with a practiced hand, brimming with childish eagerness, and refusing to answer her questions about where he was taking her. He just flashed her an enigmatic grin and kept driving.

When they finally emerged from the dense thicket, a new construction site sat before them. Beau looked through the windshield and turned to her with a grin. "My house." He hurried around to her side of the truck to open her door and help her down.

"This is technically the backyard. It needs some work, but they are still finishing up, so I can't landscape yet." There was a faint apology in his voice, as if he needed to make excuses for the muddy, bare space.

From the rear, it appeared to be a single-story modest home, with four double-hung windows across the cedar-planked siding. He unlocked the sturdy unpainted door and motioned her inside. "Welcome, my lady."

Alaina smiled at his boyish excitement. Her breath caught as she stepped through the door. Through a wall of glass, a lake of stunning beauty shimmered before her. She gasped.

When she was small, her mother gave her a box of crayons, which she used down to the nubs. Alaina decided she would have colored the lake turquoise and cerulean, with shadows of indigo. "Beau, what is this place?" she asked, her voice full of awe.

He moved beside her and took her hand, seeing the lake anew. "La Petit Pishon."

"I thought places like this disappeared after Prince Eamonn's time," she whispered.

He shrugged. "I told you, Jolie Catin, we did not rebel here. We stayed faithful to the Iron King."

Her forehead creased. "But the cars, the electricity? I thought that was rebellion."

"Tel Aviv," Beau said simply.

Alaina cocked her head, confused.

"You don't think the Iron King would have permitted Tel Aviv if technology was a sin, do you? Rebellion is in the heart, *chèr*, not in a car or a computer. Korah's rebellion was never about technology. That was just a smokescreen, a mechanism he used to seize power. And he may use it to retain that power, but you ain't going to hell for using a phone."

At eighteen, Alaina's world had been black and white, good and bad. But standing in Beau Landry's beautiful half-finished house on La Petit Pishon, she felt a great burden fall away. "Do you know what that means?"

He gave her a half-smile, watching the light beam behind her eyes.

"It means I am free to pursue my dream and not be in rebellion. I can learn, and grow, and do what I am great at." Alaina covered her mouth as the magnitude of the revelation washed over her.

As he watched, she curled into herself. He had seen her do that several times. "Hey," he murmured and took her into his arms, "don't cry."

She put her head on his shoulder and let the tears come. He could barely understand her when she sobbed. "My... my... my mother was a wonderful woman. She taught me when I was little. I love... I love the Iron King. I always have, but I could not reconcile the conflict."

Alaina pulled away, gathering herself and staring at the lake.

He let her be.

"I look a certain way, and my dad runs a bar." She swallowed back the gurgling lump in her throat. "People make assumptions about me. Most of the time, I let them." She snorted. "When I rode off with those boys, I figured if they were going to talk about me, I might as well actually do something worth the gossip, but we see how well that turned out."

"I don't think it turned out so bad, Alaina."

She wiped a tear from her cheek and gave him a watery smile. "Thank you."

He bowed his head. "Glad to be of service, Jolie Catin."

She laughed, "What does that mean? I've been too embarrassed to ask, but I don't speak any French."

Their eyes met, and a slow grin spread across his face, wrinkling his eyes at the corners. "Down here it means pretty baby doll. In France, it's somewhat wicked, but here it's an endearment."

"Well, what does it mean in France?" The little mole at the corner of her mouth danced with amusement.

"We aren't in France, are we?" Beau gave a mischievous lift of his black brow.

She advanced on him. "You better tell me."

He held up his hands and backed away. "I will not!"

Alaina cocked her head and kept coming. "You tell me Beau Landry, or I will make up some horrible nickname for you."

He laughed and let her catch him as his back hit the bar. "Oh yeah, like what?"

The sensation of his body pressed against hers sent all other thoughts scurrying from her brain. "I don't know," she declared with a saucy gleam in her eye, "but I will think of something… something rotten, and you won't like it."

He put his mouth against her ear, she could feel him shaking with laughter. "Might I suggest *mon couer*, my heart? *Mon rêve*, my dream?" He growled and nipped her neck. "*Mon loup*, my wolf?"

Alaina rubbed her head against his. "Those are not horrible."

He kissed her cheek and whispered, "No, *chèr*, they are not, for there is nothing horrible between us." Indeed, there was not. There were things he had not told her, but what lay between them was true. He realized with a rush that he did not feel haunted or broken. For the first time in three years, someone needed him. And she wasn't looking at him with sympathy. He hadn't even realized *he* needed it until a beige car with a tousled blonde in distress pulled up. "*Embrasse moi, ma chèrie*."

She did not need to speak French to know what that meant. Standing in the middle of his unfinished house, with the impossibly beautiful lake shimmering behind them, and a bright future ahead, she kissed him, promises exploding in her heart.

He took them and held them fast, and for the first time since the war, made a few promises of his own.

They had to put an end to the kissing session. Otherwise, he might hike up her mini-skirt and have his way with her right there on top of the island, and that would be very ungentlemanly. With a frustrated groan, he broke the kiss, opting instead to take her on a tour of his house.

It was unfurnished and unpainted, but otherwise complete. She realized he'd done much of the work himself. He did not brag; he was just matter of fact about the construction. The floor plan was open, simple, and spacious, the upstairs for living, and the downstairs for play, with a workshop, tack room, and a gym. Alaina's favorite room was a corner study that overlooked the lake. She tried not to picture herself sitting at a computer, working in that beautiful room.

From the dock, she appreciated the design and character of the house. Much like the owner, it fit the space it dwelt; strong, elegant, and well made.

"I'll put the boathouse there, probably be next summer. My goal is to move by October. I'll spend Tabernacles here before I move in."

Alaina's eyes lit up. The Feast of Tabernacles was an eight-day celebration, spent in camping-style tents. It commemorated the Israelites forty-year wanderings in the desert. Alaina had done it with her mother once, when she was five, and loved it. "Y'all still do that?"

"Sure. We love a party, *chèr*. Tabernacles is fun."

They unloaded some of her things into the master bathroom so she could shower and change before they returned to Landry's. "I'll take you to meet my *maman*, but we'll do it on our terms, keep her off balance a bit." He flashed his devilish grin. "I've got some work to do downstairs. Take your time. There's no hurry."

When he closed the door, Alaina thought she would take as much time as she wanted. The interview loomed like a date with a guillotine.

Afternoon Stories

Beau left her at Isabelle's, while he went to parlay with his mother. Sitting in the small living room, Alaina connected with Beau's grandmother over the most unlikely of sources, afternoon stories. They were all the rage, radio dramas broadcast to the masses. Isabelle's favorite happened to be the same one Alaina followed, and the elderly lady delighted in bringing Alaina up to speed on the three episodes she missed. An enjoyable and fitting distraction, their conversation kept her mind from swirling over what was sure to be high drama across the street.

Sipping her afternoon cup of tea, Isabelle Landry was nobody's fool, despite her daughter-in-law's opinion of her. She read the situation accurately. "Sarah, Beau's *maman*, reminds me of Phoebe in our story, *chèr*."

The segue took Alaina by surprise. "Is that so?"

"Yes, but without the murderous tendencies." Isabelle's eyes danced.

"Well, we can be thankful for that, I guess," Alaina countered with wary humor.

"Sarah is the only child of a very industrious and wealthy man from New England, although he and his wife immigrated here from Scotland. His name is Andrew ben Lenox." Isabelle paused and saw the second it hit the young woman.

"The Andrew ben Lenox… of the Lenox company?" Alaina choked.

"One in the same," Isabelle nodded. "My husband, God rest his soul, sold Lenox the drilling rights to several thousand acres back in the early 50s. That is how Jorge and Sarah met."

Isabelle turned down the radio. "In many ways, Sarah is like her father. She is organized, industrious, and if you give her a drachma, she will turn it into a galleon. What she lacks is his ruthlessness. I honestly believe the love she has for her family kept her from turning into a female version of him. Instead, she applied her talents toward this place and this family." Isabelle made a sweeping motion of her hand. "I suspect she would own half of Louisiana by now if she had not chosen to become a wife and a mother. Coincidentally, did Beau take you to the Mil-Mart today?"

Alaina's brows came to a point. "Yes."

Isabelle smiled and shrugged. "That was Sarah's store. She sold it last year."

Alaina swallowed audibly. "Sarah Landry owned Mil-Mart, the entire chain?"

Isabelle nodded.

"And she is the sole heiress to the Lenox Company?"

"Indeed, *chèr*, now you have the gist of it."

"And I am a destitute stranger who showed up yesterday in a tattered mini-skirt, no luggage, and is spending time with her only son?" Alaina's voice rose as she spoke. "Holy Cow, she is going to eat me for breakfast."

"She could, but Beau is over there seeing that she doesn't. Don't be afraid of her, Alaina. In the end, she is simply a woman."

Alaina looked across the street, "Sarah Landry sounds like a lot of things, but simple is not one of them."

The Chair

Sarah Landry sat behind her desk, working. The desk was not a petite, spindly legged, women's writing desk. No, Sarah Landry conducted business behind a great hulking creation of red oak that Jorge swore weighed more than a bull alligator. The sides and drawers gleamed reddish gold under a thick coat of beeswax polish, but the top remained in desperate need of refinishing. The only decorations softening its austere surface were six miniatures, paintings of cherubic toddlers, their true faces just emerging from their baby disguises. An enormous, variegated spider plant rested on the sunny corner, well-watered and tended, it produced offshoots in such profusion that every house in the village had one of its offspring. The center was empty, by design. There was nothing to hide behind.

Sarah Landry was not mean, nor did she have a temper in the truest sense of the word. She was rational and exacting, holding high standards of excellence, but not perfection. If any of her children or employees faltered or fell short, they received a kind reminder and correction, the first time. The second time, if it came, usually involved a visit to her study and the chair.

The chair…

Dreaded, feared, and avoided, at all costs, if anyone found themselves in the chair, it proved to be an experience they never wanted to repeat. Many a recalcitrant child, or heaven forbid, a dishonest vendor, had been reduced to a huddled, mumbling mass, in her office. The woman was legendary.

The encounters began with a level gaze, unblinking and penetrating. That established who was in charge, and it was not the occupant of the chair. A deep, chest-raising intake of breath followed the look. The interval of time between inhale and exhale signified the degree of trouble they were in. A long inhale could reduce two of her daughters to tears. It was quite effective, that breath. She honed it to perfection, along with her tone of voice, soft, modulated, and devoid of mercy.

There were no excuses accepted from the chair, for no one found themselves in that situation if excuses or explanations were plausible. No, the chair was where sentences were handed down, rendered after the evidence had been gathered and weighed, the verdict a foregone conclusion.

Of her six children, Beau occupied the chair more than any other. Thus, he was not afraid of it, at least that is what he told himself. He still did not like it, but if he was ever going to stop being her child, he had to take a page out of his father's book and refuse to sit in that damn chair ever again. His purpose for entering his *maman's* study that afternoon was to keep Alaina out of it, forever.

He entered without knocking and found her scowling at an accounting ledger, receipts and invoices spread before her like minions to be conquered.

Sarah looked up, distracted, still calculating in that magnificent brain of hers. Her head gave a slight shake as she focused. She was not a tall woman, but she had such a commanding presence no one ever thought of her as little. After six children, she wasn't. She controlled her weight by restricting sugar and calories. But according to Beau, her diet bordered on starvation. He often teased that she was so formidable because she was hungry. There was perhaps some truth to that, so he entered her study, carrying a cupcake.

She looked between him and the cupcake and laughed. "Do you think that is going to get you out of this?"

"I hope. *Allons, Maman*, I have one as well. We shall enjoy them together over tea… in the kitchen."

She raised a light brown eyebrow at him. "Very well. Put the kettle on. I will join you shortly." She turned her attention back to the receipts.

When he closed the door, she released a weary sigh, Jorge's words from the evening before still echoing in her mind. She woke this morning after a restless night, having every intention of marching across the street to confront that long-legged girl.

She showered and dressed for battle, business attire, her hair in a tasteful French twist, her make-up subtle and perfect. Jorge watched without a word, but his silence spoke volumes. When she slipped on her best diamond studs, hose and heels, he raised an eyebrow at her.

Fully armored, her weapons primed, and with righteous purpose held before her like a shield, her hand fell to her side when she reached the door.

Jorge read it all and opened his arms.

Full frontal assault aborted.

In the kitchen, Beau set the kettle to boil. Some restaurants in New Orleans did not have as much cooking, countertop, and refrigeration space as Sarah Landry. Yet she made the granite, butcher block, and stainless-steel feel homey, not institutional, and it was practical in a house that raced six kids. He had eaten some of the best meals of his life in this room.

Her one allowance to the departure of her brood was a small table for two, set in front of a large bay window that overlooked her immaculate garden. It was there Beau set the cupcakes and tea, using his great grandmother's delicate china with the purple violets that she loved. A crystal bud vase sat in the center, sporting a single yellow dahlia.

Beau rose as she entered the room, flashing his most disarming smile.

She took in the scene and him. "Pouring it on a little thick, are you not?" Her voice was low but amused.

"Is it working?" he countered in the same tone.

"It is perhaps a good start. We shall see. What you have to say will determine whether a banquet of cupcakes and a truckload of flowers will make a difference." She moved beside the chair and waited for him to pull it out for her.

He poured, and they sipped their tea. A silent battle of wills raged, not hostile or angry, but dead serious; and more important than either of them realized.

No mere boy faced her across the table. Her son was a strong, very masculine man, in his prime. She admired the flex of muscle in his forearm when he raised the delicate teacup and noted the shadow of dark beard running along his strong jawline. He'd been a beautiful child, almost pretty, with those blue eyes and impossibly long black lashes, yet there had always been a rugged maleness beneath, testosterone that would not be denied, sturdy and rough from the moment of his birth. There was a new hardness to his handsome face, as if while she was not looking a sculptor chiseled away all his childhood softness, leaving behind the planes of a man.

Beau was their only boy, the baby in a family full of girls. From the crib, he learned charm and feigned helplessness could get his sisters to do almost anything. If Sarah and Jorge had not been vigilant, he would have ruled the house like an indolent Prince, lolling about his castle, while his female servants rushed to do his every bidding. It was the primary reason she agreed to let him go to the Royal Military Academy but was shaken to the core by the haunted boy who returned.

The man facing her over the floral teacup was neither spoiled child nor shell-shocked teen, but a sum of all he had been, the promise of what he would become. Sarah could bind him in gossamer ropes of maternal care, but that was not love. That was control, and she learned the distinction from her own father.

Her capitulation to tea in the kitchen spoke volumes between them.

"There was no Army friend named Allen ben Thomas." She fired the opening shot.

Beau tilted his head and widened his eyes. "Indeed? You are familiar with the entire roster of the fifty men that served in my company, as well as the two hundred and fifty at the Academy? You memorized all the names of the squadron I was assigned and the units with whom I was deployed?"

"Pfft. Do not be obtuse with me, Beau ben Jorge ben Landry." The New England clipped tones of her birth told him exactly how much she did not believe him.

His Gallic shrug conceded her point without a battle, prepared to give her that victory. But he did not stammer explanations nor elaborate further. He simply held her gaze and dared her to go on.

"I see. It's going to be that way, is it?" She eyed him and took an aggressive bite of her cupcake.

He almost laughed, the interchange between them familiar. He loved her, even if she could be an intimidating mother lioness. "*Maman*, I am here to ensure that you don't devour her or set her in that damn chair."

She raised an imperious chin and gazed out the window. "I have no idea what you are talking about."

"Ha! And who is being obtuse now?"

The corner of her mouth quivered with a suppressed smile. "I simply wish to know who she is, and how she found her way into your bedroom."

He scoffed, "She is not in my bedroom, as you well know. I am certain you had a spyglass pressed to the window all night. Did you see me wave to you?"

"I did not have a spyglass!" She had seen him wave, though she would never admit it.

"Alaina is a friend, and she needs my help. I invited her to stay with us for a time. I quite like her and hope you will welcome her." He held her eyes, "*Pour moi, ma chère Maman, s'il te plaît?*" For me, dear mother, please?

There it was. The gauntlet thrown down between the china and the flowers.

His words echoed Jorge's, and the doubts that kept her awake all night. She pursed her lips and flared her nose. The internal battle raged. At length, Sarah Landry surrendered with a sigh. "Very well."

He drew his head back and smiled. Before he could speak, she added, "For now. Unless she gives me pause or reason to reconsider. I warn you, Beau, that girl is from Mississippi, and nothing good is coming out of that place these days. They've gone wild with rebellion, not the tech kind either, more the drunken, lawless, rowdy kind. She's got an edge to her. And I don't buy for a minute that farcical tale about her losing her luggage on the side of the road. Long legs and swishy blonde hair will besot a man, as you well know. I am no fool," she paused, her smile growing wistful as she added tenderly, "but neither are you, Son. So, I shall show a bit of mercy and offer your guest a measure of grace."

"Thank you. I think you might like her. Granny does."

Sarah harrumphed, "Isabelle would like Korah if he showed up in her parlor and turned on his famous charm. She is no expert judge of character, fooled by a pretty face just like the rest of you. We shall see over supper tonight. You will bring her?"

It was a command, not a question. But as far as interviews with his mother went, this had been a victory, so he conceded, "As long as she is not the main course, *Maman.*"

Meet the Parents

In the normal course of a dating relationship, a man rarely brought a girl to his mother's within thirty-six hours of meeting her, unless the man was disturbed, which Beau was not, at least not anymore. As he escorted his nervous date across the street, his relatives, damn their eyes, did nothing to soothe her tattered nerves. They wished her luck, plastered solicitous smiles across their doleful faces, and scurried away with knowing shakes of their heads. He felt her rising panic, saw her eyes darting back and forth. She was ready to bolt. He tightened his grip on her elbow and gave her his most encouraging smile.

Alaina felt less like Dorothy and more like Alice, headed to face the Queen of Hearts. She planned to run if anybody pulled out a croquet set.

Beau did not bother to knock, which unnerved her even further. The house smelled of pine cleaner, wood, and dinner. It was larger than most of the modest houses on the street, but everything reeked of old money and understated elegance. Beau called out a greeting and led her down a wide hallway that emptied into an enormous kitchen with a long table for twelve on one side and a family room on the other. Wood, tile, and stone dominated the space that could have graced the pages of any magazine. The homey touches of children's drawings on the refrigerator and a basket overflowing with toys by the steps gave the magazine perfection a lived-in, cozy touch.

A huge family portrait hung over the fireplace, the gorgeous Landry clan immortalized in oil and canvas. Alaina could picture Sunday afternoon dinners with the family relaxing on the sofas, among the hodgepodge of pillows and soft throw blankets. The marked contrast between this house and her father's shack made her want to vomit.

Through the bay window, Alaina saw Sarah Landry putting the finishing touches on a tastefully set table on the patio. The floral umbrella fluttered in the warm breeze, a huge purple butterfly bush providing a picture-perfect backdrop for the elegant woman. Sarah came through the door, smiling. Everything about her screamed money, from her expertly cut and colored hair to her perfect manicure. She wore a faded silk blouse and jeans, that to Alaina's discerning eye had to be custom made; they fit her to perfection.

As she shook Sarah's hand, she recognized the appraising look, identical to the one on Beau's face yesterday. Jorge rose from an overstuffed chair and greeted her with a warm smile. He was handsome, an older version of Beau, with the same coloring and easy manner, far less intimidating than his wife.

Beau watched Alaina as she greeted his parents. Her large aquamarine eyes were her most expressive feature, and right now, they were flashing fear. He moved to her side for moral support.

After the introductions, he reluctantly handed Alaina over to Sarah for a tour of the garden. As they walked through the backdoor, Beau breathed, "I swear, *Papa*..."

Jorge squeezed his shoulder. "Give her a chance. She might surprise you."

In the end, she did.

Sarah put Alaina at ease, effortlessly drawing her out. She played her role to perfection, the gracious hostess, warm, welcoming, and engaging. As the evening went on, Beau saw Alaina relax. When the discussion turned to computers, he saw potential for the evening's greatest hazard but also the greatest potential for alliance. As they spoke, the depth of passion Alaina felt toward the future of computing, and the role she meant to play in their development, flowed out of her like rushing water.

Sarah scrutinized Alaina, asking pointed and pertinent questions. She appreciated the thoughtful answers Alaina gave, and recognized the keen mind working beneath all that blonde hair. She was rough around the edges, yes. And there was a hardness to her that bespoke a tough life. But she was not ingratiating, nor was she fawning, both of which would have annoyed Sarah and made her suspicious. Alaina was motherless, the greatest of all tragedies in Sarah's estimation. As they cleared the table and Alaina washed the dishes, which she insisted on doing, she reminded Sarah of a pretty golden retriever someone dumped on the side of the road. Beau happened to be the one to pick her up and bring her home. And that's what their cupcake summit boiled down to, one simple question, 'Can I keep her?'

Whether Alaina was here by an accident of fate or a calculated plan, remained to be seen. Sarah determined if it was the former, it was her duty to help the girl, but if it was the latter, she would annihilate her.

September 18, 990 ME

Routine

It started innocently enough. Sarah invited Alaina to work with her at the store. Landry's General Store had been in the family for three generations. Isabelle technically owned it, but everyone called it Sarah's store, and had for the years she ran it.

When she got frustrated with Isabelle's refusal to grow and expand, Mil-Mart was born. For five years, Sarah built a multi-million-shekel business, that grew to fifty stores and employed over five thousand Alanthians. When Beau came home from the war and the grandchildren started coming, Sarah sold. The decision surprised everyone, except Jorge. To the casual observer, one day she was in complete command, and the next, she was done. But that was how Andrew ben Lenox raised her, and how Sarah approached life. When circumstances changed, she adapted, made decisions, and moved on.

She still worked every day, though she could have run Landry's General Store from a hospital bed. For Alaina, the store wasn't that different from her father's bar, and in their hours working together, the two women formed an unlikely bond.

Alaina became part of the family. She loved them, and the Landrys loved her.

A routine developed in the little yellow cottage with the gingerbread trim. Isabelle rose with the birds and made breakfast. Beau left with the men to fish, and Alaina accompanied Sarah to the store. Some nights they cooked, many evenings they danced, and every Thursday Alaina and Beau worked on his house. Some days, she helped him paint and did light finish work. Other days they shopped, picking out carpet or shower curtains, sometimes furniture and rugs.

It happened in mid-September, over dishes.

"I don't like those," Alaina said, curling her lip at the black square dishes Beau pointed out. "They are odd and will look strange against the granite countertop. They'll get lost. I'll be serving dinner and put a great blob of mashed potatoes on the counter because I won't be able to distinguish between the two."

The moment she said it, she realized what she had done. Her eyes widened in horror, and she turned away, tucking her hair behind her ear. "Don't... oh, never mind." She forced a smile. "If you like them, buy them. It doesn't matter to me. I don't care." She bent over and grabbed a big box of the black dishes from the shelf and tried to put them in the cart.

Beau took the box from her. "Jolie Catin, do you want to make mashed potatoes at my house?"

She tightened her lips, holding back a sudden rush of tears. "My mashed potatoes are terrible. They taste like paste."

He put the dishes down and moved to stand in front of her. "I don't care, as long as you make them for me."

Alaina blinked and a single tear escaped. "I'll make you mashed potatoes, Beau."

"Good," he said, his lips brushing hers.

October 31, 990 ME

Emite - Louisiana Bayou

Deep in the Louisiana Bayou, Mademoiselle Charlotte Durant demanded everyone adhere to strict rules of protocol. From morning greetings, to the distance between the spoon and knife on her breakfast tray, Loa Hall ran with perfection. Her long-term servants knew that even when they achieved said perfection, from time to time, Mademoiselle would imagine a slight or invent an infraction. Those sent her into a murderous rage. Thus, when the tension in the household built, they offered a sacrifice, usually a newcomer, recruited off the streets. They purposely sabotaged the unsuspecting servant. They gave them the wrong manner of address or neglected to tell them which side of the bed to turn down. The infraction did not have to be big, but it provided Mademoiselle with an outlet for her rage, and it kept the servants alive. It was an agreeable arrangement for all, except the one they sacrificed.

Into this household, the Nephilim known as Emite was born. Charlotte beat it into submission within the first hour of its birth when it attempted to bite her. She bound it, caged it, and punished it for the slightest infraction. Then she rewarded it, held it to her breast, and made it her slave.

In the darkest part of the swamp, the hapless girls of New Orleans knew they could get rid of their unwanted babes, for a price. Mademoiselle Charlotte did not do it for the money, though lucrative. She was more interested in harvesting the delicacies they provided. It satisfied the growing hunger of the monster who prowled Loa Hall, lurking outside the procedure room, anticipating his favorite treat.

She found, to her delight, that Emite could absorb any knowledge given to him. She schooled him in the old ways of the Voodoo. At two, he could pronounce and remove curses with such alacrity she secretly feared his growing skills. So, she warped his brain even further than his own nature and wielded his power as her own.

The night of October 31, 990 ME, she took him deep into the bayou for their first genuine test. She spotted their victims alone on La Petit Pishon, sitting on the dock, a Landry and his betrothed.

Mademoiselle Charlotte could not wait.

Part 5 - Joanna

October 23, 985 ME (Six Months into Rebellion)

Coronation Ball - New City Palace

At eighteen, Lady Joanna ben Luke had a talent for being invisible. The night of the Coronation Ball, she applied herself to the task and blended into the yellow and gold wallpaper like a chameleon. Invisibility, unfortunately, did nothing to ease her physical discomfort. She surmised the seventh ring of Hell was not much hotter than the Palace ballroom tonight.

Her brown eyes widened with dread as she felt a slow rivulet of sweat run down the inside of her arm. A covert glance confirmed it, wet armpits. Great, just great. Even if they dried, which was unlikely in this heat, silk stained. She resigned herself to keeping her arms plastered to her sides for the rest of the night, which did nothing to improve her mood or ease the pain from the corset stays. Those medieval torture devices were supposed to make her appear trim. Instead, they dug painfully into her soft belly and forced her ample bosom so high she was afraid one of the straining gold buttons was going to launch and put someone's eye out. She couldn't even take a deep breath, trussed up and sweating like a pale chicken ten minutes into the roasting cycle.

Her parents insisted she looked lovely, but the color was just wrong. The yellow, shimmering and beautiful in the store, made Joanna look seasick. She woke this morning with her monthly cramps and a huge pimple, ugly and red, a bullseye on her chin. She knew the second she saw it that no amount of concealer was going to cover that thing, and it hadn't.

Her elaborate upswept hairstyle collapsed under its own weight, hanging drunkenly to one side. Every time she moved, more pins fell out. They surrounded her chair like confetti. Utterly miserable, she scooted behind a huge potted palm and hid.

It was not as if Joanna ben Luke was unattractive, but she leaned toward plumpness, which was greatly exaggerated by the reflection staring back at her every morning. If she were to describe herself, at least physically, she would simply say she was fat, having reached that conclusion when she was five, the day she realized Melissa ben Horrock's thigh was roughly the diameter of Joanna's forearm, and that her leg resembled a turkey drumstick. She distinctly remembered pointing her toes, so her legs raised off the wooden chapel bench, making them seem smaller.

She started her first diet when she was seven. The egg diet… eggs for breakfast, lunch, and dinner with carrots and celery as snacks. She lost five pounds in a week and everyone was so proud, except by the end of the month, the five pounds were back, plus two more. By thirteen, she could recite the calorie count of every food imaginable. She was gaining or starving. There was no middle ground.

A curvy bombshell at fifteen, beside her willowy classmates Joanna felt like a freak. Her complete lack of fashion sense merely compounded the problem, yielding results that ranged from hilarious to disastrous, the yellow silk gown being the latest in a long line of missteps.

On the rare occasions when a boy noticed her, usually when she was starving to death or hadn't worn something that made her look like a parade float, her intense personality scared them away. Her quick mind tended to lean toward the serious, world affairs, politics, and the struggles of the poor.

Flirting was completely out of the realm of possibility because she flushed, stammered, and inevitably said something inane, which totally defeated the purpose. It seemed to come so easily to everyone else. Through the fronds, she watched a cool blonde in rose silk holding court to a bevy of admirers. To her right, the Greek Princess gossiped in scandalized whispers about the handsome Secretary Tristin, a man her father despised.

Scanning the crowd, she picked him out. He had danced with almost every girl in the ballroom, except her. With a sigh, Joanna studied the pretty little woman in his arms. She was so light on her feet, she seemed to float above the dance floor, the sort of effortless grace that came naturally to girls who did not know the meaning of the word calorie.

Joanna pushed her chair further into the alcove.

When the song ended, an imposing matron with the beginnings of a double chin and several strands of good pearls blocked her view of the party. Secretary Tristin joined her. Joanna sighed, which caused the stays to dig deeper into her rib cage. She needed to use the facilities, but if she moved they would catch her hiding back here, and that would be humiliating. When they finally left, Joanna made her escape.

In the small water closet, she wrestled with the voluminous gown and wished she could unzip and loosen the stays. Taking two wads of toilet paper, she pressed one to each armpit and squeezed, deciding she might stay here for the rest of the night. But as she contemplated doing exactly that, someone came in.

Not in a hurry to return, she stared into the powder room mirror, studying her leaning hairdo. Brown and gold curls escaped their pins, not in a winsome attractive manner, more like a rat's nest gone awry. Pushing it to one side, she was rewarded with a shower of bobby pins.

She managed a tepid smile at the girl in green who joined her at the sink. Sparkling hazel-green eyes met her own ordinary brown ones in the mirror.

"It's warm in there, isn't it?" Skinny said, washing her hands.

"Hot," Joanna confirmed, trying not to sound sulky.

"Unusual for this time of year. Have a pleasant night."

Beautiful, tiny, and nice; Joanna hated her. "You too," she called weakly.

Reasoning that it may be cooler on the veranda, she made her way outside. Near the pool, she found a suitable potted hibiscus to hide behind. This was perhaps not the best place to spend the evening because it reminded her of him… the one boy she had not scared off, and if she was honest, had still not gotten over.

He was a lifeguard at their country club, the most beautiful boy Joanna had ever seen. Theirs was a whirlwind romance, all wet bathing suits and passionate kisses, with his strong lithe body pressing her up against an old pool raft, as life jackets swung on hooks around them.

They kept it secret because her elderly parents would have never approved. Her father, Baron Luke ben Simon, was Special Council to Prince Eamonn, and her grandfather, Earl Simon ben Joshua, was the Alanthian Ambassador to the Golden Kingdom for as long as anyone could remember. Joanna's mother, Lady Elizabeth ben George, was English nobility, and third cousin to the Ruling Prince of Europe, Edward. Thus, a lifeguard, no matter how charming, funny, or incredibly tan and sexy, was not a suitable beau for Lady Joanna ben Luke. But during the skinny Summer of '83, she had not cared.

By September of that year, she realized she should have. He left her without saying a word, a backward glance, or even a lousy note. The memory of that night still haunted her, and feeling supremely sorry for herself, it came for a visit.

At Les Deux Côtés, a romantic bistro near the university, Joanna sat alone, waiting. She snuck home for the weekend from her exclusive girls' school, to meet her lover for dinner, her treat of course. He did not know it, but she rented a hotel suite. It would be the first time they were together in anything other than the lifeguard's shed or the pool pump room.

She wore a new outfit for the date, the smallest pair of pants she ever owned, and a purple knit top. Both showed off her flat stomach. In the end, he had not even seen how good she looked.

He sent a hard-eyed stranger with a pierced lip to break up with her. "You Joanna?"

Joanna's eyes widened at the spiky-haired, tattooed woman. "Yes."

The woman gave her an appraising stare and snorted, shaking her head. "Les ain't coming. He's got a live-in girlfriend, sweetheart, always has. But he said to tell you, it was fun. Have a good life."

Joanna stared like an imbecile, fixated on the poorly executed bald eagle tattooed on the woman's forearm. The words did not register. Les loved her, had told her that a dozen times. But as Lip Ring walked away, she realized in a crashing moment of clarity that she was not the only one keeping their relationship a secret.

Distantly, she thought she heard his laugh as a group walked away. She wanted to tear after him. There had been a terrible misunderstanding. That horrible woman was lying. This was a cruel joke.

But it wasn't.

She sat there, frozen. Above the pots and pans clattering in the kitchen, below the murmured conversation, and over the clinking silver on china, she heard it. A small popping noise, like a cork pulled from a wine bottle; her heart as it broke. Dipping her steaming baguette in the olive oil, she realized life would never be the same.

Back in the Palace ballroom, she pushed the memory away and her breasts up, desperate to give her lungs room to expand. It didn't matter if anyone saw her, the sweat stains were visible no matter how she held her arms. Finding her chair, Joanna wished she had the confidence of that blonde in rose silk, the haughtiness of that sultry Greek Princess, but most of all she wished she could be more like that little woman in green. She wanted to be anybody but Lady Joanna ben Luke.

March 21, 987 ME (Two Years into Rebellion)

The Wrong Side

Joanna's family aligned with the wrong side in the Alanthian Civil War. Privy to the inner workings of the Palace, they knew the truth. Vowing evil would never gain a foothold in their hearts or in their homes, her father Luke ben Simon played a prominent role in the conflict. Unfortunately for their finances, their positions in the government and society, it cost them everything.

Her grandfather, Ambassador Simon ben Joshua, did not return to Alanthia. Instead, he took up permanent residence in the Golden Kingdom where he had served since Prince Adam appointed him in the 30s. When Korah severed relations between the two kingdoms, Ambassador Simon personally financed embassy operations and continued to plead with the Iron King to have mercy on Alanthia.

Korah's government froze her parents' assets and placed them under house arrest. Their mansion became a prison. Neither could leave, nor could they have visitors. Joanna, away at university when the war broke out, did not dare go home, lest she get caught in King Korah's net.

At the onset of fighting, her father had the foresight to prepay the two remaining years of her tuition and fees. Joanna had a modest trust fund from an eccentric aunt that escaped the seizures and enough money in her personal account to see her through a year, maybe less.

Six weeks after the ceasefire, Joanna realized she had to figure out a way to make a living. The thought scared her to death. She was studying to become a social worker, surmising at the beginning of her education that it would give her the skills to administer her family's charitable trusts. Instead, a charity they supported might have to hire her. Intimately familiar with how much those jobs paid, she regularly calculated when and how to pawn her jewelry.

In the middle of her junior year, she closed her textbook, A Field Guide to Domestic Abuse Intervention, and dressed for her internship at a battered women's shelter. Her dorm window rattled in the chilly wind, and she selected a pair of warm boots instead of the comfortable slide-on shoes she wanted to wear. She grunted with the effort of reaching down to pull up the side zipper. It was a fat spring. She would have preferred her stretchy pants, but the old crone who ran the shelter told her last week that 'they were unseemly'. In Joanna's opinion, it was more unseemly to be bound in a pair of pants she had to lie on the bed to zip.

She either had to go on a diet or spend her limited resources on new clothes. Diet it was, even if her soul rebelled at the very thought. Perhaps the sweet potato diet she read about in the lady's magazine would do the trick, though she didn't really like sweet potatoes. But the before and after pictures were amazing, so she might give that one a try. Walking down the hall with her jeans making a rubbing noise, she wondered how to pull off a sweet potato souffle in the small dorm kitchen.

Two hours later, she was still thinking about sweet potatoes when a pregnant girl in her early twenties walked into her office. Joanna set down her pen and smiled. "Welcome to the Lady's House."

Enormous green eyes filled with tears, as the girl stood there with her chin quivering, clasping and unclasping her hands. Joanna came around the desk and guided her to a chair. "Can I get you a drink of water?"

The girl gave a convulsive nod, sniffing.

After she settled, Joanna began the intake process. "What's your name?"

The lip quivered again. "Judith. Judith ben Dan. My boyfriend, or my ex-boyfriend, is trying to kill me."

"I am so sorry that has happened to you, but you will be safe here. We employ full-time security, as I am sure you noticed when you came in."

Judith nodded, her hands absently rubbing her engorged belly.

"Have you been to the police?" Joanna asked, looking down at her intake form.

Judith's chin quivered again, and she poured out her tale. She moved to the New City with her husband two years ago, but that had not worked out. He was a drinker, and she left him when she met her boyfriend, who also had a substance abuse problem.

"He wanted me to get rid of it, if you know what I mean."

Joanna's nostrils flared. More and more women were coming into the shelter with that tale. The practice was almost completely unknown until recently. "I do, unfortunately. But you made the right choice."

Judith nodded, her absent stroking of her belly becoming more vigorous, so intimate, it bordered on masturbation. Joanna looked away, embarrassed.

"This is my baby." Judith declared, showing her first hint of backbone. "He doesn't want me to have it because he doesn't want to support it. But I never asked for his support. I will take care of my baby. He will never see this child."

"Well, if he is on drugs, that is a wise decision," Joanna said with an encouraging nod. "Now, let's get you settled. When is the baby due?"

The terrified look came back. "Two or three weeks. At least that is what that doctor at the free clinic said." She bit her lip and added, "I think he molested me while he was examining me. It was terrible."

Joanna felt a stab of sympathy as she helped the girl to her feet. "We'll make sure you have a female physician, shall we?"

Judith fell into Joanna's arms. "Thank you. I don't know what to say. You've been so kind. Most people aren't, you know?"

Taken aback, Joanna gently set the girl away from her. "Well, I'd be in the wrong line of work if I wasn't."

Judith laughed humorlessly. "Oh, you would be surprised."

"Perhaps." Joanna shrugged, thumbing at the waistband of her jeans. "But I know a bit about being in a tight spot."

May 3, 987 ME

Soup

The smell of beef stew caught Joanna by surprise. She looked up from the accounting ledgers scattered across her desk and blinked.

Judith stood in the open door of her office, a steaming bowl of soup in her hands. "Are you hungry? I saw your light."

Joanna made a jaw cracking yawn and nodded. "I'm starving, and if that is for me, I will call you an angel."

Judith smiled and presented the bowl with a flourish. "Why are you still here? It's late."

Joanna rubbed the back of her neck, then pushed the papers aside, making way for the soup. "We have exams this week, but I've got to finish balancing the books before I go home. Mrs. ben Fitzsimmons dropped these on me at six o'clock tonight just as I was packing to leave." She blew on a spoonful of rich stew and exhaled with pleasure. "This is divine. Thank you."

"You've got an exam tomorrow?" Judith asked, taking the chair opposite Joanna's desk.

Joanna took another bite, her shoulders slumping. "Yes, in accounting no less, my worst subject." She made a dismissive hand toward the ledgers. "I have looked at the same columns five times, and I can't get the figures to balance."

Judith pointed at the papers. "I've got a fairly good head for numbers. You want me to look?"

"No, that's okay. I'm sure you are exhausted, dealing with a newborn."

Judith stretched. "I just gave her the ten o'clock feeding. She'll sleep until two." She reached across the desk. "I don't mind. It's the least I can do."

Joanna rubbed her eyes, red-rimmed and bleary. "Glance at it, let me know if you see what I am missing." She scraped the bottom of the bowl and sat back in her chair, trying to soothe the cramp in her neck.

"Wow! We are spending a lot of money on kitchen supplies."

Joanna yawned. "Food prices have skyrocketed since the war. They did not plant last fall like they should have. And the weather has been so bad, everything is more expensive."

"I understand. But you know, there are thirty of us here. I will bet if you go to the restaurant supply companies you could get this for a lot less money."

Joanna shrugged. "Something to think about, for sure." She leaned forward to take the papers, but Judith held up her hand, staring at the figures.

She ran her finger down the columns, her mouth making silent calculations, then she brightened and turned the ledger back to face Joanna. "Right here, you've got that in the debit column, it's a credit."

"Oh, you are right. Thank you." She yawned again. "I'm so tired, I guess I missed it. I'll be glad when exams are finished."

Judith looked hurt. "So, are you done here, then?"

Joanna smiled. "No, this internship was for two years. You are stuck with me for at least another year."

"I hope I am on my feet by then, but it's nice to hear you aren't leaving. You seem to be the only one around here that has any clue about running this place."

Joanna's face pinkened at the compliment, gratified to hear her accomplishments were not completely unnoticed. "Thank you, I do my best."

May 15, 988 ME (Three Years into Rebellion)

Graduation

"Judith, you shouldn't have," Joanna exclaimed, looking at the bracelet resting in the velvet-lined box. She recognized the store; nothing was inexpensive.

Judith beamed. "Do you like it?"

Joanna slipped it over her wrist and said, "I love it. Thank you. It is so pretty."

"I thought it would go with that suit you wear when you go to fund-raisers."

Joanna held the sparkling silver bangle up, enjoying the red prisms that twinkled in the light. "Indeed, it's quite fetching, but you really shouldn't have."

Judith shrugged. "I wanted to get you something. You've done so much to help me, putting me in charge of the kitchen and the book-keeping." She leaned forward and confided, "I've got a nest egg saved up, almost enough money to buy a place in Barney's Station. I mean, it's not as nice as where you live, I am sure. But my friend and I are going in together, and there's a yard, so Amber can play outside."

Joanna flashed a smile. The industrious Judith continued to amaze her with her resourcefulness. "I am so happy for you. I know this last year has not been easy. But we are all so proud of how you pulled your life together. You are a true inspiration."

Judith dismissed the compliment. "I didn't have much of a choice, did I? I've put my resume out and have a second interview next week."

"Honestly? Doing what?"

"It's at a retirement home, and I'll be doing what I've been doing here, managing the kitchen but also procurement and bookkeeping."

"Good for you. Let me know if I can give you a reference," Joanna offered. "You've done splendid work here. Our expenditures are down twenty-four percent this quarter, and the pantry is bulging with sup-plies. Mrs. Fitzsimmons will be sad to lose you." Joanna touched Judith's shoulder. "I am going to miss you."

Judith's eyes filled with tears. "Joanna, I'm going to miss you, too."

The young ladies embraced. Now that Joanna's internship was over, the line between them blurred. Friendship blossomed. Joanna dabbed a tear at her own eye. "I'll say goodbye to you and Amber before I leave, but we will keep in touch."

October 31, 990 ME (Five Years into Rebellion)

The Pitch

Joanna knew passion would only carry her so far. It took money to accomplish anything. Dreams, desires, and good intentions would not feed, shelter, or care for a single child without the financial resources to back up the sentiment. The cold reality of commerce snaked its way into Lady Joanna ben Luke's life the day Korah's government seized her family's fortune.

She paced her small apartment, rehearsing her speech. Three boxes of glossy presentations waited by the door, ready to go. The professionally bound reports contained pictures, statistics, graphs, and personal stories Joanna gathered over the last two-and-a-half years. Funding for the work came through a field research grant obtained from the Lenox Foundation, and today she would present her findings and ask the formidable Sarah Landry to finance a center to care for the alarming number of street kids roaming the New City. Not only Lenox, but dozens of other foundations would attend, including, to her gall, the government administrator who oversaw her own family's foundation. Her father, in his covert way, ensured that many of his old colleagues would be in attendance. Joanna closed her eyes and tried to calm her escalating nerves. There would be family friends in the audience today, everything would be fine. She glanced at the clock. Time to load the car and get dressed.

The car had been the biggest surprise of her twenty-third birthday. She found it sitting outside her apartment, festooned with a giant red bow. A special messenger delivered the keys. No note, no explanation, but she knew who it was from. How her father continued to manage it, she did not know.

For her safety, she stayed away, and thus lived a life removed from her parents and their ongoing legal battles. They worked out a system of exchanging private notes, but she had not seen them in three years. Her grandfather financed a team of lawyers who chipped away at the government's case. The reports contained some hope, but it might take years, and her parents might never be free or have their assets fully restored. Until then, they remained imprisoned, and she received random deposits into her bank account, usually just before she went into overdraft.

Twenty minutes before she took the podium, Joanna stood in the hotel lavatory, trying not to hyperventilate. She reapplied her pale lipstick and smoothed her golden-brown bangs to the side. Her new hairdresser was a genius and convinced her to cut off her waist-length hair two months ago. It was the bravest thing Joanna had ever done. A few strategically placed highlights, a jagged razor cut, and a side part instead of a middle one completely transformed her appearance. She changed from a dowdy, round-faced girl into a stylish young lady. And the new hair had a new body to go along with it, purely by accident.

After graduation, she threw herself into the research with a single-minded passion. Understanding that if she wanted to help homeless kids, she had to be with them, so she followed them deep into the New City, trekking mile after mile on her feet. She got to know them, spent time in their makeshift camps, went into their squats and abandoned houses, which worried her mother, so she stopped telling her about it. She ate with them, but more often than not, gave them her own food. The manager at her apartment started warning new residents not to be alarmed. Joanna was not actually a vagabond; she just dressed that way. The ragged sweatpants and old shirts gained her entry into the kids' society, but they almost got her arrested at Prince Eamonn Park.

"Move along here, ma'am. You can't sleep on the benches," Officer Elias ben Phillip said, nudging Joanna awake with his baton.

Joanna startled to a sitting position. "Oh, pardon me, Officer. I am so sorry. I must have dozed off."

Elias drew his brows to a point over his snub nose. Her cultured voice shocked him, coming as it did, from a heap of rags. Her face and hair were clean; she smelled nice. Something was amiss. "Is everything okay, ma'am?"

She yawned and stretched, taking up a fat notebook she had been using as a pillow. "I was to meet someone, but they seem to have been waylaid."

"I think I've seen you around here lately."

Joanna smiled, her perfect white teeth gleaming back at him. "Indeed, I come here often. There are quite a few youngsters taking up residence in the park. If I want to learn about them, I must go where they are."

"You a graduate student doing your thesis?"

Joanna made a dismissive wave and said, "Perhaps one day, but honestly, for now, I am done with academia. I actually want to help people, not just talk about it."

Elias laughed. "Move along now." He motioned toward the exit. "It's getting dark. This place is dangerous at night, especially for a woman alone."

Joanna snorted and gestured to her body. "Nobody messes with fat girls. We are too hard to carry off."

Elias attended enough murder scenes in the last three years to disagree, but he did not say. He peered at her face in the fading light. "You look familiar."

She stood up, offering her hand. "We have not been properly introduced. I'm Lady Joanna ben Luke."

Elias' mind processed the name but could not place her. "Officer

Elias ben Philip, at your service, ma'am." He maneuvered her forward and asked, "So you are doing research?"

"Indeed. I received a grant to document the growing problem of homeless and orphaned children in the New City. Since the war, the increase in the juvenile population living on the streets is astonishing, and we must avert the burgeoning crisis." Joanna recited the preceding in a single breath.

Elias did not need a grant to know there was a problem. "What you are doing is not exactly safe."

Joanna scoffed. "I'm a grown woman. How safe is it for a six-year-old child?"

"You've got a point, but still." He looked her up and down. "If you don't mind my saying so, once you open your mouth, you don't exactly blend."

Joanna shot him a look. "Well, there is very little I can do about the modulation of my speech, is there?"

"The modulation of your speech? Jupiter's Moon, are they even going to talk to you?"

"Sure they are." She got a smug look and added, "They think I am here to give them money."

Elias chuckled. "And you're not?"

"I plan to help them achieve something better."

"And what might that be?"

"Hope, a home, and a way out."

All she lacked was a sword to thrust in the air, he mused. "That is a mighty tall order for a little woman."

Joanna looked up at him through her long eyelashes. "Ha! Good thing I am not a little woman."

From that point forward, Lady Joanna ben Luke and Officer Elias ben Phillip formed a friendship. In fact, she was on a first-name basis with all the beat cops that worked the areas where the homeless kids congregated. They thought she was eccentric, but so incredibly earnest and serious, they liked her and kept an eye out for her. Joanna was right about one thing. Nobody took any notice of her. And she did her research without trouble or incident.

It was divine intervention that prompted her to try on her fundraiser suit the day before the presentation. Joanna stood frozen in disbelief as the skirt fell into a puddle on the floor. The sleeves hung over her fingertips, and she could wrap the jacket around her midriff almost double. She had been wearing her comfy 'homeless rags' for so long, she had not even noticed she was no longer fat. It came as a shock since the amount of gravitational force her body was exerting on the Earth consumed almost every waking moment of her life from age five to twenty-two. Flapping her arms in the red sleeves, even the fashion clueless Lady Joanna ben Luke realized she could not wear this to the presentation tomorrow.

At 7:30 pm, she sprinted out of her apartment to find the nearest clothing store. She burst through the door fifteen minutes before closing and said, "Help!"

Standing in the hotel lavatory, she was thankful the saleswoman knew her business. The black dress and long flowing jacket made her look stylish, yet serious.

The bathroom door swung open, and an elderly lady dripping with diamonds entered. "Lady Joanna, I am so glad I caught you alone."

"Mrs. ben Lindstrom, how nice to see you again."

She walked forward; the wobbling cane juxtaposed by her lively blue eyes. "Look at you! You are the very image of your Grandmother Eloise. Alas, you probably do not remember her, but she was a lovely, fine lady. Truly the belle of the age, in my day."

Joanna flushed. Her grandmother's poise and beauty were a family legend. "Thank you, ma'am. That is quite a compliment, and I must confess, sorely needed today. I find I am rather nervous."

"Bah! Everyone comes to these things to give away money." She looked around conspiratorially, adding, "And those of us who cannot stand Korah are dying to support you just to spite him. You will do fine."

Joanna drew in a ragged breath and smiled. "That sets my mind at ease a bit."

Mrs. ben Lindstrom gave her a jaunty wink. "When you take that podium, you remember that royal blood courses through your veins. Your family served this kingdom with honor and distinction for six generations. Joanna ben Luke, remember who you are." With that, she turned and made her way into the auditorium.

Joanna squared her shoulders, left the restroom, and knocked them dead.

Her presentation was a resounding success. She earned an invitation to supper with Sarah Landry herself. Unfortunately, dinner ended before it began. Mrs. Landry received an emergency call from home that her son and his fiancée had been injured, and from Sarah's stricken expression, it was serious.

May 18, 992 ME (Seven Years into Rebellion)

Grand Opening

"Judith, where is that delivery? They should have been here three hours ago," Joanna called through the empty receiving area.

Judith's round face peered around the corner from the kitchen, brandishing a new spatula. "The driver had engine trouble. I spoke to the dispatcher. They should be here by the end of the day."

Joanna squeezed her temples and groaned. "They better. We have fifty VIP's coming to tour in less than forty-eight hours. And if the chapel chairs don't arrive, we will have nowhere for them to sit."

"Trucks break down. Do you want me to call them again?" Judith's large green eyes flashed annoyance.

"No, it will not make them get here any faster. What time do you have to leave today?"

"The daycare closes at 5:30 pm, so I have to catch the 4:15 pm train."

Joanna managed a weary smile, hiding her frustration. It was going to be another long night. Nothing new, she put in sixty-hour weeks for the last year and a half, and several nights this month simply curled up in one of the empty dorm rooms to sleep.

On the edge of the New City, in the older section of town, the abandoned winery and its dozen outbuildings were part of the grants Joanna secured to start the charity, officially named The Center for the Street Kids of Alanthia. In the last two-and-a-half years, they simply shortened it to the Center.

The principal building was a hulking structure of stone. Sometimes, Joanna thought she could still smell the oak casks and millions of gallons of wine that once flowed through the facility. The rooms were stately and rich, with beautiful wood and masonry throughout. The architecture firm hired for the project did an amazing job of using the space while preserving the character. It did not feel institutional, much to Joanna's relief.

Next week they would open their first dorm for ten permanent kids, and as funding permitted, grow to full occupancy of sixty. Each block would become its own functioning house, like a family. They hoped the bonds the kids formed would carry them through their lives, their dorm mates becoming their surrogate families, which Joanna believed was key to the residents long term welfare and stability. The facility would not solve the growing homeless problem, but for the children it helped, it would be the difference between life and death.

In a stroke of luck and good timing, Judith left the retirement community and was available. She joined Joanna three months before, and every day since, Joanna thanked the Iron King for her. Judith was a whirlwind of efficiency.

The Center was launching with minimal staff. Joanna, as the executive director, would be responsible for fundraising, vision, and overall direction. Utilizing Judith's organizational and procurement skills, Joanna placed her in charge of purchasing, accounting, and administration. Two full-time and two part-time house managers were hired to work with the kids, help cook meals, assist with homework, and keep the peace.

Only the residents would live on site, at Joanna's insistence. She believed it prevented burn out because people needed to step away from their jobs, impossible if they lived where they worked. The policy also mitigated the chances of abuse. Joanna knew from her research that adults with authority over children often became corrupt, so she determined they would not fall into that trap.

It was not only her reputation, but her family's legacy on the line. Everything about the Center would be above reproach, a beacon of hope, and integrity.

At twenty-five, Lady Joanna ben Luke overcame heartbreak, personal insecurities, a loss of fortune, and exile from her family. She successfully negotiated with the top charitable trusts in the kingdom to gain funding for her project. Through grit and determination, she stood on the precipice of making a tremendous difference in the lives of dozens of children who would have otherwise been lost in the mire.

But she did not know that great evil lurked in the shadows of the old winery. The House of Amah was within range, and Rapha, the Nephilim, waited.

Part 6 - Pepperwood

June 992 ME (Seven Years into Rebellion)

Stop and Look Around

It was a banner day at the Pepperwood Horse Ranch. A royal delegation was coming to visit with an expressed interest in two third-year mares. Persa and James were ecstatic. James, ever the perfectionist, began calculating all the work they needed to do in preparation.

Persa, who never gave a thought to decor, looked around and said, "Jay, perhaps it wasn't such a good idea to move that sofa into the house."

James looked up from his breakfast. "The brown one?"

"Well, that one too, but I was thinking of the beige one."

"Yeah, the brown one."

"Beige and brown are two different colors," Persa informed him.

He dipped his toast into the yolk and took a bite. "They're both brown."

"They're both ugly."

James lifted a shoulder. "You said you didn't care. I offered to buy new furniture for the house. But you said, 'No, let's just take the furniture from the attics at Rivergate and Leggett.'"

Persa raised her pointed chin. "Well, I've changed my mind." Eyeing the kitchen with a critical gaze, she noticed for the first time three styles of wooden chairs sat around their kitchen table.

"You are planning on furniture shopping when we have the delegation coming in two weeks? Fey, I need your help in the stables. They won't care about the house."

Persa scowled at him. "Spoken like a true man." She stood up, clearing the breakfast dishes. "They might not care, but I do."

"Since when?" James asked, amused by Persa's sudden burst of home-maker instinct. A faint spark of hope flashed in the corner of his eye. "Is there something you are trying to tell me?"

Her head snapped up, and then she seemed to collapse into herself. "No."

James moved to her side, putting an arm around her.

They had been trying for three years.

The doctor said there was scar tissue everywhere. She would probably never conceive. They could only surmise it had come from their years of training. They stopped talking about it, but they did not stop trying. And every month he heard her crying in the bathroom.

"Get your purse, my sweet darling. I will buy you a whole house of new furniture. Okay?"

Big, silent tears fell down her cheeks. "But no crib."

There was nothing to say, nothing that would take away her pain. He wiped away her tears, kissed her forehead, and took her to town.

Furniture shopping turned into more fun than Persa imagined. James was miserable. But he found the most comfortable sofa or chair in the store and let her shop. It cheered her up, and that was all that mattered. He groaned, when after four hours of furniture shopping, she insisted they go to the new Mil-Mart for whatever in the world, furnishings and home decor were. Three shopping carts later, he was well acquainted with the term.

They had been married for five years, and in one afternoon, Persa spent more money than in their entire marriage. He did not begrudge her a shekel. His mother was going to be ecstatic, having declared their home little better than a fraternity house, which was a gross exaggeration because there were no girly posters or scattered beer bottles. But she had a point.

Persa's Pepperwood renovation did not stop with the furniture. The next morning, James found her on the front porch, her hands on her hips, scowling. "What?" he asked with mild trepidation. She was in full General Mode.

"When did all the foundation plants die?"

James followed her line of sight. "I never remember them being alive." The corners of his mouth were twitching, but he tried to keep his face serious.

She turned with an identical expression, her voice cracking in suppressed humor. "I think they've been dead since we moved in."

"Are you going to make me garden today?" James asked in a tone that suggested it was a horror beyond imagining.

She covered her mouth and turned her head away, trying not to laugh. "We've lived like teenagers in this house."

A slow smile grew on James' face. "I know." He took a step toward her.

Her eyes brightened, and she stepped back. "James ben Kole, it's the middle of the morning, and we have work to do."

"Teenagers don't care about work." He picked her up and kissed her neck. "If you let me take you upstairs, I'll garden for you."

She threw back her head in laughter and passion. "Deal."

Royal Visitor

True to his word, James pulled out all the dead foundation plants. It was a considerable improvement just to have the black skeletons gone. The following morning, Persa stood in the front yard, trying to see it through the eyes of a royal.

The stables were pristine, and their original stock of twelve was now twenty, with three mares in foal and five active studs. Rivergate's renown and James' distinction in the Army lent themselves to Pepperwood's growing reputation. The letter from the Palace signaled they were finally coming into their own.

Persa turned toward the sound of a car cresting the hill. A shining black sports car, expensive and sleek, drove down the driveway. She pulled off her garden gloves and moved to meet the visitor. No one had an appointment this afternoon, but rich clients touring wine country often dropped in.

The door swung open, and a tall, thin young man emerged from the car. His golden hair sparkled in the sunlight. Persa stopped dead, blinking. Her mouth fell open, and she blurted, "Peter, you rascal, you aren't supposed to be here for two weeks."

Prince d'Or gave her a boyish shrug of innocence. "Hello, Persa. It is lovely to see you, too."

Strange visions of a portrait gallery flashed through her brain, laughter, and an overwhelming sense of gratitude. Before she could stop herself, she ran toward him, choked up, her arms spread wide. "Peter!" She hugged him around the waist, her eyes brimming with tears. "My friend."

He hugged her with one arm, palming his own eyes with his free hand, and letting out an enormous sigh. "It has been a long time."

She glowed, looking up at him. "Too long! You are so tall."

"And you are so not. Were you always this little?" he teased.

Persa drew herself up. "Good things come in small packages." She looked around, expecting others. "Where is everyone else?"

He shrugged again. "It is just me. I saw on the schedule we were coming, saw your name." He fidgeted, uncomfortable. "I did not know, well I thought, oh, forget it. Do you mind?"

Persa watched him. She'd never seen him unsure of himself. Even at seven, he was cocky. He looked lost, he looked wounded, and he looked in desperate need of a friend. She laid a hand against his smooth cheek, marred with a small cluster of adolescent acne. "I don't mind, mi casa es su casa."

He leaned his face against her hand and rested his eyes. His voice sounded weary. "Thank you. I needed to get away from the Palace."

"Well, you've come to the right place." Fury struck like lightning out of nowhere. She rose on her tiptoes, growling like a momma bear. "There is nothing that can get to you here. You stay as long as you need."

Peter drew back, surprised at her tone, and suddenly abashed. "I could not impose on you like that," he said, though his soul cried out for it. The moment he crested the hill onto the Pepperwood property, he felt free of the malevolent force that tormented him.

"It is no imposition." She took him by the arm, moving toward the stable. "We have guests all the time. You are early, so the place is a wreck inside, full of second-hand furniture, and a lumpy mattress in the guest room. Not what you are used to, I am sure, but you are welcome to stay."

Peter thought of his luxurious quarters at the Palace. Her lumpy mattress sounded like Heaven. He nodded toward the stables. "And James? What is he going to say about this? If I recall, the last time I saw him, I stole you away, and he spent the rest of the night shooting daggers at me."

Persa burst out laughing, remembering. "That was the best. But you rescued me once, I owe you one."

"Pardon?" Peter asked, confused.

Persa looked up at him, equally confused. "I don't know why I said that. Ignore me. I do that sort of thing all the time." She shook her head, as if clearing it. "Come on, let's go say hello to James. As long as you don't flirt with me, he'll be fine."

Prince d'Or gave her his famous smile. "I do not know what you are talking about."

Persa rolled her eyes and smacked his arm. "Jupiter's Moon, what a lady killer you have turned out to be. Don't do that around him, he's dreadful jealous, always has been."

They found James in Bayard's stall, grooming the stallion. Peter only had eyes for the magnificent animal. "He is gorgeous," Peter whispered in awe.

Persa was looking at James, his back to them. She elbowed Peter playfully. "Both of them."

"Fey, hand me a Dandy brush, please."

Peter looked to his left and grabbed the requested implement. Persa nodded, and Peter moved into the stall. James took it, then paused, turning to see whose hand was connected to the brush he just accepted. The play of emotions on his face was priceless, curiosity, confusion, surprise, then a mock scowl. "Come to steal my girl again?"

A dozen smart remarks died on Peter's tongue. Looking into James' face, he recognized a rare quality. The man before him commanded respect. Peter had not seen that in many men. Uncle Eamonn had possessed it. "No, sir. I came to see the horses. I beg your indulgence for arriving early and unannounced."

James took the measure of the teen. He had a scraggly mustache, which he needed to shave but hadn't. His cheeks still had the baby softness of youth, but that was disappearing. The scattered acne gave him a vulnerability, made him more human, less perfect. There were dark circles under his eyes. He'd seen that look in the boys in his command after a battle. James rose and offered his hand. "Welcome to Pepperwood, my Esteemed."

The Prince knew his way around a stable. He refused to let them treat him like a guest and changed out of his fine silk traveling clothes into well-worn jeans and work boots. James and Persa exchanged bemused glances when Peter walked into an empty stall and started working.

"You don't have to do that," Persa protested.

Peter stopped and leaned against the bedding fork. "Who is going to do it?"

Persa gave him a slant-eyed look. "Well... James or me."

Peter quirked his brow at her. "And then what am I supposed to do? Have you bring me a throne, so I can sit over there and watch you?"

When she looked sheepish, he rolled his eyes and went back to the bedding. "Go plant your flowers, Persa. I can muck out a stall."

"Suit yourself." Persa shrugged, recognizing a person who needed to get lost in stable work.

As she walked away, she heard him singing softly to himself.

Peter worked all day, doing the chores without a complaint, barely speaking a word except, "What next?"

James, the commander of men in stables and ranks, treated Peter as he would any other subordinate, with respect and firmness. Peter started at the bottom. James kept waiting for him to balk, but it never came. At noon, he went to check on Persa's progress with the plants. He nodded toward the stables. "What do you make of that?"

Persa sat back on her heels, looking at the barn, deep in thought. "Something's going on. I told him he could stay."

James widened his eyes in surprise. "You did?"

She studied her garden glove and said, "I did. I don't know where it came from, but it felt like the right thing to do. I don't know. It was like I was prompted or something. I hope you don't mind."

"I hope he doesn't mind. That bed is awful." James winked. "Cause he's not getting mine."

Persa laughed, relieved. "I warned him." She stretched her back, unused to gardening. "I better go make some sandwiches. I remember you at fourteen. You ate three or four plates every night at dinner."

"All teenage boys eat like that. Call the grocer and add on to the food order." He nodded toward the stable. "That boy, I think he's going to stay awhile."

They normally spent Sunday evenings at Rivergate. Sensing Peter was not in the mood for company, she called her father and made their excuses. She did not mention who their guest was and declined his offer to bring him to supper, claiming their guest seemed a little weary. Over the years, James' men would show up at the farm, many wearing the same haunted look Peter had now. They always invited them to stay, and most of the time they did. Yereq wished her a good evening, garnering a promise that they would come next week.

After supper, they retired to the front porch, rocking and sipping fresh lemonade. The cicada's song was pleasant and steady. Peter marveled at the stars, which seemed brilliant away from the New City lights.

Persa turned to Peter and asked, "Did you make your phone calls?"

Peter pulled the phone from his pocket and showed it to her. "Bloody hell, Pers, do you honestly think they do not know where I am? We would have a national emergency on our hands if I went to take a crap and failed to tell somebody." He sighed. "Yes, I called them. The security detail is in Redding. This button," he motioned to a large red button on the side of the phone, "is the panic button. This green one opens a direct line to the agent in charge. I told them not to, but I suspect they have several men guarding the perimeter, in case another one of those jihad assholes comes flying out of the woods and tries to kill me." There was bitter irony in his voice. "They would chip me if I permitted it. Instead, I agreed to carry this."

James was quiet, then said seriously, "That sounds like it sucks."

Peter ran his fingers through his thick blond hair. His short laugh was full of self-mockery. "Poor Prince d'Or."

"How about you just be Peter while you're here," James offered.

Peter looked out at the valley, the tops of the redwood forest visible in the moonlight. He rubbed his chin and said, "I would like to find out who that is."

"It's as good a place as any to do it." James took a sip of his lemonade. "Just don't try to steal my girl, whelp."

Peter turned a cocky grin toward James. "Sir, I would not dream of it. She only has eyes for you, always has."

James gave a harrumph deep in his throat, but Persa saw the corner of his mouth quiver. They were off to a good start.

That night, Persa fussed over him, getting him settled into the hodgepodge guest room. His new valet, Jarrod, had packed for two weeks. They loaded the entire trunk of the sports car with luggage, though he only brought in one bag. He shooed Persa out. But she kissed his forehead like he was a five-year-old and tucked him into bed.

As he dozed off, he realized for the first time in seven years he was not worried about the monster.

A New Hand

At breakfast the next morning, Peter consumed a half a dozen eggs, four pieces of toast, and eight pieces of bacon. Through mouthfuls, he mentioned his father was on an extended trip overseas. "He is going to Europe, then down to Egypt. We all know he is persona non grata in the Golden Kingdom, so he is not going there. But he mentioned taking a side trip to Persia." Peter made a dismissive gesture. "I start at the Royal Military Academy in September, which is about the time he gets home." His grin telegraphed how pleased he was with that turn of events.

James sat back in his chair. "Well, if you are looking for work. We've got three foals coming. I could use an extra hand for the summer. It doesn't pay much, room, board, and forty-five a week. It's hard work, but it's yours if you are interested."

Peter turned his emerald eyes to James. "Are you serious?"

"Are you?" James countered.

Peter looked up, considering. "I will have to work out some scheduling. There are a few things on the calendar I might have to do, but I think I can get out of them." Peter crossed his arms over his chest. "Okay, but on a few conditions."

The corner of James' mouth twitched. "Such as?"

"You cannot tell anybody I am here. And you have to treat me like you would anybody else."

"Anybody else would sleep in the tack room," James deadpanned.

Peter thought of the solid night's sleep he'd gotten in the guest room. When he smiled, his left dimple showed. "I will pull rank on the guest room, I suppose."

Persa laughed over her soapy sink of dishes but did not say a word.

Manure

The Pepperwood Ranch settled into a new routine with their summer help. Peter worked hard under James' guidance, and Persa enjoyed the conversation. James, always a man of few words, found he was not obliged to say much with the Prince in residence, which suited him just fine. The kid grew an inch in his first week. Their grocery bill doubled. But he was strong, polite, and good with the horses.

For security reasons, he made himself scarce when visitors or delivery drivers came. But one afternoon James and Persa were in the far pastures when a potential buyer dropped in. When the stranger showed up in the barn, Peter saw no way out.

He lowered his ball cap, adopted a Southern drawl, and ambled forward with an outstretched hand. "Howdy, sir. May I help you?"

The man in the suit looked at Peter with disdain, and flared his nose, shoving his hands in his pockets. "Yes. I am here to see the proprietor."

Peter narrowed his eyes, staring at the pompous man. He knew this social-climbing sycophant. Charles ben something or other, Peter couldn't remember. The last time Peter saw him, he chased him around a charity event, kissing his ass. Now, because he was dressed in a pair of jeans and work boots, the guy wouldn't even shake his hand. Peter guessed he was at Pepperwood because he heard the Royal delegation was coming and wanted to say he bought his horses from the same stable. Peter hated men like this. They surrounded his father.

"James will be around shortly, I reckon. In the meantime, is there something I can help you with?"

The man pulled out a lace handkerchief and pressed it to his nose. "You could help me by stepping away. You have a powerful aroma of manure about your person."

Peter noted the full wheelbarrow of manure sitting three feet from the man and had the insane urge to dump it on him. While that might make him feel better, it would hurt Persa and James. And there were better ways to deal with his kind. He stepped back and said, "Pardon me, sir. But you are in a stable and standing in said manure." The fastidious man danced backward. He'd not been standing in any, but Peter wanted to see his reaction. "I'll go find one of the owners."

Lightning was grazing in the front pasture. Peter whickered, and she came trotting over. He opened the gate and swung up on her bareback, going to fetch James or Persa. He found James first.

"You have a customer at the barn."

James put the long fence pliers in his tool belt, the brim of his hat shading his eyes. "They recognize you?"

"Nope. Charles ben Dickhead did not recognize me. He would not even shake my hand. He is lucky I did not punch him."

"I guess I'm lucky you didn't punch him," James said, walking toward the barn. "Go on. Make yourself scarce. I'll deal with the man." Peter did not see the smile that broke across James' face as he walked away, muttering Charles ben Dickhead.

Twenty-five minutes later, James heard the roar of a sports car coming down the driveway. How the little shit got the thing out of its hiding place and up the road without him hearing was a mystery. Bracing himself for whatever was coming, he tried to stay focused on Mr. ben Dickhead. James agreed it was an apt name for the man. He knew nothing about horses. He seemed more concerned with Pepperwood's clientele than he was about the animal he claimed to be interested in. James would not have sold the man a free cat.

Prince d'Or made a glorious appearance, literally reflecting the sun in his snowy white shirt and golden hair. James noted with some amusement that he still wore his work boots and dirty jeans.

Dickhead gasped and rushed forward, effusing greetings.

Peter timed it perfectly. He took three steps forward and pretended to trip. He caught himself, using the man, and guiding him straight into the wheelbarrow full of manure.

James pivoted away, smothering a laugh. Lord, he loved that kid.

Persa nearly choked to death over dinner that night when Peter told her the story.

James tried to look stern, but his twitching lip gave him away. "The best part was when Mr. Charles ben Dickhead tried to get up and flipped the wheelbarrow, dumping the manure all over himself."

Peter bent over, laughing, "He was at my feet, brushing turds away and apologizing."

James held up his hand for Peter to stop. "I missed that, Jupiter's Moon, he was not!"

"He… he.. was… covered in horse shit, groveling down there, saying, 'my Esteemed, my Esteemed.'" Peter held his stomach, crying.

Persa could not breathe, she was laughing so hard.

James pinched the bridge of his nose, his shoulders convulsing in laughter.

It was a good night on the Pepperwood Ranch.

Sunday Night Alone

The second week Peter was in residence, he insisted James and Persa go to Rivergate for Sunday dinner. No matter how much cajoling Persa did, he refused to join them. Truth be told, he looked forward to a little alone time. He surmised that in his entire life, he had never been in a house by himself. The guards surrounding the property did not count.

Feeling magnanimous, he dutifully informed the agent in charge that Persa and James were out for the night. "Yeah, Mack, I have the phone. It is quiet around here. You guys have been great. Thank you."

Agent Mack ben Robert looked at the phone like it was broken. In the two years he guarded the Prince, Peter never once said thank you. "You're welcome. Enjoy your night, my Esteemed."

"Good night, Mack." Peter disconnected the line and settled back on the new sofa. It was a comfortable suede, sage green with tan piping. He stretched and yawned. The house was quiet; no servants moving about. The northern California night was cool, the air still and peaceful. There were no protestors outside the gates, or security radios buzzing, none that he could hear at any rate.

His new bed was nice, and he had a sneaking suspicion they upgraded the mattress when he decided to stay; but he was not complaining. The ninety shekels in his wallet felt better than he could have imagined. He liked the horses. He even liked the work.

They were good company. James was an interesting fellow, quiet and steady, an honorable man and an amazing horseman. Persa, he adored, his genuine friend, despite their age difference. He extricated himself from his official duties and would not have to stand in a receiving line for at least six weeks. Best of all, Pepperwood smelled nice, like new furniture, hay, and the fruit cobbler Persa made tonight. For two full weeks, he had not smelled sulfur.

His stomach growled, so he got up and attempted to construct a sandwich. It was a disaster, but he ate it anyway because he made it. He enjoyed being Peter the stable hand. It beat the hell out of being Prince d'Or, unless he got to knock some dickhead in the manure. He just needed to figure out how to combine the two. But that was a tall order for a fourteen-year-old kid.

Part 7 - Joanna and Ian

July 15, 995 ME (Ten Years into Rebellion)

We Never Saw That Kid Again - Pepperwood

It happened by accident, but long ago, Ian ben Kole realized that just about everything happened by design. He traveled to Pepperwood to help James and Persa welcome a group from the Center for Street Kids of Alanthia. The campers arrived, a raggedy group of street-tough kids that did not know straw from hay, who had surely never mucked out a stall. His mother, Salome, conceived of the idea through her charity work with the Center. Her Lady's Group raised the money to sponsor ten campers to spend a week among the horses, the redwoods, and the river. James recruited Ian to help.

There he met Elijah, and from Elijah, he learned the truth about the disappearing kids in the New City. Elijah never stopped talking. But he had a keen mind and a sharp wit, which made the constant chatter tolerable in small doses. Everything on the kid was pointed, sharp elbows, nose, and ears. He reminded Ian of an elf. He was twelve but could have easily been mistaken for eight. As a consequence, he acted like a banty rooster, ready to fight, but managed to use his rapier tongue as often as his boney knuckles.

The entire visit, he never stopped talking, mucking out stalls, riding on a lead line, hiking through the forest, paddling the canoe. Elijah spoke more words in a day that Ian did in a month. Toward the end of the week, Ian noticed Elijah's stories often included the phrase, "Yeah, nobody ever saw that kid again." At first, Ian did not pay any attention. Street kids were transient in nature, drifting in and out of shelters and towns. But the frequency of the phrase quickened his spirit and brought him up short.

Walking back from the river, Ian asked, "Elijah, how long have you lived at the Center?"

Elijah's eyes brightened. They always did when somebody engaged with him. "I'm an original, been there since the beginning. It opened June 1, 992. So, I guess a little over three years."

Before the child could go into further explanations, Ian asked, "How many kids live there?"

"Perms or temps? Cause I'm a perm. I've got my own room and everything. You should see it, the best one on the hall. I will tell you, I've got—"

Ian held up his hand. "How many permanent kids?"

Elijah looked up, calculating. "Well, the Center has grown since we first opened. I'd say now there are fifty perm kids, and ten temp kids at any given time. Those temps are the ones moving in and out, usually brought in by the police after a domestic or whatnot. But yeah, that's about right. Why?"

Ian ignored the question. "How many have gone missing?"

Elijah frowned. "I don't know, loads of 'em. Happens all the time. Street kids are stupid, not like me. I know a good thing when I see it. I've got my own room, three meals a day. It's safe. Sometimes those temps are rough, and every once in a while, we get a wise guy that thinks he's going to run the place. But the Center is better than the street, drugging and pimping and dying out there."

"Where is the Center? I've never been there."

Elijah shrugged. "We ain't in the fanciest part of town. You know where Prince Eamonn's Park is?" He launched into detailed directions, highlighting his favorite restaurants, stores, and hangouts.

Ian decided to check the place out.

August 1, 995 ME

Growing Pains–New City

Judith's green eyes beamed with excitement as she burst into Joanna's office, a fat envelope in her hand. "I think this letter is what you have been waiting for!"

Joanna looked up from a complicated grant application, perturbed at the interruption, but the return address on the parcel stopped a retort on her lips. She closed her eyes in silent prayer and gingerly took the letter.

Judith sat down heavily. "Well, go ahead. Open it."

Joanna weighed the envelope, the heft an encouraging sign. Denial letters were usually a single page. "I will, but not quite yet."

"Fine. I just thought you might want someone to share the good news with. If I'm not that important..." She stalked toward the door in a huff.

Joanna furrowed her brow and said, "That's not what I meant. You know how important you are. But I need to finish this proposal and send it off. Then I'll open this. It might just be standard compliance documents."

"Okay," Judith sulked, looking hurt.

When the door closed, Joanna rubbed her temples and sighed. Judith had always been mercurial, waxing between sobs and temper. Some days, she was a lamb, some days, a bear. But the impending birth of her second child made her mood swings worse. The latest father was sadly no better than the first. The woman's personal life amounted to a series of disasters. Daily drama reduced her to tears or fits of rage.

Joanna was infinitely patient, ready with a tissue, a sympathetic ear, and a word of advice. She afforded Judith ample time to take care of the catastrophe du jour. Despite her challenges, her work got done. With the growth of the Center, the pressure rested squarely on Joanna's shoulders. She needed at least one person she could delegate to. Judith did her job on time, under budget, and without a ton of direction from Joanna. For that convenience, she put up with the tears, mood swings, and the ongoing saga of Judith's life.

Squinting at the grant application, she ignored the temptation of the envelope. She pressed on, disciplined to finish every task she started before beginning another. Otherwise, she would have half-finished things everywhere.

Her door opened again. Joanna closed her eyes, searching for patience. "Yes?" she said, an edge in her voice, not looking up.

"You have a visitor," Judith snapped.

Joanna dropped her pen, feeling harassed. "Who is it?"

"A Mr. ben Kole," Judith said, then added impatiently, "Listen, Joanna, I'm busy too. Do you want me to send him in or not?"

Joanna's brows furrowed in surprise. "James ben Kole?"

"He did not say." Judith glared, her imposing bulk filling the doorway. She looked miserable.

"Are you all right?" she asked, as much to keep the peace as to find out if Judith was okay.

Right on cue the chin trembled, and she answered in a shaky voice, "I got court papers today. Jones is seeking visitation with Amber, after all these years of not paying child support or wanting anything to do with her." She buried her face in her swollen hands.

"Oh, I'm sorry. I am sure that is very upsetting. Do you need the afternoon off?"

The corners of Judith's mouth quivered, and she nodded convulsively, tears swimming. "Yeah, okay, but I will need to place that order with Safe Supplies and finish the payables, but I think I will. Thanks, Joanna. I'll see you tomorrow."

Joanna rubbed the bridge of her nose. "No, I won't be in tomorrow. I have a lunch meeting in Sacramento at noon. Then there is the Wells Foundation fundraiser tomorrow night."

"Oh, well, have fun."

Joanna smiled weakly. A fifteen-hour day with the last eight spent in an evening gown and heels; networking and raising money was not exactly fun. "Thanks. I hope you feel better. Tell Mr. ben Kole I will be out in five minutes, okay?"

"Sure. Would you like me to bring some tea?" Judith's mood shifted to sugar. She knew she crossed a line earlier.

Joanna smiled, accepting the olive branch. "No, I appreciate it, though."

Judith returned the smile. "No problem, I'll see you on Thursday then."

Joanna pushed the grant application aside and took up the envelope. The letter was the news they had been waiting for. The Lenox Foundation approved the New Orleans project. The Center was expanding.

She had done it.

Now she just had to figure out how to clone herself.

The Right Place at the Right Time

Ian ben Kole studied the picture boards hanging in the lobby. He smiled when he spotted Elijah, sitting in the room he was so proud of. The walls were plastered with posters, ranging from sports stars to comic book characters, and his bed was loaded with stuffed animals.

He guessed the office had once been an outbuilding to store machinery. The great doors had been replaced with floor to ceiling windows. The receptionist cube sat empty and looked unused. The desk was stacked with catalogs, mail, and ledgers. They stashed assorted broken equipment behind the partition. The conference room was pristine, the chairs comfortable. Large windows overlooked a playground and a vegetable garden. Joanna ben Luke knew her business.

Though, the huge pregnant woman that greeted him was not welcoming. Surly and harassed, she seemed annoyed by his presence. But he surmised working with troubled children took a toll. Besides, she looked like she was about to give birth any moment.

When she waddled around the corner, her demeanor completely changed. "Miss ben Luke asks for five minutes but will be with you shortly. Can I get you anything? Water, tea?"

"No, thank you. I appreciate it," Ian answered and smiled. "When is the baby due?"

Her expression became dreamy, and she absently rubbed her belly, focusing inward. "In three months, we are so excited."

He controlled his expression and said, "I am sure you are. Babies are a blessing from the Lord."

"A blessing… yes." Her large green eyes became unfocused as she stared off into space, shuffling into her office without a word.

Ian watched her go, thinking she was rather odd. Moving to the second wall of pictures, he studied them, pondering what he was going to do. He woke up and felt led here.

He lived a strange life since that fateful afternoon in the MASH tent. He got up every morning, and in faith, did what the Lord told him to do, much to the hysterical nagging of his mother, who had great aspirations for her youngest son. For eight years, Ian traveled the world. He had been a truck driver, a preacher, a brick mason, a cook, a security guard, a clerk, a fisherman, and held a whole host of other jobs. He did not question the calling any longer, rarely knew why or to whom he was being sent. Inevitably, he found he was in the right place, at the right time. Today, he was at the Center for the Street Kids of Alanthia.

Seven minutes later, Ian heard the brisk tapping of high heels. He turned and got his first glimpse of Lady Joanna ben Luke. She was nothing like he imagined. His mental image had been a sturdy matron in her sixties, which she was not. She might be the fastest walker he had ever seen, moving on strong, curvy legs.

Joanna extended her hand three feet from him, coming fast. "Mr. ben Kole?" There was a questioning note in her voice, and she was trying not to stare at his hair.

He was used to the reaction and figured she had been expecting James. "Yes, ma'am. I'm Ian ben Kole, James' brother."

She gave him a firm handshake and said, "Yes, of course, welcome, I am Joanna ben Luke." She paused, and he could see her mind working. "You were at Pepperwood with the campers last week, weren't you?"

It was a statement rather than a question. He had to pass a police background check before he could visit his brother and sister-in-law while they were hosting the camp. "I was indeed."

Joanna gave a quick motion with her chin, causing her golden-brown hair to swing around her shoulders. "Come, let's go to my office, and you can tell me what brings you by today." She turned, her heels beating a rapid staccato down the hall. This time he noticed her generous rear end, and the way the black dress swished back and forth as she padded away at eight miles an hour.

Ian was tired just watching her.

Her office was a peculiar mix of children's drawings, grant proposals, and an incongruous painting that looked like it belonged in a museum. There was a plant in the corner that had seen better days and four gigantic filing cabinets. She radiated an energy that reminded him of Beau Landry's formidable mother, Sarah. It struck him in that moment why he was here. The logo on the letter drew his eye. Sarah's unmistakable signature was at the bottom. "You are working with the Lenox Foundation?"

Joanna's face brightened, and her brown eyes sparkled. "We are. They were the original supporters of the Center, and we just received word that they have selected us to open a new facility in New Orleans."

"Well, congratulations. I guess that's why I'm here." Ian settled into the chair she indicated. At her questioning look, he smiled. "Beau Landry is my best friend. He has been for more than a decade. I believe I might be of assistance to you."

Joanna's head tilted as she regarded him, her mind running through his family tree and the advantages of having a personal intimate of the Landry clan working on the expansion. Joanna had run the Center long enough to know talk was easy. A parade of volunteers came and went, very few stuck around. However, Ian's family fell firmly in the 'actually did something' category, so he might be serious.

She heard the lobby door shut as Judith left. She glanced at the clock, 3:00 pm, almost a full day by Judith's standards. Joanna returned her attention to Ian, who was bearing up under her scrutiny well. That was one of the ways she vetted them. If they wouldn't meet her eyes, they weren't serious. At length, she asked. "I certainly appreciate the offer, Mr.

ben Kole. In what capacity do you think you might be able to assist the Center?"

The corner of Ian's mouth lifted. She got straight down to business, with no hint of flirtation or coyness. She was simply direct. He could tell she was taking his measure, and she wasn't quite sure she liked what she saw. This amused him because women tended to fall all over themselves around him. Great before the war, a terrible temptation since. Ian sensed in Joanna ben Luke a woman he could be friends with, and that was refreshing. "In any capacity you might need me."

She crossed her arms over her ample bosom. "Well, what can you do?"

He mimicked her arm crossing. "Just about everything."

Joanna narrowed her eyebrows, amused. He was teasing her, which nobody ever did. "What do you do for a living?"

He returned her expression and repeated, "Just about everything."

She remembered his background check. But what was missing in his roster of jobs was charity work. She had no idea what brought him here today, other than the fact that Lenox might want an inside person on the expansion. But the grant had not stipulated that. A more likely scenario was that Beau Landry told him about the grant, and he swooped in to help. Dozens of folks came and went. In her experience, it was best to weed them out before she wasted time. "Mr. ben Kole, I appreciate the offer. I honestly do. But I have to warn you. This is not glamorous. Most people operate under the delusion that they are going to change the world, that the work is going to fill a hole in their lives, they are going to help these kids, and everything will be fabulous. The reality is many of these kids are troubled, and they will break your heart. The hours are long, the pay is terrible, and we lose more than we win. There is never enough money. The need is greater than we are equipped to handle. We drown in paperwork. There is a constant need to fundraise. Half the people don't care and start avoiding you because they think you are going to ask them for donations. In all, we spend as much time on peripheral items as we do on our mission."

"Sounds familiar," Ian said, enjoying the little speech.

"Why do you want to get involved?"

Long ago, he stopped answering that question because the Lord told me to. He watched her closely and waited, waited for the answer to come. He smiled, gratified when it came. "Because there are not two of you, and you are going to need my help."

Joanna drew back in surprise. Moved by an impulse she did not understand, she stood up and reached across the desk, offering her hand. "All right, Mr. ben Kole. Get ready to work harder than you've ever worked in your life."

Ian rose and shook her hand. "When do you want me to start?"

"Tomorrow. We've got lunch in Sacramento and a black-tie fundraiser at the Ritz tomorrow night. I assume you have formal wear?" At his nod, she added, "If you are still around, we'll talk about Thursday then."

August 2, 995 ME

Friends

"Do you actually live with your mommy?" Joanna asked by way of greeting, as Ian climbed into her car.

"Good morning to you, too," he answered, sliding the passenger's seat back to make room for his long legs.

"Did she pack your lunch?"

Ian buckled his seatbelt and gave her a baleful stare. "I take it you are not a morning person."

Joanna reached into the center console and chugged a cup of coffee. "No, I'm not. There's a coffee for you, if you want it."

"I think you need it more than I do," Ian said, watching the trees fly by. She drove as fast as she walked.

She shrugged but remained silent.

Settling into the passenger seat, he did not say a word as his life flashed before his eyes. She was a maniac, muttering curses at the other drivers, flying past everyone. The irony of her impatience amused him. Even at thirty miles an hour, they were currently traveling faster than the rest of the world, who still relied on horsepower.

"Nice car," Ian said, breaking the silence at 10:30 am.

"Thanks. It's just a tool, though. I couldn't do what I do without it," she answered absently, her mind elsewhere.

"You work a lot?"

Joanna gave a dismissive shrug. "It's pretty much all I do."

He gathered that. She had not said a single thing that was not related to the Center. Other than the crack she made about him living with his mother, which he only did when he was in the New City. He did not have a permanent residence. His lifestyle never called for one. "What else do you do, hobbies, friends, significant others?"

"I have friends. You will meet many of them tonight at the fundraiser." Joanna grinned as she overtook the pack of cars and moved into the lead.

"Friends you see outside of fundraisers?" Ian pressed.

Joanna looked at him with hooded eyes. When she ran her tongue over her upper teeth, it looked like she was contemplating taking a bite out of him. "Why all the questions?"

"I suppose we will be spending time together. I am trying to get to know you," Ian answered, completely nonplussed by her demeanor.

"Oh," she answered, as if holding a conversation was unusual, a foreign concept that she was willing to try. She spent the next ten minutes telling him about her work, how the Center started, and the projects she was overseeing. Then she launched into their objectives for the luncheon and the fundraiser tonight. The only human she mentioned was Judith.

"So, Judith is your friend?" Ian asked at the end of her recitation.

Joanna let out an exasperated laugh. "That is complicated. But I suppose over the years we have become friends. We've been together a long time, since the beginning. I attribute much of the success of the Center to her. She is brilliant at what she does."

"But?" Ian prompted.

Joanna sighed. "She can be difficult. Most people can't work with her, which is why I moved her to the business offices with me." She gave him a rueful smile. "But that is just Judith. I'm used to her."

A long silence ensued before she added, "I guess I know how it feels when people don't care for you because you are different. If you seem intense or focused or passionate, they don't understand you."

Ian looked out the window. She just described his life for the last eight years. He lived in a world that he was not part of, existing on the periphery, alone. And no one understood why he did it. "Joanna, I understand that completely."

She turned, and he saw something in her golden-brown eyes. They reflected his own feelings. A kinship passed between them, comfortable and kind. Joanna smiled, and Ian smiled back. On the road to Sacramento, a friendship was born.

Runaways

Twenty minutes later, Joanna declared, "Ha! I do have a friend."

Ian gave her a half-smile, leaned against the door, and crossed his arms. "Do tell."

"Well, I've been sitting here thinking about what you said, and I do have a friend." She grinned, oozing smug satisfaction.

He raised a brow at her. "One not related to work?"

She pursed her lips, staring at the road. "Well, sort of." Ian gave a bark of laughter, which she ignored. "He's a police officer. As a matter of fact, I have a bunch of friends, an entire precinct."

"That you met through work," Ian teased.

Joanna made a frustrated snort. "That's not fair. Just because I met them through work, doesn't mean they aren't friends."

"Okay. Do you go to their houses for dinner? Do you call them to chat or catch up?"

"No. But if I need any of them, they will come. Elias was at the Center the other day," she declared and raised her chin in defiance.

The hair on the back of Ian's neck stood up. "Why was a police officer at the Center?"

Joanna's shoulders drooped. "We had another runaway. I have to report them."

Ian chose his words carefully. "Elijah mentioned that happens often."

Joanna got a faraway look. "Unfortunately."

"That must be hard."

He saw the first crack in the shell around Lady Joanna ben Luke when she answered in a quavering voice. "More than you know."

Working with this woman and these kids, Ian ben Kole had a pretty good idea he was about to find out.

August 11, 995 ME

Chinese Takeout

On his tenth day at the Center, Ian walked into Joanna's office and asked, "What are we eating?"

She looked up, distracted. "What? Food?"

"Yes, Joanna, we mere mortals have to eat."

She rubbed her eyes, clearing away the cobwebs. "Didn't we just do that?"

Ian shot her a look. "At noon, it's seven o'clock."

Joanna took a drink of water from the massive tankard she kept on her desk. "I'm going to get fat hanging around you."

He ignored her. She obsessed over her weight, and he was done telling her she wasn't fat. "Chinese?"

"Are you going to go get it?" She narrowed her eyes at him.

"I've gone the last three times, it's your turn."

"Pfft, you are the one who's hungry." She made a face at him, which he returned. Joanna laughed and rifled through the takeout menus. "Tell me what you want."

Ian heard her car start a few minutes later and went back to the plans spread across his desk. He took up residence in the small office beside Joanna's, moving in under the suspicious glare of Judith. Joanna had been right about three things. He had never worked harder, Judith was a character, and the work was going to break his heart. He felt a presence in the room and looked up. Elijah's pointed face peered around the door frame.

"Are we alone?" the elfin boy whispered.

"Yes," Ian answered in a normal tone of voice.

Elijah shushed him and slipped back into the darkened hallway. "Come out here. I don't want anybody to see me through the windows."

Ian got up and joined him. "Why the secrecy?"

"I heard you and Miss Joanna are leaving, going to New Orleans."

Ian studied the youngster who was wearing a purple comic book t-shirt and bright red socks. "That's right. We are opening another facility."

"You remember when we were talking about those kids that went missing?" Ian nodded. "Well, I been thinking. Every time Miss Joanna leaves, that's when the kids go missing."

"What do you mean?"

Elijah shrugged, "Might be nothing, maybe just a coincidence, but the Center ain't the same when Miss Joanna's not here." He shot a meaningful look at Judith's office. "It turns into something out of Charles Dickson."

"Charles Dickens?" The corner of Ian's mouth lifted.

"Yeah, whatever." Elijah pointed at Judith's office. "That's a mean one in there. She walks around like she owns the place, screaming and yelling at everyone. She's run off three or four house managers, including Joe. He was slow and kind of lazy, but we kids liked him. He was nice." Elijah made a low noise in his throat. "Miss Judith hated him, hounded him to death, until he up and quit."

"What are you getting at, Elijah?"

Elijah shrugged his pointed shoulders and moved toward the door. "Nothing. It just occurred to me if she's running off the staff, maybe she's running off those kids. Goodnight, Mr. Ian." With that, he slipped outside.

Ian stared after him for a moment, then walked across the hall and turned on the light in Judith's office. He had avoided it since he started.

The woman bristled with hostility toward him, so he ignored her. Looking around, he saw stacks of files piled two feet high in the corner. Tiny notes of intermittent age covered her desk. A four-level bookshelf overflowed with bags of snacks, candy, and canned goods. Three drinking glasses held pens in a rainbow of colors, and she had vendor branded paraphernalia scattered everywhere. A new computer, monitor, and calculator sat on a guest chair, the new boxes covered in dust. The general atmosphere was unkempt and disorganized. Paper clips, staples, and tiny shreds of paper littered the floor. She refused to let maintenance clean. A gorgeous peace lily thrived on the windowsill, but the matching one in Joanna's office was nearly dead from lack of water.

He heard Joanna come in with the food. His stomach growled. "Conference room?" he offered.

She paused on her way back to her office, looking uncertain.

"Come on, Joanna. It won't kill you to take a minute to eat."

She sighed and followed him.

August 12, 995 ME

Road Trip

Ian waved the piece of paper in Joanna's face. "This document says that I am the official co-head of the New Orleans project and as such, I have an equal say in our operating procedures."

Joanna bulled up at him. "A document which you obtained in an extremely underhanded manner, Ian ben Kole," she shook her head, giving him a baleful look, "by calling your best friend."

"At least I have a friend," he teased.

She crossed her arms over her chest and harrumphed. "Equal say or not, we are not discussing operations for the Center. We are discussing our route to New Orleans, for Heaven's sake."

Ian smiled and leaned back in his chair. He knew he had her. "I have the checkbook."

Joanna tilted her chin at him. "I have the car."

"I've made hotel reservations." He recognized the poker game, so he saw her chin tilt, and raised her a brow. "Along the route I have chosen."

"A route that will take an extra day and a half," she said petulantly.

"Joanna ben Luke, how long have you lived in California?"

Her nose flared. "My entire life."

"Have you ever driven the Ocean Highway to Cambria?"

She looked away, refusing to answer.

"Santa Barbara? Malibu? San Diego?"

She sipped her coffee and looked at her watch, pretending he did not exist.

"Since the grant in '88, have you taken more than two days off in a row?" Ian pressed.

Joanna shifted in her chair, uncomfortable with the turn of the conversation. "What's your point?"

He leaned forward and said, "There is more to life than work. You have a chance to drive down the coast of one of the most beautiful places on Earth, and you are complaining that it is going to take an extra twelve hours."

She set down her cup with a thud. "Fine. Then you are driving all the way to New Orleans. I am going to ride with my feet up on the dash and be a lady of leisure for the next four days."

He smirked, a decided gleam in his eye. "If I'm driving, it will be five." Her eyes bulged, and he barked with laughter. She was so easy.

Ruins

"Why are we stopping?" Joanna looked around at the deserted road. "I thought we were going to eat in the car."

Ian waggled his eyebrows at her. "It's bad for the digestion. Besides, I want to show you something."

"We are never getting to New Orleans," Joanna murmured under her breath.

Ian locked the car door. "Quit moaning, Princess Workaholic. Follow me." With three long strides, he disappeared.

Joanna stood by the car for a moment, shook her head in resignation, and went after him. He set a fast pace, and she had to struggle to keep up, her breath catching. When she crested the hill, she found him waiting for her, an expectant look on his face. She gasped in surprise. "Ian, what is this place?"

He gave a formal bow, making a grand sweeping gesture. "Lady Joanna, these are the ruins of the Hearst Castle. Archeologists have been excavating for the last six or seven months."

"Oh, it is magnificent!" Joanna covered her mouth in awe.

"Pleasant spot to eat lunch." Ian gestured to the mountainside.

Joanna gazed at the fairy-tale castle in wonder. "Can we look around?"

"I thought we were on a strict timetable?" he teased.

Her look told him exactly what he could do with his timetable. "There's more to life than work!" She scampered off, calling over her shoulder. "And I am going to explore!"

Ian heard her laugh as she ran down the hill. He paused for a moment, smiled up to the sky, and winked.

Fish Tacos–Santa Barbara

The wind from the Pacific Ocean blew Joanna's blunt-cut hair off her face. The setting sun cast her skin in a pink glow, and the vague pinched crease between her brows relaxed. She pushed her half-eaten taco away and covered it with a napkin, settling into the slat backed chair. Taking a sip from her large mug of beer, she looked over Ian's shoulder at the sand-hill mountains through hooded eyes. "Santa Barbara is beautiful."

Ian dabbed the corner of his mouth and followed her gaze. "It is." He took a sip of his own ale. "Aren't you glad we took the scenic route?"

Joanna rested her head and exhaled, deep and slow. "I am not even going to rise to that bait. I am too content."

Ian toasted her with his taco. "Exactly my point, Princess Workaholic." He devoured it in a single bite.

"You should be gargantuan, the way you eat."

Through a full mouth, he said, "Fast metabolism."

She snorted. Her metabolism ran a degree faster than a corpse, but she deigned to comment, enjoying her surroundings. The sunset painted the sky in brilliant hues. The water lapped against the pier's pylons, hypnotic and soothing. Late on Tuesday night, they were one of the last diners on the pier. "This is a pretty spot for dinner," she said through a yawn.

He pulled her unfinished food in front of him. "You mind?"

She waved a dismissive hand. "For what we are paying, somebody should eat it."

He rolled his eyes. "You're paying for the ambiance." He chased the taco with a gulp of beer, following it up with a small belch.

Her mouth dropped open in mortified outrage. "Did you just burp in front of me?"

Ian shrugged. "I'm a man. We burp."

"Gross!" she exclaimed in laughing outrage.

Ian snorted at her. "Like you don't burp, Princess."

"Shut up!" She covered her eyes with one hand, shaking her head with embarrassment.

He chuckled and settled back, sipping his beer. He motioned with his glass to the fishing boats. "I spent a summer on one of those a couple of years ago."

She drew up in surprise, considering him. "You have lived an interesting life, Ian ben Kole, but I would not have pegged you as a fisherman."

Ian yawned. True to her word, she made him drive the whole way, and he chased after her for three hours while she frolicked among the ruins. Fatigue and alcohol loosened his tongue. "I get called to do a lot of things. Sometimes I'm a fisherman, sometimes a fisher of men."

A quip died on her lips. He was serious. In the eleven consecutive days they spent together, this was the first truly personal thing he shared. She accepted the gift. "I know a bit about difficult callings."

A slow smile spread over his face, which was amazing. It was a genuine smile that showed both upper and lower teeth all the way back to his molars. It lit up the pier and demanded one in return. Her smile was not so spectacular, but she gave him one anyway. Their eyes met, soft and hooded, companions and friends, easy in each other's company.

August 15, 995 ME

Chicken Fried Steak - Houston

"That is the biggest plate of food I have ever seen in my life." Joanna's eyes bulged as the waitress set a platter in front of Ian, sporting an enormous batter-fried, gravy-covered piece of beef, so large it hung over the plate.

Ian rubbed his hands together in anticipation, not sparing her a glance. "And I am going to eat every bite of it."

"What in the hell is chicken fried steak?"

He moaned with delight, chewing with his eyes closed. "The only kind of hell I will ever get close to, Princess."

"Isn't there a commandment against gluttony?".

"No." Ian patted his flat stomach. "My body is a temple to the Holy Spirit, and the Holy Spirit loves chicken fried steak." He took an enormous bite and said, "My brother loves it, too."

She shook her head, picking at the house salad dressed with lemon juice. "Well… let me try it." He cut her a generous piece and passed her the fork. "Not that big," she protested.

Ian gave her a long-suffering look, then sliced a microscopic piece. She laughed. "You are a brat."

He agreed, chuckling. "My brother will tell you that, too." He handed her a normal, human-sized bite.

She eyed it dubiously but went for it. She chewed absently and then shrugged. "It's okay."

"Okay?" He took back his fork, scandalized. "You don't know anything about good food, with your dry salads and your half sandwiches on wheat bread with no mayo."

"Huh," she snorted, "I know enough about food to know that if I ate a quarter of what you do every day I'd be sitting here on two chairs. I've gained at least five pounds since I met you, and that's eating those salads."

Ian raised an eyebrow at her.

She tried to scowl, she really did, but was completely unsuccessful. "Shut up."

Between bites of mashed potatoes, green beans, and chicken fried steak, he threw out a comment that stopped her cold. "So, when are you going to ask me? I know you are dying to."

Joanna scratched her head and pretended she had no idea what he was talking about. "Ask you what?"

Ian looked at her from beneath his long dark lashes and pointed to his white hair. "How I got it." He tilted his head, considering. "I think you've gone the longest of anyone I've ever spent time with and not asked."

Joanna crossed her arms over her chest. "Well, I'm not going to ask. I figured you would tell me if you wanted me to know." She hoped he would tell her. She hoped he would tell her right now, but she was never going to ask.

The corner of Ian's mouth lifted. He recognized a challenge. He'd been prepared to give her the fake story, the one he told the world; hereditary trait, a fluke, ran in his family. He eyed her and then started nodding his head slowly, his chin thrust out. "Hmm. Fine. Then I won't tell you."

She matched his raised chin. "Fine. I don't want to know."

He chuckled. "You are the worst liar."

Joanna suddenly found the old wooden plow hanging from the rafters in the rustic restaurant fascinating. At that moment, she decided she would cut out her tongue before she ever asked him.

Ian ben Kole studied her; he was going to have so much fun with this.

August 16, 995 ME

Bienvenue au Bayou - Louisiana

"I really don't feel comfortable with this," Joanna grumbled for the third time that hour. "Please, just take me to a hotel. I have a lot of work to do."

Ian shook his head and kept driving. "That's not how they do things."

Joanna flipped the sun visor down and applied a fresh coat of lip gloss in the mirror. She morphed into her professional persona. A dramatic change from his traveling companion of the last four days, who wore jeans, t-shirts, and not a speck of makeup. Riding through New Orleans, she looked like the woman he first met. But now he knew who hid behind that mask.

"Ian, I don't even know these people. I met Sarah Landry once, and then only briefly. They are my patrons. I've corresponded with them for years, but to stay at their house? I would be much more comfortable at a hotel."

"I have no doubt you would, but this is the best way." Ian was completely immovable on this point. "The Landrys are a huge family. You have no idea how many there are. They all have money, they all have influence, and they will volunteer to work at the Center... if they like you. But they will only like you if they get to know you. And that will not happen if you stay in a hotel and meet them in a boardroom with a bunch of plans and proposals."

She huffed and muttered in sulky resignation, "I'm more comfortable in a boardroom with plans and proposals."

Ian winked at her and adopted a lazy Cajun cadence, "Life ain't all about work, *chèr*. Sometimes you got to sit back and relax, eat some crawfish, and enjoy a fais-do-do."

Impatient and incredulous, she scowled. "What did you just say?"

He chuckled and turned off the main road, *"Bienvenue au Bayou, chèr."* Welcome to the Bayou.

No Warning

Beau Landry was perhaps the most beautiful human she had ever seen. Joanna's mouth hung open while the two men embraced in a friendly masculine hug. She smoothed her black dress, silently heaping curses on the back of Ian's head. He could have warned her, could have prepared her. Instead, she was poleaxed and completely mortified by her stammering greeting. Feeling a hot blush, she blinked rapidly and composed herself, muttering something inane like, "Hi."

Neither man noticed, a small blessing. She was going to wring Ian's neck. That was just wrong. You shouldn't do that to somebody. He could have said, "Oh, by the way, my friend Beau is a blue-eyed, black-haired, French Cajun god." And that voice, for the love of all that is holy, it should be illegal to have a voice that sexy. With an effort, Joanna relaxed her face, fearing she might look constipated. She whispered a silent prayer, "Please, Father in Heaven, don't let him flirt with me."

The Lord did not answer her prayer. It was cruel.

Ian ducked his head, studying her. "You okay?"

Her smile was overly bright, her voice two octaves higher than normal. "I am just a little tired from the road."

Ian stretched his neck forward, weaving his head like a turtle. "You sure? Your face is flushed."

If looks could kill, Ian ben Kole would be dead. He drew back, and she hissed through clenched teeth for his ears only. "I am going to murder you."

Ian threw up his palms in surrender. "What?"

Joanna rolled her eyes. Truth be told, Ian ben Kole was just as handsome, even shocking with his white hair and his winter blue eyes, but he was her friend. Beau Landry belonged on one of those 'Hot Guy' posters the girls hung in their dorm rooms. "You could have warned me," she muttered, giving a quick nod toward Beau, who was unloading their luggage.

Ian's confusion cleared and the corner of his mouth lifted. "Oh, because he's handsome?"

She tossed her short hair and stalked away, muttering, "That's the understatement of the year."

Best Friends

Joanna regained her composure a half hour after they arrived at Beau's beautiful lake house. Their host had an easy manner, and after the initial abortive attempt at light-hearted flirtation, he had mercy on her. She was tired, which she should not be since the trip was the most leisurely four days of her adult life. Despite that, or perhaps because of it, she excused herself for bed at sunset.

Beau and Ian sat on the back deck, staring out at the lake. Ian said into the darkness. "Where y'at, Beau?"

Beau stroked his short beard and shrugged. "Been a good month."

Ian was encouraged by that. "Put a few of those together, and that's a path forward."

"Could be." Beau did not sound convinced.

"You reach out to her?"

Beau turned his head slowly. "No."

"She's in New York right now," Ian said offhand.

Beau raised his brows and said with exaggerated slowness, "I know where she is, Ian."

Ian shrugged. "Just thought I'd tell you."

"Six months, I put together six solid months, and I'll call her." Beau relaxed back in his chair, his face resolute.

Ian did not pester him. It was an old argument. One that spiraled out of control in '92. They did not speak for two years afterward, Beau referred to them as 'The Dark Years'.

"I see Hector is gone." Ian said, referring to Beau's live-in caregiver.

"Yep. He went home a couple of months ago to take care of his *maman*."

Ian took a swig of his beer. "Are you replacing him?"

Beau rubbed the back of his neck. "I've considered it and will if it gets bad again." He raised his green tea in salute. "I stay out of the alcohol, and I run five miles a day. I watch my diet. I pray, a lot, and spend most of my days on the water. It seems to do the trick." He shook his head ruefully. "I sound like an old man."

"Least you don't look like one," Ian quipped.

"That's true, Whitey," Beau said, watching the fireflies dance at the water's edge. "You ain't never gonna tell me, are you?"

Ian crossed his arms over his chest. "One day, when the Lord tells me I can. I promise, Beau. I will."

Beau drummed his fingers. "That's a bitter pill, *mon frère*."

"Yeah, and one I wouldn't have chosen, but the gift came with a cost."

"That war came with a cost," Beau's quiet voice held the empty haunting of old ghosts. "It comes to me sometimes when I'm sleeping. I wake up, and I can't remember; but it's horrible." He paused. "I know it's got something to do with the Major and his little wife. I know it. You don't have to say, but I see it when I sleep. I reckon you see it when you're awake."

Ian absently pressed a finger in his eye socket but did not speak.

Beau stood up and walked to the railing. The sun disappeared, painting the sky brilliant orange and red. The azure lake looked purple, its waves calm. "I faced it again in the bayou with Alaina, but I can't remember shit." He stretched and continued. "It's like being locked in a prison cell." He gave a humorless laugh. "The thing is, and I can say this to you, I'm not sure I want out. Whatever drove me into the darkness, is still out there. And sometimes it seems safer in this cell. At least when I'm lucid. During the other times, ain't nothing reaching me.

"That's the reason I don't call her, Ian, why I don't go find her." Beau vibrated with self-loathing. "The longest stretch I put together was three months. Then it comes and finds me."

Ian went to stand beside his friend. "I'm sorry."

"The irony of this, *mon amie*, is that two of the people I love most in the world know the truth about what happened, about what I saw, and neither of you will tell me. Y'all each got a key. I haven't asked her in five years." Beau turned and gave Ian a half-smile. "You're easier to pick at."

"Thanks," Ian retorted sarcastically.

Beau motioned toward the house. "We brought that girl down here 'cause she's doing fine work in the New City, and there is a dire need in New Orleans. Something wicked is going on. I can't put my finger on it. But there is a darkness growing, and it ain't just Korah and his mess. That's bad enough, but this feels sinister."

Ian sharpened his attention but held his tongue, afraid he would blurt out the truth.

"You warn that little lady in there?" Beau asked.

The hair on Ian's arms stood on end. "What do you mean?"

Beau's intelligent eyes pierced the darkness. "Maybe nothing, maybe I'm just out of my head. But I'm telling you, I got a bad feeling that those kids ain't running away. Something is getting them."

Ian covered his face and muttered, "Jesus."

Beau snorted, "*Vous êtes un homme courageux!*"

"English…"

"I said, you a brave man to speak that name like you do."

Ian scratched his head with both hands. "Comes with the hair."

"Talk about." Beau gazed out at the dark lake, his lips pressed in a firm line. "Before this is all over, we're going to need what caused that hair, Whitey."

Part 8 - Concurrence

February 14, 997 ME (Twelve Years into Rebellion)

Refugee - Pepperwood

A loud bang on the front door caused Persa to sit straight up in bed. James moved before she could blink. "Stay here!" He barked and pulled on his boxer shorts, padding barefoot out of the bedroom.

Persa threw back the blankets and dressed in haste, listening from the doorway. At James' exclamation, she raced down the steps. Huddled on their front stoop, writhing in agony, was Prince Peter ben Korah. James picked him up with little effort. Peter looked like a prisoner of war, all skin and bones, pasty white with his blond hair long and matted.

James yelled to Persa, "Call an ambulance."

"No," Peter said weakly. "He will find me and kill me for sure. No ambulance. No doctors."

James laid him on the sofa. Persa covered him with a blanket, falling to her knees. "Peter?" She stroked his forehead, noting he was cold. "Oh, Peter, what's happened?"

His nose ran blood and water, and he cradled his right hand. Struggling for words, his breath came in shallow pants. "Torture."

There was a fresh basket of towels at the foot of the steps, Persa dove for one to staunch his wounds. "What do you need? Where are you hurt?" Persa dabbed carefully, muffling her cries.

"There is medicine in the car... in a bag." His lip cracked and blood leaked down his chin. James grabbed a coat, running out the door before he finished the sentence. Peter moaned. "Sorry, Persa, did not know where else to go."

A veil momentarily fell away, and Persa growled. "Marduk! That fucking bastard did this to you, didn't he?"

"Korah did this to me. But he had help. They wear hoods." He closed his eyes in profound sadness and resignation. "Palace… monster lives there… only time it left me alone… when I lived here." Peter lifted a limp hand out to her. She pressed it to her cheek, bathing the cuts in her hot tears. "It hates us. So jealous when I am here."

He swallowed, grimacing at the pain in his throat. "I thought he was going to kill me when I got home in '92." A wracking shudder seized him, and he curled into a ball. "That is why I did not come back." He rolled over, staring at the ceiling. His eyes were bloodshot, his pupils huge.

Persa laid her head beside his, feeling helpless as waves of fury and pain washed over her.

Peter's voice cracked. "It was the best summer of my whole life."

Persa wrapped her arms around him, holding tight. "We love you, Peter."

He started to cry, soft and pitiful. "I am going to die, Pers. But I did not want to do it smelling sulfur."

"No, you aren't going to die." Persa kissed his forehead gently, containing her rage. "He does not have that power. He will not get you. We won't let him."

When James stepped through the door, all thoughts and knowledge of Marduk vanished back into the abyss where they belonged.

James and Persa got down to the business of saving Peter's life. His story unraveled through the long night and into the dawn.

"Told him I would not marry that Egyptian cunt," Peter mumbled. "Still not going to. I do not care what he does to me."

Persa wiped his forehead, pressing kisses to his cheek, reassuring him she would protect him, keep him safe.

Peter's valet, Jarrod, smuggled him out of the Palace, packed a medical bag, and got him in his car. How he managed to drive the three hours north in his condition was nothing short of a miracle. "I thought if I made it here, I might have a chance."

James squeezed his shoulder. "You did good, man. We're glad you're here."

Peter snorted a weak laugh. "You do not seem concerned about me stealing your girl this time." His head lolled toward Persa, and a ghost of his dimple appeared. "Just wait until I am recovered, you little hottie."

Persa laid her cheek on Peter's chest, giving a sad laugh. "Oh, Peter, there you are."

He closed his eyes. "My bones hurt, Persa. Get your head off my chest." He swallowed painfully. "What day is it, anyway?"

James looked at his watch. "It's February 14th."

Peter groaned and covered his face with his hands. Persa saw his right one was a vibrant shade of purple, and the pinky appeared broken. "Bloody Hell, they have been shooting me up since my birthday."

Persa smothered a gasp, noticing for the first time the puncture wounds up and down his arms. "Peter, honey, when is your birthday?"

His voice became dreamy as the medicine took effect. "January 6th. I turned nineteen." He slept.

James let out a deep groan. "What kind of monster does this to their own son?"

"I don't know."

"I'm calling Ian. This boy needs prayer."

Persa turned her head sharply and said, "Don't tell him who's here. No one can know. His life depends on it."

February 24, 997 ME

Home

The rhythmic sound of the bedding rake confirmed James' suspicions; Peter was in the stable. That was a good sign. He entered the barn with a nod, greeted with a chorus of morning whickering from the horses. They worked in silence. Peter kept weaving and bracing himself against the stall time and again, but he pushed on with dogged determination. When he threw the last fork of bedding into Lightning's stall, he slid gracefully down the wall and sat at the old mare's feet.

James handed him a cup of water. Peter accepted it with a trembling hand. "You should go back to the house. Johnson will be over in a bit, he'll finish. Persa has breakfast ready."

Peter rubbed his face, then grabbed the back of his head. When he spoke, his voice sounded listless and bleak. "It is the absolute betrayal. That is the hardest part." He looked up, eyes swimming in pain. "I am his son."

James let out a deep sigh. "And one day you will sit on the throne."

Peter laughed without mirth. "No, that is where you are wrong, my friend. I will never be the Ruling Prince."

James sat down with him, resting his wrist on a bent knee, his face thoughtful. "I don't see where you have much choice in the matter."

Peter cleared his throat and took a drink of water. "I actually do. Alanthia has another choice." There was steel in his voice. "My Cousin Josiah is not dead."

James sucked in his breath with a hiss. "Seriously?"

Peter nodded. "My mother and I helped him escape."

James made a low whistle. "When? Josiah disappeared a few days after Prince Eamonn died, right?"

"Yes." Peter closed his eyes. Every bone in his body hurt. "I think I told Persa, or maybe I dreamed it. I spilled my guts, did I not?"

James looked away. The horror that sprung forth in Peter's delirium was chilling to hear, let alone live through. "We weren't sure what was real, and what was you being out of your head."

Peter rubbed his forehead and snorted. "Well, being tortured for forty-five days and turned into a drug addict ought to give you a pretty good idea what living in Korah's House of Horrors is like."

James set his face, but Peter read the pity in his eyes.

"Poor Prince d'Or." Peter snorted ruefully. "Bit different from the public image, is it not? The world would be shocked." He thumped his head on the back of the stall. "Most of what they print about me is lies. I play the role though, ridiculous, empty-headed, playboy. Up until now, it kept me alive, but he believes it." He blew out a shaky breath and rested his elbow over his eyes. "I think he has always hated me."

James' nose flared. Korah systematically painted his son as a wastrel and an idiot. He did it with such covert manipulation that very few ever saw beyond the lies to the truth. It was strategic, designed to weaken and undermined Peter. It kept him from becoming a threat to Korah's power. "I should have never let you go back in '92," James said through gritted teeth, vibrating in fury. "I had a bad feeling when you left."

Peter banged his head against the stall, the chords in his neck taut. "We could not have stopped him." Images of fists flying and his mother screaming flashed across his brain. "Not then, maybe not now. But if I can stay for a while, I might be able to figure something out." His words were a mix of desolation and determination.

James swallowed a lump in his throat and said thickly, "Peter, you can stay forever, if you want. You always have a home here."

Peter's face contorted, and he turned away. "Damn, James, do not make me cry."

James put his arm around Peter's shoulder until he gathered himself.

Peter palmed his eyes with the heels of his hand and said, "I appreciate it. I have a lot to figure out."

"How do you know your cousin is still alive?" James probed tentatively.

Peter wiped his hands on his jeans and stretched his neck. When he spoke, James got a glimpse of the man the Prince had become in the intervening years, calm, calculating, deadly. "I have my ways, James. I am not without resources."

A slow smile built, one of James' toothy ones that lit his brown eyes and wrinkled the sunbaked lines at their corners. "So, you're going to fight that son of a bitch?" At Peter's nod, James grew serious. "You know I did, right? We never really talked about it, but I fought that wicked bastard in the '86."

Peter set his mouth in a firm line. "What the Civil War taught us, is that we cannot fight him that way. I am working on a different plan."

James narrowed his brows. "You still need to know how to fight. While you are here, we'll make sure you can defend yourself. I have a thing or two I can teach you."

Peter held out his bruised right hand, the pinky finger splinted and wrapped. The bruise extended up his arm, yellow and deep purple, ugly. He pulled up his sleeve. Needle marks covered his forearm, a roadmap to hell. His nose flared as he stared at the wounds. When he looked up, there was hatred in his emerald eyes. "I think that is an excellent idea."

James nodded in cool determination. "Come on then, we'll start with breakfast."

March 2, 997 ME

The Anger Stage

The power of anger swept away the pain, the betrayal, the fear. Free of the oppressive presence of Korah and Marduk, Peter felt as if a millstone had been removed from around his neck. He slung it into orbit. Addiction clawed at him, so he substituted it with caffeine and nicotine. He smoked like a chimney and drank pots of coffee.

On day sixteen, Persa found him at 4:00 am working on a computer that mysteriously arrived at the house. She stood in the doorway of his bedroom bleary-eyed, her strawberry blonde hair a tangled mess. "Are you still awake?"

He looked up with a guilty expression. "Sorry, Fey."

She rubbed her face and moved beside him, resting her small hand on his shoulder. "Are you talking to somebody on that thing?"

He dropped a weary head to her hand. "Not talking exactly." He yawned, loud and masculine.

The screen was hard to look at, the glare rough on her sleep sensitive eyes. She squinted at the strange characters, the lines loading and flashing. "What is that?"

"Computer code."

Persa yawned and asked, "Can you read what it says?"

Peter stretched long arms above his head, his shoulders making a loud popping noise. "Enough to be dangerous." He smiled up at her with impish mischief. "Which is exactly the point, right?"

Persa wrinkled her nose at him. "Be careful. I didn't nurse you back to health for you to go out and get yourself killed." Her tone was light, but her words were serious.

"I am no hacker, Pers, but I believe I found a couple."

"Don't tell me." She held up her hand, "I do not want to know."

The program finished, and the screen went blank. Peter rose from the chair like an old man. Hours in the same position, the lingering effects of his ordeal, and lack of sleep made him creaky. At 6'1", he towered over Persa. He pulled her into a hug. His hair, which had not been cut for several months, hid his face when he kissed the top of her head. "No, you do not want to know. The less you and James are involved with what I am doing, the safer you will be."

March 14, 997 ME

It's Time

"How old is this horse?" Peter asked, brushing Lightning's white coat.

James snorted. "Old as Methuselah."

Peter ran his hands over her fine flanks. "She is in good shape. Did I hear Persa say this was her horse when she was a little girl?"

James leaned on the stall door. "She was Persa's mother's. We don't know how old she is. We brought her from Rivergate, but there are no records on her."

Peter gave Lightning an affectionate pat on the rump. "I have never heard Persa mention her mother. What happened to her?"

James shook his head. "That's a touchy subject with Fey. She ran off when Persa was a baby."

Peter paused, "I wish my father would have run off when I was a baby."

James gave a humorless chuckle. "We'd have all been a hell of a lot better off if he had." He hefted a bag of feed and resumed his work.

Peter picked up the brushes. Lightning nudged him affectionately as he exited the stall. "It has been a month. I think it is time you teach me how to fight."

James froze mid-stride and turned, his eyes cold and calculating. "Well, you can ride. Why don't we start there?"

May 15, 997 ME

Serendipity–Montreal - Alaina

"Serendipity" was the name of the photograph that changed the course of Alaina ben Thomas' life. Taken on December 12, 990 ME, she was sitting at the edge of Prince Eamonn's Fountain, staring across the bay, unaware of the photographer. Some argued it was her body that made the picture so arresting, long-limbed and perfectly proportioned. Others said it was her classic California girl next door blonde beauty that captured the attention of the fashion world and the kingdom. Art critics claimed the mystery came from her enigmatic expression. Was she happy or sad; it was impossible to tell, but everyone wanted to know. Serendipity became the Mona Lisa of the Millennium. It launched Alaina's career and made her a Super Star.

French Bread - Montreal - Alaina

Fashion Week, Alaina vowed this was going to be one of her last. She was too old for this, and she was hungry. Who visited Montreal and did not eat bread? Who? Fashion models, that's who. "Ellen!" Alaina called from her dressing room. "I want food when I get done. Do you hear me?"

Alaina's business partner and executive assistant, Ellen ben Quincy, replied in a sing-song tone, "I have grapes and carrots out here."

"I hate you," Alaina retorted. She applied the final touches to her makeup and sat back, studying her face with a critical eye.

"You hate being hungry. You don't hate me," Ellen answered, still in the next room.

Alaina could tell she was distracted, the keystrokes of the computer discernable as Ellen took care of the innumerable details that came with being the world's foremost fashion model. "What time is it?"

"You have a clock in there," Ellen countered. "It's 3:30 pm. We have to go in five minutes."

Alaina made a sound of disgust deep in her throat at the perceived imperfections on her twenty-six-year-old face. "I don't want to do this anymore."

The typing stopped, and Ellen appeared in the doorway. Alaina watched her in the mirror's reflection. Ellen was as tall as Alaina, dark-haired and sultry eyed. Since giving up modeling and becoming Alaina's assistant, she had filled out from bone-thin to bombshell. She had full hips, big breasts, and a tiny waist. Alaina whirled around and stared at her in outrage. Ellen was eating a piece of French bread with what looked suspiciously like butter. The bitch!

Ellen smiled, sly as a cat. "You are making two-point-five million shekels a year for walking down a runway and shaking your ass. So you're hungry? Who cares? Shut up."

"Bah! Easy for you to say, standing over there eating your bread." Alaina sulked, but the corner of her mouth quivered. "I never really wanted to do this."

A black brow lifted in an expression that clearly telegraphed that Ellen heard that particular lament about a billion times. "Yes, Alaina. We all know."

Alaina turned her attention back to the mirror and fluffed her hair into its signature tousle. What they did not know was that she secretly pursued her actual dream. She rose from the chair, the gold dressing gown slithering over her body. "Give me a bite of that."

Ellen laughed and handed her the last bite. "It's lingerie," she warned, "you'll have a pooch."

"A freaking bite of bread will not give me a pooch." She gave a catty look down at Ellen's rounded belly. "A loaf might, as you seem to have discovered this week."

Ellen chuckled and rubbed her stomach in satisfaction. "It's divine, and I am eating bread."

"Ugh, I should dock your salary for torturing me."

Her Strut - Montreal - Alaina

Alaina slipped on the lacy boy shorts with a pang. They crawled up more than her backside. Memories of a long ago summer day in the bayou with a man with blue eyes and black lashes crashed. Her left hand trembled as she reached for the matching bra, the two-carat diamond engagement ring still on her finger. "I hate red boy shorts," she complained to Ellen.

Ellen rolled her eyes. "I know you do, honey. But Arturo and I got you a one hundred-thousand-shekel bonus for it."

"You are a vampire," Alaina said flatly.

"I am brilliant." Ellen fastened the brassiere. "Come on, they are about to queue your music."

"Her Strut… my song…" Alaina sighed. She wasn't sure if she loved it or hated it but could not deny it was powerful. Bedecked in red lace and heels, she went to work. At the end of the runway, Alaina stopped and struck her pose, looked down with her signature enigmatic expression and met a matching one. Golden hair and emerald eyes stared back at her. Intrigued, she held his gaze for a moment longer than normal, smiled, and winked.

The cameras erupted into a frenzy.

Not So Secret - Montreal - Alaina

Alaina's hotel room smelled like a floral shop when she returned. Ellen stacked invitations in a neat pile on a silver tray. Two burly security guards stationed outside her door had instructions to keep everyone out. She was not to be disturbed. She swept past them, every inch the pampered diva in a foul mood. It was the French, spoken all around her. It kept hurling her back in time. It hurt. Still, it hurt. She was hungry, too. She ate the mini sandwich Ellen left for her in three bites, grumbling there wasn't more. She showered and watched body paint and glitter snake down the drain. It felt good to be clean.

Feeling defiant, she ordered half the room service menu and fell onto the couch, exhausted. She lounged in old blue jeans and a faded t-shirt that read, 'Louisiana Crawfish - Suck the Head, Pinch the Tail.' Twenty minutes later, her order arrived, the cart laden with enough food for seven people. She motioned the steward inside without noticing him.

"My, someone is hungry," said a sarcastic voice, not French, but a posh, upper-class accent.

Alaina's head snapped up, meeting the devastating countenance of Prince d'Or, dressed in hotel livery. She crossed her arms and cocked her head in amused regard. "Well, I'll be damned. Look what the cat drug in."

Peter chuckled. "I have been called worse."

"With good reason." Alaina countered, annoyed at the intrusion.

They never met face to face, had never been in the same room, before today. But it was inevitable. Alanthia's two most beautiful people would one day cross paths. She just never expected it to be so clandestine.

Peter shrugged and gestured toward the heaping cart. "Shall we eat?"

Alaina narrowed her brows, careful to not crease her forehead when she did it, which took talent. "Fine."

She informed the guards she was going to have company. They nodded, keeping their faces impassive. But she caught the speculative glint and imagined them elbowing each other and laughing. She rolled her eyes and slammed the door. "Did they recognize you?" Alaina asked with petulant annoyance. She hated having her business splashed all over the tabloids. This story was worthy of the front page.

"If they are good bodyguards, they should have," Peter replied with bored cynicism.

"Well then, you can pay them off when you leave… shortly." Alaina moved to the cart.

"We will talk after you eat." Peter backed away in mock fear. "Models are always starving."

"You would know." Alaina dug into the breadbasket and took a heavenly bite of a steaming baguette.

Peter poured her a glass of wine and retorted in sardonic humor, "Like attracts like."

The French onion soup was divine. She settled back in her chair, accepting the wine, her peevishness fading with the food. "You taking up the runway, Prince d'Or?"

A golden eyebrow raised. "No. Everyone in your industry wants to fuck me."

Alaina nearly spit out her soup. It was true. He was so incredibly beautiful; men and women alike fell in love with him. "Everyone except me."

Peter folded his hands over his lap and leaned back with a playboy's confidence. His expression said he could change her mind if he wanted. "Refreshing, I assure you." His eyes rested on her ring, but he did not comment. Prince Peter ben Korah knew quite a lot about Alaina ben Thomas.

"Why the secrecy? Why not just come to the room?" Alaina studied him. He was not what she expected. There was a steeliness to him that surprised her.

He held the wine glass up to the light, watching the prisms sparkle from the crystal. "I have my reasons." The playfulness was gone from his voice. "As do you, Miss Pink."

Alaina froze, the fork halfway to her mouth, the bite of salad *niçoise* quivering on her fork. Her eyes darted around the room, expecting the secret police to explode in and arrest her. The food in her stomach rolled over, and she was suddenly very nauseous. The inevitable upon her, she was exposed. She forced herself to eat, adopting a confused expression. "Pardon me?"

Peter rubbed his chin. "I am not here to arrest you. I am here to recruit you."

October 23, 998 ME (Thirteen Years into Rebellion)

The Answer is Still No - Pepperwood - Ian and James

Every year on the anniversary of the Coronation Ball, Ian traveled to Pepperwood. No matter where he was in the kingdom, he made a point of being here. James and Persa never put it together, not that they mentioned anyway. It had been thirteen years since Persa disappeared. He was the only human alive that remembered that event, and he carried the knowledge like a festering wound.

Everyone operated in complete ignorance, except for the occasional odd statement. James might say, 'When I was racing,' or 'when I was drinking.' He'd hear Persa remark, 'When I was gone.' Momentary confusion would cloud their faces, then recede into oblivion. They chalked it up to the war. No one remembered the groom, Joshua.

Ian did not begrudge them their blissful ignorance, was thankful for it. But when he heard that Persa would never conceive, Ian understood why. They no longer talked about having children. Instead, they filled their world with horses, each other, and the kids from the Center.

James built a permanent dorm on the property. It housed ten kids and two adults. Each group spent ten days at Pepperwood. The Center sent six groups a summer, and Persa mothered them all. It was the highlight of their year. The kids loved Jay and Fey's ranch. It was a powerful incentive to keep them in line for the other fifty weeks of the year.

James braced his arms against the railing, watching the horses graze in the numerous pastures and paddocks. "You can ask her, but she won't go. She hasn't left the ranch in a year and a half."

Ian joined his brother at the railing. "It's not better?"

James snorted. "Worse, if anything. Some days she struggles to get to the stables, especially when the kids aren't here."

"Not even Rivergate?" Ian whispered.

James pursed his lips. "Nope. We do Sunday dinners here now. She claims it's because Cook has gotten old, but that's just an excuse. Ian, it happened so gradually, I didn't even notice. We've always been pretty solitary, dealing with the demands of this place." He threw a casual hand out at the sprawling ranch and shrugged. "But she would go with me to shows, fairs, to town." James grabbed the top of his head and squeezed. "I don't know what to do, E. I feel like the answer is just out of my reach, like I should know why she's so afraid. There is a part of me that understands, but then I don't. It's maddening."

Ian closed his eyes and whispered a quick prayer for wisdom. The immediate answer was, "Not yet." He took three steps away from his brother, frustrated. Steepling his fingers over his mouth and resting his thumbs under his chin, Ian literally held his lips shut. He inhaled deeply and said, "We do not always understand how the Lord works, but I have faith that one day we will. Beau struggles. You know what's happened to him."

James picked at a fleck of paint. "He's not the only one. Guys from our company show up here periodically. But that is why this is so confusing. We were in the war. Persa was home. She wasn't on the battlefield with us. She didn't see the things we saw." He mussed his hair in frustration. "I don't even remember that last battle, nothing. It's blank. Do you?"

Ian drew back at the direct question. His introspective brother never asked him about the war, ever. Ian answered very slowly. "I remember everything, but I don't talk about it." He spit over the railing. "Beau has asked me a number of times, badgered me all the way back to Louisiana. He stopped speaking to me for two years over it." Ian turned, his teeth gritted. "Even now, I can't tell him. I can't tell you, and I can't tell her! So don't ask me because I am not strong enough to keep saying, no." With that, he stormed off.

More Than Friends

Ian found himself in the woods, the quiet surrounding him, the giant redwoods loomed above. To keep saying no… to Beau, to James and Persa, but most of all to Joanna. To keep saying no…. He said yes to the Lord every day. But it was a battle. A battle to keep silent, to keep Joanna at arm's length.

Their gentle, companionable friendship had deepened into an all-consuming love that lit his days and haunted his nights. They maintained a facade of friendship, working side by side; long hours at the Center, long nights at posh fundraisers. They traveled together for days, shared meals and laughter, supported and encouraged each other, disagreed periodically, sometimes loudly. He teased her. She challenged him.

He woke up every morning and waited. He waited for the Spirit to move and give him the freedom to pursue her. He lived with a sick dread that it did not come because he would soon be called away. So, because of that, he would not risk her heart. At her core, she was quite fragile, which was in direct opposition to the image she showed the world. But Ian knew better. He knew the real Joanna, every wonderful, hard-working, vulnerable part of her, and understood why she did not force his hand, it came from a place of deep-seated fear. She had been an equal participant in the facade until two nights ago.

Her father died; peacefully and suddenly. Ian was with her when she got the news. He went with her to make the funeral arrangements, then sat in the pew and listened with pride as she delivered a moving and eloquent eulogy. He stood by her side while she received hundreds of mourners and hosted an elegant reception afterward. He watched Joanna do it dry-eyed, competent, and composed.

Then he witnessed her fury, in the form of a lamp crashing in her office. He rushed in, found her crimson faced and gasping. The broken lamp lay in three pieces against the wall.

"What's happened?"

She covered her mouth and turned away. "Look at the papers."

Ian picked them up. Legal papers, officially freeing her parents and restoring their fortune, twenty-four hours after the funeral.

"Come on. I'm taking you home. You shouldn't be working." Ian took her elbow, guiding her to the door.

Judith stood in the lobby, ashen-faced. "Go get her purse!" Ian barked. "I'm taking her home." Judith did not hesitate, and for once, did not give him an attitude.

Joanna lapsed into a semi-catatonic state, looking lost. She hadn't slept well for a week.

"Come on, Princess. Let's go."

She blinked, brown eyes brimming with tears. "Those bastards freed him… after his death." She buried her face in her hands smothering a low cry. Her knees buckled, and Ian caught her before she sank to the ground.

"They kept me from him, all these years, and now he's gone." There was no moving her. He just held on as she wept her heart out. The part-time receptionist looked down at her feet, unable to bear the sight of such raw grief. Judith handed Ian the black leather purse that bulged with twenty pounds of gear that ranged from keys, to makeup, to headache pills, to tissues, to chemical spray. Ian had once seen her produce a full-size hammer from its depths.

Judith laid a hand on Joanna's back, murmuring softly.

This seemed to recall Joanna to herself. She straightened with a great sniff, wiping her eyes and donning the mask of the professional director. "Thank you, Judith. I appreciate your kind words. I am going to take Ian's advice. Is there anything you need from me before I go?"

Judith smiled with sympathy. "I have this under control, Joanna. You get some rest. Take care of yourself. We will be fine here."

Joanna's face faltered, and she nodded convulsively. Judith held out her arms. Joanna went to her, a cry caught in her throat. "Thank you. I will call you tomorrow."

Joanna's bungalow was in a quiet neighborhood, in the old part of the New City, convenient to the Center. Her neighbors were a mix of elderly couples who lived there for decades, and young people, busy restoring the houses to their former charm. A huge oak tree dominated her front yard, an ill-advised choice. Planted decades ago, someone failed to consider the size of the tree when it matured. In the fall, it dropped acorns like missiles onto her roof, clogging the gutters and making a terrible racket. Worse yet, the acorns turned her sidewalk and driveway into a set from a slapstick movie. Speed walking Joanna, more than once, limped into the Center cursing the oak tree and nursing a skinned knee.

Mindful of acorns, Ian guided her into the side door, handling her like a patient who just had surgery. She accepted his help without telling him she did not need it. He settled her at the kitchen table and put on the tea kettle. In the small cupboard above the stove, he brought down a bottle of whiskey. Today, called for more than tea.

"I should go to my mother," Joanna said, looking tired and listless. Then she added with bitter irony, "Since I can now."

"You're not going anywhere tonight." Ian retrieved two cups. "I'll take you over tomorrow."

He heard her sniff in quick succession. "Ian, what would I do without you?"

He smiled. "You would well and truly be a workaholic, of that, I am certain. And," he winked and put the teacup with a generous slug of whiskey in front of her, "you would have never learned to appreciate chicken fried steak."

"I do not love that concoction as much as you do, but I will admit to a passing fondness." She sipped and grimaced, but obediently drank, letting the warmth fill the empty spaces.

"Come on, take your tea. We'll go into the living room and get comfortable." Ian rose, bringing the bottle of whiskey.

Two hours later, she had a hazy look, her eyes turning to small slits when she smiled. "I don't normally drink."

Ian chuckled. "I know, Princess, but tonight you have license."

"I'm just so tired," she said, absently running her fingers through her razor cut hair. "I'm sad, too." With an effort she launched herself off the couch, weaving as the alcohol hit her hard.

Ian rose to steady her, and she stumbled into his arms. She rested there a moment, her chest heaving as another wave of grief washed over her.

When it passed, her hands climbed his chest and rested on his jaw. "Ian, I missed my time with him. I missed it, and now it's too late."

"I know." He nodded. Warning bells blared in his mind, the way she was looking at him, with her body pressed fully against his.

She gave a drunken shake of her head, her words slurring. "You don't know. You can't possibly know how bad I hurt. How everyday it hurts." Tears spilled unheeded down her cheeks as she held his face. "How I look at you... and love you. I never do anything about it. I never do this." She raised up on her tiptoes and pressed her lips to his, soft and tender, chaste and innocent.

Joanna lost her balance and caught herself against his chest. "But I can't tell you. Because I can't lose you, too. I would rather cry myself to sleep every night than tell you and have you reject me, have you leave me. Don't leave me, Ian." She swayed and stumbled, he caught her as she passed out in his arms.

October 31, 999 ME (Fourteen Years into Rebellion)

Usernames

Pishon990... Alaina looked at the username on the screen with her heart pounding. Her hovering fingers trembled over the keyboard. The dark chat room's private message request blinked like a beacon. She gave a whimper and hit the accept button, feeling like she just launched a nuclear bomb.

Pishon990: Jolie Catin...

She covered her face, refusing to believe her eyes. Nine years and never a word, and with two simple French words, her world shattered. While she was sitting in her computer room, in ratty shorts and a faded t-shirt he bought her, wearing a ring she could not bring herself to take off, he finally reached out.

MissPink: Beau?

Pishon990: Alaina.

She gave a strangled cry, as if she had just been struck. It echoed in the cold space. Alaina trembled and slipped on her sweatshirt. At least this piece of clothing was new, it felt like armor. What to say?

MissPink: Hi.

Pishon990: Where y'at?

Alaina smiled at the familiar expression.

MissPink: Living the dream, you?

Pishon990: Fishing, thinking about you today.

MissPink: Damn you.

Pishon990: It was today.

MissPink: You think I don't know that?

Pishon990: I wasn't sure.

Alaina threw her chair back and stalked away from the computer. She wanted to pick it up and smash it, she screamed at it, "You aren't sure!" She stood over the keyboard and typed in angry pounding strokes.

MissPink: Like you care, like you ever fucking cared.

In the corner office, overlooking the pristine lake, Beau pressed his palms over his eyes. He deserved that.

Pishon990: I never stopped.

MissPink: Liar!

Pishon990: Never lies between us, Jolie Catin, only truth.

The message board hovered empty. Beau watched the screen, his hands sweating, and waited.

MissPink: Are you better?

A huge exhalation escaped Beau as he read the words, and he shook his head in disgust. How to explain a twelve-year battle with PTSD in a chat?

Pishon990: Most of the time.

MissPink: I would have stayed.

Pishon990: My fault.

MissPink: Not all. How is your mother?

Pishon990: Still running the world.

MissPink: LOL, I bet. Granny?

Pishon990: She died last year.

MissPink: I'm sorry. She was nice. I still make gumbo thanks to her.

Pishon990: I miss her biscuits.

Alaina laughed; Isabelle's biscuits were legendary. Her mouth watered just thinking about them.

MissPink: How many nieces and nephews do you have now?

Pishon990: Too many to count.

MissPink: Are you still in your house?

A deep longing hit the base of her gut at the thought of him in the beautiful house that should have been hers, too. She pictured him, could see in her mind's eye, where he was sitting.

Pishon990: I'm in your office right now.

It was like a body blow, she recoiled, 'your office'. She looked around the windowless freezing room, the contrast was so stark, she typed the next words before she could stop herself.

MissPink: Is the sun setting?

Pishon990: Orange and violet, the water is calm tonight.

MissPink: I can see it.

Beau kept the door shut and locked on this space, hidden from the prying eyes of his family. Framed magazine covers blanketed the walls from floor to ceiling, snapshots of them together held places of honor on his desk. The original Serendipity print, purchased from the artist, dominated the back wall, a four-foot by three-foot masterpiece.

Pishon990: I see you everywhere. You have done well.

He wanted to type, "Come home. Come back to me. I love you," but he did not. He'd gone five and a half months without an episode, but she still wore his ring, and tonight he took a chance.

MissPink: I never wanted it. I had other plans.

Pishon990: Yes, we did.

We... the simple word that captured everything they were supposed to be, everything they were not.

MissPink: Serendipity... I've been asked a thousand times what I was thinking. I've never told.

Beau turned his chair and stared at the photograph. He memorized every pixel.

Pishon990: What were you thinking about, *chèr*?

MissPink: You.

She ended the chat and fled the computer room, through the secret panel, into her bedroom. Secret, like so much of her life. Alaina fell onto her bed, alternately cursing and crying, slamming her fists into the pillows, and then hugging them to herself. Emotions, long held at bay, smashed like a battering ram against the fortress she built around her heart. It spilled out. From old heartbreak and shock, to hope and fear, she could not stop the flood.

She rolled from the bed and opened the trunk. Buried beneath the new blankets, wrapped in a pink and rose handmade quilt, was their engagement portrait. Untouched for years, with shaking hands, she pulled Isabelle's soft blanket away and stared at the exquisite oil painting. Beau and Alaina, standing on the dock at his house, La Petit Pishon shimmering in the background, the sun setting behind them. Young, beautiful, and looking at each other with love that she believed would conquer everything, everything except a Nephilim.

November 11, 999 ME

London

Ilsidor landed atop One Aldwych Hotel seconds after the Archangel Michael dispatched Gabriel, Uriel, and Raphael to confront Marduk in New York and Zeus in Athens. "Thou summoned me, my Prince?" Ilsidor asked.

"Aye, Ilsidor. Go to the home of Persa ben Yereq and James ben Kole as sentinel and guard."

"To engage, my Prince?" Ilsidor put her small hand to the golden sword at her side.

Michael shook his head and said, "Nay, the shield still holds, but the veil will begin to fall away. The first memories will be revealed tonight. Stay close to Persa. It has begun."

Romantic Tryst - Pepperwood - James and Persa

"Persa," James called from outside, his voice holding a note of urgency. She paused with a handful of pasta over a pot of boiling water, debating if she should drop it. She let the noodles fall back into the canister and turned the burner off on the spaghetti sauce, putting the lid on to keep it warm. They had a mare in foal, and it sounded like she was needed. Her stomach growled, so she ate a hunk of cheese as she slipped on her boots. Instead of finding James at the door of the stable, he was mounted in the yard with Lightning saddled.

"Get on. I need to show you something." James handed her down the reins.

She did not immediately take them. "What? I've got dinner started."

"It's a surprise." He grinned and rode off.

Persa's heart began to pound. She looked around, uncertain. She hated the fear that gripped her, but it seemed part of her now, as if it embedded within the molecular structure of her body.

"Fey," James encouraged, "you can do it. Come on."

She stood frozen, gripping the reins. Persa ben Yereq, former World Champion and veteran of a hundred competitions held across the globe, who at eight years old executed a handstand on the back of a cantering horse, was afraid to ride on her own land. Her eyes went blank as she stared at Lightning. Nervous sweat bathed her as her insides turned to liquid.

James rode back, his expression grim.

Persa looked away because she could not explain it and was bone-tired of fighting about it.

His voice held a note of pleading desperation. "Please? It's not far."

Her breath came in short gasps, and it felt like her heart might pound out of her chest. She grimaced and mounted with a stifled sob. When she opened her eyes, James was smiling at her with pride, as if she had just done a ballerina lift. The degree to which she had fallen galled her, prompting her to speak sharper than she intended. "I'm on a horse. It's no big deal."

His smile faded, replaced by the long-suffering look he wore all the time now. Without a word he turned and rode away, expecting her to follow. She did, with extreme reluctance.

James battled frustration so intense he wanted to scream, but he had gone to quite a bit of trouble to set up this surprise and would not let an argument spoil it. With a determined force of will, he relaxed his shoulders and slowed his mount. He had to break through to her. She seemed to be spiraling into a bottomless pit of fear. He worried that soon she would fall beyond his reach.

Back at the house, the phone rang, long and insistent. After a brief pause, it started again. The caller was desperate, tears falling on the other end of the line. "Please pick up, please pick up," he whispered.

The ring echoed through the empty house, but there was no one at Pepperwood to answer the frantic call from New York. Peter dropped the phone and picked up the gun.

At the fence line, James dismounted and waited for her to catch up. She still rode with an effortless grace, but the grim set of her jaw told him she was fighting for every step.

Persa stopped and glanced around. "Why are we here?"

"Get down. I have a surprise."

She pressed a middle finger to the bridge of her nose, hard. He looked so hopeful that she could not bear to disappoint him. Gathering herself, she managed a weak smile, feeling ridiculous for being so afraid.

He took her by the hand and led her through the gate, into the woods. Her voice trembled. "Jay?"

"Shh." He pulled her tight to his side. "I've got you."

She saw the dancing lights ahead of them, casting shadows against the redwood trunks towering above them. The dusk of the field was swallowed in darkness. A vase of flowers sat in the middle of a red blanket, spread on the soft forest floor. Two glasses and a bottle of their neighbor's wine invited the lovers.

Persa froze.

James turned to her, his eyes shining with expectation. "Do you like it, Fey?"

Her face paled in the candlelight, and her hand flew to her mouth. He thought she was delighted; she was terrified. She stumbled backward, muffling a cry. James took a step toward her, and she screamed. "No, no, no! Not again! No!" She tripped, caught herself, and ran.

"Persa!" James called after her, but it was too late, she was gone. His chin dropped to his chest. He stood there, deflated and defeated. The flickering candles cast grotesque shadows on the blanket. He gave a vicious kick to the vase, and it exploded with a shower of glass, water, and greenery. Venting his frustration, he hurled a wine glass against a tree. The wine bottle in his hand was ready to fling, but he changed his mind, pulled the cork, and took a long slug. Stomping the candles into embers and wax, he left the utter destruction and stalked to the edge of the fence. She was gone, riding furiously... away from him.

Disgusted with the whole farce, he mounted the horse, carrying the bottle. Instead of going to the house, he turned toward town and the bar.

Locusts Remembered - Pepperwood - Persa

Persa ran. Not a fitness run, the type athletes used to stay in shape, she fled in tripping, stumbling, ankle-twisting, terror. Small whimpers burst from her chest. She tried to smother them, lest he hear. He came for her, just like last time.

Rape!!

He fooled her again. How could she be so stupid? James would not make her leave the property. It was him! He was here!

Tristin...

His name hit her like a bullet to the head. She face-planted, eating grass and dirt. She scrambled up and crashed into the gate.

He bellowed her name, then started smashing glass. Persa surged ahead, tears blinding her, sobbing.

She saw an image of Tristin sliding a piece of paper across the table, heard his guttural voice, "Sign it. You belong to me, Persa."

She grabbed her head and swayed, dizziness and nausea swamping her, making the world spin. She staggered and fell against Lightning. Another crash of glass. She leapt onto the back of the mare and kicked the horse in panic. They took off toward the house, riding like the hounds of hell chased her, when it was just the memory of one.

A terrible hollow voice echoed in her brain, "Say my name, Persa. Say my name."

She smelled him, smoke and sulfur. She gagged and vomited over the side of the horse. But she did not stop, urging Lightning forward. The porch light beckoned. She focused all her attention on that pinprick of light, leaning over the saddle, flying. If she could make it to the porch, she would be safe. If she could make it inside, he could not get her. She did not dare look back.

Lightning drew up in a skid, a foot from the porch. With a litheness she had not exhibited in a decade, she jumped. She pounded across the wooden planks, inside the house in two strides. She twisted around, locking the door.

Terror overwhelmed her. She knew if he wanted in, no lock would keep him out. That certain knowledge sent her to her knees. She had to hide; he must not find her. Running up the steps, she felt him at her heels. She screamed and remembered him chasing her at the House of Amah, taking off his clothes as he did it.

"I get my ninety minutes, Persa!"

She sobbed, stumbled, climbing on her hands and knees.

"Take off your clothes."

She sprang into the hall, hit the wall hard, bounced off, and kept moving. "No! No!" she shrieked.

Peter's room. She had to hide in Peter's room. His ragged voice echoed in her memory, "He does not get me when I am here." Persa seized that thought. She slammed into Peter's bedroom door with both hands, leaving bloody handprints on the white paint. It flew open with a crash, and she slammed it behind her. Persa looked around, frantic. Taking the fluffy green blanket off the bed, she sought refuge inside the closet, hiding.

James finished the bottle of wine before he got to the Cipollini Bar in Redding. He gave a curt nod to several neighbors and took a stool in the corner. The crowd was sparse, but it was a Thursday night, and that suited James just fine. He was there to get drunk, not to socialize.

The scant crowd did not dissuade the band warming up on the small stage. Their eager faces glowed with excitement, thrilled to be performing in front of a crowd instead of in their parent's barn. James scowled from his dark corner, upended his beer, and ordered a second.

Bracing his hands against the side of his head, he stared at the tiny bubbles in the golden lager. He jerked up, dread and pain washing over him. Looking around the bar, he saw another in the New City, long ago. Was it during the war or before? He gave an imperceptible shake, like a horse with a fly on its withers, and gulped the beer. The mug came down hard.

Drunkenness hit him, like an unexpected blow from behind. He belched, the taste in his mouth was vile. He felt in his breast pocket for a cigar. A cigar? He didn't smoke cigars… or had he during the war? Yes, he had in the war. He had forgotten that, hadn't smoked one since. Tonight, he wanted one.

He took another drink. Persa… she was so far away, lost to him. Physical pain wracked his body. Persa was gone. She didn't love him anymore. He buried his face in his hands and felt like weeping.

The band finally stopped sound checking and started playing, the opening chords sent shivers down his spine. He wanted to stand up and yell at them to stop, but he was frozen on the bar stool. Each deep strum of the guitar was a blow to the gut.

He hunched his shoulders against it. "Oh God, she's gone," he railed in his mind. His breathing became rapid, and he slid off the barstool, absently waving to the bartender. "Put it on my tab."

He had to get out of here.

When the singer grabbed the microphone and sang the opening verse, James threw back his head in agony. He stood, rooted to the floor as images battered him. Persa running from him. Him watching her through the trees. Persa dressed in midnight blue, "I don't love you anymore." He covered his mouth, trying to stop it, fighting it. He fled the bar.

Mounting his horse, he sped away, cursing the drink. With each stride, memories hit him, until he was sobbing with each strike of the hooves. "She left me. She left me." Desolation washed over him, as bone chilling agony gripped his soul. "She took another lover."

Then with sudden clarity, he pulled back on the reins, his eyes wide with horror. "I left her there."

Ian's pleading echoed in his mind. "I'm telling you, Brother. Something is wrong. She's in trouble."

He grabbed the back of his head and buried his face in his elbows. Mortification and shame swamped him. He had left her with a monster, just as he had left her tonight. With a strangled cry, he called her name into the blackness and flew towards home.

The bloody handprints on Peter's door sent a cold chill down his spine. "Persa?" A small noise from the closet told him she was hiding, and he felt bone-deep shame. All these months he had not understood. Now he did. "Fey, come out baby. I'm here, you're safe. I won't let anything happen to you."

She did not come out or open the door. "Tell me something only James would know."

He closed his eyes and thought, then said quietly, "You had on a pair of sparkly green cowboy boots the first time I saw you. You took me to see Rain, who was a yearling. Then you said you could do a backflip."

She cracked the door and peeked up at him from her cocoon. "What were you wearing?"

He got a blank look and shook his head. "I have no idea."

She let out a sigh, pulling the blanket up to her chin. "I know what you were wearing. He would have jumped in my mind and told me."

James fell to his knees. "Oh God, Persa."

His anguished face was pale and bloodless, hers dirty and bruised. Their eyes met across the darkness, crimson and tears.

"I'm so sorry. I remember," he whispered. "Do you?"

Her sudden sob was all the answer he needed. He reached into the closet and pulled her out, carrying her to their bed. She whimpered and wrapped her arms around his neck, burying her face in his hair.

He set her down gently and removed the boots from her limp legs. She was filthy, covered in dust and dirt. There was vomit on her shirt and dried blood on her chin and hands. James felt wretched. He had left her, again. He brought her a glass of water and knelt in front of her, carefully washing the dirt from her face and hands.

"He took me," Persa said quietly. "He tricked me, and he held me."

James buried his head in her lap. She stroked his hair absently. "It was terrifying."

Without a word, he undressed her and then himself, moving beside her as if she were spun glass that might shatter under his touch. He kissed her, murmuring his love into her ear, telling her all the things her heart needed to hear. "Fey, you are safe in my arms. I will not let him hurt you."

They had not made love in months.

She blinked back tears and stroked his cheek. "He's held me again. I've been in bondage."

James' nose flared as he rolled on top of her, anger flooding his soul. He remembered their wild ride when he rescued her, the same power overtook him.

She read it in his eyes and rose to meet him, her teeth scoring his lower lip.

He pulled away. "You are my wife!" James growled.

"Please." Persa reached between their bodies and gripped him. "Please, bring me home!"

With a fierce thrust, he took her, tight, hot, and infinitely his. "My love," he ground out.

She met his eyes, the fire back in her soul. "Never parted, never again."

James braced on one arm, positioning his powerful hand under her buttocks, pulling her against his hard thrusts, burying himself deep inside her, touching her womb. She gave herself to him completely, reveling in the power that surged between them. She arched into him, force meeting force. It asked, 'Are you with me? Will you fight for me? Are you strong enough? Are you ready?' As the shudders wracked their bodies, the overwhelming answer was, 'Yes!'

They lay together breathless, entwined, preparing for war.

I Know Someone Who Can - Pepperwood

Ilsidor guided Persa's mare along the twisted path through the dark forest, it grieved her to watch the pitiful flight Persa made as the memory veil began to lift. She stood sentinel until her husband arrived, then went to retrieve Lightning, forgotten in the chaos. When they came upon the clearing the mare froze. Ilsidor stopped cold.

Marduk lay huddled on the red blanket, writhing in pain, covered in black blood.

For a millisecond, Ilsidor wanted to run to him, to fall to her knees by his side, to gather him in her arms and comfort him. But he was lost and had been for a long time. Her voice was resigned, the end was upon him. "Thou art mortal."

He groaned pressing the blanket to the stump where his mighty arm hung askew. "Ilsidor, help me."

She refused to look at him. "Where is thy whore? She should be helping thee. Go to Egypt and dig up her bones!"

Marduk turned on Ilsidor like a rattlesnake, spewing venom from his black tongue. "You fucking jealous bitch. I am hurt, and you pick a fight with me?"

Ilsidor drew her golden sword. "I will cut thee down! Take thyself off to thy lair to die."

"I was headed there, but decided I was not going to hide." He stood up, awkward and unbalanced, swaying. His face contorted with pain and rage. "I'm not dead yet." He took a menacing step forward. "And there is unfinished business, between you and me, and that little cunt inside." He gestured toward Pepperwood.

Ilsidor scoffed. "Thou canst touch either of us," She tilted the tip of the sword under his chin and taunted, "As thou knowest well."

He raised a black lip at her, his giant fangs dripping with spittle.

She pressed the blade harder, feeling his leathery skin give under the pressure. "Thou art chained, like a dog."

He snarled. "The thousand years are almost up, Ilsidor. And then we will see. This shield won't hold much longer. Even if I do not take her out, I know someone who can!" He spat acid at her face and disappeared a second before Gabriel landed in the clearing.

Ilsidor wiped away the vileness and turned to her companion. "I should have listened to thee, brother. You always said he would come to a bad end."

"Ils, they are truly mortal now. Tonight, Raphael and I watched Zeus die. We had a fierce battle, and I thought Marduk fled to Babylon. When we meet again, I am going to kill him."

Ilsidor stared off into the distance, shaking her head. "No." She whistled for the horse. "For Philomela, for Persa, for Peter, for Setayish Quraishi…" She closed her eyes. "And for the millions through the ages, I will kill him."

Part 9 - Parallel

November 12, 999 ME

The Box - Pepperwood

The first thought that crossed Persa's mind when she woke the morning after her wild flight was that her hand hurt. She gingerly pulled it from under her pillow and studied it with sleepy eyes. It had several small scratches and one nasty cut. There was dirt under her nails, and blood crusted the angry wound. She felt nothing last night.

James lay beside her. His eyes were closed, but his breathing was shallow, signaling he was not in a deep sleep. She had vague memories of waking up several times and finding him watching over her.

Persa felt numb to everything except the throbbing pain in her hand, but she supposed she had been numb for years. How had she forgotten? How had they all forgotten? She shuddered. James rolled over, gathering her in his arms and pressing a warm kiss to her cheek. The gentle affection made her want to cry. "How did we forget?" she whispered.

He shook his head. "I don't know." His voice sounded thick with fatigue. "I've wondered that all night. I think it was a gift, so we could live."

So we could live... the words echoed in her brain because they *had* lived. They had an amazing life. They prospered, loved, and laughed.

"I remember the beginning and the end." Persa hugged James, pressing into him. "I remember you rescuing me."

James swallowed hard. "I remember being drunk, a lot. I smoked cigars and raced horses. In the bar last night, I remembered how it felt to be without you."

The desolation in his voice brought her to tears. She remembered that, too. They lay together in the stillness, him holding her as she sobbed.

"Jay," she said through tears, "I think that's why I can't have children. He did something to me."

"Shh." He squeezed tightly, holding her as her tiny body convulsed.

With a superhuman effort, he tamped down the rage. As she poured out her heartbreak, his eyes were drawn to their closet. In the back, on the top shelf, sat an old box covered in dust. She thought the contents were secret, but he knew. Inside she hid baby clothes, small items she picked up when she shopped without him. Purchased, then hidden away, pink dresses, blue overalls, a bib that read, 'Daddy's Little Girl'.

A dam broke, and he cried with her for the first time in many years. Together, they mourned the children they never had and never would.

Missed Call

A phone lay on the kitchen counter. Sent to Pepperwood in March, it arrived with a simple note, 'I will call you when it begins.' There was no signature, return address, or indication of where it came from, but they knew. And every day since, Persa kept it by her side, until last night.

When she stumbled into the kitchen to make coffee. The smell of old tomato sauce made her grimace. She glanced at the phone before slipping it in her robe and froze in fear.

"Jay!" she yelled.

He tore around the corner, ready to fight. "What? What is it?"

"Two missed calls."

"Oh, no." He took the phone from her, staring at the screen. "Should we call him?"

Persa closed her eyes and held out her palm. "We have to try. If he's running, he will have thrown his away. There will be no danger if we call it." Her hands shook as she pressed the button.

It rang three times before Peter's voice came over the line. "Fey."

She expelled a huge sigh of relief. "Are you okay? I just now saw… I'm so sorry… we had some… interesting events happened last night." Persa made an incredulous snort.

"You, too?" Peter asked, running his fingers through his disheveled hair and gripping the back of his neck.

"Yeah, somewhat mind-blowing."

Peter cradled the phone, flopping back on the pillows. "Yeah, me too. Quite an adventure."

It smashed into her brain. "A spur-of-the-moment adventure?"

They were both silent as memories of them running through the Capitol Building played across their minds.

"Bloody hell, Persa?"

She covered her mouth. "Oh, Peter, do you remember?"

Peter squinted his tired eyes, his mind reeling. "That we were together on 9/11? How did we forget that?"

"We don't know. James and I remembered last night, too." James looked at her, making an impatient gesture. Persa held up a finger for him to wait.

Peter shook his head. It was years ago. But he thought the events of that day were etched on his mind forever, the bombings, the chaos, their mad flight away from the New City with fire and destruction raining down around them. When he spoke, he did so slowly, "Persa, who the bloody hell was Secretary Tristin?"

December 12, 999 ME

Birthday Girl

James rolled over and kissed Persa, his breath tickling her neck. "Happy Birthday, my love."

Persa made a sleepy smile and stretched. "I'm old."

He snuggled deeper against her body. "You don't feel old."

She gave a jaunty shake of her shoulders, burrowing under the covers, seeking his heat. He felt warm and solid against her in the chilly morning air. She drew his work-roughened hand to her lips and kissed, studying it in the gray light. He had a scratch on his forefinger, a day or two old, well healed. He kept his nails trimmed and clean. Their half-moons were well defined in the nail beds. She outlined the shape of his fingers, thinking of the hard work they did every day, how they were capable, strong, and beautifully fashioned. His hands had once held her aloft in impossible feats of daring, took her to wondrous heights of passion, and would protect her to their last pulse of life. She loved these hands.

They lay in the dawn, quiet save their breathing. In the weeks since the memories began to return, they faced each day and each revelation. But they did so without a spirit of fear, and they did it together. The ordeal became a chain that drew them closer, bound them tighter. They reawakened and came alive.

For a couple who had never been apart, the realization that they lost each other was akin to throwing gasoline on an old cook fire. They exploded. Morning kisses were no longer distracted pecks on the cheek; they morphed into countertop, panties pulled to the side, passionate romps. When they spoke to each other, they listened, made eye contact, instead of mumbling, "Yes, dears." The good and the bad, they remembered, and in so doing, rediscovered each other. On the morning of Persa's thirty-fourth birthday, despite everything, they were strong, and they were happy.

This was why her birthday wish sent an icy chill down James' spine. "Take me to Zuzah's Chocolates and Confections. I want my birthday truffle."

Ramen and Chocolate

"No, sir, I'd like room 404, please. It has a nice balcony that overlooks the Bay and the park. I stayed here a few years ago, and it's my birthday." Persa flashed a sweet smile at the gangly youth behind the front desk.

He shot her a helpless grimace and pushed his glasses up the bridge of his nose for the third time in as many minutes. He kept typing, looking up, then back down. James stood behind Persa, giving the clerk a deadly look, one honed in the army for new recruits under his command. The clerk's palms were sweating as he frantically tried to rearrange reservations. Persa was oblivious to the interplay. She thought she was getting her way through charm and persuasion. Cold menace was making it happen.

The clerk let out a deep sigh of relief, thankful he avoided a smack upside his head. "Yes, we can accommodate you. The room will be available after 4:00 pm." He pushed his glasses up and smiled down at Persa, avoiding James.

Persa beamed. "Perfect. Thank you so much." She turned to James, taking his arm, and said under her breath, "See, all you have to do is ask nice."

James moistened his lips, hiding a smile, "Yes, dear."

They exited the hotel, walking hand in hand down the crowded sidewalk, mixing with the tourists and professionals scurrying back to their offices as lunchtime came to a close. They slowed their pace, trapped behind an elderly couple and a harried mother wrestling three children. Persa kept her eyes averted and pushed past them. Their first destination was in sight, Kogane No Hikari Ramen House. She sucked in a deep breath, and her mouth watered in anticipation.

Down a narrow alley, the battered yellow and red sign made Persa clap her hands in delight. Even after the lunch rush, the small restaurant was crowded. Dark-haired customers hunched over steaming bowls of deliciousness. A young waitress hurried over, a clean towel and an empty tray in her hand. "Let me wipe down that table in the back."

The kitchen was open. There was a counter for ten, and six small tables lined the windows. The restaurant smelled heavenly, like rich broth, roasted meat, and fresh seafood. Persa discovered this place on her frequent forays into the city, her weekend escapes. Ramen... oh, she remembered ramen.

James realized they could easily be in Japan. Stepping through the doors felt like they entered another country, another world. The menu comprised four pictures with the words written underneath: Shio, Tonkotsu, Miso, Shoyu.

"I have no idea what to get."

Persa looked up and said, "You should order the Tonkotsu, it's a rich pork broth and will fill you up. This place makes the best Shoyu. That's what I'm getting."

A few minutes later, the server place steaming bowls in front of them. James raised a straight brow at Persa. "Fey, there is no way you can eat all that."

She inhaled with a deep moan, closing her lovely hazel eyes in ecstasy. "No, but I am going to try."

At the first bite, James knew it was the most amazing soup he ever tasted. Persa was making slurping noises, her face inches from the bowl, using chopsticks and the soup spoon like a pro. They ate in silence, interrupted by incoherent sounds of awe.

James leaned back in his chair, stifling a burp, a lone noodle and scallion floating at the bottom of his bowl. "I am in heaven."

Persa flashed him a brilliant smile. She still had three-quarters of her food left but was slowing down fast. "I knew you would like it. The eggs are my favorite," she said, eating one and closing her eyes in delight.

"Can you make this at home?" James asked with dubious hope. The chef behind the counter was a wonder to behold.

Persa laughed. "Not with a hundred years of practice."

They left the ramen shop, pleasantly full and warm. Their next stop, Zuzah's. With peaceful determination, they ambled toward the open square.

James gestured to a park bench. "Let's sit for a minute. I'm not hungry yet."

Persa tucked her leg under her rear and leaned into him. "Me either."

They sat for a time, people watching the tourists and the college kids.

"I sat in front of Zuzah's all day. I didn't know what else to do." His voice was low and steady.

Persa met his eyes. "A part of me knew you would be here." The wind ruffled her hair, and a stray curl blew in her mouth. She sputtered and spit it out.

James smoothed it behind her ear, the beginnings of a smile on his face. "But you were disguised."

"I was?" Persa frowned and looked across the lawn. "I don't remember."

James nodded. "On second thought, let's get your truffles. We've had a nice day, and I don't want to spend the rest of it digging up bones. It's over, you're safe, and we are together. That is all that matters."

"True." Persa gave him a quick kiss.

Holding hands, they strolled across the lawn. Persa tucked the errant strand of hair behind her ear again and mused, "Ian said something to me a few years ago that I've been thinking about."

"Oh yea, what's that?"

"He has always been so sweet to me, very kind and patient. I think he knows. I think he's always known. Do you realize he's come to Pepperwood every year on October 23rd?"

James looked up, furrowing his brows. "You might be right on both counts. He got testy with me a while back and stormed off. But he said something that never made sense. In a good imitation of his brother, he repeated the words, 'I can't tell you. I can't tell Beau, and I can't tell her, so stop asking me because I might not be able to keep saying no.'" James paused. "We were talking about the war. I thought the person he was referring to was Joanna."

Persa flicked a hand in exasperated dismissal. "I don't know what he is doing with Joanna. It's obvious to anyone with two eyes they love each other." She shook her head, returning to the subject. "You are right, though. He might have been referring to me. If he remembers, that explains a lot."

James cleared his throat.

Persa watched his mind working. "He was frank with me about the agoraphobia. We all danced around it, but Ian didn't. He called me out on it."

James turned in surprise. "He did?"

Persa nodded. "He told me to read 2 Corinthians 12, so I did. It gave me a lot of comfort, especially the part about His strength being perfected in my weakness. But Ian wanted me to glean something else, and I did not understand, until now."

"Which is?" James prompted.

"The passage talks about the thorn in the flesh coming from a messenger of Satan." She shrugged. "We skip those parts, so we know nothing about what we are up against because we've never faced them."

James rolled his eyes. "Not Sunday sermonette material, is it? Seems like we get the same thing from the pulpit every week, don't we?"

Persa lifted her shoulder, cringing at the truth of his words. "Sadly, yes. I had no idea what to do. I did not know how to fight him. Honestly, I can't even remember praying, I just remember being afraid… and angry."

James nodded; his eyes grim. "I was furious the whole time you were gone." He smiled, making a valiant effort to leave the past in the past. "But we are back together, and your chocolate cherry truffle is waiting."

As they strolled across the lawn, James added. "Regarding Ian, when he gets home from New York, we need to have a conversation, and I think Beau Landry needs to be a part of it."

December 22, 999 ME

Grocery Shopping

"Are you sure?" James asked, careful not to raise his voice and scare Persa from her stated course.

She stiffened her spine and drew herself up to her full 4'10". "I am. They did not deliver the lemons I ordered, and I need them."

"Lemons?" James raised a brow at her. "Lemons are important?"

Persa tilted her chin up and quipped, "They are if you are making a lemon cake."

"Hmm, who knew?" Sarcasm dripped from his tongue, but he offered, "You want me to go?"

She tapped her toe, considering. "No. I am going by myself."

He studied her through narrowed eyes. "You riding or driving?"

"I'm riding." A slow smile broke across her face. "I see that look."

James sauntered over to her. The light filtering into the barn cast her in a warm peach glow. She looked better than he'd seen her in years, strong, substantial, feisty. His Fey was back. "What look?"

Her hands went to her hips. "The one that says that there is no way I am taking your new truck to town."

"You cannot blame me, considering you've only ever driven on the ranch," he laughed and pulled her into his arms, burying his stubbled chin in her neck and nibbling her ear.

Persa squealed and wiggled away. "Stop it, you wicked man. I know you are trying to distract me." She rose on her tiptoes, giving him a quick kiss and a butt squeeze. "Saddle Lightning. She hasn't been to town in a while either." She turned, shaking her small hips and her ponytail as she sauntered away, giving him a show.

James leaned against the door frame, appreciating the view, a smile in his eyes. It had been almost three years since she left the ranch alone. It felt good to have her back.

Prince Eamonn's Fountain - Elijah - New City

It always cracked Elijah up when girls tried to dress like boys and thought nobody would notice. To Elijah, it was plain as day. It was their hands. Girls had different hands than boys. They could change the way they walked, even change the way they talked. They might disguise their faces and play all kinds of tricks, but unless they wore gloves, the hands gave them away. He'd been watching a girl for the last week, from his favorite place in the park. She was good, he'd give her that. But she was not a boy.

Years ago, Elijah nominated himself and became the unofficial patrol of Prince Eamonn's Park. He monitored this place, watching for predators, human or any other kind. Parks attracted street kids. Open spaces, public bathrooms, and benches created the illusion of safety. Elijah knew, in Prince Eamonn's Park, safety was an illusion. By his estimation, fifty kids disappeared from this place.

Elijah had not lived on the streets for a long time. At seventeen, he was an established member of the community, a senior at the local high school, and the ranking member at the Center. However, Cynthia and Samantha had been originals, too. They became his sisters, and they both disappeared walking through this park.

He approached Officer ben Phillip about it once or twice. But he didn't have any proof, and cops didn't take kids seriously. He confided his suspicions to Mr. Ian, who convinced the police to investigate. They increased personnel and patrolled the park for three months. During that time nobody went missing. But resources and funding pulled the regular patrols away, and the disappearances started again. That was when Elijah appointed himself the unofficial guardian.

The wind felt bitterly cold, and the sun was setting. He approached the girl, who pretended to be a boy. "Hey," he called, leaving twenty feet between them. She was about to run. "You need to be careful around here. It gets dangerous after dark."

The girl jumped at the sound of his voice. She turned big brown eyes on him and pulled her hood tight over her hair. "Thanks."

Her gruff voice did not fool Elijah, and she did not move.

Elijah shrugged his thin shoulders and walked away. He'd warned her. Glancing back, her black clothing seemed to disappear in the falling darkness. He hoped it would hide her from whatever hunted here at night.

Solstice - House of Amah - Rapha

Eight days, eight days left until they released Lucifer. Rapha, the Nephilim, relaxed in the enormous chair he fashioned, on the spot where he was conceived, at the center of the labyrinth. Flames burned around him as he watched the drama unfolding in his garden with dispassionate amusement. He flicked his huge hand, setting another fir tree aflame. He grinned as his prey recoiled against the heat and sought another means of escape.

Rapha narrowed his burnt orange eyes, focused, and lifted his prey into the air with the power of his mind. Holding it suspended, he tilted his head to the side. The prey tilted in the same direction. He grinned; it screamed. He forced it higher until it silhouetted against the full moon hanging low in the sky. It kept squirming, which displeased him, ruined the art he was creating. So, he paralyzed it. He leaned back, enjoying the effect, an X against the pale light. When he flicked his finger, it spun like a pinwheel.

When he tired of toying with his food, he finished it and got to work. This was an important night on the calendar, and as they had done every Solstice and Equinox since they were seven, he sent his spirit beyond the labyrinth for a meeting.

They collided in the ether, cunning, malevolent, and vicious. Rapha saw a fire that mirrored his own, though this one shimmered deep in the Louisiana swamp. Drums beat an ancient and primal rhythm. He smelled the fecund earth, tasted the blood in the air, felt the anticipation. Their time was coming.

"Hello, Brother."

December 30, 999 ME

Audit - Landrys - Sarah and Jorge

Sarah Landry sat at her oak desk, wearing a pinched expression, a report spread before her. She shook her head in bemused denial, but after two hours of pouring over the figures, she conceded the auditors were correct.

Jorge's handsome face showed his concern. "Is it bad?" He moved beside her, picking up the papers.

"Worse."

Jorge's lips tightened. "Come on, sit down with me. You been at this for hours."

Sarah slumped and gave a weary ascent, allowing him to guide her to the sofa. He settled her against his side, draping an arm around her shoulders. "I cannot believe it."

"What does the audit say?" Jorge rubbed her arm.

"It goes back years, from the very beginning. It started small, just negligible amounts, here and there, but lately the transactions have grown larger and more frequent." Sarah whispered, "Joanna's signature is all over the papers."

Jorge made a deep sound of regret. "You sure?"

Sarah nodded, weary and resigned. "Yes."

"I don't buy it." Jorge's body tensed. "Ian's been there, what, four years now? We've been involved with Joanna ben Luke since the late 80s, right?"

"Money makes people do strange things. You know that." Sarah rose and went to the bar. "The government took all her money, held it for years."

"But she recently got it back, right? You say the fraud has gotten worse. That doesn't make sense." Jorge accepted a glass of rum.

Sarah narrowed her eyes. "That's true. The first big hit happened right after we authorized the grant for New Orleans."

Jorge gave her a sidelong look. "She was here, *Doudou*, remember? It was the first time she and Ian came to visit. They spent about three weeks here."

Sarah's mind calculated. "I do remember that. They stayed with Beau. It was right after Hector left. I was relieved to have Ian at the house with him."

"When was that? Seems to me, we got a picture of them, don't we?"

Jorge looked off into the distance, trying to recall.

Sarah was moving before Jorge finished his sentence, thumbing through the photo albums on her shelf. "It was at Sarah Ann's christening, wasn't it?" She took the hefty book from '95 down and flipped through the pages. "Yes, here it is." She pointed and turned it to Jorge.

He picked up the album. Ian's broad grin shone out from the page; his white head bent forward toward Joanna's golden brown one. She wore an expression of suppressed humor. Ian was pulling her onto the dance floor. "The date of this picture is September 1, 995, so that's a Sunday. They left out of here a couple days later. What's the date on that first big transaction?"

Sarah hurried over to the audit, scanning the paper with her finger. Her face fell. "September 9, 995."

Jorge held up a finger. "Well, hang on, let's walk this through. That's a Monday. Joanna ben Luke... that woman's a lot like you, *Doudou.* Do you think after spending three weeks down here with us, getting a two-million-shekel grant, and driving all the way from New Orleans to the New City, her first day back she's going to commit major fraud?" Jorge frowned, shaking his head. "For that matter, why would she wait until Ian came to work with her full time to start doing it? That don't make sense."

Sarah froze. "No, it does not." Her eyes narrowed and her voice became deadly. "Something's not right."

Part 10 - Ringing in the New Year

December 31, 999 ME

Not Another Day Without You - New City - Ian and Joanna

Not quite awake, Joanna stumbled to her front door, certain the insistent pounding just after dawn heralded bad news. "Ian! What are you doing here? You are supposed to be in New York."

Ian pushed past her, gasping like he had run from the Bronx. His hair bore finger marks through it, and his eyes blazed with a wild intensity that elevated her already coursing adrenaline. Taking her by the shoulders, he gave her a small shake and croaked, "Are you okay?"

"I'm fine. What in the world is wrong with you? What's happened? Is it the Centers?"

"You're fine." He covered his mouth and closed his eyes, sagging into the door. "You're okay?"

"Yes," Joanna replied with an edge of impatience. "What is going on?"

Ian pulled her into an embrace, his arms surrounding her like bands of steel. "I was so afraid that something happened to you."

Joanna held him, feeling the fine tremors coursing through his body. In all the years they worked together, she never saw Ian ben Kole afraid, ever. "I'm fine. But are you okay?"

Ian groaned and rubbed his cheek on the top of her head, his chest rising and falling in short pants. "Yes."

They stood together, holding in the most prolonged physical contact they ever had. She did not know what he was on about, but did not move, absorbing the feel of him in her arms.

He broke the embrace, and she stifled an involuntary groan to have him gone so quickly. But instead of moving away, he leaned down and cupped her cheek, staring into her eyes. She watched the play of emotions cross his face, fatigue, relief, then something enigmatic, an expression she had never seen. A slow smile built, all Kole Brother's teeth and charm. The light caught something in his eyes that captivated her anew.

With a rush of breath, he blurted, "I love you."

Of all the things he might have said, this sent her sideways. She blinked up at him. "You what?"

"I love you, and I cannot hold myself from you anymore."

"Ian?" She turned away, afraid to let him see what his words did to her. One kiss, one drunken night, one disastrous moment of weakness fifteen months ago, she said the words, he did not. "I thought you would never say that."

"Say?" he murmured and moved in front of her. His blue-gray eyes shone with every unspoken emotion between them. "No, but I showed you."

Joanna stiffened. Having played the role of 'friend' for so long, she could not abandon it, not if this was some temporary break in his iron will. With a sad shake of her head, she gave him a way out. "Friends... we're just friends."

"Friends?" he snorted and backed her against the door. Molding his body into hers, he kissed her.

In the years she had known him, he never did anything halfway, and apparently that extended to kissing. An inferno blazed between them, and she melted like candle wax.

Trailing kisses down the side of her neck, he whispered, "You know I love you. You know I do. I have since the beginning."

The sound she made was a cross between a groan and a moan, as his touch rendered her utterly incapable of speech.

Ian's eyes locked with hers, and he whispered, "Marry me, Lady Joanna ben Luke, my heart, my soulmate, love of my life."

A thousand nights, a thousand tears, a thousand moments of unrequited love passed between them.

"Do you mean it?"

He held her gaze, and from beneath the stormy gray depths she saw a side of him she had never seen, as if he had unleashed a wolf. And she was going to enjoy every second of being devoured by him.

"Y-Y-Yes," she stuttered.

He picked her up, giving a shout of victory, then abruptly set her down and moved to leave.

"Where are you going?" she demanded, thoroughly off kilter.

Ian grinned, looking at her.

Her hand went to her hair, which was surely messy from sleep, and she realized her ratty black bathrobe had toothpaste splatters down the front of it.

"I'll be back at ten. I've got a marriage license to get. Be ready, we're getting married today."

"Today? It's New Year's Eve."

"And I'm not closing out this Millennium without being in your bed, without being inside you."

The unflappable, unapproachable, austere Joanna ben Luke began to orgasm, right there on the threshold of her bungalow, with Ian ben Kole standing a foot and a half from her. She shivered and moved his hand over her pounding heart inside her robe. "Hurry back."

He closed his eyes and moaned, teasing her taut nipple with his thumb, lust thrumming between them.

With an audible gulp, he removed his hand. "Go get ready. You're coming with me. I am not leaving you for a second."

Spur of the Moment, Four Years in the Making

At four o'clock sharp, Officer Elias ben Philip offered Joanna his arm and led her up the aisle. Her father's absence weighed heavily for a moment, but this was her wedding, not her father's funeral, and she put it out of her mind.

Judith pulled the wedding together in hours. Her two daughters, scrubbed and pink-cheeked like their mother, were pretty in their matching dresses as they scattered rose petals. Judith looked at them with pride from her place at the altar. The tiny bouquet shook in her hands as she fought back tears.

All the residents and staff of the Center were in attendance, along with most of Precinct Eleven. Joanna's elderly mother stood frail and happy, just a shadow of grief etched on her face. Ian's parents, Salome and Kole, occupied the front row. Persa looked overwhelmed, surrounded by the kids who jostled for a position near their beloved Miss Fey. At the altar, the two Kole brothers wore matching grins and formal attire. But Joanna only had eyes for one.

The Center's volunteer pastor opened his prayer book, and the service began. The Spirit that lived in Ian ben Kole burst forth, filling the air with the most beautiful presence the guests ever encountered. A soft weeping filled the chapel as the Spirit of the Living God settled upon them, blessing the holy covenant of Ian and Joanna's marriage.

They transitioned from best friends to husband and wife in the space of a day. A deep abiding bond sealed their hearts, as they acknowledged a love that lived in their souls for years. They declared before the world and to each other what everyone knew for a very long time.

Joanna wore a gown purchased for a Passover fundraiser three years ago. It had been relegated to the back of her closet because she thought it looked too much like a wedding dress. Only in the dark, as twilight sleep hovered, did she imagine wearing it with Ian standing by her side. It was merely a dream until today.

Ian smiled down at his bride. She was outwardly calm, but the slight trembling of the bouquet gave her away. The roses were a perfect representation of her. Delicate petals of cream turned to pink, like her skin. Sharp thorns protected her and the children from predators. The deep evergreen leaves were steadfast and humble, like the amazing woman who held them. They smelled heavenly. He always loved her scent.

Ian could not truly convey to her or anyone else, the frenzy that drove him from New York yesterday. Accustomed to the leading of the Lord, he felt an overwhelming urge to get to her. It was time. Something was coming, and there was no way he would leave her without the protection of his name, his life, and his body.

Holding her hand, he spoke the words that had been in his heart since she scampered over the hill to explore the ruins of Hearst Castle. The memory of it was permanently etched in his mind, her laughter, the way she turned over her shoulder to call back to him, his Princess W.

Beau was the first to notice the growing bond between them. He felt his best friend's absence but reasoned if the time had come for him to take Joanna to wife, perhaps soon Beau would be released from his bondage. Persa's presence in the second row told him that the truth was breaking free.

They did not linger at their own reception. Neither wanted to spend their wedding night at the Center, even if it was where they met.

As dusk settled, Persa grew anxious. Ian saw her pull James' sleeve as her eyes darted around the room. She sensed it, too. Something was coming.

Ian took Elias aside. "Elias, can you post a couple of men here tonight? I've got a feeling."

Elias scanned the room, his cop senses alert. "You, too? Something's brewing, and I don't like it." He nodded toward Joanna, who was hugging one of his fellow officers. "Though, I am mighty happy for you two today."

Recalled to his joy, Ian smiled. "Thanks, man."

"About time, too. I thought about asking her, just to get you off your ass."

Sudden possessiveness swamped Ian, making him cold inside, but he kept a teasing note in his voice when he said, "Glad you didn't. I would have hated killing you."

Elias cut him a sidelong look and quipped, "I ain't that easy to kill."

"Which is why I'd like you here tonight." Ian scanned the crowd. The children he loved were jostling Persa.

Elias nodded and elbowed Ian in the ribs. "Go on now, take your wife to bed. It's long overdue. You two have been walking around burning up for three years."

"Four," Ian said and stalked off to do just that.

Bungalow Home - New City - Ian and Joanna

Every hotel in the New City was booked, at least the ones worthy of a honeymoon. Joanna did not mind, insisting her bungalow was perfectly fine. It occurred to Ian as he carried her over the threshold that for the first time in his adult life, he was home. His one-bedroom apartment did not qualify. Her house, he supposed, was now his house too. The realization made the events of the day seem more real to him than anything else.

He did not put her down until they were in the bedroom. Through a tender kiss, he asked, "Did I tell you today, how beautiful you are?"

"I'm not beautiful, Ian, but I am glad you see me that way." She blushed and turned away, feeling shy.

"Not beautiful?" Ian pulled her back, refusing to let her hide. "You never see yourself, not truly. There is some wicked spell that lies to you every time you look in the mirror." He ran his thumb over her eyebrow. "It tells you that your gorgeous brown eyes, like chocolate flecked with gold, are ordinary." He kissed them.

Her breath shuddered.

"It lies to you and says that your cute turned-up nose is unattractive, when it is adorable." He kissed the tip.

She blushed and batted her lashes.

He ran his hands over her curves. "And your body?" He growled, excitement building in his veins. "Your body, that you hide under black dresses and baggy sweaters, with its curves and its softness that you think is fat. Your body has tempted me beyond reason."

She pressed into him, feeling his arousal.

"I am going to make love to you with the light on, so I can see every tantalizing inch of you."

"Ian." Old insecurities rose out of the grave. She wanted to believe him. She bit her lip. "I've only done this once."

He looked down at her, his eyes turned into pale blue fire. "I haven't done it in a long time. Not since the war and never with anyone I loved."

She blinked at him, a high blush running from her chest to her cheeks. "Make me your wife."

"Princess, do you know how long I have wanted to do just that?" He cupped her breasts, feeling their weight, caressing her. She made a soft feminine noise of pleasure as he moved his mouth to the tender skin.

They undressed with slow deliberation, exploring each other. He was tall and lean, taut muscle over long limbs and strong bones. When she ran her hand over the planes of his stomach, she delighted in the shudder he made.

"Come and lay with me, my love, and we will become one flesh," he whispered, "man and wife." His fingers teased her thighs, brushing over her most intimate places, hovering, caressing, waiting.

She pushed against him, panting. "Ian, touch me."

Ian gave a low noise and found the place that burned for him, slick, moist, and holy. With reverence, he explored her until she cried out for him, and he could restrain himself no longer. He pushed into her body, inch by inch, taking his time, enjoying the moment. This was the reward for every long night, for every long day. He knew the wait had been worth it. Fully inside her, he pushed hard, and she arched against him in ecstasy.

Making love to his wife, Ian ben Kole finally found a place on earth for his restless soul.

They made love twice, and lay together, languid and sated. Caressing each other as if this was a dream. The clock in the living room chimed the eleventh hour, and Ian grew tense. A sudden shudder came over him.

"What's wrong?" she asked in a lazy voice.

He gave a rueful sigh. "There is something moving in the air tonight, Princess. Something moving in the spirit. It's been heavy on me for three days. I've been about to jump out of my skin."

"Why?" Joanna was not alarmed, too relaxed to let anything shatter her peace.

He took her small hand and placed it on his head. "I need to tell you how I got this. I should have told you long ago."

She stroked the white hair at his temple, shimmering in the cool light of their room. "I knew you would one day."

"I have seen the Lord, Joanna." Ian kissed the pale skin above her breast. "He came to me after the last battle of the war."

A small smile lit her eyes. "I know. You brim with it. You always have."

He grew puzzled. "You know?"

She laughed quietly and shifted, staring into his blue-gray eyes. "Do I know that the man I love is full of the Holy Spirit like no man I have ever encountered? Do I know you discern things on a higher plane than the rest of us? Do I know that you have an intimate relationship with The King once reserved for the Gune?" She brushed her mouth over his lips. "I am no fool, Ian ben Kole. There is very little about you I do not know."

"But you never said," he breathed, in awe of her.

She trailed kisses down his face and nipped his ear. "Neither did you, but you showed me."

It Begins - New City - James and Persa

The phone Persa carried chirped to life as they were leaving Ian's reception. With shaking hands, she pulled it from her reticule. James wrapped a strong arm around her shoulders, lending his support.

"Fey, it goes into motion tonight. I wanted to call you, to say goodbye." Peter's voice on the other end of the line was businesslike and distracted.

"By grace, we are in the city. Where can we meet?" Persa's heart raced.

"There is no time."

"No. I won't let you do this without saying goodbye, not when I am here." Persa understood the moment he put this plan in motion he would be in mortal peril, and there was no way he was going into that without one last hug from her.

Peter's composure broke. "Come to the Palace and go to the stables. I will send word you are coming."

Persa turned to James and said, "We're going into the lion's den to say goodbye to our cub."

James nodded. He agreed with Persa. There was no way he was letting Peter embark on his plan without a word. He was, in some ways, the son they never had. They loved the Prince as if he were their own. Someone had to.

James gave his name at the guardhouse. He held Persa's hand across the bench seat of the new truck and felt the nervous energy pulsing through it. They waited for what felt like an eternity. The Palace bustled with activity, preparing for the New Year's gala. At length, the guard motioned them through, pointing to the stables.

Persa studied the grounds, thinking of the horrors Peter recalled in his delirium, and the truth of what went on in this place. "Deceptively beautiful, isn't it?" she remarked, with a hard edge to her voice.

"That he has survived here…" James made a rueful snort.

"There is a part of me that will want to knock him over the head and take him back to Pepperwood, to keep him safe, to stop him from doing this, whatever it is he is doing." She frowned and shook her head. "Don't let me do that, Jay. Let me give him strength."

James nodded. "We knew this day was coming, has been since he showed up on our porch, strung out and half dead. Hold that image. He has to do this."

Peter waited alone in the stables. He dismissed the grooms, and the curt manner he delivered the order shocked them into quick acquiescence. The staff here rarely, if ever, saw that side of his personality. But he did not want any witnesses and would not expose James and Persa to danger in the closing moments before he broke free. For three years, he did everything possible to keep them out of this, to keep them safe. He listed their names with the Guard, there was not time to fabricate anything else, but their work at Pepperwood created a cover. No one would question why Prince d'Or met with two acclaimed horse breeders, even if it was New Year's Eve.

Strolling from stall to stall, he spoke to each of his prized horses, saying a private farewell, suddenly grateful he had this time with them, alone, before it all began.

He had not counted on seeing James and Persa and was afraid he might fall apart when he did. But he could not deny them, or himself, these few precious moments. He heard the truck doors shut and waited in the cool darkness of the barn, letting the smell of feed, horses, and hay calm his thundering heart.

The tiny woman who came around the corner made his eyes sting, beloved Persa. Peter opened his arms, and she flew to him like a sprite. He picked her up and held her tight, burying his face in the curls of her strawberry blonde hair. "Fey," he breathed and gave her a chaste kiss on the lips before putting her down.

Turning to James, he offered his hand. James pulled him in for a fierce hug, and Peter held on.

He looked from one to the other, his surrogate family. They were the only stability he had ever known, the only people he truly and unconditionally loved. "I am exceedingly glad to see you, but what are you doing here?" Peter took in their attire, adding in a low whisper, "Please tell me you are not coming to this gala tonight."

James' somber face broke into a smile. "I am last on the guest list. No, we've been to a wedding. My brother Ian married Lady Joanna ben Luke today."

Peter's brow furrowed. "Those two run the Center for Street Kids, right? They were here a few months ago for a luncheon." At Persa's nod, Peter smiled. "Please offer them my warmest congratulations."

Peter glanced around and said in an overly loud voice, "Come, let me show you the mare we have been corresponding about."

They chatted for fifteen minutes, trying to stop time, pretending it was just a normal interlude, together, in the stables, with the horses. They refused to accept that these might be their last moments together, delicate, infinitely precious, and all too brief. When Peter looked at his watch and back at Persa with a knowing expression, tears began coursing down her cheeks.

It was time to say goodbye.

She wrapped her arms around his waist and squeezed, her heart breaking. "Win!" she implored. "Then come home."

He could not promise that he would do either.

She read it, and before losing her composure, left.

Peter squared his shoulders and turned to James.

Their eyes met, and James said quietly, "He won't suspect it of you. You've got that advantage. Don't flinch, don't second guess yourself. Whatever you do, do it at one hundred percent. Take that son of a bitch down." They hugged. "Go with God, Peter. We'll be praying."

Peter swallowed as an understanding passed between them. The man

Prince Peter ben Korah had become, at least the good part of him, was emulated after the humble, quiet soul who stood before him, the debt, unredeemable. "I will make you proud."

James' mouth quivered. "You always have."

Peter nodded and walked away, leaving James alone in the stable. James bowed his head, silent tears falling into the dust.

Just a Moment - Landrys - Beau

The noise from the band drifted over the water, raucous and loud. Beau stood alone at the end of the long pier, the Landry New Year's Eve party in full swing behind him. Feet danced on wooden planks. Voices raised in laughter and song. His own melancholy made him feel guilty because he should be celebrating tonight, for Ian, and ninety percent of him was, but ten percent… was nothing but seething black envy.

Alaina, he wanted Alaina.

As if she read his mind, the phone buzzed in his pocket. Her picture lit up the screen. The wistful expression the photographer captured mirrored the pain and longing in his heart. "Happy New Year, Jolie Catin."

"Happy New Year, Beau. I only have a minute, but I had to call. I needed to hear your voice."

"Chèr, is everything all right?" Beau paced the pier.

She gave a husky laugh. There was noise in the background, female voices and keyboards tapping. "We're going live tonight. I'm nervous."

Beau let out a deep whistle. "What do you need?"

Alaina was silent on the other end. He sensed her moving, the background noise fading to silence. She whispered into the phone, "Just tell me I'm good enough. Tell me I will not get anyone killed."

The soldier in Beau, long dead and buried, rose from the grave and took over. "Alaina ben Thomas, you have one of the most brilliant computer minds of the age. I have seen you in a fight. You can do this. You will not fail."

"And that is why I had to call. I knew you'd have the right words," Alaina whispered. "Beau, pray. Everything hinges on the next few hours."

"May the spirit fall upon you, Jolie Catin." He heard her shaky exhale. "Call me later and tell me how it turned out. I don't care what time it is."

Loosed

There was no time in the pit, no light, no noise save the interminable rattling of the chains that bound him. Alone in the silence, Lucifer filled the endless hours with boiling hatred and plans for revenge. He plotted and relived the mistakes of the past. In the pit, he formed a thousand plans, one for each year of his imprisonment.

He quit looking up, waiting for the door to open, had gone mad for years anticipating, knowing that the day would surely be soon, only to languish year after year without a measure of time or place to anchor him. When he heard the great seal move. He did not raise his eyes, certain it was his wishful imagination. But light flooded the abyss, blinding him.

His sentence was over.

But his enemies had no intention of letting him leave this prison in peace. They swarmed the moment he was free. Not foolhardy enough to single-handedly fight all of them, he rocketed into orbit and hovered above the crowned jewel of the universe, Earth.

Below, he felt their sin, but the absence of his elohim, the absence of the demons, made their wickedness seem paltry. It did not draw him, did not feed him. He quieted his mind, feeling and listening. His eyes widened in recognition; a truly great power beckoned.

"Great Master, I call thee forth. For I have made a place for thee. Rest in safety until thy glorious victory."

Lucifer laughed. It had been three thousand years since he heard a voice like that. He did not know how one came to be on the Earth, but he was about to find out.

The master of the House of Amah welcomed him with open arms.

January 10, 1000 ME

Yellow Dress - New City - Ian and Joanna

"Ian, we have to go. It is the height of social suicide to not attend an event for which one has Rsvp'd yes," Joanna said over morning coffee.

Ian lowered the newspaper. "You Rsvp'd to Prince Peter's wedding, not Korah's."

Joanna gritted her teeth, recognizing the stubborn set of his jaw. "It does not matter. If our places at the table are empty, they will note our absence." She stood up, clearing the breakfast dishes away. "I don't want to go, you know that, but I've spent the last fifteen years rebuilding, networking, fundraising. One does not snub the Ruling Prince, even if he is a reprehensible madman."

Ian threw the newspaper in the garbage bin and dried the dishes she handed him. "The Palace is a dangerous place. You remember, I felt an evil spirit there the day of the luncheon."

"And if you feel it again, we will leave. But we must make an appearance. Missing this could set us back decades." Joanna pled with him, "You know how important this is."

The hair on the back of Ian's neck tingled. He closed his eyes, and against his better judgment said, "If I get the slightest feeling, we are out of there."

Joanna smiled. "It's just a wedding, Ian. Besides, with all the influential people in attendance, we might cut down on our fundraisers this year, which means more nights at home."

Ian gave a lecherous chuckle and ran his hands over her curves. "Well then, how could I possibly say no?"

Joanna emerged from the bathroom to find Ian going through her closet. "What are you doing?" she asked, vaguely perturbed.

"Picking out your gown." He looked over his shoulder. "I can tell you one thing, it won't be black. You have fifty black dresses."

She sat down in a huff. "Black is slenderizing."

Pushed to the back, he glimpsed color. He fought his way into the depths and wrenched it free. Yellow silk, fussy, and sweat-stained. In contrast to the sleek black gowns, the dress was as incongruent to the rest of her wardrobe as a Roman toga.

She saw what he held in the mirror's reflection and gave a startled cry. "Take that thing to the trash!" she said, her face flaming.

An eerie dread washed over Ian. Something dark hovered. "Tell me about this gown."

Joanna made a dismissive wave. "It's hideous, a relic. I don't even know why I still have it. Throw it away."

Nausea swamped him, and he sat down on the bed. Desperation and pain pulsed from the fabric. The gown slithered off its hanger and fell to the floor, puddling at his feet. "Tell me," Ian croaked.

Her hand froze midway between her face and the moisturizer pot. She recognized that tone. The Spirit was heavy upon him, crashing with increasing frequency since their wedding night. She prayed it wasn't their marriage that caused it, but suspected it was by design. He was not supposed to be alone. Joanna moved to his side, taking his hand. He patted it but kept his eyes closed.

She looked at the puddle of yellow silk and made a sound in the back of her throat. "I wore that dress to the Coronation Ball when I was eighteen."

He let out a low growl, pain mixed with sadness. He squeezed the bridge of his nose and asked, "You were there?"

"Yes," she drew out the word, "with my parents."

"Tell me what you saw." He reached down, picked up the dress, and thrust it into her lap. "Go back there. Tell me everything you remember."

Joanna looked between her pale husband and the yellow dress. Closing her eyes, she felt drawn back in time, seeing it clearly, the colors, the gowns. "It is hot in the ballroom, and I am absolutely miserable. There are people everywhere. My father is across the room, talking to his colleagues, Prince Eamonn's advisors. I don't know their names, but they are angry. I can tell by their expressions. Dad is trying to hide it, but he's furious. He's looking at somebody, one of his enemies."

Ian squeezed her hand but remained silent.

"Nobody has asked me to dance, which is okay because it feels like a sauna in the ballroom, and I'm pretty sure I'll melt if I dance. So, I push my chair behind a huge potted tree so I can watch, but I'm really hiding. I don't want anyone to see me."

"What did you see from behind that tree, Joanna?" Ian asked, his voice low and somnolent.

"Dancing and groups of ladies holding court. There's a pretty blonde woman in rose silk. They are speaking French. She is," Joanna paused, searching for the right word, "she is aloof and imperious. Despite that, men swarm around her. One suitor offers her a drink, and when she looks at him, I push my chair deeper. It's like looking at a dead person. There is something wrong with her.

"They exchange pleasantries, but I can't hear what he's saying. I think it's French... yes, it is. He calls her Mademoiselle Charlotte, and she takes the cup he's offering her and drinks. This pleases him, but when he turns, I see his expression, and I want to run."

Joanna clutched the yellow silk and opened her eyes. "Ian, I don't like this."

"Shh," he soothed, "go on. I'm with you, you are safe."

Joanna closed her eyes and continued. "There's another group of women, Greeks. They are all huddled around the Princess. That man, the one my father was staring at, the one that gave the other woman the drink, he insulted her on the dancefloor, and she is furious."

Her breath shuddered as she continued, "I see him watching her. It gives me the creeps. She's in danger, Ian. I think that man is going to hurt her." Joanna fought off the urge to fling the gown from her lap.

He put his arm around her waist and held her tight. "Go on, you are doing fine. It was a long time ago."

Joanna groaned, beginning to tremble. "Then he moves on. I'm watching him now and so is my father."

She exhaled, feeling the heat and the sweat running down her sides, the stays pressing into her stomach, and the old discomfort of her heavy body. "Everyone is dancing and having fun, and I'm sitting there sweating like a cow, hiding. There's this pretty little lady in green, floating above the dance floor, laughing and having a fantastic time. I hate her because she is everything I am not."

She choked, coughing and shaking her head.

"Go on," he urged.

"Someone moves in front of me, and I can't see anymore. I have to use the bathroom, but if I move, they will see I am hiding and that would be humiliating. I'm trapped. They talk, and the man, when he spoke this time, I could hear his voice. It sounded hollow. The woman reached in her purse and gave him a card."

Joanna broke off with a sob. Shaking her head, the shadows cleared, and she saw their faces. "No!" She threw the dress from her lap and started to rise.

Ian held her, his voice gruff. "Finish it."

Joanna closed her eyes, fighting the memory, "His name was Secretary Tristin. The man my father hated, the one who gave the woman in the rose silk the drink, who was going to hurt the Greek Princess." She covered her face. "The little lady in green, it was Persa. Oh, my heavens, Ian, it was Persa. Tristin asked where he could find her." Joanna sobbed, "Ian, he was talking to your mother. She invited him, gave him a card, and told him to call."

It was a body blow, a shot to the gut he had not seen coming. He bent over with it. The ramifications of her words rocked him to his core. His mother… his mother had set up the events that destroyed James and Persa's lives, that robbed them of their memories, and their children. His mother, with her wicked ambition and selfish scorn against Persa's perceived lower birth, loosed hell upon their family.

In the Spirit - New City - Ian and Joanna

Ninety minutes later, driving to the Palace, Joanna attempted to lighten the mood. "Well, I guess on the bright side. There is no way this ball can be worse than the last."

Ian raised his head and turned to give her a baleful look. "Joanna, we are walking into a viper's nest."

A year ago, she would have been irritated with him, but no longer. He was increasingly abiding on a spiritual plane she could not fathom. It came on him, sudden and powerful, often bringing him to his knees, sometimes, with fervent prayers whispered in a language no one could understand.

It happened on their wedding night, right before the power went out. He'd risen from their bed to bring her a glass of water and collapsed. At first, she thought he was having a seizure, then she thought he was going mad.

When it passed, she asked in a tiny voice. "Ian, are you okay?"

He gave her a grim look but nodded, pulled on his robe, and returned with his well-worn Bible. He pointed to a passage and walked away.

Joanna read the words, '*Likewise the Spirit helps us in our weakness. For we do not know what to pray for as we ought, but the Spirit himself intercedes for us with groanings too deep for words. And he who searches hearts knows what is the mind of the Spirit because the Spirit intercedes for the saints according to the will of God. Romans 8:26-27.*'

Joanna pulled on her robe and found him staring out the window, looking at nothing. Their reflection from the glass highlighted his bright hair in the candle lit living room. She wrapped her arms around his waist and rested her cheek against his back, understanding dawned.

When he spoke, his voice was deep. "It's why I did not come to you earlier. I did not have leave to do so."

She drew in a quaking breath, all this time, she never understood. "I thought you did not love me."

He turned and kissed the top of her head. "No, Princess, that was never it."

She swallowed and cleared her throat. "So, do you know things the rest of us don't?"

He laughed silently. "It doesn't work that way, but yes, I know some things that others don't."

"Like what?" Joanna met his eyes.

He bowed his forehead to hers. "It's our wedding night, my love.

We've got a lifetime ahead of us, and I promise, I will tell you. But I must confess, when the Spirit comes upon me, it's exhausting. Take me back to bed, Wife. Let me rest in your arms."

Wife... the word sent a thrill up her spine.

As she pulled the blankets over him and snuggled beside his long lean body, he sighed. Visions of a mad escape, running people, a racing car, and an open-pit faded away as Ian slept in the arms of his love.

The line waiting to get into the Palace grounds was at least a mile long. Joanna eased the car to a gentle stop. "Tell me what I saw. Who was Secretary Tristin, and what did he do to Persa?"

Ian looked at her with sad eyes.

"What?"

He sighed and bowed his head. She left him alone as the car inched forward. When he turned, she could not read his expression.

"I have been given permission to tell you."

She blinked.

Ian began the story in the MASH tent, keeping the emotion out of his voice, simply relaying the facts. For more than a decade he held those secrets, but telling brought no relief, only sadness and fatigue. He looked around and regretted coming here. Yet the Spirit moved, and he felt compelled to attend, like it was an execution he was duty-bound to watch.

Joanna eased the car to a stop, directed into a parking space on the great lawn beside the Palace. She turned off the ignition and faced him, pale and trembling. "You've known this all these years and never said? They do not remember?"

"It was the most direct instruction I ever received, from the lips of the Lord himself, the day I got this." He pointed to his hair. "I was not to speak of it until the end."

"Which is when?" she demanded.

Ian gave a wry laugh. "If I knew that, Princess, I would tell you. Alas, Persa was at the wedding, and she has not left the ranch in almost three years. That alone tells me something has changed. I could tell James wanted to speak with me, but he held his tongue."

Joanna nodded; thankful her brother-in-law did not overshadow their wedding day with such a horrific subject. "What do we do now? Do we leave here and confront your mother? Do we drive to Pepperwood and tell them what we've learned?" Joanna ben Luke, a woman of action, doer of deeds, did not sit idly by when circumstances demanded her attention.

"I wish." He dropped his hands to his lap, his countenance aged beyond his years. "It does not work that way. I often wish that it did. No, we wait. We wait until the Spirit moves, we wait until the Word comes, then we act."

"Oh, Ian, that is horrible. How have you lived this way?" Joanna whispered.

He moved slowly, pulling her face toward him. "Like this," he breathed, his lips hovering above hers.

Peace flowed through her, relaxing the tension in her limbs, calming her. Clarity came to her mind like a dirty window wiped clean. All was in control, the only thing required, obedience. Distantly, she heard Ian pray, unintelligible, but for the first time it did not seem strange; and she joined him.

Power exploded around them. Joanna gasped, threw back her head, and raised her hands in abandoned worship. In an instant, it was gone. Joanna collapsed like a deflated balloon, her breath coming in slow deep exhales. When she opened her eyes a half slit, she found Ian looking at her, the corner of his mouth lifted in a smile. Joanna blinked in astonishment.

For thirteen years, the unfathomable experience kept him separate from those he loved. In a vehicle parked outside Korah's Palace, his beloved wife experienced the Lord in a manner beyond human imagining. As they strolled hand in hand toward the wedding, they did not understand how much they were going to need the Spirit tonight.

When You Just Know - New City Palace - Ian and Joanna

The wedding was a glittering affair. They were accustomed to splendor, moving in the circles they did. Galas, fundraisers, operas, theaters were all part of the swirl that surrounded Ian and Joanna's lives, though this was their first event as husband and wife. They received hearty embraces and congratulations from their scores of acquaintances and friends. More than one remarked that Lady Joanna inherited her grandmother's vibrant spirit. She looked stunning and positively glowed with love.

The same could not be said for the couple exchanging vows in front of the oddly cloaked "priest" performing the wedding ceremony. Joanna recoiled when the bride appeared at the doorway, festooned in ancient Egyptian attire befitting Cleopatra.

Ian's hand snaked out and grabbed Joanna's, seeing her quick desire to flee. His eyes communicated with her. Be still. Stand.

A name crashed in on her, "Jezebel!" She mouthed it to Ian.

Ian nodded and motioned to Korah. "Ahab."

"Lord Jesus," Joanna breathed in prayer.

Ian broke into a true smile, one of the glorious ones, and it seemed as if a dome of protection fell over them. They became observers, removed from the pretty sounding but utterly blasphemous words spoken at the altar. Side by side, they drifted through the reception, even danced, though they did not eat or drink.

Toward midnight, Ian looked at her and said, "It is time for us to depart. Lucifer is coming."

Part 11 - Puzzle Pieces

January 24, 1000 ME

Two Jacks & Two Wild Cards - Louisiana - Beau

"Pishon!" Alaina screamed into the phone. "Falcon in the wind. Pick up four packages. Now! I just sent coordinates."

"Miss Pink," Beau said, keeping his voice calm. "I've got it. Are you okay? *Dis-moi la vérité.*"

"Scared, Pishon. They are pursued."

Beau took a deep breath. This was his chance, finally. "I will not fail you, Jolie Catin. Not this time."

Alaina made a hissing intake of breath and cringed at his misguided words. "You did not fail last time. You saved me, saved both of us."

Beau rubbed his eyes, wincing at the pictures that flashed in his mind. He pushed them aside as a sense of purpose dawned bright and clear. He seized the moment before it fled. "I love you."

It hung in the air, long felt and long unspoken, almost ten years between this utterance and the last.

"As I you, every day since we met." She swallowed hard. "Be careful."

Beau smiled into the phone. "Nay, *chèr*, I've been careful long enough. I'll call you in a bit."

He glanced at the coordinates, the old Landry boathouse and dock near Delacroix. He did not know who he was picking up, but when he saw the driver, it rocked him to the bone. As the sedan pulled into the metal shed, he had a new understanding about why Alaina called him on

New Year's Eve. *Mon Dieu.*

Prince Peter ben Korah was formal, dignified, and furious. Anger rolled off him in waves, though his manners remained above reproach, impeccable. In person, Prince Josiah ben Eamonn was a much bigger man than Beau imagined. The mental picture he and the rest of the kingdom had was of the teenager, believed dead for more than a decade. Prince Josiah, like his cousin, was unerringly polite and dignified, though he carried an air of resigned chagrin. Beau refrained from asking questions, suspecting a family quarrel, familiar ground given that dozens of Landrys surrounded him at any given time. Experience taught him the wisdom of minding his own business. From Beau's perspective, the Alanthian monarchy showed little compunction about killing one another, and he had no desire to get in the middle of that.

The two young ladies came as a shock. Everyone knew who they were. Davianna ben David and Astrid ben Agnor dominated the headlines for months. That the foursome traveled together, and that Alaina orchestrated this rendezvous, simply cemented what he suspected, she was knee-deep in The Resistance.

Leading them toward the flat-bottomed boat, he looked up at the sky. For years, he prayed for an opportunity to redeem himself, and the Lord came through in the biggest way imaginable. His passengers were the four most sought after people on the planet.

Tell Me of Her - La Petit Pishon - Beau and Peter

"Do you need some water, *chèr?*" Beau asked as Astrid slumped into her seat, a decided green tint to her pale skin.

She nodded from behind dark sunglasses that hid the migraine pain pulsing behind her extraordinary cat-eyes.

His instinct was to open the throttle and get the foursome out of plain sight as quickly as possible, but he experienced migraines after the war and knew the racket of the engine would wreak havoc on the suffering girl. So, he charted a leisurely pace, kept his voice low and soothing, and attempted to distract his passengers with a tour of the bayou.

They were strung tight as bowstrings, undercurrents flying everywhere. It made his head spin, but Beau pieced it together. Josiah and Davianna did something that nearly got them captured, which enraged Peter. Josiah all but growled at Beau every time he smiled at Davianna, but the two of them were not together, though it looked like they wanted to be. Conversely, Peter and Astrid were conducting a passionate affair, and their declaration of love was new, perhaps the first time they had spoken the words. Beau grinned, touched by the poignant moment that passed between them; he remembered that feeling. Josiah turned away, and Davianna bit her bottom lip and looked like she was about to throw up. Astrid did, but that was from the headache. *Mon Dieu.* They were as bad as one of Granny's afternoon stories.

At the house, Beau helped Peter settle Astrid into one of the guest rooms. In the hallway, he asked, "*Mon* Prince, may I have a private word?"

Peter nodded, his manner distracted, his movements stilted.

Beau motioned to the steps that led downstairs. They emerged into the gym, Beau filled with free weights, heavy bags, and the cardio equipment he used during the rainy season. He kept the curtains open, and the wall of glass gave him an unobstructed view of the dock and the lake beyond when he worked out. He spent a lot of time down here.

"You have a beautiful home, Mr. Landry," Peter complimented. "I thank you again for your aid."

"I would have done it for duty, my Esteemed," he shrugged, slightly embarrassed, "but she asked it of me, and I'd pick up the Devil himself for her."

Peter turned his head slowly, considering Beau. "Miss Pink?"

Beau met his speculative gaze and gave a sheepish smile, feeling like an adolescent with a secret crush. "Aye, my Jolie Catin."

Peter drew back, then raised a golden eyebrow and laughed. "I believe that is rather rude, is it not?"

Beau shook his head, smiling. "Not here."

Peter started pulling pieces out of the air, random statements, ratty T-shirts, a stained coffee cup, and a two-carat diamond ring. "Bloody Hell, you are the Mystery Man."

"What?"

"The love of her life, the one she will never speak of, to my knowledge has never spoken of. Is it you?" Peter stepped forward, suddenly angry again. Alaina was his friend, and he did not have many, not real ones anyway. He thought the Mystery Man was dead, but this guy appeared whole and healthy.

Beau stiffened under Peter's angry royal regard. "I suppose I am."

"Where the hell have you been?" Peter demanded, thinking of the sad, far away looks he witnessed over the years.

Beau gestured around them and snapped, "In our house."

That stopped Peter in his tracks. "Our house? This is her house?"

"It was to be... when we married." He nodded toward the rose beige wall. "She painted that wall. I wanted gray."

Peter turned and looked at the paint. "Her entire house is this color."

When Beau spoke, his voice was soft, but a note of desperate longing crept in. "You've been to her house?"

Peter wanted to retort that he had been in her bedroom, but a vulnerable pain clouded Beau Landry's face, an emotion he would not have understood before Astrid. Two months ago, he would have torn into the man. Instead, he considered what it would feel like, seeking information from a stranger about the woman he loved. "What do you want to know?"

Beau let out a tremendous sigh of relief. "Everything, *mon* Prince, everything."

Eavesdropping - La Petit Pishon - Beau

They passed a peaceful day, albeit a strange one. Beau liked Davianna, even if she messed up his spice cabinet and shooed him out of his own kitchen, twice. She sang while she worked, and cooking settled the restless, nervous energy surrounding her. Over sandwiches, her bubbly personality asserted itself, and she made him laugh. Astrid emerged from the bedroom at dusk, bleary-eyed and quiet, but functioning, to everyone's relief.

Prince Peter simmered like a rice pot with the heat turned a tad too high, the lid clattered, and the contents oozed out, dripping down the side and scorching the burner. As the sun set, his anger finally boiled over. He bowed to Beau and excused himself to have a private word with his cousin.

Prince Josiah sat for a moment, rocking in his chair, and watching the water.

"Best to have it out, I suppose," Beau said quietly.

"Indeed," Josiah replied with a bow and left to face the wrath of Peter ben Korah.

Beau remained on the deck and heard Josiah tell the ladies to stay inside. He had no interest in eavesdropping, but the rage flashing behind Peter's green eyes caused Beau a bit of concern. The last thing he wanted to do was explain how the two Princes of Alanthia killed each other in his backyard. He could only imagine what his *maman* would have to say about that, let alone Alaina, who sent them here for their safety. Intending to avert violence, he moved to the side of the house and watched.

What he saw, and what he learned, changed everything.

Beau froze when he heard the words Peter hurled at Josiah, a monster… stinking of sulfur and death, that would invade his mind, throw him up in the air, and spin him around.

His world stopped.

Beau could not breathe, and a scream caught in his throat. "What is that thing?" he wanted to yell. "I have seen it too. It stalks my dreams and robs me of my sanity. One of those things stole my life, my love, my future. It stole everything!"

But before he could form the words, Peter threw a wicked left hook, and a melee erupted.

Beau took a step forward to break them up but arrested mid-stride when Davianna shrieked, "It's on!"

The Princes broke apart. Then true darkness fell.

Lucifer landed in his backyard.

Beau could not move, paralyzed where he stood, like the worst PTSD nightmares. However, he was lucid, present, and aware of his surroundings, knew what was happening.

It was horrid.

Then blinding flashes of white light fell out of the sky. He remembered that light. All those years, he thought he imagined it, thought it was a dream, part of a delusion or a hallucination. But it was not. He saw them for what they were, angels with gleaming swords and huge wings. And in an instant, they vanished, all of them, including the devil.

When the voice came out of Heaven, Beau fell to his knees. No one in hundreds of years had heard him speak, and it was terrifying, like a crash of thunder, judgment, and power; The Iron King.

Beau did not know how long he sat there with the words reverberating in his mind. He came back to himself when he imagined a slither and remembered the snakes. That broke the paralysis. Beau fled into the house, his heart pounding in his chest.

"*Mon Dieu!*" he cried. A pot of etouffee billowed black smoke. He ran to attend it, lest it burn his house down. Turning off the stove, he coughed and slammed the backdoor.

Running his fingers through his hair, it stood on end, electrified. He found his phone and dialed Alaina.

Revelation - Louisiana - Beau

The road stretched before Beau, dark and empty, as if he were alone out here. He chose a touring vehicle for the trip, comfortable, with enough power to make it interesting. He usually rode in the back of this car when he went to town on business or picked up his formidable *Grandpere*. Soft blue lights illuminated the interior, which smelled like soft leather and money. But for the first time in thirteen years, Beau Landry could not detect the stench of fear.

After tonight, he should have been huddled in a corner, babbling and drooling, the white coats called to carry him off to a padded cell with the rest of the lunatics. But he felt fine, and that simple fact filled him with elation. He understood, at last. His mind was clear, like a black shroud had been pulled away. And even though it was dark outside, no darkness occupied his soul.

It was real, that apparition on the battlefield. All these years, he believed it was a delusion, a trick his mind played to help him deal with the slaughter he witnessed that day. He convinced himself of it, and when he met Alaina, he had found peace.

Only after encountering something like it again, did he break, for real that time. If Alaina had not been there, he probably would have let it kill him. He had gone berserk in the bayou, of that he was certain. She said he saved them, but he could not remember. Twice today, she brought up that night. He never spoke of it, and he gathered from Peter, neither had she. But she still wore his ring, and he was done hiding.

As the sun crested above the mountains, the road sign read: New City - 750 miles.

January 26, 1000 ME

The Largest Emotional Bank Account Withdrawal in History

Beau walked through the doors of the New City Center for Street Kids of Alanthia at 10:30 am. A yelling woman cut his greeting short, "Amanda-AAHH! Get in here!"

"Sorry," said the harried, twenty-something receptionist, he assumed was Amanda. She skirted her desk, wearing a glum expression. "I'll be right with you."

Beau pretended to study the photographs in the reception area, but he was listening to the tirade coming from the office down the hall.

"What is wrong with you? How many times do I have to show you how to do the inventory receipts? Look at these mistakes! I swear, if I don't do everything around here, it doesn't get done. Bring me last month's invoices and shipping manifests!" The woman's voice reached a crescendo. "Now!"

Quick tapping heels heralded Joanna, who barreled around the corner, fuming. She froze when she saw him. "Beau," Joanna exclaimed, her face changing from fury to delight. She moved to hug him but drew up short as the tantrum down the hall escalated. Holding up a finger, she said, "I will be right back."

She stomped off. When she stopped at the open door, her voice cut through the ruckus. "Amanda, please return to your desk. Judith, I need a word with you."

The young girl rushed past Joanna like a rabbit fleeing a wildfire. Instead of returning to her desk, she ran to the bathroom, trailing sniffles. Joanna stepped into Judith's office, closing the door with a decisive bang.

"I thought I smelled swamp water," Ian drawled from around the corner.

Beau turned with a grin. "Ian, where y'at, old married man? She got your balls in her purse yet?"

Ian laughed, reached between his legs, and checked. "Nah, still here, though you've seen that purse."

"That thing is legendary," Beau said with a chuckle.

Ian nodded and pointed to Beau's clean-shaven cheeks. "You're naked. I haven't seen that guy in a decade."

Beau raised a brow and grinned. "Neither has Alaina, but she will tonight."

Ian punched Beau in the arm, giving a whoop. "No way!"

Beau adjusted himself in exaggerated maleness. "Hopefully, all the way."

Joanna emerged from Judith's office, flushed, but her professional mask in place. "Beau, it is so good to see you. Please come in." She gestured to the conference room.

Beau's eyes shifted to the open door across the hall, then back to Ian and Joanna. "Let's do this in your office, Joanna."

The color drained from Joanna's face when Beau picked up his briefcase.

Ian froze, the hair on the back of his neck standing on end. He leveled a look at Beau, nodded once, and led the way. Beau had not left New Orleans in a decade, so to show up unannounced, on what looked like official business, seemed ominous. He could see by Joanna's expression she drew the same conclusion.

Ian closed the door, taking a seat in one of the comfortable chairs across from Joanna's desk. Beau took the other. Joanna perched on the edge of her seat and leaned forward. "Beau, what brings you to the Center today?"

Despite the ominous foreboding, Ian admired his wife, the consummate professional, getting straight to business.

Beau's expression revealed nothing as he met their eyes. "Well, if I'd have been here a month ago, it would have been worse news than I've got today." He let that sink in, Sarah Landry's boy to the life.

"On December 30th, the accounting firm of Bradshaw, Clarke, and Simpson delivered this audit report to the Lenox Foundation." He tossed a bound set of documents onto Joanna's desk.

Joanna moved it around to face her. Ian leaned forward so he could see as well. Beau watched their faces as they read the opening lines. Joanna's eyes widened, her jaw dropped, and she covered a gasp with her palm.

Ian burst from his seat, snatched up the report, brandishing it like a weapon. "This is a lie!"

Beau cocked an eyebrow. "Sit down, Ian. We know." He nodded to Joanna. "You narrowly escaped prosecution, my dear."

Ian was not certain Joanna's face could get paler, but it did.

"I have never stolen a shekel from the Center."

"No, but your fingerprints are all over the fraud perpetrated against this place since the beginning," Beau said, cold and unflinching.

Ian reared back and pointed a finger in Beau's face. Through clenched teeth, he snarled, "I don't know what you are playing at here, Beau. But I will kindly ask you to quit fucking with my wife. She is not a thief!"

Joanna did a double take. She had never heard Ian use a foul word, ever, and certainly never toward his best friend.

Beau did not back down, answering in a clipped tone. "Granted, but she bears some responsibility for this." He pulled out another sheaf of papers, dropping them on the desk with a thud. "Those are the complaints the personnel company has received against Judith ben Dan." Beau held Joanna's eyes and said, "I believe I received a demonstration of her behavior when I walked in?"

Joanna's shoulders sagged. "Yes, unfortunately."

Beau gave her a sympathetic smile. "Joanna, I'm sorry to have to be the one to tell you this, but that woman out there is not your friend."

Joanna blinked at him, not making the connections.

"This is the forensic accountants' report. We have credible evidence that Judith ben Dan stole your identity and opened at least six bank accounts where she deposited the embezzled funds. The paper trail runs back to you. Joanna, she set you up to take the fall."

Ian watched it happen. Joanna recoiled as if she had just taken a hit from a slow-motion cannonball. Her mouth dropped, and she covered her face. A moan of pain filled the silent office.

Joanna could not breathe. Judith, her most trusted colleague, the woman she helped, counseled, and protected, not only stole from the Center, but tried to frame her. She fought with Ian about her continually. He wanted Judith gone, especially as the hostility between them grew. But Joanna stood up for her, always seeing the good, even when no one else did. The treachery blindsided her. Ian took her in his arms, and she buried her face in his chest.

"Give us a minute," Ian said to Beau, then added, "and make sure that bitch doesn't leave."

Beau flashed a grin. "With pleasure, *mon frere.*"

Beau closed the door quietly. The red-eyed receptionist sat behind her desk, sniffing. He nodded towards Judith's dark office. "She still here?"

"No, sir. She left the minute you walked into Miss Joanna's office. Took her computer and a bunch of papers and ran out of here."

Beau shook his head and walked to the window. "Good riddance." Then he turned and said, "Call the locksmith."

Amanda blinked up at him. "I'm sorry, sir, but I didn't catch your name."

"I'm Beau Landry and effective two weeks ago, I'm the head of the Lenox Foundation. And that woman who just left out of here? She's been stealing from me."

Amanda's tear-stained eyes widened. "I'll call the locksmith, Mr. Landry."

Beau's nose flared. "You do that, Amanda. After that, call the police."

A slow smile spread across Amanda's face. "Yes, sir, gladly."

What to Wear? - New City Bunker - Alaina

In the month they holed up in the bunker, Alaina and Himari bonded with Peter's former nanny, Genevieve ben Willard. She mothered them, made sure they got enough sleep, and kept them fed. Going through Alaina's closet, she pulled out a simple, yet elegant, black gown. "You must wear the Shatan, Alaina." Holding it up, she admired the cut, the movement of the fabric. "This will look striking on you."

The memory of her first day in the bayou as Beau's sisters dressed and clucked around her, hit Alaina with sudden, unexpected clarity.

Himari leaned in the doorway. "No. That makes it look like she's trying too hard. Jeans and a sweater, Al." She cut a glance at Genevieve who was about to argue. "She does not need to be strolling up in haute couture. The paparazzi might notice her." Himari snorted and pointed a finger. "He's lucky she even bathed."

Genevieve laughed.

Alaina made a dismissive wave at Himari. Standing in her dressing gown, she sorted through her selection of clothes. "I doubt very much the paparazzi will be there, but I don't want to look over-eager." She took the black gown from Genevieve and held it up. "Regardless of what I wear, I am dying to get out of here."

Genevieve chuckled. "Well, you deserve a break. Our two Princes are safe, for the moment. Though, I must confess, I was speechless when Peter told me Josiah proposed to Davianna ben David." She shook her head at the gray silk Alaina was considering. "Don't misunderstand me. I am happy for them, but it is out of character. He was always such a serious, dutiful young man. I expected him to take a bride as part of an alliance."

"Like Keyseelough?" Himari spat the name of the Egyptian Princess. Her left hip still bore the yellow remnants of a bruise from her encounter with the wicked bitch.

Alaina cocked her head and frowned. "It doesn't surprise me. I watched the tape of them in Windsor several times. The way he chased after those girls, there was something about it."

Himari chuckled. "And that video of them in New Orleans?"

"That nearly got them killed," Genevieve said gravely.

Alaina smiled. "Yes, but it brought Beau here." She looked through her lashes at her companions. "I'm nervous." She plopped down at her dressing table, fluffing her hair. "I was eighteen the last time I saw him."

Himari rolled her eyes and threw her palms up, encompassing Alaina's stunning beauty. "And you are worried why? Look at you!"

Alaina gave her a sidelong glance. "I'm pasty and pale after spending a month down here."

Himari tapped her temple. "I will tell Peter we need a tanning bed."

Genevieve gazed off into the corner. "That is actually not a bad idea. If we've got to be down here for any length of time, the sunlight could be beneficial." She rubbed her chin and wandered away.

Alaina shared a secret look with Himari and said, "She is just using it as an excuse to call Jarrod. You know she is."

Himari grabbed the back of her neck, stiff from hours at the computer. "You don't need an excuse. Don't dawdle, Al. Get dressed. It's time."

"Maybe I'll wait for the tanning bed."

"Stop." Himari sat down on the bed and held her eyes. "We talked about this already, so I will not get all sappy and serious with you again. Get dressed. Go see your man. Get laid. I don't expect to see you back here for a couple of days. Peter told me they are staying in New York for at least a week, maybe more. Go have fun."

Fun was an alien concept for Alaina. When had life been fun? The last nine years had been work, days and weeks on the road, long nights in the lab, long days in front of the camera. Her professional life entailed travel, fashion shows, and shoots on location. Only in the last couple of years did she spend more than a day or two at her house.

In retrospect, the only time in her life she could truly call fun was spent in a yellow gingerbread cottage and wooden meeting hall on the bayou. She could still hear the accordion, still smell the Cajun spices, and remembered dripping with sweat, swinging around the dance floor, partnering with the French-speaking Landry men. One in particular, the most fun of all, waited for her tonight. Alaina closed her eyes and nodded. "You are right. Now scoot, I know what I'm wearing."

Waiting - New City - Beau

The staff at the Lenox Mansion in the New City welcomed him, surprised, but unruffled by his appearance. Beau had not been here since the Academy, but little had changed. After his brutal meeting with Ian and Joanna, he prowled the compound all day, waiting for Alaina to arrive for dinner, as nervous as a boy at the eighth-grade dance.

He changed clothes four times, vacillating between jeans and a suit before settling on a pair of charcoal silk trousers and an electric blue dress shirt. He was vain enough to recognize the blue set off his eyes, and the athletic cut of the clothes showed he kept his body in shape. The tie posed a bit of a conundrum, but in the end, he decided the occasion warranted it. Fashioning a full Windsor knot, the silk charcoal added the right touch.

Studying his reflection, he recognized his forehead was higher than it used to be, but his black hair was still thick. He'd worn a beard and mustache for nine years, albeit a close cut one, not like some of his uncles. But he was clean-shaven tonight. A stranger looked back at him, a man he had not seen in years, clear-eyed, unhaunted.

He checked his watch for the fifth time, and with a rueful shake of his head, went to the living room to await the most important date of his life.

The Lenox Mansion - New City - Beau and Alaina

Alaina drove through traffic, ignoring the honks and flashing lights of the other cars flying by. Alone with her thoughts, she did not join them in their haste, though she had for many years, taking up the rhythm and rush of this place, her adopted home.

The overhead streetlight caught the glint of the diamond on her left hand, and she considered taking it off, though she never had. It served as a constant reminder of him and the day he slipped it over her knuckle with a promise to love her forever. It felt like a banner, a flashing neon sign of vulnerability, proof she never moved on, never got over him. He had hurt her, abandoned her, and with every passing mile, she gave him the power to do it again. But she kept driving.

Pulling up to the guardhouse, she laughed. Even after all these years, she struggled to wrap her head around who he truly was. It was easier to think of him as the young man driving a wagon to his mother's general store, or the fisherman standing in a flat-bottom boat, teasing her with a wiggling worm on a hook. That was the Beau she knew, the one she agreed to marry. She never quite reconciled that boy with the man who would inherit one of the greatest fortunes in the world.

The Lenox Mansion served as a forceful reminder of who waited on the other side of those gates. It wasn't a home. It was a compound, occupying fourteen thousand acres of prime real estate. Alaina lived in an exclusive area of the New City, and her house would fit in the garage of this sprawling Spanish grande dame. Pulling up the driveway, she gave a wry snort, thankful she wore the black Shatan.

She handed her keys to the attendant and followed the butler inside. He took her wrap, handed it to a maid, and then there was Beau. When he stood, her breath caught. He had lived in her memory, fixed in time as a twenty-two-year-old. But when he smiled, the years melted away, and so did her heart.

Beau drank her in like a man who had been in the desert for a decade. He had seen her on film, in print, but the woman, the living, breathing, flesh and blood woman was a sight to behold. She was more beautiful than he remembered. It had been too long, a lifetime. When he spoke, his voice was low, awestruck. "Jolie Catin, *mon amour*, it is good to see you."

She imagined this moment a thousand times and picked her favorite. Alaina threw her clutch on the couch and walked toward him. It was a walk that made her millions, that set the fashion world on its head, and turned mortal men into quivering puddles of jelly. It was armor, that walk, power, grace, sexy as hell, and she knew it. Alaina stopped in front of him, a foot between them, her left hand on her hip, aquamarine eyes staring him down like a tigress.

"*Mon Dieu*," Beau murmured in appreciation, "can you do that again?"

Alaina burst out laughing. "Oh, Beau."

She held her arms out, and he came to her. When they touched, it felt as if they had been holding their breaths for years. They hugged in fierce desperation, squeezing tight, clinging to each other.

Alaina's chest constricted, and she gasped. She felt like she held a dead man, suddenly restored.

He buried his face in her neck and relished her soft skin, the scent of her, soap, hair products, and Alaina, his sweet Alaina. When she whispered his name, his throat tightened, and he could do nothing but growl.

She brushed her cheek against his head, and with a laughing sob, said, "*Mon loup*."

He answered the call, nipped her ear. Then he kissed it, moving up her jaw until their lips brushed.

Like that first night on Isabelle's porch, they set the Lenox Mansion on fire.

Beau broke away, gasping. "*C'est bon*, that has not changed." He shot her his riverboat pirate grin.

Alaina's legs turned to jelly as her arms hung limp at her sides. She blinked and said, "Beau, I think I had forgotten that."

Beau exhaled through his nose, shaking his head. "I did not." He tried to recall himself and his manners. "Are you hungry?"

Her eyes darted around the room, then she answered in a low, quavering voice, "No."

"Good!" The word came out in a shuddering rush. He took her by the hand and nearly ran with her to the bedroom. Ushering her inside, he went to the windows, closing the blinds on the six sets of French doors that led out to the pool. He shot her a lecherous grin. "There are servants everywhere."

"Should you tell somebody we will be late for dinner?" Alaina leaned against the door, one foot propped behind her, watching him as he moved.

"*Non*," he grunted, looking pained. "I am not waiting for you, not for one second longer. The servants *n'a pas d'importance*."

They met in the middle of the room, lips and tongues, hands and clothes, pulling, tugging, grabbing, feeling. Beau unzipped the black dress, and she let it slide down her body.

"Red boy shorts," he said through clenched teeth, then he spun her around, and pushed her toward the bed. "Do that walk."

She stopped and posed, her million-shekel ass on perfect display. Over her shoulder, she looked him up and down and purred, "You have too many clothes on."

He did not by the time they reached the bed. They fell among a tangle of gold pillows and down comforter, desperate to touch, as they had never done before.

Beau smoothed his hand inside the red lace and found her moist and wet, pulsing with need. He climbed atop her, his body on fire.

"Beau, wait," she said between kisses and breathless panting.

He looked down in confusion, half-mad with lust, moving against her, seeking.

"I've... I'm... I..." She turned her head aside and squeezed her eyes tight. Then she blurted, "I waited for you." Color crept up her chest, turning her pink.

It took a moment for her words to register. He froze; his blue eyes grew large as the impact hit him. His mouth fell open in astonishment, and he buried his face in her hair, whispering, *"Mon amour, mon amour, ma fille précieuse."* My love, my love, my precious girl.

She moved her hips against him. "Well, don't stop."

He chuckled and rolled off her, wiping tears from his eyes. "Jolie Catin, there is not a power on this earth that would make me stop, but I perhaps need to take a bit more care, no?" He kissed her ear. "Not rush, your first time." His words caught.

She slid her hand to his silk erection, stroking gently. "I don't mind. I just did not want you to be surprised."

He closed his eyes, responding to her touch, moaning. "I am surprised." He moved against her, reveling in her gentle stroking fingers. "Pleased, honored, and undone by you."

"Don't make me wait," she whispered, running her tongue inside his ear.

With a shudder, he unsnapped her bra and pulled the panties over her long legs. Beau crawled up the bed, the wolf back, his blue eyes blazing. He pressed his face between her thighs, nuzzling the well landscaped blonde curls, growling deep in his throat. He kissed her stomach and teased her with his fingers.

She moaned and called to him, *"Mon loup."*

His restraint broke. "Jolie Catin, I have loved you every day that we have been apart, every day."

Then Beau Landry and Alaina ben Thomas were separated no more.

Later, Beau stroked a lazy hand down the long curve of Alaina's hip. They lay side by side, their eyes lidded in sated pleasure. A single tear fell over her lashes and disappeared under his gentle kiss. "Do not cry, Jolie Catin. I am here now."

She could not fathom how he knew, when she had not realized until that very moment how much she needed to hear those words. Something cracked, deep within her female soul. She bowed her head, hiding the sudden rush of vulnerability.

Since the day she drove away from him, she felt alone. Surrounded by friends, by hundreds of fans, by colleagues, she held part of herself back, apart from them. She learned to do it growing up, out of place in a Mississippi beer joint, the computer genius, doing homework on top of a case of beer.

Colleagues and friends would have scoffed at the notion that Alaina spent the last decade afraid, but Beau wasn't the only casualty of that Louisiana encounter. It haunted her dreams, waited in shadowy corners, and lived in every creak of her dark house. She despised scary books, masquerade parties, and never, ever, got on a boat.

But it was more than that. A woman alone was vulnerable in a way no man could truly understand. It could manifest anywhere, a walk to her car in a dim parking lot, an elevator ride, an empty gas station in Texas. The fight between the two boys in Mississippi, that prompted her to steal the car, had been over which one was going to have sex with her first. She experienced it as she strutted down the runway, enduring lusty eyes that feasted on her, imagining what they would do if they lured her to their beds. Everywhere she went, it stalked her, haunted her, frightened her. With Beau's simple words, 'I am here now.' a lifetime of cumulative fear crashed in on her.

She had no shield, laying before him naked. With her blood mixed with his seed warm between her legs, Alaina quietly and completely fell to pieces.

Beau soothed and stroked, speaking to her in French. When she responded to his touch, he kissed and cajoled, "Alaina, I won't leave. I am here now. You are safe."

"Make love to me," she whispered.

Her ragged cry tore his soul in two. He smothered it with his lips, coaxing her with his body. "Hush, *mon amour*. We are together. I am yours, and you are mine."

Her hands pulled his hair back, her expression becoming fierce. "I have always been yours, Beau Landry." She turned her left hand, bringing it to his face. The diamond sparkled in the dim light. She arched her back, and pulled his mouth to her breast, as wild passion overtook her.

Beau made a deep growl and rolled with her to his back. She seemed startled to find herself atop him, but he guided her hips, showing her the way to take her pleasure. "That's right," he murmured as she found the rhythm.

Moving his hand between them, he teased and enticed, fanning the flame. He felt it begin, deep within her. Incapable of coherent speech, he muttered a patois of English and French as they shuddered together, the fires burning away the years of loneliness and fear.

At dawn, Alaina murmured, "I need to get in my car."

"You don't think I am letting you out of this bed, do you?" He snuggled closer, growling in satisfied pleasure.

"Then you go get it. I have no idea where the attendant put my keys." Alaina wiggled into him.

Drowsy and distracted by the delicate mole at the corner of her mouth, he whispered, "What do you need in your car, *chèr*?"

Alaina laughed, "Himari insisted I bring a shack pack."

Beau choked and sat up. "A what?"

"A shack pack. You know, toothbrush, change of clothes, that sort of thing… in case I got lucky."

"Lucky?" Beau snorted, nipping her ear. "Is that what you call it?"

Alaina settled in the multitude of pillows; her hair fluffed in the sexiest tousle Beau had ever seen. She smiled and said, "I think the only time I ever got lucky was when I asked you for directions."

Beau propped his head on his palm. "And I got lucky when you came back, that first time and now."

She turned toward him, laying her hand on the side of his face, the shadow of his black stubble giving him a pirate look in the dawn light. "I was never gone, not truly."

He closed his eyes. "I was."

"I know. That's why I waited. I knew one day you would come back."

Beau gave a rueful snort and dropped his head onto his outstretched arm, nose to nose with her. "I wasn't sure. I was never sure."

Alaina's voice was just above a whisper, vulnerable but brave. "Are you sure now?"

Beau brushed his lips against hers. "I wouldn't be here if I wasn't."

Alaina returned his kiss, their urgent need long spent. They touched, gentle and quiet. "What changed, Beau? What brought you back?"

"Later, Jolie Catin, we have lost too many years. Right now, just let me love you."

And she did.

January 30, 1000 ME

Three Days - Lenox Mansion - Beau and Alaina

They spent three days in bed. Their meals appeared on carts outside the Master Bedroom door. They soaked in the hot tub, made love in the shower, slept in each other's arms, laughed, cried, and fell back into sync. It had always been the way of them, instinctive and natural, no contrivance or falsehoods. However, they avoided discussing the events that drove them apart, understanding that it robbed them of a decade, and refusing to give it power over the first days of their reunion.

Alaina cracked her eye at 8:00 am on the morning of the fourth day and found Beau fully dressed. From the way he stood, she realized their fragile bubble was about to pop.

The time had come to deal with the tough subjects.

Beau faced it without fear. He would be strong enough, this time. Offering her a cup of coffee, he invited her to join him at the small table set with a light breakfast, a view of the bay beyond the pool and large manicured gardens. They sat in silence while she sipped her coffee and picked the delicate raspberries out of the fruit salad.

When she seemed sufficiently awake, he cleared his throat and began. "I need you to tell me what happened that night in the bayou."

Alaina put her cup down. "You don't remember?"

Beau gazed out the window. "Not much. I have flashes, like a lightning storm at night, bits and pieces. It's confused."

She nodded, and he saw her keen mind working behind the aquamarine depths of her eyes.

When she remained silent, he marshaled his strength and said, "I don't know what is real and what's a nightmare."

"It was a nightmare."

"I remember the war. That has become clear." He tapped on a stack of papers she had not noticed. "We're not the only ones dealing with this. And after the other night, I have a much better idea of what it is."

The blood left her face, "You mean after what happened with Peter and the others?"

He met her head-on. "When Satan and the angels showed up in my backyard? That is exactly what I mean."

Alaina looked away, the rumpled bed inviting. She glanced between it and him, imploring.

He shook his head. "Jolie Catin, we have to talk about this."

She stood up, her chair tottering on the tile floor. "Why? Why do we have to talk about this? It's over. You are better. Let's be done with it." She turned her back on him, rubbing her hands up and down her arms, hugging herself.

"It's not, and you know it." He pulled her against him, resting his chin on her shoulder, holding her tight. "If you don't want to talk about the bayou, we don't have to right now. But we will soon, Alaina. There are things in play here I don't quite understand, and I need your help figuring them out."

"I lost you over this. I don't want to take that chance again. It's too soon." She turned in his arms, fragile. "Can you understand that?"

Beau laughed with bitter irony. She only understood a fraction about the years he spent struggling between delusion and reality. He could not convey the darkness, or the frustration of being consumed by an endless battle with depression, delusions, paranoia, and night terrors. It was like living in quicksand, but he had pulled himself from the mire and was not going back. "Things are different now. I am different. But I understand."

He set her away from him, serious and determined. "If you're not ready, we can put that aside for now." He looked out the window and came to a decision. "I'd like you to get Prince Peter on the phone. I've got questions, and he's got answers."

"Peter?" Alaina asked, surprised.

"Seems there is more to Prince d'Or than what comes across in the news, now isn't there?"

Alaina put her hand on her hip. "You don't know the half of it, Beau."

"I would have never believed it, but I've been able to deduce quite a bit." Beau's blue eyes flashed shrewd intelligence.

Glad for a distraction, Alaina tilted her head and teased, "And what, pray tell, have you deduced?"

He stretched, the tension in his body abating. "Well, he's up to his eyeballs in The Resistance, if he's not the one behind the thing."

Alaina's eyes widened. Only a few people knew of the covert organization, even fewer were privy to Peter's role in creating it. "What makes you say that?" She settled into her chair, interested, but alarms blaring in her brain.

Beau held up his hand, counting down his points, "First, the network is well-financed, which I know a bit about." He flashed her a millionaire's grin. "It's big money behind that organization with power and resources coming from inside."

Alaina ran her tongue over the inside of her teeth, crossed her arms, and sat back, curious. "Go on."

He gave her a sultry look. "Second, when you asked me to pick them up, you called him Falcon." Her eyes widened at her mistake. He narrowed his and delivered a bombshell. "That is the name of the organization's leader."

"How do you know that?" Alaina paled.

"Jolie Catin," he wagged a finger at her, "do you think my *grandpere* has not looked into this?" He swept his hand around the grounds. "You think the man that built this is not gathering intelligence on every organization and fringe group that might disrupt our business?"

Alaina saw him transform, no longer the amiable Cajun, the playful teasing boy who danced with her at a *fais-do-do,* nor the haunted soul struggling with the aftermath of war. He was the son, and the grandson, of tycoons, and that DNA did not skip a generation. Standing before her was the Beau Landry she had never seen. The power he exuded was formidable and incredibly sexy.

"Don't worry. I saw the report. They know very little. I figured out the rest on my own, and I've kept it quiet."

Alaina's aquamarine eyes dilated; treason was dangerous business. "What else?"

"It does not take inside information to pull together the third thing. It's the timing of Prince d'Or's disappearance and reappearance with Prince Josiah and those girls. I got to admit, though, they were a hell of a shock, Jolie Catin." He penetrated her reserve, and she felt like she was sitting in Sarah Landry's famous chair. "You helped them get away?"

There was no sense denying it. He was in on this now. "New Year's Eve, when I called you."

"That's what I thought, good girl." He leaned forward, kissed her mouth, then whispered in her ear, "Fourth, because I met Prince Peter, and he ain't nothing, I mean nothing, like we all been led to believe. There is nothing stupid about that man."

Alaina remembered thinking that in Montreal all those years ago. "You are right." She relaxed; he had indeed used his extraordinary mind to make these connections. "I believe we could say the same thing about you."

He flashed her a grin and continued, "Fifth, because he knows you. And from our conversations, I figured out you work directly with The Resistance leaders. Why do you think I told you I wanted to be involved?"

"Your patriotic duty?" she teased.

The joke missed its mark. "I left my patriotic duty in the dirt with the severed heads and exploded bodies of my friends, Alaina."

She flinched. He had never, in all the time she knew him, mentioned the action he had seen in the Civil War. She did not look away. "Well, that's why I got involved, because of what they did to you. You saw something on that battlefield that hurt your mind."

She looked down at her hands and said, "There were things you told me that night in the bayou after it was over, when you were bringing me home, before you stopped talking." She covered her face, beginning to cry. "Before you went away and wouldn't come back."

Beau's heart broke. "What did I say?"

She lifted her head slowly. "You said that was the second time you'd battled something like that."

Beau closed his eyes and pursed his lips, seeing it, and for the first time in his life he did not fight it off. "We were lined up, behind enemy lines. My unit had broken through, and we were hellbent on taking out the command because old Korah was on the field."

"You don't have to do this," she whispered, taking his hand.

He ignored her and continued, "I remember the smell. It was awful, rotten eggs. I could taste it. This thing, this being, came out of the smoke. It wasn't human, though it dressed like a man. I never knew what it was and never could wrap my head around it.

"But the other night, Prince Peter had a come apart at Prince Josiah. He went *coullion*. I wasn't eavesdropping for the sake of snooping, but they just looked like they were about to kill each other; and I did not want to have to explain that. So, I was on hand to keep the peace."

He took a sip of lukewarm coffee. "Josiah said something to Peter about him getting the life that should have been his, and I will tell you what, *chèr*, those two men went ballistic. Turns out, Korah killed Josiah's momma and daddy, but he also killed Peter's momma."

Alaina gasped in horror. "Oh, that is awful!"

"That ain't the worst of it. Old King Korah, he got himself a monster. Peter freaked out and yelled that it lived in the Palace and would mess with him, but it was what he said the monster did, how he described it…

I knew that was what I saw on the battlefield."

Beau gestured to the table. "Those letters over there are from my old Army commander, James ben Kole, that's Ian's brother. He and his wife Persa, they're involved in this thing, too. Ian knows the truth, always has, he just won't say."

He pressed his lips in a firm line, the weight of responsibility resting on his shoulders. "I'm not exactly his favorite person right now." Beau gave a rueful smile. "It's like we've all got bits and pieces. I think it's time we put it all together."

Alaina nodded, feeling resigned. This was coming for them, whether she liked it or not. "Sit down, Beau. Before we call Peter, I need to tell you about the Black Key."

By late morning, Beau made two emergency calls: one to Pepperwood, one to the Center. His message was simple, "Get to the Lenox Mansion by tomorrow morning at 8:00 am, do so with the utmost stealth and secrecy because their lives depended on it."

January 31, 1000 ME

A Time of Reckoning

Alaina insisted that any contact with Peter happen at the bunker. "There is absolutely no way we can make contact outside the secure lines we've set up. I've put my tail on the line to even suggest it. And trust me, there was a battle *royale* to get permission." Alaina met the eyes of the assembled group, James and Persa, Ian and Joanna. "The location is secret, so for security reasons we'll have to drive together."

"I've got a vehicle that will do the trick," Beau said.

Ian snorted. "How many cars have you got now, Beau?"

Beau flashed a grin. "A fair few, Whitey."

"Shocking."

"Just like your hair," Beau teased.

"You're just jealous, cause I'm prettier than you." Ian mimicked Beau's accent and patted his face.

Alaina giggled. From the things Beau told her about Ian, she expected a solemn, aloof man. She should have known better. His wife, Joanna, reminded her of Beau's mother, not in looks necessarily, but in demeanor and intensity. Ian's brother James was sunbaked and tough as rawhide. He said little, but when he did, she found his melodic Irish burr soothing. He fairly oozed integrity, a stalwart, steadfast presence. It did not surprise her he rose in the ranks of the rebel army. Standing beside Persa, Alaina felt like a giant, though the little fairy woman carried an innate aura of strength that belied her stature. She expected Persa to take charge, and she did.

"We will do absolutely nothing that puts Peter in further danger. Do all of you understand me?" Persa looked around the room, settling on Alaina. "If it's safe, can you arrange a video conference? I would like to see him." She pressed her lips in a grim line and raised her pointed chin. "I've been worried."

James put his arm around his wife, patting her shoulder in silent reassurance. He nodded in concurrence but did not elaborate.

Joanna and Beau sent questioning looks toward the silent couple, unable to fathom how two horse ranchers from Northern California knew Prince Peter.

Ian long suspected but was never certain. Over the years, he caught their looks when Prince d'Or was mentioned and saw the way Persa leaned forward if his picture came on the news, love and longing in her face. He remembered a frantic phone call in the middle of the night from James, "Pray! Pray for a young man fighting for his life." Ian realized with sudden clarity; it had been the Prince. He shocked the group by saying, "We will not discuss this further until we reach the rendezvous. It is the leading I feel."

Alaina did not understand what he meant, but the rest of them did, so she did not argue. She was the outsider in this group, existing on the periphery, a ghost in Beau's life, his missing half.

Joanna caught Alaina's eye and said, "Alaina, we are all so glad you are here, and we are happy for you and Beau."

Alaina glanced away, trying to hide the emotional impact of those words. "Thank you."

An odd peace settled over the room, bringing clarity and purpose. They all struggled to reach this moment, this time, and a sense of destiny fell.

Beau broke the silence. *"Mon Dieu."*

James rose and lifted Persa to her feet. "Let's go."

Video Conference

"I expect we are having a video conference because a certain 4'10" Commander-in-Chief insisted," Peter drawled, as he moved away from the camera and took his place on the couch between Astrid and Davianna. Prince Josiah sat at the end, tall and regal. Out the window, the New York skyline loomed in the background.

"I'll box your ears, Peter," Persa said affectionately, eating him up. "You've had me scared to death."

Prince d'Or flashed his famous smile. "Fey, this was not a spur-of-the-moment adventure, you know that."

Persa harrumphed, her mock fierceness dissolved, and the other ten people did not exist for a second. Hazel eyes held emerald ones, and she said, "It's good to see you."

"You, too." He smiled and turned to the pretty redhead beside him. "May I introduce you to Astrid?" He cleared his throat. "Astrid, the little lady in green is Persa. That stern-looking brute beside her is her husband, James." Peter kissed Astrid's cheek, claiming her in front of everyone.

Astrid brought her thumbnail to her mouth, but dropped her hand, looking uncomfortable. "It's nice to meet you both."

Persa gave the girl a speculative look, and it hit her broadside who Astrid resembled. She fought to keep her face neutral, but she was unsuccessful.

Peter read it. "Yeah, I am a sick bastard."

James pinched the bridge of his nose and shook his head. Dropping his hand to his lap, he looked at Peter and said, "Boyo…"

Peter laughed. "I better watch out, or he will have me shoveling manure for a year." He patted Astrid's knee, then looked back in the camera, his face teasing. "Mr. Landry, it is a pleasure to see you again, sir. I regret our hasty departure."

Davianna snorted. "We did not have the opportunity to say goodbye."

Astrid's shoulders shook with suppressed laughter. "Party crashers ruin everything."

"Snakes ruin everything," Davianna deadpanned.

Josiah leaned down and looked at his three companions, his lips parted incredulously as the three of them cracked up. He turned back to the camera, maintaining his royal dignity, though it was apparent that the laughter in the New York Penthouse was infectious. "I trust there were no ramifications, sir?"

Beau rubbed his chin. "Not immediate, although that was the catalyst for the conference today."

Thus, they called the meeting to order.

Ian began, "If I might, I'd like to open us in prayer?" Nods of ascent and the clasping of hands brought them before the Lord. "In the name of the Father, the Son, and the Holy Ghost, we pray that you grace us with your presence. Protect us, guide us, and reveal what you would have us know. For you alone are omniscient, and we sense each of us has bits of a great puzzle, that in your wisdom, you might reveal, for your glory and purpose. In Jesus name, Amen."

Genevieve ben Willard rose. "Alaina, when you called and asked for this meeting, I prayed, and feel prompted to start at the beginning." At the chorus of head nods, she folded her hands and said, "On the evening of April 30th, 985, Prince Eamonn left the Palace stables for an evening ride. He was unaccompanied, as was his habit."

She nodded toward Peter and Josiah. "Josiah, you were home, on leave from the RMA, and the three of us were together. I was in mortal dread, but at the time I did not understand why. Josiah, you were furious at being kept in the children's wing that night."

Josiah nodded, looking grave. "You were a force to be reckoned with, Auntie. You would not let me leave, no matter how loud I blustered. I suppose I owe you my life. I never thanked you for that, but I'd like to express my gratitude now."

Davianna looked between them and added, "As do I."

"Congratulations on your betrothal, by the way," Genevieve said, her light gray eyes flashing with delight.

Josiah turned to Davianna, touched her hand discreetly and announced, "Wife, Auntie. We were married two days ago."

The bunker erupted in mass congratulations.

Persa kept her eyes on Astrid, interested in the young woman who seemed to have captured Peter's affections. She caught the subtle withdrawal from Peter's arm slung around her shoulder at the mention of marriage and saw the way Peter pulled her back. His expression remained mild, but his body language was resolute. Persa turned to James. He'd caught the subtle interplay too.

Peter cleared his throat, and they quieted. "As Auntie explained, Uncle Eamonn disappeared off the Palace grounds that evening. His body was later staged, to make it look like a riding accident, but he was murdered. Korah killed his brother."

Silence fell. Most of them suspected, but to have it confirmed like that, just matter of fact, shocked them.

The two Princes exchanged a look, and Ian deduced they had carried that certain knowledge for a long time.

Peter continued, "We believe Korah performed a ritual with the aid of some ancient tech, and in so doing, released a supernatural being he calls the Dark Master. But his actual name is Marduk."

James growled, hearing the true name of his enemy.

"Who paid me a visit the other morning," Astrid said dryly, her voice, full of loathing.

Persa met Astrid's eyes across the screen. "Did you see him?"

Astrid's tweezed brows came to a point over her nose. "He bit me."

Persa drew up. "He has done that to me, too." Knowledge passed between them, fury and disgust over the act, mutual hatred, then something deeper. Persa ground out, "Do not let him touch Peter again."

Astrid nodded, and across the airwaves they reached an understanding. "I won't."

Himari paled. "Peter, the old tech Korah used, was it a cell phone like the Black Key?"

Peter nodded, looking troubled. "I believe it was. Korah obtained it a couple of years before he used it."

Himari grimaced. "Damn."

James leaned forward. "And one of those things freed Marduk?"

Peter stared into the camera. "Yes."

Ian took a drink of water and said, "Joanna, please tell everyone what you saw the night of the Coronation Ball."

Persa turned to Joanna, confused. She assumed Joanna was merely accompanying Ian. Her family was in exile, long removed from court intrigue, but they were an integral part of Prince Eamonn's reign, so she supposed she might have something to say. "You were at the Coronation Ball?"

Joanna took Persa's hands. "Yes, I was there that night."

Persa felt her stomach drop.

"We met. You probably don't remember. It was in the powder room."

Persa wanted to tell Joanna to shut up. She did not want to hear anything, not in front of all these people. Instead, she issued a low warning. "I don't remember the ball."

"I didn't either until a few weeks ago, not the important part anyway." She blotted away a tear, and gratefully accepted the tissue Genevieve handed her. "I was hiding because I was fat and hot, wearing a horrible dress."

"Jupiter's Moon, was it yellow?" Persa's eyes widened in surprise.

A spurt of laughter escaped Joanna. "Not one of my best fashion choices, but yes, a hideous thing."

Persa smothered a giggle with the back of her knuckles. "I don't think it was as bad as the hair," she broke off, seeing the vision clearly.

They erupted in giggles.

Davianna and Astrid turned to each other and joined in, kindred spirits. "What about the hair?" Astrid squeaked.

Joanna held up a palm and said through choked giggles, "It was terrible. It looked like a rat jumped on my head and did a dance."

The girls howled.

Himari looked at Alaina and shrugged. "I do not know what they are talking about."

Josiah and James exchanged a bemused look.

Ian rolled his eyes.

Beau, the baby brother to five sisters and lover of women, sat back, enjoying the show.

"I'm sorry. Okay, hold on." Joanna took a drink of water, composing herself with effort. "I was hiding."

"Because of the hair," Davianna prompted.

Everyone laughed.

"I'm sorry, I do that when I get nervous," Davianna apologized.

Josiah turned to her. "You do that when you are not nervous, Minx."

Ian raised a straight eyebrow at Joanna. "Do you need me to tell the rest of it?"

Joanna waved him off. "No, I'll do it. I'm sorry. I don't know why I keep laughing. This is serious."

Peter chimed in. "I know exactly why. If there is one thing Josiah and I have learned in the last month is that you have to laugh." He took a deep breath. "I expect you are going to tell us you encountered the infamous Secretary Tristin?" Peter's eyes became murderous. "Marduk, in the flesh."

All laughter stopped. Persa put one hand on James' knee and the other on Ian's, her arms stiff. From behind closed eyes, she issued a command, "Say it, Joanna."

"He was hunting," Joanna said in a small voice.

"Bloody Hell!" Peter exclaimed. "He was. I knew it. I hid."

Persa's chest convulsed, but she held on, "What did you see?"

Joanna stared at the floor. "He picked three women: a Greek Princess, a blonde French Creole woman… and you, Persa." She collapsed into Ian's arms, burying her face in his chest.

Persa spun into James, and he held on.

Beau Landry bolted to his feet and shouted, "Mademoiselle Charlotte!"

Alaina's eyes grew to the size of dinner plates. "The witch!"

Prince Josiah sat erect; an army commander's voice erupted from his chest. "Princess Philomela of Greece, Antiochus' sister."

The stunned silence was broken only by Persa's faint crying. She had not known there were others. Marduk held her, but she never knew there were others.

"My Esteemed," Ian's voice cut across the silence, "please tell us what you know of Greece."

Josiah turned to Peter and gave a meaningful look at the girls. After the massacre, Greece was a painful subject for them. Peter pulled Astrid across his lap. She and Davianna snapped together like magnets. With a nod, Peter acknowledged his understanding, accepted their care, and freed Josiah to speak.

"For several years, I served in the King's Army, assigned to a unit that patrolled the pilgrim road. Our territory encompassed a large part of eastern Greece, to the Macedonian and Turkish borders. As such, I am familiar with the area and the political environment."

Josiah shot Davianna a private look, she patted his knee, encouraging him to continue. "Princess Philomela died under mysterious circumstances shortly after returning from the Coronation Ball."

Peter nodded. "That was the catalyst for the fall out between Alanthia and Greece. She was injured at the Palace. I was young, but I remember there was quite a stir. It shook my mother to her core. She was very frightened by the events, but I never knew the details. Afterward, Antiochus and Korah loathed each other. Diplomatic relations between our kingdoms have been strained ever since."

The weight of responsibility to repair the errors of the past and to chart a new course rested firmly on Josiah and Peter's shoulders. Mutual understanding passed between them, and Josiah remarked drolly to Peter. "Quite a pair, those two, Antiochus and Korah."

Josiah turned his attention back to the group. "It was rumored that Princess Philomela died in childbirth, though no child was ever publicly acknowledged." His mind pulled random bits of information together, a hypothesis forming as he spoke. "Afterward, Antiochus became a recluse, some say he went mad. I am inclined to believe it, based on how he ruled. The Iron King rebuked Greece, and it descended into chaos. It is a hotbed for violence and rebellion, a training ground for jihadists. Great evil has grown in the region in the last fifteen years."

He patted Davianna's knee. "Unfortunately, the pilgrim roads from the west run straight through there. Camp Eiran was not the first Pilgrim slaughter I encountered. Though that was the sole purview of man, many others were not." His face grew grim. "It started small, missing kids along the road."

Joanna gasped.

Ian stiffened.

Josiah continued, the Captain of the King's Army delivering a report. "There were wild stories, which we dismissed as flights of fancy, at first. The locals bore witness to a creature of immense stature and strength, with the appearance of a mythical god of old. In '96, we gathered the first hard evidence that we were not dealing with a legend but a vicious, cannibalistic beast. The culprit embarked on a reign of terror, slaughtering anyone who stumbled into his territory. Witness' statements, plaster casts, and physical evidence pointed to the truth. The Israelis in my unit called it by name, Nephilim, a supernatural being, created as a byproduct of a sexual union between a fallen angel and a human woman, a giant."

Alaina became an ice sculpture, frozen and beautiful.

Josiah's concentration shattered at the dual howls of pain that erupted at opposite ends of the kingdom; one from Persa, the other from his wife. "Davianna!" He wrenched her away from Astrid. "What?"

"Daddy." Her face contorted. "We were in Greece when he died. I was the one… I found him. All around the area were huge footprints in the sand. And, and… there was a spear buried in his chest the size of a tree." She shook her head, her voice hoarse and halting. "We couldn't get it out. It was too big."

The story pulsed out of her like blood gushing from an arterial wound. "My mother wanted to leave him there, but I couldn't," she said, begging for understanding. "You know I couldn't. I couldn't just leave him there."

Her eyes glazed over. "So, I tried to bury him, with that giant spear sticking out of the ground. I just threw dirt on top of him because I couldn't move him. It was just too big. And then the birds came," Davianna sobbed. "My daddy…"

Josiah picked up his young wife, cradling her like a baby, and left the room.

Everyone stood at once.

Peter's urgent cry cut across the chaos. "James!"

James looked up at the video screen, Peter's worried face in closeup. "Persa!"

James nodded. Persa was wrapped around him, her chin on his shoulder, sobbing uncontrollably.

Peter's voice broke. "Pepperwood is safe. It always has been. It's protected. Get her home."

"Exactly what I was planning to do." James' brown eyes burned. "Peter! Be safe, we love you." With that, he too, carried his wife out the door.

Peter looked at Alaina, her normal peaches and cream complexion had gone stark white. "Alaina, go with them, keep me informed." The video screen went black.

Beau turned to Himari and Genevieve. "Are you two coming?"

Himari shook her head. "Hell, no. I've got my own shit going down around here. You all go figure out how to fight the fucking giants."

All Six of Them

Twenty minutes after leaving the bunker, Joanna's phone chirped to life. "What in the hell have you gotten yourself into, Lady J?" Elias ben Phillip whispered into the phone.

"What are you talking about, Elias?"

"I'm talking about the all-points bulletin I am holding. You, Ian, and several others, are wanted for questioning."

"For what?" Joanna whispered.

The phone shook so hard in Joanna's hand that Ian took it from her. Elias quickly and quietly relayed the message.

Ian's face went stony, and he signed off, thanking Elias.

"Mon frère, where y'at?" Beau adjusted the rearview mirror to see Ian.

"Where we're at, is on the run. Seems the Prince of the Power of the air intercepted our call. All of us are wanted for questioning."

"On what charge?" Beau asked.

"High treason."

James swore with violent creativity. His anger burned against Korah, hot and bright, which felt better than desolation.

Alaina pulled out her phone like a gunfighter. "Sunflower, we're in the wind. Going dark, I know the drill." She disconnected and turned to the group. "Give me your phones, now!"

With ruthless efficiency, Alaina dismantled them and flung them out the window, one at a time. Joanna made a pained noise as hers sailed into a sandy bank.

"Beau, there are three safe houses in the vicinity."

"List 'em off, Jolie Catin."

"There is a large one right on the Bay, though it is in the New City. We have a remote cabin in Rancho Corral, and a house disguised as a vacation rental at Mill House Beach."

In unison, Joanna and Ian called out, "Mill House Beach!"

Beau pulled his sunglasses down from the visor. "The beach it is. *Laissez les bons temp rouler."*

Part 12 - Mill House Beach

January 31, 1000 ME

Car Rides Make Good Musings

Beau cast Alaina a sidelong glance and asked, "How many safe houses does The Resistance have set up?"

Alaina blew out a quick breath, considering. "I don't know. Honestly, I believe Peter is the only one that knows them all, but I'd estimate there are at least a hundred from here to the Golden City."

Beau whistled. "That takes serious money."

Alaina gave him a sly smile. "We didn't steal it. We made it."

Beau turned a speculative glance at her. "Talk about?"

Alaina's aquamarine eyes slanted, and she ran her tongue over her upper teeth, her head tilted to the side. "Tech."

Beau chuckled, recognizing she was mimicking his penchant for understated, one-word answers. He made a low growl. "I love sexy, smart girls."

"I can walk a runway, too."

"Oh, Jolie Catin, like nobody else."

Heat passed between them.

Ian piped up, "Do I need to drive? Watch the road you randy Cajun, I don't want to end up in the ditch."

Minus the ladies, Beau would have informed Ian that the strength of his erection could lift the vehicle out of any ditch, but Sarah Landry's son refrained. Instead, he waggled his eyebrows at Alaina in comic exaggeration. "Old married men don't understand, do they, Jolie Catin?"

Joanna scoffed.

James' voice cut through the air. "If you two rutting stallions are finished. I'd like to get my wife to the safe house, please."

Beau felt transported back to the Army, under James' command. 'Sir, yes, sir," Beau barked. Then lowered his sunglasses and winked at Alaina.

There was more to talk about, more to uncover, but the human mind and heart had limited capacity on how much pain it could absorb in a single sitting. When Prince Josiah lifted his heartbroken wife from that sofa, they reached their maximum; except for Persa and James, who could not stop it.

Persa rested her head in James' lap, curled on the bench seat in the back of the SUV. The truth had been lurking in a corner of her mind for months, as if she knew on a soul-deep level the genuine horror of her captivity, Rapha.

James stroked her head, unable to think of a single word to make it better. He remembered the alley outside the chocolate shop, the feel of her hard stomach against his palm. He heard the doctor's devastating words, 'Too much scar tissue, I'm sorry.'

In the space of a morning, the maniac Korah was hunting them, the sanctuary of Pepperwood denied, and they had another horror to cope with. A pasture flew by on his right, reminding him that at least his horses were taken care of. Johnson was an excellent manager. If Persa was a mare, he would know what to do. But she was infinitely more precious, and he was utterly lost on how to care for her.

In the second row of seats, Joanna made notes to herself, fretting over the Centers. The day-to-day activities would be fine. She and Ian had excellent staff. In fact, since Judith's departure, the spirit and mood of the entire organization from the New City to New York changed for the better. Amazing how one negative force could affect so many people. It was the children that Joanna worried about. Prince Josiah's words echoed in her mind. 'It started with disappearing kids.' Leaning her head on Ian's shoulder, she whispered, "How many of our kids have disappeared?"

Ian brought a fist to his mouth. His eyes turned stormy gray. "Seven here, two in New Orleans." He followed her logic. They had been searching for the culprit since Elijah first mentioned it to him all those years ago.

At the front, Alaina navigated in quiet, confident directions. They drove in silence for twenty miles. Beau said low, for Alaina's ears only. "Mademoiselle Charlotte."

Alaina crossed her arms over her chest. "That witch!"

Ruthless, cold vengeance passed between them. "We are going to annihilate her."

Alaina looked like a Valkyrie of Norse legend. "Burn her to the ground, *mon loup*. To the ground."

Who is to Blame?

At Mill House Beach, James and Persa stood on the well-appointed deck. A persistent wind blew, but Persa seemed oblivious to the chill.

"No, it's okay. I need to be alone." Persa let go of James' hands and turned toward the sea. "Well, maybe not alone. I need to have a talk with someone."

James rested his hand on the railing. The low hanging sun glinted off his auburn hair, touched with flecks of platinum. "I'll watch from here. Don't go too far, Fey."

"I won't, Jay, just far enough to find Him," Persa said in a reedy voice. She looked ethereal and seemed to float away.

Ian moved beside James at the railing. "Is she okay?"

James dropped his head, studying the sand beneath the deck. The sea oats rustled in the wind, making a soothing sound. "She doesn't have much of a choice in the matter, does she? She never did."

Ian watched Persa disappear down the steps onto the beach. She looked impossibly small against the backdrop of the Pacific. "She's an amazing woman, always has been."

James' lips pressed into a firm line. "You knew, and you never said."

Ian dreaded this for more than a decade. "Not everything, but I did not have leave to speak, Brother, or I would have." He rubbed the back of his neck. "Or perhaps not. I'm not sure what good it would have done."

"I've had several months to consider that," James said evenly. "The memories started coming back in November."

The impact settled between them.

"When I saw you both at the wedding, I suspected they might have," Ian said, then turned, watching Joanna through the window. "There's something else."

"Something other than a devil kidnapped my wife, raped her, held her captive, and forced her to give birth to a hybrid?"

Summarized in such a straightforward manner, the horror of Persa's ordeal made Ian recoil. To deliver the final devastating blow seemed cruel. He closed his eyes and begged for wisdom.

It is time.

Ian obeyed. "Brother, it was our mother who invited Secretary Tristin to call on Persa. She told him where to find her."

James brought his left hand slowly up and covered his eyes. "Tell me that is not true," he said in a harsh whisper.

"I'm sorry." Ian focused on Persa's tiny figure at the water's edge. "Joanna overheard the conversation. She recalled it a couple of weeks ago." Ian scoffed. "I am certain Mother did not know what she was doing. She was just stupid and ambitious."

James erupted. "All those months we searched for Persa, and she never said a word. She watched me tear the city apart looking for her, watched me go crazy." He whirled, picked up a chair, and heaved it over the balcony. "She betrayed my wife into the hands of a devil! Robbed me of my children! And you say to me, 'She was just stupid'?" His chest heaved, and he had a maniacal look in his eye.

Ian stood stock still.

James snarled, "Do you know what she has been through? Do you have any idea the horror she endured those fifteen months he held her? I remember more than she does. I remember what she told me the day I rescued her." James came within inches of Ian's face. "He threatened to kill us, all of us, including that bitch of a mother of ours. Everyone! He invaded Persa's mind and found everyone she loved, including Mother. Including Mother!" he screamed. "She stayed, she submitted, she endured... to save us all."

James buried his face in his elbows. "I left her there. I crawled into a bottle, and I left her there. You kept trying to tell me, but I did not listen. I knew where she was. I would go watch her, and I did nothing!" He fell against the house. "I left her there, E. I left her there."

Ian gathered his weeping brother and held on. "None of us knew. I've dealt with this for years. We did not know. You cannot blame yourself."

James choked, "Then who else is there to blame?"

A strange, yet familiar, voice answered from behind the brothers, "Marduk."

They froze, then slowly turned to face the man who had spoken.

Joshua held out his hand, a nail scar visible. "Come with me. James. Let's go find Persa. She's out there looking for me."

The Best Medicine

Joanna decided she was the best candidate to figure out dinner. The safehouse had a stocked pantry as well as a freezer. She had no appetite. but it gave her something to do, and that was better than being idle. When she heard James shout 'Mother', she cringed.

Beau and Alaina were talking in low voices on the couch, but their conversation halted as the drama unfolded on the porch.

Joanna busied herself filling a stockpot with water. Beau and Alaina moved to the bar. "You need some help, *chèr*?" Beau asked.

Joanna shook her head, pushing her fringe cut hair off her forehead. "No. I am just making a pot of chicken and rice soup. I figured it might be soothing. My stomach is in knots."

"Been a hellacious day." Alaina said, rubbing the back of her neck.

Ian came through the door, his face as white as his hair. "It just turned into a heavenly one. The Lord is outside."

Everyone stopped.

No one doubted the truth of his words, but they exchanged mystified looks. Inexplicably, a hissing, hysterical laugh built deep within Beau's chest. His shoulders rocked with it. The corners of Alaina's mouth twitched as she joined in. Joanna coughed and wheezed, her own laughter breaking through.

Ian moved like a sleepwalker. "It's not funny. He really is out there."

Which sent the three of them into peals of hysteria. The look on Ian's face was absolutely priceless. He was aghast.

"You people are crazy. I think those two girls rubbed off on you."

Joanna moved around the corner to hug her ashen husband. "I hope so. We will need a bit of humor."

You Can Always Find Him at the Beach

For some people it was the mountains, for Persa it was the sea. The vastness, the power, the immensity, the unknowable depths, and mystery, she always felt Him at the beach. It just usually wasn't literal. She knew the moment she saw him walking with James.

Joshua.

Her feet were running before she gave a thought, flying above the sand, water spraying up her calves. She ran like her life depended on it, toward the source, toward the Savior.

He caught her as she leapt, spinning her in a wild embrace. His daughter, beloved Persa.

He lowered her, and she stroked his face in awe. "You were there. How had I forgotten you were there? You were there through it all, weren't you?"

Joshua's hazel eyes shone with love. He kissed her hand and said, "From the beginning to the end, and every day in between." He drew James beside them, and they walked down the beach. "You two have done well. I've sent many to you for refuge. You've cared for them, given them shelter, safety, and love."

"You protected us, Lord," James murmured, dumbstruck, nearly speechless.

"There was a great evil done to you both. But the Father is rich in mercy and steadfast love. He set a great hedge of protection around you. It still holds and will until the end. You can return to Pepperwood soon."

"What would you have me do, Lord?" James requested his orders with a military bearing, ready for battle.

"Remember the night that we met. Our companions will see you through the trial to come." In an instant, He vanished.

February 1, 1000 ME

The Last Field

"*Cher*, you the color of your shirt," Beau observed over breakfast the next morning.

Persa blew her cheeks out and glanced at her apple green shirt. "That bacon smells terrible. Who eats bacon that comes out of a box in the pantry?"

Ian shoved an entire piece in his mouth, chewing with enthusiasm. "It tastes good to me."

"Whitey, you'd eat a turd."

Ian considered for a moment. "I might if you battered and deep-fried it."

Persa covered her mouth and ran from the table.

James scowled at his breakfast companions.

Alaina threw up her hands. "Don't look at me! I am innocent in the whole fried turd affair."

James shook his head and went after his wife, muttering under his breath, "Children." Then he faltered mid-step. The horse breeder in him knew the cycle of every female under his care, including his wife. He calculated… October, it had been since late October.

He found her huddled on the bathroom floor. She was green, pale, and clammy. He handed her a warm washcloth for her face, then switched the tap and gave her a glass of water.

Persa looked at the glass dubiously. But she took a swish and spit it out in the commode, laying back on the floor with a groan. "I can't eat any more of that pantry food. It's killing me."

James sat on the floor, cross-legged, with his back against the wall. "I don't think it's the pantry food, Fey."

She moaned in misery. "I'm sick, Jay. It's got to be the food."

He closed his eyes and swallowed against the sudden hard lump in his throat. "Nobody else is sick, Fey."

"Well, I am." Her eyes were slits.

"I don't think you are sick, baby."

"Are you crazy? I threw up last night, again this morning, and at least half a dozen times in the last month." Persa countered, becoming impatient. He had all the sympathy in the world for one of their horses who fell ill. She was going through hell. Now she was sick, and he had the audacity to sit there and imply it was in her mind. She raised up on her elbow, glaring at him. "What do you think, I'm making it up?"

His eyes were enormous, alive with mirth. He shook his head and broke into a full Kole Brother's smile. "I think you are pregnant."

An immediate denial sprang to her lips. "No, I..." Then her mind began the calculations, her eyes blinking rapidly. "I, um, I uh... don't remember the last time..."

"October," he whispered. "It was October, Fey."

Her hand covered her mouth, eyes widening with shock. She extended her arms to him, and he pulled her close. They were both overwhelmed.

Planted the night the memory veil lifted and watered by their tears, the last field the locust destroyed bloomed. Persa and James were expecting a baby, at last.

Jarrod the Wonder Servant Strikes Again

It was almost a vacation, with three couples sharing a beach house. Short of a worldwide rebellion, global warfare, and the collapse of the Alanthian Government and civil society, it was a peaceful time. Isolated along the Pacific shore, removed from the chaos and violence, the three couples lived outside of it.

The evening of February 1st, a delivery van pulled up to the beach house. Joanna opened the door to the driver and got swept away.

The driver came in like a whirlwind. "You, go get the men. Tell them to unload."

Joanna stood in the doorway with her mouth hanging open. The woman was the most beautiful person she had ever seen, statuesque, raven-haired, blue-eyed, and bossy!

"You catch flies with your mouth open like that! Move, woman. I've not got all day."

"You're a… You're a…" Joanna stuttered.

"A Gune, yes, of course!" Jelena dismissed her. "And apparently I am still in logistics because we could find no drivers to do this delivery, so I had to do it myself. Now go on."

Ian appeared at the door and froze. He cleared his throat. "Jelena?"

"Ian," she rushed forward and swept him up in a big hug, "it is nice to see you again. Go get Beau and your brother to unload this truck. I brought you groceries." She winked at him.

It was more than groceries. The delivery included clothing, supplies, and weapons. Alaina realized the moment she opened the first box of clothes whose handy work this was Jarrod, Peter's valet.

"He is a wonder," Alaina declared. "He operates right under Korah's nose, cool and dignified. You would never know he was a revolutionary, if you met the man. I think he and Genevieve have had something going on between them forever, but she won't say. Turns red in the face and scurries off every time Himari teases her about it."

They unpacked the boxes like kids at a birthday party, perfect sizes, tastes, and attire for each of them. Alaina's face flamed when she got to the bottom of her box.

"What you got there, Jolie Catin?" Beau looked at her from beneath black lashes.

Alaina pushed the box away, fluffing her hair self-consciously. "Nothing." She tried to sound nonchalant.

"Pass it over." Beau was envisioning an entire box of lingerie.

She picked it up and tried to scamper off.

He scrambled up and caught her around the waist. "Oh, no. Let me see."

"Go away, Beau Landry!" Alaina squealed.

Ian leaned back in his chair, arms crossed over his chest, chuckling. "You may as well show him. You know he won't quit, stubborn as a mule, that one."

"Shut up, Whitey, 'for I come over there and kick your ass." He reached around Alaina. "Come on, give it over."

Alaina bit her lip and bowed her head in surrender. With sudden defiance, she shoved the box into his hands. "Here then." Her face blossomed pink with embarrassment.

Beau waggled black brows and gave her a lecherous grin. He opened the box, and his face changed, becoming sober. He closed the lid and carefully put it on the coffee table. Then he took her left hand, brought it to his lips, and got down on one knee.

Alaina covered her mouth with her free hand and squeezed her eyes together. The room went still.

"I asked you once, a very long time ago, but the question bears repeating. Alaina ben Thomas, I love you with my whole heart and have since the moment I laid eyes on you. I loved you when you were a child, and I loved you when we were apart. But my Jolie Catin, I never knew how much I was going to love the woman, until I got you back." His cobalt blue eyes shone, his voice husky. "I want to wake up with you every morning, and I want to go to sleep with you every night. I want to give you babies and dance at a *fais-do-do* with you when we are ninety years old. Will you please do me the very great honor of becoming my wife?"

Alaina brushed away a tear. "In my heart, I have always been your wife, Beau Landry. So yes, I will marry you."

Beau shot her his riverboat pirate grin, rose, and dipped her in an extravagant kiss. She came up tousled and glowing.

He pulled her by the hand, laughing. "Come on Jolie Catin, I think I saw red boy shorts in one of them boxes."

On February 2, Ian married Beau and Alaina in a touching ceremony on the beach. Alaina looked stunning in the white beaded gown that had been in the bottom of the box.

February 3, 1000 ME

McSwilley's Revenge

Persa and James emerged from their room to find the group huddled around Alaina's tablet. Alaina moved her finger over the video. "You two ought to enjoy this one." She beamed with satisfaction. "They released a whole series this morning."

Persa sat down gingerly, woozy. But now that she understood the reason, she was sublimely happy about it. "What is it?"

"Prince Peter's revenge, is what it is," Beau laughed.

King Korah's face came into focus, livid and leaning forward. The angle was odd, obviously shot without his knowledge. He had Ebenezer ben James, a man they watched on the news for years, by the throat. "If you run a story like that again, I'll string you up by your balls. No interviews with my son without my approval. He does not set policy. He does not speak for my administration and knows nothing about modernizing food production! You crossed the line with that interview, Ebenezer. If you do it again, I will shut this fucking place down."

James ben Kole grinned. "That son of a bitch."

Alaina took back the tablet. "That's the least of them. Korah is done. The entire world is about to find out, Prince Peter ben Korah is no dummy. You do not know how much I love this. I wish I could see his face when he sees this video."

Persa exchanged a look with James, who nodded. "Well, I'd like to see his face when I tell him a bit of news, too. We'll share it with you in the meantime. James and I are expecting a baby."

Ian flew off the couch and lifted Persa up with a whoop of joy. "Pers, congratulations!" He gave James a backslapping hug.

Beau turned to Joanna and Alaina. "I told y'all it wasn't the bacon."

February 5, 1000 ME

Himari Does Not Mess Around and Neither Does Alaina

Himari may have sent them off to figure out how to fight the giants on their own, but the intrepid little hacker had been busy. While the six beach house residents were having a pleasant interlude, Himari was researching. Hacking her fingers to the bone is how she put it to Alaina during their daily chat on February 5th. She followed it up with a dozen encrypted videos and internet links from the Last Age. Nobody in the Millennium could mine the databases of the old internet like Himari, which made perfect sense, considering she was one of the original pioneers in its rediscovery.

Nephilim had been a hot topic in obscure prophecy circles in the Last Age. There were volumes of research on them, hours of video, and at least a hundred books. Nasty creatures, though none existed in the age of the Gune, which was a testament to their inquisitive nature and desire to discover the deep things of God. It put the lackadaisical Millennials to shame, who had the evidence of God right in front of them and never dug below the surface.

Beau was watching a video, his long legs stretched out on the sofa. "Ooh-we, check out this dude's tie." He froze the screen and showed it to Alaina. "They had some fine clothes back then."

Alaina laughed and mimicked his accent. "You *coullion*, Beau Landry. It's your hour to be doing research, and you over there looking at clothes."

Beau shrugged off her mild rebuke. "I reckon you and me have a good idea about what we up against. We already faced it."

"Yeah, but it was little then," Alaina said under her breath.

"You gonna hafta share… *chèr*." There was a serious edge underneath the teasing.

Alaina stared out at the ocean; her eyes hooded. "I haven't wanted to spoil the mood."

"You avoiding it, and you know it," Beau countered. "You remember way more than I do, Jolie Catin. Hiding out ain't gonna make it go away."

"It's my honeymoon. How's that, for a where y'at?"

"Girl, you sound like you from Delacroix." Beau teased in an exaggerated accent.

"I'm practicing." Alaina moistened her lips. "So, I'll fit in when we go home."

Beau sat up and put the tablet on the coffee table. He rested his elbows on his knees, his face serious. "We don't have to fight. We can just go on with our lives, stay in the New City, or go to New York." He shrugged. "We can leave it. Let the authorities take care of it. We can just be done. There's nothing written that says we got to go face that damn giant again. I figure we've lost enough."

It was tempting, and she had been contemplating it for weeks. She even said it back at the Lenox Mansion, but something changed, and she wasn't sure when. Perhaps it was the night James threw the chair off the porch, or maybe it was the day Beau proposed to her, or more than likely, the day she finally became his wife.

"I want my office back. I want my house. I want Landry's, and I want to dance with you at a *fais-do-do* when I'm ninety. We can't have any of that if we run."

Beau nodded and grabbed the tablet. "Fair enough." He stretched back on the sofa. "Then let me figure out how to kill that orange-eyed bastard."

February 6, 1000 ME

Not What I Expected

The evening of the seventh day, Joanna and Ian lay awake with the sound of the ocean coming through a crack in the French doors. "It's a strange world we live in now," Joanna whispered, smoothing Ian's thick eyebrow. The coarse hairs were a deep brown at the roots, such an interesting contrast to his hair. She reveled in the freedom to touch them.

Ian relaxed under her hand with a contented, sleepy smile. "It's been a strange world for me for many years." He pulled her against him with a satisfied grunt. "Until I finally got you in my bed."

"For a man full of the Holy Ghost, you are exceedingly wicked in this bed," she said with a smile, rubbing against him.

He gave a low, dastardly chuckle. "Who invented sex? There is no sin in the marriage bed, Princess. Just you, me, and this nice round derriere of yours." He grabbed said body part with both palms and squeezed, emphasizing his point.

"I just did not think it would be this way." Joanna brushed a light kiss over his full lips.

Ian murmured, enjoying the feel of her breast against his chest. "What way?"

"Hot."

He rolled, putting her on top, appreciating the view. "You thought it would be… chaste?" He brushed his thumb between her legs and rocked his hips upward in invitation.

Joanna shuddered and arched her back, breathless. "I suppose."

Ian gave a deep chuckle. "Guess I fooled you."

February 7, 1000 ME

What Money Can Buy

"What is it, Jolie Catin?" Beau asked in response to the sick expression Alaina wore as she disconnected with Himari.

Alaina pressed a finger to her temple. "Astrid left Peter yesterday. He's not doing well."

Beau sat down heavily, empathizing with Peter. "That surprises me. They seemed bonded at my house."

Alaina snorted. "We were bonded, too."

"My fault."

"Not all. I believe a voodoo witch and her evil spawn played a part."

Beau glanced up at her and snarled, "Every year, every night, every tear… I'm gonna take it out of their hides."

Alaina's aquamarine eyes showed deadly intent. "With pleasure, *mon loup*."

Beau nodded, rubbing his stubbled chin, considering. "I don't think we should tell the major and his little wife about Peter. These things have a way of working themselves out, and those two, well, they dealing with enough. Let's give them a minute."

"Joanna told me they have been trying for a decade. The doctors told her she could never have children."

"I've never seen a man so happy as the major is right now. He'd carry her everywhere she wanted to go if she'd let him." Beau took a step closer to Alaina, nose to nose. "You ain't as easy to pick up. You an Amazon beside that woman."

Alaina put her hands on her hips and drew herself up to her full height. "Makes me a better giant fighter."

Beau narrowed his eyes at her, a memory flashed. "I seem to recall you beat the shit out of that witch, *dis moi la vérité?*"

The corner of Alaina's mouth twisted. "I grew up in a bar, honey."

"Ha! I can just see you strutting down the runway with a baseball bat, busting heads."

Alaina laughed ruefully, "I fought off more than one ardent admirer."

All teasing banter evaporated. The mental image of her at the mercy of lusting men made him furious. He ground out, "Well, you won't have to ever do that again, *chèr*. I will destroy any man that tries to lay a hand on you."

Alaina gave a dismissive wave. "It came with the territory. I did okay."

Beau ran his fingers through his hair and laced them behind his neck. "I should have just come. I knew where you were." He leveled a look at her. "I kept tabs on you. Did you know that?"

She raised her eyebrows, the little beauty mark between them emphasized their lift. "And how did you do that?"

His arms fell to his sides, just a bit ashamed. "Money."

Alaina's jaw dropped. "Money?"

He lifted a shoulder. "I'm rich."

"You are a spying scoundrel, that's what you are!"

He pulled her around the waist and buried his face in the crook of her neck. "I figured if you ever got in trouble, I'd come. That's what I told myself, at least."

"You are Sarah Landry's boy to the life. That's the sort of thing she would do."

Beau pulled back from her, smiling. "Well, she did it first. When I was out of my head. She made sure you were okay. Used our money to make sure you did not fall into the hands of anybody unscrupulous, especially in the beginning, when you were just getting started."

Alaina pushed away from him, stumbling back. "What?"

"She didn't do nothing wrong, *chèr*, just had our lawyers go over your contracts, and made sure you signed with the right agency." Beau met her outrage, completely unrepentant.

Alaina was opening and closing her mouth like a fish on land, could form no words as her mind spun backward. It had been so easy, or so it seemed. The right agency, the right contracts, while the rest of the models she knew scraped by hand to mouth, Alaina skyrocketed to stardom, never paying serious dues.

"Did you honestly believe that *Maman*, who loves you, was going to send you off alone to the New City with a few shekels and a set of pink suitcases? You think the Landrys would abandon you because I got sick?" He shook his head. "You know Ellen is my cousin, right?" he asked, referring to Alaina's executive assistant and business partner.

With sudden clarity, she knew, black hair, blue eyes, languid grace. "I'll be damned. She is a Landry. I should've known. That treacherous bitch."

Beau chuckled. "She did you no harm, Jolie Catin. Wouldn't tell me much, she kept your confidence. She was no spy, even though I picked at her. She'd tell me things like you were hungry, or tired, or working too hard. Ellen loves you, like the rest of us."

Alaina stood, dumbfounded. "All these years… I thought I was alone. Come to find out…"

"That you were never really alone, *ma fille précieuse*." My precious girl.

"Money," she said with a rueful roll of her eyes.

He shook his head and pulled her close, "*Amour*."

She should have been angry, outraged even, to discover the life she was so proud of had been a product of manipulation and Landry machinations. But then the truth dawned on her. It had been her work that made it happen, long hours in the gym and in front of the camera, commitment, being half starved. It was no contract or bevy of Landry lawyers that burned up the runway, that had been her.

"I don't know whether to kick you or kiss you."

"I'd prefer a kiss but gimme a warning if you plan to kick me with those lovely long legs. You got some slutty black pumps with silver buckles in that closet, put those on if you are going to kick me. I might even like it."

Alaina got a calculating gleam in her eyes, pushed him onto the bed, and turned toward the closet. She emerged from the bathroom a few minutes later, dressed in black lace and those shoes... Beau was exceedingly happy to take his punishment.

Several scratches and bite marks later, Beau said seriously, "Before we leave, you and Persa are going to have to tell what you know. We can watch all the videos, read all the research, Ian can move in the Spirit, but the fact of the matter is, you two have first-hand knowledge about what we up against."

Alaina covered her eyes with her elbow. "She hasn't seen one since it was a baby. The one we saw was four years old. I cannot even imagine what they have grown into now."

February 8, 1000 ME

Throwback

Persa cracked an eyelid and waited. She was not sick this morning, so she smiled and yawned, giving a lazy stretch. They had the Master Bedroom with its enormous king-size bed and luxurious down comforter, which she inhabited with her strong man. Rolling to her side, she stroked his chest, twirling the hair with her forefinger. "You've gotten hairier."

"I have?" he asked through a yawn.

She propped on her elbow and moved her questing finger to his temple. "Uh-huh, and I like this silver."

One corner of his mouth lifted. "Just look at Ian. You'll see what I'll look like when it goes completely white." He moistened his lips, adding in wry humor, "Bless his heart."

Persa chuckled. Alaina gave them an extensive lesson on the phrase a few days before. "They are an interesting pair, aren't they?"

"Ian and Joanna?" James stretched, shaking off the remainder of sleep.

Persa ran her fingers through James' hair, massaging his scalp. He snuggled back into the pillows with a groan of contentment. He did not need much, a decent dinner after a hard day, a kind word, and petting, not even sex, just rub his head or the shoulder that bothered him, scratch an itchy spot on his back, and he was pretty happy. At the beach house, their long-term relationship juxtaposed with the two honeymooning couples. "I guess both couples when you think about it. I wonder if we ever acted like that?"

"What, in heat?"

Persa snorted. "I seem to recall several years of that for us, my love."

James gave a lazy smile, enjoying her touch. "I suppose now, we go for quality over quantity." He squeezed her shoulder. "Though we have to suspend that for about seven or eight months."

Her stroking finger stopped. "What do you mean?"

James leaned up and kissed the end of her nose. "It means, Fey, that until the baby comes, I'm not doing a single thing that might put you or that little one in danger."

Persa flopped back into the pillows with an exasperated outcry. She knew him well enough to realize he was serious. "We have been going at it like teenagers these past few months, and I am perfectly fine."

"Yeah, but I didn't know." He rolled over on his side. "I do now." He moved the tip of his finger around her engorged breast, full and hard, the pink nipple turning rose with pregnancy. "Though, these are nice."

She gave him a half-lidded pout. "They also hurt and itch. I had to run in here yesterday and rip off my bra to scratch. It felt like I was being stung by a thousand ants."

"Well, don't hurt them. They're pretty." He weighed one in his hand. "It really is not fair. It's like the boobie fairy came overnight and left these behind." He leaned over toying and teasing the nipple with his tongue.

Persa whined, "You can't do that and then turn celibate on me."

"Who said anything about being celibate, Fey." He moved a hand over her little pouched belly. "The first twelve years we were together, we did not have sex. But I imagined all manner of interesting things we could do."

He spent the next twenty minutes showing her exactly what he had in mind.

War Stories

"I'm warning you, Joanna, don't play poker with him," Ian said from the kitchen, stuffing a whole cupcake into his mouth.

Joanna bridged the cards with a flutter. "I'm not afraid of this Cajun."

Ian took a huge gulp of milk, chasing the cupcake, and wiped his mouth with the back of his hand. "He'll cheat, and if he doesn't cheat it won't matter, because he does not lose."

Beau leaned back in his chair, balancing on the back legs. "I'm sitting right here, Whitey. I can hear you. You realize you and she aren't communicating on that higher plane you walk around in."

"I don't need that higher plane to tell me you are a rascal and a cheat. I've known you since we were fourteen years old. You forget, you showed me some of your tricks back at the Academy."

Beau gave Joanna an innocent look. "Don't believe him, *chèr*. He's telling you tales." He leaned in and whispered conspiratorially, "It goes with the hair, gone a bit senile."

James gave a low laugh, pulling out a chair. "Don't let that lazy bayou persona fool you, Joanna. This man is a shark. Money chases him down, tackles him, and begs to jump in his pockets. I've never seen anything like it. He can set up a good race, though. I made a ton of money before the war with him booking and holding stakes on races across the territory."

Persa raised her head from the book she was reading. "What?"

Ian called from the kitchen where he was scoping out the refrigerator, absurdly thrilled to be able to talk about that time. "Oh, you should have seen it, Pers. He was amazing. Nobody ever rode a horse like that. Drunk or sober it did not matter, James was something. Nobody beat him, ever." He pulled a cold chicken leg out of the refrigerator and took a bite. "And when we fought? There was no distinction between him and the horse; they were one and the same. It was a sight to behold."

James' voice was low and held an edge of command. "And what did you see, Lieutenant?"

A long-forgotten cannon exploded in Beau's mind. He froze. Everyone else leaned in. Ian's chicken leg fell to the plate. It was time, and only Ian truly remembered.

Ian wiped his mouth with his hand and ran the water in the kitchen, washing up. He shook off the excess and took a towel from the rack, all eyes on him. Making his way to the table, he pulled out a chair.

Alaina moved behind Beau, resting her hands on his shoulders. Persa came beside James, who scooted over, making room for her beside him. Joanna closed her eyes for a moment, then met Ian's and nodded.

Ian folded his hands on the table and said, "We had one objective that day, take out Korah and his command." He nodded to James. "Those were our orders. The night before the battle, you came riding in with Persa and six other horses. I couldn't believe it when I saw you, Pers. You were so little, wasted away to nothing, and your eyes?" He shook his head. "They were huge, full of fear but a fierce determination that I recognized. It was the same expression you used to get when you would push yourself to some crazy trick on the back of those horses with James. The one that said you were doing it, even if you died trying." Ian gave her a two-fingered salute.

"I'd seen that thing that held you, on the Capitol steps on 9/11. Do you remember Beau? It struck me blind."

"*Mon Dieu*!" Beau made a low growl. "I do remember that Loa."

"Well, that was the first time I encountered it. I am pretty certain I ran into it again several months ago at a luncheon we had at the Palace. But the day of the battle? That was the worst."

He looked between Beau and James. "You sure you want me to tell this? I don't know what good can come of it."

"I remember most of it, *mon camarade*. You ain't gonna hurt me."

James gave a silent nod.

Ian braced himself, said a quick silent prayer, and continued, "We fought our way through the lines. Nobody could stand against us, not mounted and armed like we were. It was the last battle, and we wanted to win. We tore through them like it was nothing, in a straight line. They fell by the hundreds, and we did not lose a single man in the charge. I could see them, Korah and his generals. He thought he was safe, but he did not know who was coming to kill him."

Ian took a drink of water. "I swear I made eye contact with him, he sneered at me. Then he raised his arms above his head and shouted, something guttural and nasty. I really wanted to kill him then. I realize now, he was calling something down. We saw what it was a few minutes later."

Beau took up the story. "That devil came out of the mist dressed like a medieval knight, all in black. It looked to me like his horse was breathing fire. For years, I thought I imagined that, but I don't think I was."

Ian held his gaze. "You weren't. It stunk. The whole battlefield reeked of it, sulfur and brimstone, nasty. He killed the entire line, everybody on either side of us with just the flick of his hand."

All three men raised their hands to their faces, their eyes closed against the memory.

"He turned to you, Beau." Ian swallowed heavily. "He called your name. You floated out of the saddle and just hovered there. Then he looked at us," the Kole Brothers held each other's eyes, "and he called, James and John, sons of thunder!"

A clock ticked in the silence, no one moved. "I knew we were going to die, right then. The hatred that pulsed off that creature wasn't of this world. It did not have an age." Ian's heart was pounding, his breathing labored. "Then he took off his helmet and showed us who he was."

"A huge reptile, black as coal, with fangs that drip blood, and a forked tongue," Persa said through clenched teeth.

Ian nodded. "I lost my bowels. It was the vilest, scariest thing I ever saw."

James' face was pale. "It yelled something at us, in a language that made me want to vomit."

"It did. And right before it raised its hand to kill us, the Lord came between us. There was a flash of lightning, and the entire world went white. I looked around, and all three of us were up in the air, surrounded by light. It was quiet, peaceful. No sounds of battle, screaming men, or firing guns, just us in a cloud or a dome or something. Beau, you smiled at me. Then it was over. You and James passed out, and I was sitting there in my own excrement. I looked around, and the battle was over. The guns were quiet. The fighting stopped. I dismounted, heaved you both up on your mounts, and took you to the hospital tents.

"The next day, nobody remembered anything, including you, Pers." Ian looked away. "All these years… I never told. Because I promised I wouldn't, but I told Him I wouldn't be able to do it on my own. So, I lived a life by myself. I stayed away because even with the gift, I might tell. And what good would it do? What difference does it make? Even now, all it's done is bring it back to mind." His voice shook with emotion.

"Ian," Joanna's voice cut across the table. She fell to her knees beside him. "It shows how he can be defeated, honey. Beau did not die that day, because he was covered in your love. Otherwise, he would have died with the rest of that line. You two brothers, your bond gave him pause. That's why he was cursing."

The answers came so clear to her. "It was love that kept you alive. The strength of your love carried you through it." Joanna stood up, her face shining. "You prayed, all of you. I know it, all of you prayed in Jesus name and it brought them down."

Beau's mouth fell open. "You did! On the steps that day, and then you could see."

Persa leaned forward, "And when James and I married each other the day before the battle, we did so in His name."

James was still, "That's who I called on in the battle. I screamed it at the top of my lungs."

Standing straight and tall, Alaina said, "And that's how we did it in the bayou."

An Uncle Boudreaux Tale

Beau covered Alaina's hand, tan and dark, over slender and manicured. His blue eyes were intent, she met them, silently begging him not to say what she feared. "It's time to tell, Jolie Catin."

Her voice cracked, sounding tiny. "No, please don't make me." She stifled a sob, "Please, Beau don't… don't make me."

He came out of the seat, holding her close. "I'm sorry, *Bébé*."

"It's too terrible. It's too scary! No," she cried and tried to push away. "There were dead things everywhere. It was voodoo, Beau, with bones and skins and blood."

Alaina hit his chest, her head thrashing back and forth. "She was dressed, oh God, she wore clothes like something out of a nightmare. She painted her face white, like a skull with black lines all over it. Her eyes, there was no color, like a corpse. Don't make me go back there. Don't make me remember it!"

Joanna moved behind Alaina and laid a hand on her back, whispering a silent prayer. Ian moved into position behind Beau, doing the same. Persa wrapped her arms around Alaina's waist, resting her head against her arm, murmuring soothing words. James stood to one side, a hand on Beau's shoulder and one on Alaina's.

Alaina's frantic gasping slowed, as she absorbed the love surrounding her.

"We are all here, you can do this," Beau whispered.

"I'm afraid, Beau. You weren't the only one scared that night. I never let myself remember. I saw what it did to you, what if I lose you again? What if I can't come back?" Her voice squeaked, like a small child afraid of a monster, hiding in the dark. "What if I get lost in the bayou?"

Beau closed his eyes, pressing his forehead against hers. "I won't let you get lost in the bayou, Jolie Catin. I promise, I'll come get you. Tell me the story, pretend it's just a tale like we did that first day. You remember, the one where you were the governess?"

Alaina laughed, an edge of hysteria to it. "You didn't believe the governess story, but I can, maybe tell it if it's just a tale."

"That's right, like Uncle Boudreaux."

"He tells the worst stories, Beau. Nobody ever believes him." She sounded drunk.

"It's just an Uncle Boudreaux story. Come on, tell it like that."

"Just a bayou tale, designed to scare the kids so they won't go running around after dark and get lost in the swamp?" Alaina floated backward in time.

"That's right, just like that," Beau whispered, floating off with her.

"Well, it started the night of the Coronation Ball when the king's wicked brother stole the throne. There was a price to pay for that throne. A wicked god demanded his choice of all the fair maidens in the land. The wicked king, he don't care about the ladies, he only care about his kingdom, so he agreed. That wicked devil, he showed up to the ball, and he picked out three pretty girls, so he could make his own sons."

Alaina swayed, but the hands of her friends steadied her. "One was a Creole Princess, she pretty on the outside, but inside she full of rot, wicked to the core. A voodoo priestess, dressed in silk, she took that devil to her. The other two maiden's, they was scared of him, not Charlotte.

"When that baby was born, it wasn't right from the start, but she twisted it all up and trained it, like a pet. She ordered it around, and it would do anything she told it to do. But its daddy was a devil, so it could lift things up in the air and spin 'em around with its mind.

"He was a huge and ugly thing, with a giant misshapen skull and teeth that protrude, even when its lips were closed. He had orange hair and eyes the color of hellfire. It could utter curses, make people see things that weren't there. It was always hungry, and its favorite treat was little kids, they tender and soft, like veal.

"On Halloween in 990 ME, Charlotte decided it was time to move from the little kids and babies she was feeding it to a young couple she'd seen on a lonely lake. They were minding their own business. The girl, she'd made her boy a supper, and they were eating it on the pier, sitting on a blanket. They had wine, and it was a fine dinner. The girl was so proud because his granny taught her how to make that food, and she knew he loved it. He told her so and leaned in for a kiss. It was the last kiss she got from him, and it tasted like wine and gumbo."

"It was good gumbo, *chèr*," Beau said in dreamy remembrance.

Alaina's smile was otherworldly.

"But then the witch came, and the boy and girl, they just floated into the boat. They didn't scream or nothing, they couldn't. The devil did something to their voices, and they couldn't yell. They couldn't move, just floated. The girl thought about all the bad things she'd done in her life, the things she'd stolen, the people she'd lied to, all the selfish and mean things she'd done. She was dabbling in stuff she shouldn't, things that were forbidden. And the boy? He was just too good for her, too smart, too kind, and too rich. Her life with him and his family had been a dream. She weren't nothing but Mississippi bar trash, and now she was going to suffer. And that devil made her think she deserved it.

"They took them to a place, a terrible place, with burning fires and things hanging from the trees. It smelled horrible, blood and rotten flesh. Flies buzzed everywhere, big fat green ones. They were feasting on the dead animals, whose glassy eyes were shining in the firelight. That witch, she was twirling around the fire, shaking a skull full of bones, cackling and calling out instructions to her boy. He was taller than a tree, his hands the size of frying pans, and his face was painted like the witch's, like a skull, black and white. He stood off from the fire, watching, licking his lips at the boy and the girl like they was dinner. They still couldn't move. They were stuck, paralyzed.

"Then that witch, she pulled out a big ole knife and started toward the girl, and that's when the spell broke. For the boy, he loved the girl, and he'd been praying. She heard him, then he said it, he said the most powerful name given unto man by which we might be saved, Jesus. Jesus.

"And he took that knife and broke the witch's hand when he did it. It snapped, loud. The girl could hear it even above the sound of the buzzing flies and the scream of the giant, who was coming after the boy, fast. That witch turned on the boy, she was going to hurt him, and that made the girl mad. She wasn't scared no more. She picked up a stick and beat that witch near to death. And the boy? He took after that giant with that big knife, chased him down. That giant, he saw death in that boy's eyes. and he ran.

"Then the girl got scared again. She started crying real loud, I bet they heard her in Delacroix that night. Once she got to crying, the boy stopped chasing that giant and came back to get her. He loaded her up in that boat and took out of there, took her to a safe place, where people took care of the girl. As soon as he docked the boat, though, the boy, he couldn't talk, just like back at the voodoo fire.

"The girl, she cried and begged and pleaded, but he wouldn't come back. Then the girl got scared. She started thinking that the witch was still out there, and she was going to be angry. The giant, it was still out there, too. They weren't going to forget, and without the boy to protect her, she was a goner. All those things she thought when she was floating, well, they seemed real, too. She was just trash. So, she ran away."

Silence hung in the air. Alaina opened her eyes, "And now you see why nobody ever believes Uncle Boudreaux's stories because they are terrible."

Beau's eyes shone, stormy blue and intense. "You forgot the ending, Jolie Catin." He cupped her cheek. "After a long time, the evil witch's curse was broken, and the boy woke up. He went searching for the girl and found that she still loved him. He married her on the beach, and they lived happily ever after."

All You Can Do

Ian woke in the night to the sounds of muffled tears and found Joanna curled in the fetal position, crying into her pillow. He reached out, struggling out of a deep sleep. "Hey, what's wrong?"

She turned, engulfing him in a desperate hug. "I'm a noodlehead."

He gave a faint laugh. "What?"

Joanna sniffed. "I've been laying over here thinking about my life, how the biggest thing that I ever worried about was what size my jeans were. Alaina and Persa and," she broke into fresh sobs, "our kids! They were disappearing. What got them? What they must have gone through?"

"Princess, we don't know that, not for sure." He kissed her tears away. "I'm glad you didn't go through what those other ladies have, but don't think for a minute, you lived your life only concerned with your jean size. Look at me." The pale moonlight filled their bedroom, casting ghostly shadows on the walls. "Nobody has worked harder for those kids. You've saved hundreds of them, and never once have I heard you ask, 'What's in it for me?'"

Her voice was small. "It's how I was raised, 'for whom much is given, much is expected'."

Ian laid his hand against her cheek. "But you lost it all. You had nothing when you started. You could have used your family connections to do anything you wanted. Joanna, you could have gone to the Golden City and lived with your grandfather and never worked a day in your life. You could have just found some rich guy and married him, played tennis at the club, and sat on a charity board once a month. You did not have to work seventy hours a week, going into abandoned buildings, drug houses, and brothels to pull those kids out, to show them a better way, to give them a home, and a hope. You didn't have to do any of that," he kissed her gently, "but you did."

She closed her eyes, her voice a broken whisper. "What if it wasn't enough? What if I am not enough?"

Ian snorted. "Let me tell you something. When I was first filled with the Holy Ghost, I was frantic with the work that needed to be done. I tried to rush from place to place, from person to person, to do it all." He stroked her arm. "Then I got sick. I wasn't sleeping. I wasn't eating."

Joanna laughed, and he gave her a crooked smile.

"I ended up in the hospital, down in Miami. I was there for several days, dehydrated, exhausted, with a fever they could not get under control. But I kept trying to leave, and they kept putting me back in the bed. Finally, this Cuban nurse came in and told me if I did it again, she was going to restrain me. She dug in my bag, pulled out my Bible, and said, 'Read it.'"

He laughed ruefully. "I was so pissed. I thought, 'Who does that old bat think she is, to tell me, who has seen the Lord, to read the book? She does not know who she is talking to.' I was nineteen."

She smiled, her eyes full of fondness.

"I flipped it open and started reading, because I had nothing else to do, and I was pretty certain she was going to restrain me. So, I read." He rolled over, staring at the ceiling. "I figured out that Jesus, when he was walking the Earth the first time did not run around like a maniac, rushing from place to place, trying to get it all done. Then I started thinking about the Iron King. He doesn't leave the Golden City; we are commanded to go to Him." He turned and said matter of fact, "Which we need to do."

Before she could argue, he resumed his story. "So, there I was, stuck in that hospital bed, and I got convicted. I was trying to make myself more important than the Lord, trying to rush, trying to do more, do it faster. Do you know what happened, Princess?"

She got a flash of mischief in her eye. "You ate all the food in the hospital?"

He cracked up. "Well, that… but too, He started sending them to me. The people He wanted me to touch, orderlies, nurses, doctors, once even a little girl whose brother had been in an accident. They came to me. I just had to be still."

Ian rolled to his side, admiring her profile with its cute turned-up nose. "The thing is, He gives us the work He wants us to do, no more, no less. Don't hold yourself to a higher standard than He does. He knows we have to sleep. He knows we are human. Don't make the same mistake I did and believe otherwise."

Without opening her eyes, she gave him a sleepy smile. "Thank you." With those words, Joanna truly rested for the first time in her adult life.

February 9, 1000 ME

Game Night

It was James' idea. Perhaps because he was about to expire with lust for his wife, or because he did not wish to lose any more money to Beau Landry at poker. More likely it was because he knew there was one more story that needed telling, and he dreaded it. Then again, it might have just been that he was a competitor deep in his soul, who craved competition and loved winning. If it wasn't going to be at poker, then he would find another mechanism. Nobody believed it when he emerged from the bedroom with a Pictionary game in his hands.

Industrious entrepreneurs were recreating the toys, games, and videos from the last age, rediscovered in the files of the old internet. Alanthians bought them by the truckload, especially the Superhero videos. The beach house was full of them, left behind by vacationing families over the years.

Persa jumped to her feet, just as competitive as her husband. "Boys against the girls!" she declared, and no one argued with her.

It was a disaster for the boy's team.

The girls mopped the floor with them, much to Ian's outrage. "Now that is not fair! How in the world did you get 'Horizon' with one straight line?"

Joanna raised a haughty chin at him. "We're just smarter than you."

Ian pointed at her. "You'll pay for that, Princess."

"Get back over there with your scientific drawing," Persa teased.

"What?" Ian motioned to his last drawing in frustration. "It was a water molecule!"

The girls exploded with laughter. A single wave drawn on the paper got them to 'water' before Ian finished his molecule.

Alaina rolled the dice and moved her piece on the board, an "All Play". She picked the card and looked at it, then covertly passed it to James, who studied it, and nodded. The two teams huddled around their drawings.

James was fast. He drew a stick figure with a triangle on the bottom, pointing to the triangle.

Beau yelled, "Skirt!"

James nodded furiously and drew a crosshatch pattern on it.

"Plaid!" Beau guessed again.

James nodded with enthusiasm and drew a long penis hanging down from the triangle.

Beau yelled out, "A plaid schmeckle skirt!" Simultaneously, Persa blurted, "A kilt!"

James dropped his pencil and looked at Beau in disbelief. "A plaid schmeckle skirt?"

Ian fell off the couch, howling.

Persa croaked, "A what?"

Beau turned red, his chest starting to shake. "A plaid schmeckle skirt, you've never heard of one, *chèr?*"

"A schmeckle?" Joanna was wiping tears from her eyes.

"It's what my granny called it."

Alaina was losing it. "Beau, your grandfather is Scottish!"

He threw up his hands in surrender. "We don't wear kilts in the bayou."

February 10, 1000 ME

Well Beyond These Walls

After lunch, Persa cleared her throat. "I'd like to say something."

Joanna turned off the water in the sink and dried her hands. Ian finished the half a sandwich Joanna had left on her plate. Beau put down the glasses he was clearing and straddled the chair backward, facing Persa. James made a grunt deep in his chest, pocketing the screwdriver and leaving the door repair for later. Alaina lowered her tablet, her hand slightly shaking.

"I've been thinking about how brave Alaina was the other night when she told us what happened in the bayou." Persa gave a small bow toward her new friend. "I have similar stories, many are worse." Persa sighed, staring at her feet. When she looked up, her face became resolute. "I don't need to rehash them or relive them. In some ways, that feels like it gives glory and power to him, and I'm not going to do that."

"Amen, Sister," Ian agreed.

"The fact is, I survived. We've all survived him. There's not a person here, his wickedness hasn't touched, and it goes well beyond these walls. We saw that on the conference call." Persa tucked a loose strand of hair behind her ear.

"What you need to know from me, is what I remember about the beasts." Her lower lip quivered, and she placed a protective hand over her stomach.

James came forward, but she held up a palm, halting him. "Stop. I have to get through this, and if you touch me, I won't."

He nodded but did not look happy.

Persa steeled herself and looked directly in Ian's eyes. "I didn't see it very often, only a few times. It was dangerous and vicious from the second it was born. I thought I'd die during the birth. I was only pregnant sixteen weeks, but it was enormous when it was born."

James reeled backward, that was why he had not seen her pregnant all those months when he was spying on her. She'd already given birth, and it nearly killed her. He brought his hands to his lips to keep from crying out.

"Tristin," she tsked, "which is what he called himself, kept me from the creature, for my safety. He liked to dance with me and pretend I was somebody else." She shook her head with a humorless laugh. "It's why he took me, why he held me… because I was a dancer." She shrugged, wearing the armor of sarcasm. "I couldn't dance, if that thing chewed my leg off, which it tried to do when it was three days old." Persa pulled up her pant leg and pointed to a bite mark on her ankle, old and faded, white with age, but still visible.

"The worst thing they can do, both of them, is jump in your mind. They can get in there and mess around. I don't think they can read your thoughts, but they can see your memories, at least the pictures you hold in your mind. They are experts at interpreting facial expressions, and they understand body language. They can send their thoughts into your brain and plant things that never happened. They tell you lies." She looked straight at Alaina. "They will tell you that you aren't good enough, that you deserve what they are doing to you."

Persa's nose flared. "I got damn good at keeping him out. The only time he'd get me was when I was sleeping, even then I learned how to fight him off." Her eyes were lidded in remembrance. "Wicked bastard.

"In the end, the Lord put a hedge of protection around us. It's held to this day. Tristin… Marduk has never penetrated it, and it wasn't just us it protected." Her voice faltered. "It protected Peter, too. When it got too intense, when that beautiful boy could take it no more, the Lord sent him to us, and he was safe. None of us understood it. I think he did a little. He knew…" She covered her face, then laced her fingers together. "He knew that Marduk did not touch him when he was at Pepperwood." Persa let out a shuddering breath and continued, "He told me as much, the last time he came to us. But it disappeared in the crisis of trying to keep him alive, and I forgot again. That's when the agoraphobia started. That's why I became so afraid to leave the ranch."

"I'm so sorry, Pers. I was hard on you about that." Ian looked crestfallen.

"You didn't know what precipitated it." Persa forgave him. "The thing is, perhaps Pepperwood isn't the only place with a hedge around it. Beau, is Landry's protected?"

Beau's face became veiled, but he gave her a sarcastic smile and said, "No, Persa. Among other nefarious creatures, the Prince of Darkness came for a visit."

Persa dropped her hand and lifted her eyes to the ceiling, a laugh escaping. She held up a finger, signaling he should wait while she giggled. "Well, there's that, but he didn't come to visit you, did he? He was after Davianna, wasn't he?"

"It's more accurate to say he was after what Davianna is carrying, poor *Bébé*."

Persa held up her hand in surrender. "I can't go down that rabbit hole with you, Beau Landry. It is taking every bit of energy I've got not to freak out about what we are facing. If I worry about what Peter and Josiah and those girls are up against…"

Alaina chimed in. "I'm not even going to tell you what else has gone on with Himari and several others in the Resistance. It would curl your hair."

Joanna and Ian exchanged knowing looks. Ian bobbed his head in agreement and spoke. "The question becomes, what work are we being called to do?"

Beau rested his chin on the back of his palm. "Well, Whitey, I think that's where your expertise comes in, now isn't it? You the one with the calling." There was no rancor or sarcasm in his voice, just a simple statement of fact.

Ian winked at Joanna. "Well, Beau, it seems like I'm not the only one these days. My beautiful bride joined me in that calling the night we almost met Satan."

Alaina stood up. "Oh, mercy, y'all wear me out." She stalked off. "I'm going to the beach."

The room was dead quiet. James looked out at the beach and murmured, "That's a good idea."

Joanna turned to Ian. "I hate wearing a bathing suit beside her."

Beau's eyes went to the bedroom door, and he grinned. The faint notes of a bayou song followed him down the hall.

Persa stood alone in the room, dry-eyed, and bemused. She guessed she was going to the beach. It was as good a place as any.

February 11, 1000 ME

Rock Around the Clock

At 1:12 am, Joanna and Ian both sat straight up in the bed.

"Did you hear that?" Ian asked.

"Another brick in the wall?"

Ian shook his head, looking haunted. "That's not what I heard."

"What did you hear?" Joanna asked in a breathless whisper.

"Not that…" Ian blinked.

A light came on in the living room. They scrambled to get dressed. Beau stood in the middle of the room, blinking against the light. Persa and James appeared in the doorway. James looked thunderous. "Who is blasting the music?"

They exchanged sleepy, confused looks.

"What did you hear, James?"

"What?" James grumbled and rubbed his face. "Somebody yelling and cracking a whip. It scared me to death."

Persa looked up at him. "No, they were singing about a tornado."

Beau argued, "Uh oh, that's not what I heard."

Alaina appeared in the hallway, her face frozen in terror. "I heard something else, a song from the Last Age. I think that means… the Black Key… he's found it."

They fell to their knees in unison.

They prayed for twenty solid minutes until Ian raised his head and said, "Amen."

Persa's voice was quiet. "Did you see anything, Ian?"

"Not clearly, but I think Davianna and Josiah are okay." He shook his head in resignation, "I've got nothing on Peter. He and Astrid… it's just blank."

Alaina buried her face in her hands. "Persa, he's not good. I didn't want to tell you, but Astrid left him a couple of days ago. He's been out of his head. Genevieve is worried about him; we're all worried about him."

Persa dropped her hands to the floor in frustration. "You should have told me."

"I told her not to, *chèr*. You two got enough to deal with, and you happy with the baby…" He nodded toward the couple. "We took it up for you, though. They've been in our prayers."

Persa's voice strangled as she said, "You don't know what he's been through."

Beau tilted his head and gave her a knowing glance. "I know more than you think, and I can imagine the rest."

Huge hazel eyes bore into cobalt blue, of all them, Persa, Peter, and Beau bore the deepest scars, Marduk's greatest victims.

"And so you can," Persa whispered. "Thank you for your prayers."

Alaina leaned against the wall, her long legs stretched out in front of her. "If we all heard different songs, then that means it released them, the rest of the elohim."

"Today is February 11th, right?" Persa asked, sounding defeated.

James looked at his watch, "Yes, why?"

"I watched a video that Himari sent over, and one speaker had a theory. It was complicated, based on bible numerology that I couldn't follow." Persa made a listless shrug. "He hypothesized the Nephilim did not come into their full power until they were fourteen." She looked at each of them, "That would be today."

"Great. We not only get to take on giants; we get to take on full power giants! Damn, like Thor and shit." Beau looked at Ian, the corner of his mouth twitching. "We need a vat of toxic waste or something, so we can fall into it and come out Superheroes. You can be Spiderman. The major, he can be Superman. Me? I'm an Ironman kinda guy."

Ian shook his head, laughing, "You are a bat shit crazy kinda guy, is what you are."

"Not anymore, *mon ami*. Though after all this, I might be again. But I reckon this time, I'll have company."

They went back to bed because there were only two things to do at that hour, sleep or worry. As they were dozing off, Joanna whispered, "Ian, what song did you hear."

He gave a snorting laugh and rolled toward her, taking her firmly in hand. "Do you really want to know?" He brushed a light kiss over her parted lips.

"Yes," she said, enjoying the feel of his full lips against hers.

He squeezed and whispered in her ear. "Fat Bottomed Girls"

February 12, 1000 ME

One Last Battle Plan

"Well, we are no longer wanted," Alaina announced to her breakfasting companions. Beau followed her into the room, smiling. "I just got off the phone with Himari. The worst of the fighting has stopped."

"Good news," James said and took a drink of his coffee. "Guess we are leaving then." Pepperwood was weighing heavy on his mind, among other things.

Alaina handed him her tablet. "Look at this! Korah's government is on the verge of collapse. It is rumored the Ruling Princes are going to support a change in leadership." She moved to the kitchen for her tea. "We have been working toward this for years."

Persa leaned over James' shoulder and said, "Wow! I think they did it!"

"Did what?" Ian emerged from his room, toweling his hair.

"Took thirteen years, *mon frere*, but we are on the verge of seeing Korah's government declared illegal and watching Prince Josiah assume the throne. There was a lot of blood spilled in the mud to get to this day." Beau snapped his heels together and gave a smart salute to James. "Major."

Ian looked between the two, threw his towel on the sofa, and joined Beau.

James rose from his seat, tall and proud. Persa had a sudden vision of him in his blue officer's coat and vest, wearing a battered cavalry hat. She remembered the two First Lieutenants, gangly with youth, but with battle hardened eyes. James saluted, an easy, effortless gesture. Tears burned the back of her eyes as she watched the touching scene.

"At ease, gentlemen. We have one last battle plan to review before we discharge you," James said with authority bestowed upon him through rank, experience, and honor. There was no question who was leading them into battle.

Nope

"No, absolutely not. You are not leaving me at Lennox." Persa crossed her arms. "I'm going home."

"We're not staying at Pepperwood, Fey. I'm taking the horses over to Rivergate. Then we are going to fight, and you are not coming. You are pregnant." He punctuated the last three words.

"I'm well aware of that," she countered, "but of all of us, I have the most experience with these things."

"And we have the most experience fighting." James stonewalled.

"I gave birth to it; I'm going to kill it."

"You weigh ninety-seven pounds."

She drew herself up, offended. "I'm at least a hundred by now."

James reached out, running his finger over her jutting chin. "And our baby is about four ounces."

Her enormous hazel eyes pled with him, "Don't leave me at Lennox. Let me come home to Pepperwood and say goodbye to Dad. I'll go to Lenox when you fight. I promise." She laid a hand on his chest. "It's safe at home, even the Lord said it was."

"I'm not worried about Pepperwood. It's not safe out there. You've seen the pictures, the news reports, the whole damn world has gone crazy."

"Jay… I'm afraid. If you go to Pepperwood without me, I'm scared you won't make it back. I don't want to be apart from you. He's searching for me. I feel it." She rubbed her head absently. "I can't explain what it's like when they probe your mind, but he is pushing the boundaries of mine. What if he finds me, and you are far away? That mansion or even the bunker will not be any protection against him. Trust me."

"Dammit, Persa." James pulled her into a rough embrace. "You always turn those eyes on me and make me do things I know I shouldn't do."

February 13, 1000 ME

All Good Things Must Come to an End

They packed the SUV, but everyone lingered for a moment, looking back at the beach house. It had been an extraordinary two weeks, in some ways the most horrible time of their lives, and in others, the best.

"I've never had two weeks off," Joanna said wistfully.

"Neither have we," agreed Persa, pulling James tight around the waist.

Beau tossed the keys into the air. "I never worked two weeks." Alaina gave him a look, and he relented with a roll of his eyes. "In all seriousness though, if I had to spend my honeymoon with four other people, I guess y'all were all right."

Part 13 - The Greatest of These

February 13, 1000 ME

We've All Been There

They were hours outside the New City, and what should have taken an hour had taken four. "I can't believe it. Look at all this," Alaina said into the silence of the SUV. Cars were crashed, flipped, and burned, some still smoking. Charred remains and black skeletons of twisted metal blocked the road every hundred yards. Long stretches of the highway became impassable, the detours just as bad. Trash was strewn everywhere, remnants from looted vehicles. The eerie absence of people punctuated the devastation. Fighting and chaos rocked most of metro Alanthia for twelve days, and everyone was in hiding.

Joanna felt the destruction to her core. This was her home, her city. "Why did everyone leave their clothes on the side of the road, who would do that?"

"Look away, Princess, those aren't clothes," Ian said in a low, steady voice.

Joanna flinched, closing her eyes. "Oh, Lord. I thought they were clothes, they're all over. Ian, there have been dozens and dozens of them."

"I know."

"The Centers, what's happened to the Centers? If this is everywhere… the buildings burned, people dead on the side of the road?" Joanna started overloading. "Our house? The kids? Ian, where are the kids?"

"We'll get there soon." Ian patted her knee, not letting his own anxiety show. "We left Maribel and Jonas in charge. They are good, and they are competent. I'm sure they are fine."

"Beau, take Ian and me to the Center." Joanna dug in her prodigious purse, then realized her phone was on the side of the road.

"Lady J., I wish I could, but with all this wreckage, I don't think we are taking this vehicle into the city." As if to emphasize his point, metal scraped the underside of the SUV, making an otherworldly screech.

"Beau's right," James confirmed. "We do not want to get stranded out here." He surveyed the devastation. "Gentlemen, I think a change of plans is in order. We need to turn north, go to Pepperwood. We'll ride back into the city."

Joanna made a low, keening sound. James was not without sympathy, concerned about the kids, too. "Joanna, I understand how much you want to check on things, but this is our best course of action." He leaned forward. "Beau, find a place to pull over. Persa needs to use the bathroom."

Persa fidgeted in extreme distress. She'd had to pee for an hour and a half. "I'm about to have you pull off to the side of the road."

Alaina turned in her seat. "There should be a rest area up ahead." She looked down at the screen. "The GPS has our ETA at three minutes."

Persa did not open her eyes, all concentration directed at not wetting herself. "What does that mean in real-time?"

Alaina grimaced, looking pained, though nowhere near as pained as Persa. "Fifteen minutes?"

Persa made a pitiful groan. "Hurry, Beau, I don't care if you flatten all four tires doing it. Just get me to a bathroom."

Joanna smiled. "Well, I've got this bowl with a lid in my purse." She held it up. "If you want it."

"Shut up, Joanna. I'm not peeing in a bowl."

"We men don't have that problem."

"You shut up, too, Ian."

"Geez, she's mean since she's gotten pregnant," Ian said to Joanna. The smack to the back of his head came from his big brother. "Ouch!"

Ian turned and saw James with a satisfied grin on his face. Ian rubbed his head, which no longer hurt, but it was hard coded in the DNA of little brothers to pretend otherwise. "You hit me!"

"I'll do it again, too. Quit messing with my wife."

Joanna giggled. "Poor, Ian. Come here and let me kiss it."

"Yeah, you saw what he did." Ian shot a veiled look at James, playing the role.

"I'm going to kill you both," Persa growled. "As soon as," her voice climbed, "Beau Landry gets me to a bathroom!"

"I'm driving as fast as I can, Persa. Use the bowl!"

"Not using the bowl! Just drive!"

Smothered laughs came from several places in the vehicle. Persa whimpered.

February 14, 1000 ME

Ian's New Calling

It took hours to navigate the destruction, but the further north they traveled, the less concentrated it became. James drove down Pepperwood Lane at 1:00 am, to their collective sighs of relief. The headlights illuminated the pretty white house with its sparkling green roof. Persa had a vivid memory of the first time she'd seen it, riding out of the woods, the day James brought her home.

Ian unlocked the gate while they waited. James turned to Persa and murmured, "Welcome home, Fey."

Absurdly, she wanted to cry. Emotions, hormones, and an endless day hit her behind the eyes. "Welcome home, Jay. Love you."

He winked at her. "Have we got food at the house? I'm sure my brother is hungry."

"Your brother is always hungry," Joanna piped up from the back seat.

Ian hopped in the car. "You guys are hungry, too? Good, cause I'm starving." Tired laughter greeted his words. "What?"

"I was just saying you should take up the runway, Ian. You'd fit right in with all the starving models," Alaina teased.

Ian gave her a toothy grin. "Well, I'm handsome enough."

"Jolie Catin, you be sure and set that up as soon as we get home. Phone your agent. Ian's got a new calling. I don't think he's ever been a model."

"I need him to be a soldier before he's a model," James deadpanned as he pulled the vehicle up to the house.

Persa yawned. "I think I need him to be a cook, if he's hungry. I'm tired."

First Born

Persa walked down the dark hall, hiding in the shadows. An inhuman cry came from under the door, shrieking and wailing, calling for her. It beckoned, but she knew death lay in wait, greedy and grasping, reaching for her. She covered her mouth to keep from screaming. It must not know she was there. It must not see her fear, for if it did, it would consume her, bite by bite.

She ran, but in the way of dreams, did not move. Panting and pumping her arms and legs, she could not escape. The voice exploded in her head, dark and evil, taunting her. "Mother, I am coming for you. I see you in your bed."

It felt like she was being strangled. Blackness covered her, sucking her down into the pit, alone and forsaken.

James heard her moans and struggled awake, but a weight pressed him into the mattress. He could not move. A sense of dread washed over him. He felt her slipping away and could not reach her. His breath came in rapid gasps. He broke the invisible bonds that held him and flung himself on top of her, protecting her from the malevolent spirit in the room.

"Persa," he cried, his vocal cords thick with sleep and cracking in terror, "wake up!"

She fought him, pushing and struggling, crying now. "No, no! Leave me alone."

James felt himself being lifted from the bed. His blood ran like ice water, but he clutched his wife, lifting her with him. "Lord, Jesus!" he called.

Invisible strings severed, and he fell atop her with a whoosh. Persa gasped at the impact, coming fully awake. James raised his weight to keep from crushing her. In the bedroom's stillness, the sound of their labored breathing echoed in the cocoon he wrapped her in.

Her eyes were enormous, visible by the bright moon shining through the blinds. Her voice, when she spoke, had such icy dread it stopped his heart. "He is coming."

Better Off Alone

Rapha liked these Redwoods. They were tall like him. He considered the irony of traveling a road the humans called the Avenue of the Giants, somewhat amused by it. He was half-human, after all. Though he did not care much for that part of himself. The weak part that needed to sleep…

and eat. He preferred the other part, the powerful part, that could bend objects with his mind and manipulate matter.

He had vague memories of the woman he was hunting. Primarily, he remembered wanting to hurt her. That sadistic desire that drove him forward, plus the promise of greater power. His brother, Zuzite, had killed his mother at birth and enjoyed immense freedom before making the fatal mistake of allowing his hunger to overrule his mind.

Rapha recalled his father more, received missives and notes through the years, had an unlimited bank account, and completed all the tasks Marduk set before him. Both his parents abandoned him, which was really shitty when he pondered it. Unlike his two brothers, who had guidance, Rapha raised himself.

His other brother, Emite, was so twisted up by that sick mother of his, Rapha decided he was better off by himself. One day soon, he planned to travel down to the bayou because Emite wasn't likely to leave Charlotte without Rapha's help. Together, they would accomplish marvelous things. Emite, for all his insanity, was exceedingly talented in curses and mind manipulation. Rapha anticipated a glorious future. Barred from taking his revenge, held prisoner at the place of his birth, he was free at long last. The first item on his agenda, kill his mother.

Darkness Before the Dawn

Two loud bangs on the guest bedroom doors and an even louder call to arms drove Ian and Beau from their beds in the space of a heartbeat. Before their wives rolled over, the two soldiers were dressing and arming themselves, preparing for battle. Among the supplies delivered to the beach house were gear and weapons. None of them said a word when they saw the bounty at the bottom of their respective boxes. They exchanged glances and closed them up, until the time.

"Beau?"

He sat on the bed beside Alaina, pulling the laces tight on his black boots. The tunic and fitted trousers seemed to fade away, blend into the darkness. "Don't worry about me, *Bébé*. I'm one hell of a fighter."

"I know that. I've seen you." She sounded breathy.

"It's because I'm a bit crazy. You know that, right?"

She snorted. "Crazy like a fox."

His blue eyes flashed, cold and deadly. "And vicious as a wolf. Ain't nothing gonna hurt you, or any of these people that I love. I ain't gonna fall apart this time, you got my word."

"I never doubted that for a second, *mon loup*."

Ian dressed in identical gear. Joanna fluttered around the room, desperate to find the place of calm, somewhere she could go in the Spirit to still the pounding of her heart and alleviate the panic pushing in on all sides. She failed miserably. "You need to pull up that hood! You need to tie that string! Your hair! It will see your hair!" She ran to him, trying to pull the hood over his head with her shaking fingers. "Ian, it's like a beacon."

"Hey, stop!" Her agitation unnerved him, and he stilled her hands.

"Don't fight me on this." Joanna wrenched away, frantic to hide his hair. "Beau... James... their dark hair... but yours?"

Anger erupted in Ian, and he gave her a small shake. "Stand down, woman!"

Joanna drew back in shock and startlement.

"We are not given over to a spirit of fear, but of power, and of love, and of a sound mind." Ian's tone softened. "Be strong. He will fight this battle."

Joanna's female heart broke. She had to give him back to the Lord. "I just got you. He's always had you, but I just got you."

Ian pulled her into his chest and let her cry.

"Where in the hell did you find that sweater?" James asked through gritted teeth.

Persa gave him a defiant look. "It's what I wore when he took me, what I wore when I left the House of Amah, and what I will be wearing when we take him down."

"Take it off and burn that damn thing!"

"No."

"Dammit, Persa! I don't want to fight with you." James loomed over her, but his face broke, and so did his voice. "And I don't want it to be the last thing I see you wearing."

Persa recoiled as if he had struck her. "Don't even say that!" she cried in horror.

"We do not know." James regained his composure. "Any battle you go into, any one, it does not matter the odds, you know you might not come out."

"James... James... no..." Persa threw the sweater off and came toward him in only her bra and jeans she could no longer button.

His brown eyes softened with old love and knowledge. He stood, battle-hardened, resolute, and ready. "Fey, this has been coming since he took you. One day, I was going to fight. I wasn't going to standby any-more." He picked her up. "You've always known that."

"We've lost so much, but we have it all back. Why do you have to fight? Let's run." She knew, even as she said the words, that he wouldn't, but she had to try.

"You didn't marry a runner, darling."

She leaned her forehead against his, tears falling on his chest. "No. I married a man."

Full Armor

It was a prayer for the ages, one said before battles both physical and spiritual, recited and memorized a billion times since the Apostle Paul penned the words to the Ephesians three thousand years before. It was as true in the predawn hours of February 14, 1000 ME as it was in 62 AD. For they did not wrestle against flesh and blood, but against spiritual wickedness in high places, against the powers of darkness pressing in on the Pepperwood Ranch.

It was Beau who took up the prayer, recited a thousand times, over a thousand days. He sent it over the waters of his quiet lake, cried in the blackness of his room, gasped it with every footfall on the punishing, long runs, and whispered it in the silence of his porch. It became his shield in the hospital as he fought memories and visions, struggling to regain his sanity and reclaim his life. The prayer served as a balm when he missed Alaina with such force and power that it brought him to his knees.

Standing in the living room of Pepperwood, holding the hands of his wife and his best friend, Beau's voice rang strong and powerful, the words warm and honeyed, spiced with heat and danger—no fear.

"We come to you today, Lord, seeking your protection as we go into battle. We gird our loins with the belt of truth, that we might discern the lies of the enemy in the pit of our stomachs. For we know lies are their natural language. Help us recognize their words for what they are, lies.

"We put on the breastplate of righteousness, not righteousness ob-tained through ourselves, but through the forgiveness you bestowed upon us through your work at the cross. Protect our hearts, Lord, with that breastplate, let them not be troubled.

"And we strap on the shoes of the Gospel of peace. That as we walk forward, we do so in your perfect will, on the path you have set, embold-ened by the peace that surpasses all understanding, and the truth that you will never leave us or forsake us.

"We hold up the shield of faith to extinguish the fiery darts of the enemy. May our faith protect us, as we face more than fiery darts. We pray today like the man with the demon-possessed son, 'Lord, I believe, help my unbelief.'

"Then Lord, we put on my favorite, the helmet of salvation, the helmet of deliverance, the helmet of Yeshua. It covers our ears and protects our minds. I pray you anoint us with its power, but especially me, you know why.

"Finally, we take up the sword of the Spirit, which is the Word of God. Our only offensive weapon. We are thankful tonight to be standing beside our brother, Ian, who you saw fit to give that gift all those years ago. We remember how your Spirit showed up, how it saved us, how it protected us. The powers of darkness flee before it, give us that protection, pour it out, and bathe us in the light of your glory. In Jesus' name. Amen."

And all God's children prayed, "Amen."

The Line

He was a big son of a bitch was the first thought James had when Rapha emerged from the trees. The second was how inconceivable it was that his tiny wife bore such a monster. However, the third and final thing that occurred to James ben Kole was that he was going to kill it.

They were mounted, facing the giant. James freed the horses in the stables for their protection. He would not leave them trapped if the beast broke their line. But instead of fleeing, the horses formed a phalanx around them. Five from the House of Amah were still at Pepperwood. They wanted to kill the giant as much as he did; he could feel it.

Lightning was riderless as she moved to the head of the line. Her coat began to glow.

"*Mon Dieu*, what have you got there, Major?" Beau breathed in awe.

Realization hit James as he remembered Joshua's words on the beach. He patted Bayard's neck and said with a wry smile, "Apparently a companion."

Ian looked up at the predawn sky and said, "And behold, a white horse… faithful and true."

James smiled and looked between his Lieutenants, then gave a great cry, the call to battle. They went out to meet the giant in full force and fury, mounted, mighty, and deadly.

When the World Stops Turning

It would be better to be in the action, to be in the thick of it, fighting. At least that's what it felt like inside the house. Alaina was a wreck, visions of the bayou crashing in on her from all sides, pummeling her like body blows.

Joanna saw what was happening and ran to her. "Alaina, don't go back there. Don't let the enemy get a foothold in your mind. Stay here. Listen to my voice. Pray, come on. You can do it."

Persa watched them from across the kitchen. She could hear the battle outside, the pounding hooves, the shouts, then the call when it came. "Mother."

Her entire married life, she longed for a child and thought she would never have one. But she did. Not a child, Spawn. Until that moment, she'd forgotten the name she called it, the loathing she had for it, viperous, poisonous thing.

"I will kill him if you don't come outside," he said in her brain.

She moved, walking through a fog. It came down to this, from the moment Marduk took her. She looked around her kitchen, wearing a sad smile, noting the mismatched wooden chairs where they had eaten hundreds of meals, remembering the night when she, James and Peter laughed so hard about the man in the manure.

Pausing in the living room, she gazed at the sofa where she and James had lain side by side, reading, visiting, relaxing. She touched the soft suede, seeing Peter as he recovered, making her laugh and cry. She fingered the glass vase Dad gave them as a wedding gift and smiled at the silver cup sitting on the mantel, the crowning achievement of their youth.

The front door did not make a sound as she opened it, its hinges well-oiled and cared for, maintained like the rest of this beautiful home they built and loved. Her boots echoed on the porch, the white paint faded and embedded into the grain. Pepperwood lay before her, and the battle raged.

The giant stood in the middle, with horses and riders furiously circling. The men fired and feinted, slashed, and drove. Their expressions were something to behold, fierce, determined, deadly. It was a glorious scene.

Then it stopped.

With one wave of the giant's great hand, everything froze, except mother and son.

Rapha turned with a malevolent smile. "Mother Cunt."

"Devil's Spawn."

"It's been a while." He bowed with mock gallantry, the long tails of his tunic fluttering in the wind.

"Not long enough," she said, oddly unafraid, donning armor honed during thousands of hours of captivity, hardened in the fires of hell, and prepared for this day. She slipped it on effortlessly and walked down the steps of the porch.

"I've enjoyed devouring your children. Sometimes they call out for you. Did you know that?" He grinned, showing her two rows of fangs. "Momma Fey..." He imitated a falling child's voice. "You've got one now. I smell it on you."

Persa glared at him. "I should have killed you before you were born."

Rapha scoffed. "I was too strong for you, even then. So was he... I know he'd like to see you again, perhaps have a dance. Do you want to dance with Daddy, go for a little tryst in the garden?" He laughed at her horrified expression. "I did not tell him I was coming. I think he still has a soft spot for you, but I vowed that one day I would make you pay."

A whip uncoiled in Persa's hand. She did not brandish it, did not let her eyes leave his, but the competence with which she handled the implement demonstrated her prowess with it. "You will not touch me or any that I love," she said calmly and traced her nail over the corner of her eye down her cheek.

The giant blinked, his own hand going to the side of his face, where a wicked scar marred his skin.

"I gave that to you," she said softly, the words almost a caress, full of menace, and the promise of pain.

Rapha laughed. "Perhaps my memories of you are a bit faulty. You are not a cowering little worm, are you?"

"Never."

"And you think to beat me into submission?" he asked, his eyes watching the end of the whip that flickered on the ground, alive and menacing. "You think to kill me?"

"No," she said, making eye contact with James, Ian, and Beau, who, while paralyzed, were very much present. "They are."

Rapha sneered in an expression so reminiscent of Tristin it made Persa's blood turn to ice. "I do not think they are."

She did not flinch, did not take a step backward as he scented the air, his eyes turning to hellfire.

"Should I fuck you first or just devour you one bite at a time?" He licked his lips, and the true evil of him, the eternal damnation of his wicked soul blotted out the watery sun peeking over the trees. "Come here. I'm hungry."

With a flick of his hand, Persa felt her body jerk, bonds lashing her arms and legs. She closed her eyes, drawing all her strength, refusing to cry out, refusing to cower as an invisible rope dragged her toward his drooling mouth.

She had not seen Lightning, not focused on any of the riderless horses, but her beloved mare moved forward between them. She reared, as tall as the giant. A pulse of blinding white light flashed, and Rapha stumbled backward. The three men, who had been held in suspended animation, yelled the name of Jesus.

The action unfolded in slow motion. Events that were only seconds felt much longer. Released from their bondage, man and beast moved in unison. Beau and Ian drove swords into the giant's heart. James, astride Bayard, flew to Persa, rose in the saddle, and caught her mid-air. But as James rose, Rapha struck a mighty blow.

When Bayard landed, the giant fell dead. But the light in James' eyes began to fade. He smiled at Persa and said, "I didn't let you fall."

Then he died in her arms.

It was a noise Ian ben Kole would never forget, one he never wanted to hear again, the sound his sister-in-law made the moment the life left his brother's body. It echoed in his brain, reverberating like a gong, blocking out everything. He shouted; he knew he did. The foul giant crashed to the ground, that must have made a noise, as did the pounding hooves of his horse as he flew to his brother's side, catching his lifeless body before it toppled into the dirt, taking Persa with it.

His mind refused to process the reality, could not accept that in a single instant James was gone. But Persa kept screaming, begging James not to leave, calling him back. And when he looked into his brother's lifeless brown eyes there was no denying the truth.

That was when Ian made his own sound of agony.

Suspended between them, across the backs of two of his beloved horses, Ian and Persa clung to James.

"*Mon Dieu*," Beau choked, wrapping an arm around James back, steadying his body. "*Descendons-le.*"

"Yes," Ian sobbed, "help me get him down."

"Don't let him fall," Persa cried.

"I won't," Beau assured her, and the steadiness in his voice brought Ian back to himself in a manner reminiscent of the battlefield so many years ago. There was duty to attend, action to take.

"Alaina, Joanna, bring me two blankets from the stable," Beau shouted to the horrified women frozen on the front porch.

"He can't be gone," Persa sobbed, stroking James' back as Ian and Beau struggled to hold him on the saddle.

"Oh, Yeshua," Ian cried, "no."

"Mon ami, laisse-le partir," Beau said, moving between the horses and taking the weight. "Let go, I have him."

True to his word, Beau eased James off the saddle, a soldier's competence, and efficiency in handling the remains of a fallen comrade, a skill long forgotten, too horrible to remember, but one Ian was grateful they had been taught.

Persa sat backward on Bayard, and Beau lifted her off with reverence and gentleness, as if she might shatter.

"Take him upstairs, to our room," Persa said, keeping her back to the abomination behind them.

Ian nodded and together, he and Beau carried James into the house and up the steps. They laid him out carefully. He looked asleep, a smile on his face. There was no blood, except for a tiny drop inside his nostril.

"Can you please leave?" Persa asked, broken, but resolute with steely determination. "He's... he's still warm."

Ian's throat closed. He could not breathe, so he nodded, and left his sister-in-law lying beside the body of her dead husband. As the door closed, the agony of her weeping tore his heart into a million pieces.

He stood in the hall, utterly incapable of functioning, the loss too incomprehensible. James, stalwart, honorable, and true, was dead. He shattered under the weight of it... his brother. He could not pray, could not think, or imagine a world that did not have James ben Kole in it.

"Ian," Joanna whispered, touching his arm.

He turned, staring into her red rimmed eyes. The unwelcome thought flashed that he was grateful she was not crying over his body right now. It made him feel guilty, horrible, but it was there, nevertheless. "Princess," he croaked.

"Come with me," she said, employing the strict, motherly tone she used with distraught children.

For once, he did not mind and let her lead him into the guest room, where she lay beside him and held on as he wept.

"Bébé," Beau said, pushing a chair into the narrow hall. "Sit here, in case Persa needs you. I'll go tend to things outside."

Alaina balled her fist over her mouth, as her face contorted.

He kissed her temple and went to work. The horses were utmost in his mind, as if James were encouraging him. He would not want harm to come to them, not in the hour of his death.

The sun rose above the trees, casting Pepperwood in cool shades of winter green. The smell of trampled earth, horses, and dew greeted him. He averted his eyes from the fallen giant, unable to look upon the thing, unable to process any more ugliness and horror.

The white mare, the one who led the charge, patrolled her herd, keeping them within the open paddock and away from the body of the beast. He recognized the behavior of the guardian, a bit of herd dynamics, wisdom James imparted before and during the war. No one in Beau's acquaintance understood horses the way James ben Kole did… had… Beau closed his eyes against a rush of pain and grief.

Wind kicked up from the south, bringing the scent of forest, water, and earth. It lifted his hair and seemed for a moment as if the hand of God touched him. He nodded, accepting the gesture.

Driven to do something, to set things right here, as much as he could, Beau whickered, and Lightning turned her ears forward. Her intelligent blue eyes appeared watery, as if she, too, wept. She trotted over to him, and a gurgling knot lodged in his throat. He realized that these magnificent beasts had been missing from his life for too long. Immersed in his cars and his boats, a fundamental connection had been severed, and he vowed to remedy that when he got home. There was room at La Petit Pishon for stables, and he needed one of these horses, to remind him, to anchor him if the darkness pushed in again. He wanted a Pepperwood horse. With that conviction, Beau got to work.

Upstairs, Persa determined she would not weep in their final moments, not send James to his reward with the sound of her wailing following him into Heaven. He was gone, true, but while a remnant of life remained in his body, she would say her goodbyes with dignity. He deserved that from her.

There were a thousand things to say, a thousand memories to recall, a lifetime of being the other half of his soul. Even their names were rarely spoken without the other's. From the moment nine-year-old James walked through the door of Rivergate, wearing his new boots, and carrying his leather suitcase with his initials engraved within his family crest, they were inexorably linked; James and Persa, partners, friends, lovers, husband and wife.

She touched the silver hair at James' temple and whispered, "If it's a boy, I'll name him Joshua, for I'm sure that's who you are with right now."

As It Will Be

The stables James walked were the finest he had ever seen, pristine, clean, and shining. Even James' eye for perfection could find no fault. He stopped at each stall, every horse more magnificent than the last. He faltered at the end of the row, recognizing the occupant.

"Rain, oh, girl," he breathed in awe. She nuzzled him affectionately, and he buried his face in her mane, tears streaming from his eyes.

"She is a magnificent horse, isn't she, my friend?"

James turned with a smile. "Indeed, my Lord. She carried Persa and me many hours."

"It was the first of sorrows for you both, losing that horse," Joshua said with perfect knowledge.

James smiled ruefully, stroking Rain's nose. "It was."

"But Rain's death is nothing compared to what Persa is going through right now."

James looked confused. "My Lord?"

"Your dead body is currently occupying your bed at Pepperwood with your widow mourning over it. Do you know why?"

James' brown eyes bulged. "No, Lord, tell me."

"Because, James, you could never forgive yourself for what happened to Persa. You would have lived the rest of your life in agony over your failure to stop something you were never meant to stop." Joshua shook his head. "I told you that day on the beach, it was not your fault, yet you would not let it go. You did not stop for one minute, blaming yourself." He paused. "So, I gave you what you wanted. I let you die over it."

The truth of Joshua's words convicted James to the atomic level of his soul. He fell on his face, at the feet of the Savior, in repentance. "Forgive me, Lord."

"That is the truest test of faith, isn't it, James, to accept the things you don't understand, to take the Scripture that says, 'My ways are higher than your ways and my thoughts are higher than your thoughts,' and apply them to your life. It takes faith to move forward when you don't have the answers."

James closed his eyes, nodding without words or defense.

"Do you think you can do that, James?" Joshua reached down and lifted James to his feet, his hazel eyes intent. "Do you think you can stop playing God in your own life and let me do it?"

"With your help, Lord, I will try," James said hoarsely.

"And in that, my son, I have no doubt. Give my love to Persa, tell her I like the name."

Joshua laid a hand on James' head and disappeared into the mist.

Marsupial

"I saw Rain."

Persa scrambled off the bed, screaming at the top of her lungs. Alaina burst through the door, ready for action. Ian hit the wall as he stumbled out of the guest room. Joanna rolled out of bed, exhausted with fatigue and grief.

Shouts of thanksgiving echoed off the bedroom as everyone piled on top of James, crying with relief and amazement.

He had been dead for over an hour, well and truly gone.

Persa showered him with kisses.

Ian kept saying, "Praise God."

Joanna leaned up against the wall, like a rag doll, arms and legs limp.

Alaina sprinted from the room to find Beau.

He was in the stables, nuzzling an old white horse, tears coursing down his fine face.

"Beau?"

He squeezed his eyes together, cutting off the flow and backhanding the tears. "Jolie Catin, there's something special about this horse. I think we need to take her with us to the bayou."

"Honey, you need to come inside. There's somebody in there that wants to talk to you."

"If it's all the same, I don't really feel like talking right now."

"Beau, James is alive."

Beau covered his face with his hands and groaned. "Oh no, not again."

Alaina flew to his side. "No, no. You are not going crazy. Come on. I'll show you." She pulled him by the hand, back to the house.

She threw the door open and yelled up the steps. "James ben Kole, you better tell Beau you are alive, right now."

"I will if he gives me back all the money he won off me at poker."

Beau dropped Alaina's hand and mounted the stairs like a man walking to the gallows. He stopped in the doorway and took in the scene. James sat upright on the bed, smiling, with Persa's arms wrapped around his neck. Ian stood off to the side, his face glowing. Joanna collapsed in the corner, looking like a happy drunk.

"Well, I'll be damned. You were playing possum."

Instructions, Sir

"Yes, that's fine. Please do what is necessary. Of course, thank you for calling. Have a nice evening." Beau handed the phone back to Alaina and grinned. He turned to Joanna and said, "Lady J., it seems I made a bit of an impression on your little secretary, Amanda."

Alaina narrowed her brows at him, but he ignored her. "That was the butler at Lenox. There are sixty residents from the Center living it up in high style right now."

Joanna rushed toward him with outstretched arms. "My kids? You've got my kids?"

Ian collapsed into a chair. Persa buried her face in James' chest, refusing to let Rapha's words spoil the moment of relief.

Forty Pieces of Silver

That evening, as Ian dozed, Joanna came to their room, pale and withdrawn. "What did Elias say?" he mumbled from his cocoon of blankets and pillows.

Joanna sat down on the edge of the bed, pulling off her socks. "He was relieved to hear the children were safe. He and a few others will go to Lenox and transport them back to the Center. The fighting has largely stopped."

"What's wrong?" Ian rose onto his elbow.

"He's been over to the Center several times, checking on things."

"And?"

Joanna looked off in the distance, not seeing anything. "He found Judith there."

Ian sat up now, fully awake. "Doing what?"

"Being dead," she said in a monotone. "She hung herself. Left me a note."

"Oh, Princess, I'm so sorry. Did Elias tell you what it said?"

Joanna started to cry. "He wouldn't tell me. He said it wasn't rational, that she was out of her mind, consumed with jealousy and envy." She sniffed and wiped her eyes. "He discovered that family court deemed her unfit and took the girls. Our wedding weekend was her last unsupervised visitation. He suspects she embezzled the money to pay the lawyers."

Ian pulled her to his chest as she wept long, wracking sobs.

At length, she whispered into the darkness, "She was my friend, Ian."

February 15, 1000 ME

Only in Wartime

At first, Beau thought the noise outside was thunder, then, wealthy man that he was, he recognized it. In Alanthia, in wartime, short of an invasion, only one person would arrive at Pepperwood in a helicopter. Persa heard it too and screeched with joy, running out the door.

It landed in the top pasture, great blades sending dust and debris flying. Prince d'Or knew how to make an entrance. Persa stood on the front porch with her fist balled at her lips.

The apocalyptic scene of the day before was nothing but a memory. While Beau was in the stables, and James lay dead, Hell claimed the body of the giant, just like his brother. The Earth opened and swallowed him whole. She could not even detect a disturbance in the soil.

When the whirlwind settled, she saw Peter's fine form emerge from the helicopter. He offered his hand to a small woman whose red hair fell down her back in long waves. Persa's mouth dropped as she recognized Astrid. Her appearance transformed from the short-haired and withdrawn girl on the video conference to a serene and confident beauty walking beside Prince Peter.

Persa felt James move behind her, draping his arms over her shoulders. His warmth was welcome in the chilly morning. He spoke quietly, "It was three years ago yesterday, that we found him strung out and half dead on this porch."

Her eyes narrowed as the armor slipped on. "Well February 14th didn't claim either of you, did it?"

James kissed the top of her head. "I suppose you wouldn't let it."

"I had little control over it, but I appreciate the sentiment, Jay."

A sunray broke through the persistent cloud cover, shining like a spotlight and setting off gold sparks from Peter's hair. James chuckled, remembering Peter at fourteen.

Persa looked up at him. "What are you laughing about?"

"Nothing. It's just good to see him at Pepperwood." He nodded toward the couple. "She's pretty, but I'll be interested to see what she's like. He's never brought a girl home."

Persa rubbed a knuckle over the back of her lips, considering, "I think she's more than a girl, Jay. Beau told me about the afternoon they spent at his house. He loves her."

"He's only known her for a couple weeks," James snorted, spoken like a man who had been with his wife since they had baby teeth.

"That didn't stop Prince Josiah and Davianna, they're married. Peter and Astrid have been together the same amount of time."

James grunted. "Yeah, but she left him."

Persa took care not to move her lips as the couple got closer. "Well, she's obviously back, so be nice, boyo." She smiled and moved forward, grasping Astrid's hands. "Welcome to Pepperwood."

Turning to Peter, her eyes watered, and she said, "And you? Welcome home."

"Fey." Peter picked her up and spun her around. "It is good to see you."

Persa kissed him on the cheek, laughing. "Put me down… you are going to squish the baby."

Peter closed his eyes and leaned his forehead against hers, resting it there as the impact of her words settled between them. He realized who had robbed her of her children the moment he remembered Tristin. "Truly?"

"Truly." Persa cupped his face.

"That's good." He beamed. "I've got news, too, but it can wait."

Peter straightened and moved into James' outstretched arms. "Congratulations, man." He reared back and studied James. "You look rough. Are you all right?"

Persa and James thought that was funny. Peter and Astrid exchanged bemused glances and greeted the rest of the Pepperwood crew.

Friends in High Places

After lunch, Peter drew Beau aside. "I need a word." Peter winked at Alaina. "And you too, Mrs. Landry, please sit down." Peter indicated to a couple of overstuffed chairs and pulled Astrid down beside him on the sage green sofa he loved. It had aged to a soft patina, but its familiar comfort spoke of home more than any other piece of furniture on the planet.

Peter looked between them but addressed Beau. "You recall when you assisted us that day we fled New Orleans that Josiah and I promised if there was ever a service that we might render to repay your kindness, we would do so."

"I do, my Esteemed."

"For several years, dark occult practices have festered and grown in Alanthia." He and Astrid exchanged a veiled look. "New Orleans has become an area of particular interest. There have been rumors, but little hard evidence, surrounding a certain witch operating in the region.

Whilst in New York, we met with the lead investigator." His voice held a note of sympathy. "After the conference call and our meeting, we determined there was ample reason to focus attention down there."

Prince Peter, born to duty and service, blossomed under the promised righteous rule of his cousin. His manner and speech were formal. "We will no longer tolerate wickedness, nor allow it to prosper in Alanthia. One of Prince Josiah's first orders of business will be the complete eradication of subversive and dangerous groups operating inside the Kingdom. Mr. Landry, we would like to give you the opportunity to take part in the investigation and subsequent action against them. We will authorize the full force and power of the Federal Investigative and Armed Services to act with extreme prejudice."

"To send them straight to Hell." Beau's eyes flashed, and he grinned. "My Esteemed, I would like nothing more."

"Beau?" Alaina's voice climbed. "We won't have to do it alone?"

Beau laughed, deep and rich, "It appears not, Jolie Catin. It looks like we might just dance at a *fais-do-do* at ninety, after all."

Alaina's smile was gorgeous, her eyes aquamarine pools of light and love. "And Uncle Boudreaux's story really will have a happy ending!"

To Be True

"I met him when he was seven," Persa said, taking a seat beside Astrid and nodding toward Peter who stood beside James at the horseshoe pit. Ian and Beau were at the opposite end, shouting good-natured ribbing and placing wagers across the distance.

"Your husband or Peter?" Astrid asked.

Persa laughed. "Well, both of them, I suppose, though technically, James was eight when we met, but I was referring to Peter."

Astrid turned her blue cat eyes on Persa. "If he was seven, his mother was still alive."

Persa gave the girl credit for perceptiveness. "Indeed, she was. Princess Alexa was a lovely woman."

Astrid gave an ironic laugh. "Should I say thank you for the compliment?"

"So, I am not the first person to bring that up?"

"No... I believe Korah brought that to my attention while he was torturing me."

"Jupiter's Moon," Persa said, burying her face in her hands.

"But I survived. Peter helped me through it, because, as you know, Korah did the same thing to him."

"He told you that?" Persa studied the young woman.

"Well, otherwise, I would not have mentioned it." Astrid turned serious. "Peter would have died without you, without this place, in more ways than one. After his mother passed, this was the only place he ever felt safe, the only times in his life someone cared for him, loved him. You and James have each other, but you made room for him in your family, and gave him sanctuary. I do not know if either of you realize how important you are to him. He loves you and this ranch." She bit her thumbnail and said, "Thank you."

"We love him, too." Persa folded her hands over her little belly. "I do not mean to be blunt, but I need to ask you something."

"Okay."

"Do you love him? I mean, well and truly, love him? And not just because he's beautiful, or charming, or powerful. Because he is those things, but he is so much more." Persa smiled sadly. "Not all of it is light; there are dark shadows in him. He hides them, even from me, but we've lived through the same hellfire, so I see them, where others don't."

Astrid nodded. "I know what you are talking about."

"I expect that's why you ran."

"Actually, quite the opposite. I tried to pull it out of him and take it with me, so he wouldn't have to carry it anymore, so he could be free."

With wisdom beyond her years, Astrid continued, "The thing is, love doesn't work that way. You can't run away from somebody that loves you, no matter how good and noble your motives are. It is a mistake to think you can set them free, and they will be fine; that you can just hold on to their love and be the only one to suffer."

Astrid shook her head. "I didn't do very well without him, and he sure did not do very well without me."

Astrid reached across the distance and took Persa's hand. "So, I suppose the answer to your question is yes, I well and truly love him, and not just because he's beautiful, which he is." She smiled broadly and winked.

Persa matched her smile and said, "Oh, I think you and I are going to get along just fine."

Thank You

I hope you enjoyed the second installment of The Millennium Series. This one was truly a labor of love.

M2-Rise of the Giants proved a much more difficult book to write than M1-The Black Key for a variety of reasons. Like any good second child, it refused to act like its obedient older sibling.

I wrote M1-The Black Key linearly, from start to finish. M2 came in segments. Some days, Persa and James were talking; other days it was Beau and Alaina. Ian was not supposed to have a major role in M2, but along the way I realized he was the lynchpin, and Joanna was born the following day. The voice memo I recorded the morning I realized I had three couples to contend with is still one of my favorites.

M2 spans fifteen years and is both a prequel and a companion novel that runs concurrent with M1. The characters and events cross over, weaving between books. I did not realize it at the time, but M2 set the tenor, tone, and structure for the rest of The Millennium Series. Readers may notice recurring dates from M1. I thought that was fun, and it gives depth to the stories, Easter eggs to hunt.

M2 is scary; the villains are terrifying. I don't like to be afraid, nor do I care for dark subjects, but evil is real. What emerged in the first days of writing shook me. I was overjoyed to find my beloved Peter in the receiving line of the World Equestrian Championships. Prince d'Or does indeed spread sunshine wherever he goes.

Alaina's terror and reluctance to talk about the Bayou... well, that was me. I did not want to go there. But when the time came, the amazing characters surrounded me with love, as did He.

While writing M2, I'd fall against the wall of my co-worker's office and say, "This second book is going to be the death of me." By the time I was done, I had no skin left, but all seven major characters got everything I had to give.

I hoped you loved M2-Rise of the Giants, in the end I sure did.

It is truly the greatest honor and privilege of my life to have you on this journey. I am humbled and incredibly grateful for your time, encouragement, and patronage. You deserve my best, as does He.

The adventure continues in M3–The Outsiders. Take my hand; I am going to tell you an amazing tale.

In Christ,
Staci Morrison